YEARNING

Christopher Mitchell is the author of the epic fantasy series The Magelands. He studied in Edinburgh before living for several years in the Middle East and Greece, where he taught English. He returned to study classics and Greek tragedy and lives in Fife, Scotland with his wife and their four children.

BY CHRISTOPHER MITCHELL

THE MAGELANDS ORIGINS

Retreat of the Kell
The Trials of Daphne Holdfast
From the Ashes

THE MAGELANDS EPIC

The Queen's Executioner
The Severed City
Needs of the Empire
Sacrifice
Fragile Empire
Storm Mage
Soulwitch Rises
Renegade Gods

THE MAGELANDS ETERNAL SIEGE

The Mortal Blade
The Dragon's Blade
The Prince's Blade
Falls of Iron
Paths of Fire
Gates of Ruin
City of Salve

Red City
City Ascendant
Dragon Eyre Badblood
Dragon Eyre Ashfall
Dragon Eyre Blackrose
Dreams of Kell
God Restrainer
Holdfast Imperium
World's End

The Magelands Dominion

Serpent Dominion
Demon Witch
Death Seer
Blood Burden
Kin Strife
Tempest's Edge
Creator of Worlds
Palace of the Almighty
Sapphire Throne
The Lost Ascendant
Yearning for Evermore
Holder of Worlds

Masters and Makers

Fall Seldom Kings
The Making of Abigone

Whalebone King
Lies the Prince
Suffer the Heir
As Makers Dreamt

Cover Design by Sasha Almazan and Gene Mollica, G&S Cover Design Studio. LLC.
Maps by Irina French

Brigdomin Books Ltd
First Edition, November 2025
Ebook Edition © November 2025
ISBN 978-1-915978-75-2

ACKNOWLEDGEMENTS

I would like to thank the following for all their support during the writing of the Magelands Empire - my wife, Lisa Mitchell, who read every chapter as soon as it was drafted and kept me going in the right direction; my parents for their unstinting support; Marilyn Hopwood and Lisa Hoffman for reading the books in their early stages; James Aitken for his encouragement; and Grant and Gordon of the Film Club for their support.

Thanks also to my Advance Reader team, for all your help during the last few weeks before publication.

DRAMATIS PERSONAE

Sapphire Empire – Imperial Court (in Order of Seniority)

Thorn Holdfast, Empress (53)

Kelsey Holdfast, Herald of the Empire (50)

Lucius Cardova, Imperial Constable (54)

Brogan ae Bridget, Chamberlain (47)

Fenu, Imperial Chancellor (54)

Cael Holdfast, Imperial Adjutant (33)

Martius Claudian, Imperial Chief of Staff (51)

Toripadeni, Chief Jurist (41)

Slaeon, Imperial Treasurer (59)

Position Vacant, Lord Marshal

Quill, Imperial Quartermaster (48)

Cole Holdfast, Imperial Secretary (34)

Arrosa Holdfast, Postmaster (32)

Plateau City - Others

Carden Holdfast, Karalyn and Cardova's Son (18)

Caitlyn Holdfast, Karalyn and Cardova's Daughter (17)

Calpurnia Holdfast, Kelsey and Van's daughter (23)

Caelius Holdfast, Kelsey and Van's Son (20)

Cowie Holdfast, Cael and Arrosa's Son (10)

Kelvin Holdfast, Cael and Arrosa's Son (6)

Carrie Holdfast, Cael and Arrosa's Daughter (6)

Caelius Logos, Former Quartermaster

Van Logos, Ambassador from the City of Salve

Nestorian, Rosie Jackdaw's Husband

Frostback, Silver Dragon

Halfclaw, Blue/Green Dragon

Colsbury

Shella, Retiree

Postmaster's Agents

Saewa, Imperial Spymaster

Alva Holdfast, Agent

Muriel of Hold Terras, Agent

Clackenbaird – Marchbrae Holdfasts

Aila Holdfast, Purveyor of Whisky

Naxor, Aila's Cousin

Carter Holdfast, Corthie and Aila's Son (21)

Clova Holdfast, Corthie and Aila's Daughter (20)

Carron Holdfast, Corthie and Aila's Youngest Son (17)

Ceres Holdfast, Corthie and Aila's Daughter (15)

Carla Holdfast, Corthie and Aila's Youngest Daughter (14)

Hold Fast Estate, Holdings

Killop Holdfast, Corthie and Aila's Eldest Son (28), Estate Manager

Celine Holdfast, Retiree

Ulna, Dragon Eyre

Blackrose, Queen of the Eastern Rim

Maddie Jackdaw, Blackrose's Rider

Beth Jackdaw, Maddie's Daughter (22)

Amy Jackdaw, Maddie's Daughter (15)

Oto'pazzi (Topaz), Maddie's Husband

Sable Holdfast, Retired Agent

Alara'osso (Lara), Sable's Partner

Anaj'osso (Joss), Sable and Lara's Son (21)

Alindi'osso (Lindi), Sable and Lara's Daughter (16)

Athumia – Inopei

Kyra Holdfast, Karalyn and Lennox's Daughter (33)

Konna Holdfast, Corthie and Aila's Eldest Daughter (25)

Edgar, Brother of Edmond, Lord of Nom Karta

Edward, Kyra and Edgar's Son (14)

Alfred, Kyra and Edgar's Son (14)

Elmhirst, Ancient, Edgar's Aide

Esher, The Ninth Ascendant

Famula Min Gahad, Queen of the Dominion

Abda Min Gahad, Famula's Sister

Saphben Mon Gahad, Famula's Brother

Konran Mon Gahad, Famula's Brother

Tirna Min Gahad, Famula's Sister

Sigra Min Sigmund, Lord Sigum's Niece

Laverne, Governor of Tempest Mine

Achan, Exile from the Empire

Athumia – Zamata

Bailey, Theodora's Brother

Bauchlie, President of Zamata

Gunstians

Paltanai, Missing Gunstian Archpriest

Galina, Gifted Agent

Aitan, Gifted Agent

City of Salve

Emily Aurelian, Queen of the City

Daniel Aurelian, King of the City

Elspeth, Emily and Daniel's Daughter

Maxwell, Son of the God-Queen

At the Salve Mine

Lahnos Laimos, Former Commander, Imperial Army

Sigum Mon Sigel, Dragon, and Friend of Lahnos

Ora'lya, Dragon Rider

Dermot Laimos, Lahnos's and Dolwyn's Son (14)

Lana'lya (Lana Laimos), Lahnos's and Ora'lya's Daughter (9)

Jade, Demigod of the City of Salve

Dawnflame, Lostwell Dragon

Firestone, Dawnflame's Young Son

Others

Karalyn Holdfast, Immortal Dream Mage

Cairney Holdfast, Corthie and Aila's Son (24), Exiled

The Magelands
The Unknowable Ocean
Realm of the Holdings
Shield Mountains
Royston
Holdings City
Blackwater
River Holdings
Barrier Mountains
Plateau City
Inner Sea
Sanang
Twinth
Broadwater
Mya
Beechwoods
Tritos
Black Mountains
Arakhanah
The Plateau
Rainsby
Forbidden Mountains
Basalt Desert
Grey Mountains
Akhanawarah
Tahrana City
Jade Falls
Rahain Capital
Calcite City
Rahain Republic
Brig
Kell
Lach
Domm
Fire Mountain
N

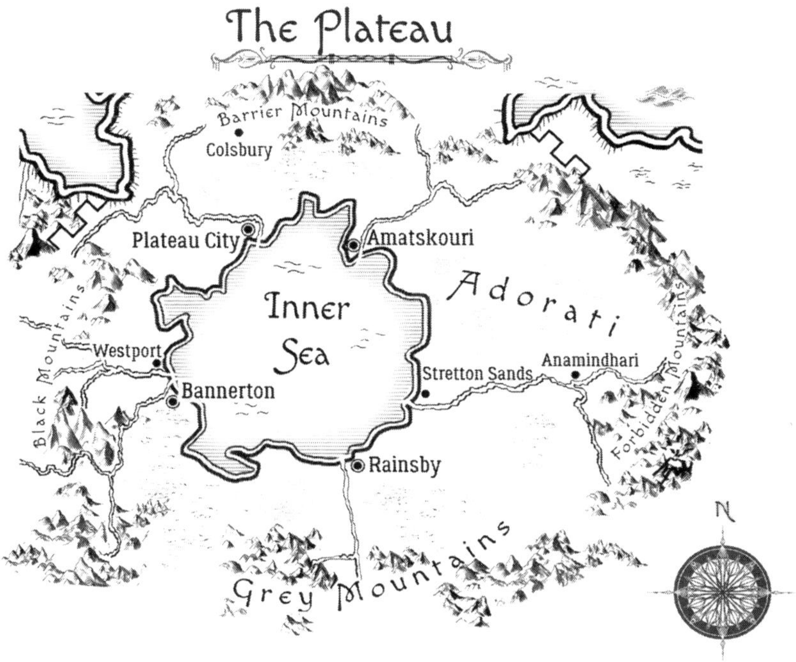
The Plateau
Barrier Mountains
Colsbury
Plateau City
Amatskouri
Adorati
Inner Sea
Black Mountains
Westport
Bannerton
Stretton Sands
Anamindhari
Forbidden Mountains
Rainsby
Grey Mountains
N

CHAPTER 1
HAVEN FOR OLD GODS

Nom Karta, Inopei – 2nd Abrinch 1613

'Why not?' said Konna.

Lord Elmhirst eyed her. 'It's nothing personal. Now, if you would excuse me, I have much to do.'

Konna narrowed her eyes at the Ancient. 'I have been in Nom Karta for eight years,' she said. 'Tell me why my application has been refused.'

Elmhirst glanced at the four other gods on the veranda, who were standing next to their luggage, ready to be transported to one of the Doomed Worlds. 'Please bear with me for a moment,' he said to them, 'while I deal with this interruption. Miss Konna,' he went on, 'eight years may seem like a very long time to you, but, to us gods who survived the destruction of the Ascendants, you are but a child. You are far too young to be assigned any responsible role in the government of the Dominion, whether here on Athumia, or upon any of the Doomed Worlds under our control. Apply again in a century or two, after you have gained some experience. Besides, you are a Holdfast; and I do not deem it wise to hand over power to a member of that family.'

'Kyra is only seven years older than me,' said Konna, 'and she is Edgar's chief advisor, as well as a Holdfast.'

'Lady Kyra is a mortal,' said Elmhirst. 'At thirty-three, she is nearly halfway through her natural life span; whereas you, Miss Konna, are at the very beginning of your journey into immortality. For Lady Kyra, it is now or never; but you should be enjoying yourself in this, your first of many centuries to come. Now, if you please, I have business to conduct.'

Konna fell into silence, her eyes tight with anger.

Elmhirst turned to the four other gods. 'You all know what is expected of you upon the world of Apharan,' he said. 'Protect the lives of the mortal miners, and ensure that the deliveries of oil, gold and copper continue to flow into Nom Karta. Keep a very close eye on volcanic activity, and take all precautions against the earthquakes that trouble Apharan. If the world becomes too unstable, evacuate without delay. When your decade of service is complete, you will be entitled to a decade of rest here on Inopei, or upon Aucteran. Good luck.'

One of the four gods withdrew a Quadrant. 'Thank you, my Lord Ancient,' she said. 'Glory to the Dominion.'

'Glory to the Dominion,' said Elmhirst.

The god swiped her fingers over the copper device, the air shimmered, and the four gods and their luggage disappeared.

'Tell me, Elmhirst,' said Konna; 'how I am supposed to gain experience if you won't even consider my application to work on the Doomed Worlds?'

'Are you still here?' said Elmhirst.

'Answer me.'

'I had assumed you were being rhetorical. Miss Konna,' said the Ancient. 'Are you genuinely seeking my advice? Very well – here it is. Study languages for the next twenty years, along with the histories of every world governed by the Dominion. After that, apprentice yourself to another god for a few decades. Act as their servant, and learn all you can from them. Following that, I would recommend that you attend the military academy in Teros City for a further decade or two. Train with the army, and then turn your attention to the navy. Sail the oceans between Inopei and Aucteran; start as a midshipman, and work your way up to captain. There are many other avenues you could explore –

the study of Tempest, for instance, or the arts of civil administration. I can write this all down for you, if you like.'

'Don't patronise me,' said Konna.

Elmhirst raised a hand for silence, and the air shimmered again. Four different gods appeared on the long palace veranda.

Elmhirst smiled. 'Welcome back to Inopei,' he said. 'I trust the situation upon Apharan is stable?'

'For now, my lord,' said one of the gods. 'Seismic activity continues to worsen, but I would estimate that the world has a few decades left in it. The supplies of oil and gold remain abundant, but some of the other mines are beginning to be exhausted.'

'And the mortals?'

'All miners, staff and soldiers are accounted for, my lord,' said the god; 'no fatalities.' He glanced at Konna. 'Who is the woman by your side? I do not recognise her.'

'She arrived here after you were dispatched to Apharan,' said Elmhirst. A faint smile crossed his lips. 'Prepare yourselves for a surprise, gentlemen – this is Miss Konna Holdfast, a demigod who has defected to the Dominion from the Sapphire Empire.'

'A Holdfast?' said one of the gods.

'Indeed,' said Elmhirst. 'An *immortal* Holdfast. Lady Kyra's cousin. Death, vision, shape-shifting; she is quite accomplished, despite her youth. We are not to hold her family name against her; so it has been decreed by Lord Edgar. Through her great grandfather Lord Malik, Miss Konna is descended from the line of King Nathaniel.'

A few of the gods eyed Konna with suspicion.

'Might we assume that her father was Corthie Holdfast, my lord?' said one.

'You assume correctly,' said Elmhirst. 'Make your way to the palace of Lord Konran Mon Gahad, where you will be thoroughly debriefed. Quarters have been set aside for you, and you may remain there while you decide how to spend the rest period you so richly deserve.'

The four gods bowed to Elmhirst, then they vanished. Elmhirst gazed out at the city of Nom Karta, then he raised his hands.

'Do you see this, Miss Konna?' he said. 'Look at what we have achieved in such a short time. When we arrived here from the Doomed Worlds, Nom Karta was in ruins, and its neighbouring city of Sat Orma was in an even worse state. The civil war between Queen Famula and Lord Tegru destroyed most of the buildings, and many thousands of mortals were killed. Look at it now. The palaces have been repaired, the roads re-laid, the harbours rebuilt, and Sat Orma is rising from the ashes. In fifteen years, we have resettled over two hundred thousand mortals from the Doomed Worlds. We have found them homes and jobs, and their hard work has transformed Sat Orma from a rancid slum into one of the jewels of the Dominion. Under our guidance, the continents of Inopei and Aucteran are experiencing an economic boom beyond all reckoning. Iron, coal, gold, oil, silver – all are pouring into the Dominion; and yet the Holdfasts continue to claim that the gods should not rule. What folly. You, Miss Konna, are immortal, yet you are still living within the bounds of a mortal life span. You have been alive for a mere twenty-six years; it is not enough to learn the complexities of rule. Come back after a century, and we shall talk again about your prospects. Good day.'

Elmhirst took his own Quadrant from a pocket, swiped it, and vanished, leaving Konna standing alone on the palace veranda. She walked forward and stood where he had been standing, then she gazed out over the splendour of Nom Karta. When she had arrived eight years before, several of the palaces were still damaged from the civil war, and from the terrorist attacks carried out by Cael Holdfast. The roads had been ripped up, the harbour was derelict, and Sat Orma had been in ruins. Had the gods been responsible for the restoration of the two cities, as Elmhirst had stated, or was it due to the industriousness of the two hundred thousand mortal evacuees from the Doomed Worlds? They spoke the same language as the native Aucterians, and had brought with them a host of skills – building, carpentry, metal-working; along with a fierce desire to turn their new home into somewhere magnificent. Ten thousand Banner soldiers had also been transported from the Doomed Worlds. They had been reorganised into a single

Banner of the Dominion, and had recruited among the natives, allowing their older veterans to retire in comfort and honour. With no new Bullan soldiers arriving from their lands to the far south, the Banner had taken over the defence of Nom Karta. They had each sworn an oath to Queen Famula Min Gahad, but everyone knew that Lord Edgar was responsible for the running of the government. The dragons seemed to like it that way – they had every privilege and luxury they could desire, without the burden of having to govern millions of humans.

Konna turned and approached the massive Palace of King Naghad, where she lived with several other gods. The dragons who had once inhabited the huge building were long gone, massacred on the ill-fated invasion of Gunst some twenty-five years previously, or in the civil war that had followed, and Konna had an apartment far bigger than anything she could possibly require. She even had a dozen mortal servants to see to her every whim, and yet Elmhirst and the others saw her as little more than a child.

Banner soldiers stood to attention as she passed into the great entrance hall. The temperature immediately dropped, from the ferocious heat of the Nom Kartan summer, to the cool interior of the palace. Still indignant about her treatment at the hands of Elmhirst, Konna made her way to the large section of the palace where Lord Edgar lived with his wife Lady Kyra. King Naghad had been one of Gahad's eldest sons, and his palace was among the biggest in Nom Karta; and it was there that Edgar had chosen to set up his government. He had modelled it on a royal court, despite being, in theory, merely the chief minister of Queen Famula, who had remained in the palace of her mighty father Gahad.

Mortal courtiers and servants mingled with Banner soldiers as she walked through the ornate and grandiose hallways. The scale of the palace was enormous, its ceilings high enough to accommodate the largest dragon, and the effect made Konna feel small.

The great audience chamber was empty, so Konna walked up a long ramp and entered an upper level of the palace. She went to Edgar's private chambers, and was allowed through by the soldiers on duty. Inside, she found Edgar dining with Kyra and Esher in a small room that had a long balcony overlooking the city of palaces.

Konna halted before the table, and curtsied.

'Join us, Konna,' said Edgar, his eyes tight. 'Have you eaten lunch?'

'I have not, my lord,' said Konna. 'I hope I am not intruding.'

Edgar frowned. 'Of course not. Sit.'

Konna took a chair, and wondered if something was wrong. Edgar had been more reserved than usual over the previous few months, as though he was being distracted by bad news he was keeping to himself. Esher gave Konna a smile, then he poured her some red wine from a vineyard in the west of Inopei.

Kyra eyed her. 'How did it go with Lord Elmhirst?'

'Badly,' said Konna. 'He refused to even consider my application. He told me to come back in a century.'

'That's what we expected,' said Esher.

'It's what *you* expected,' said Konna. 'I had naively hoped a personal appeal might sway him. I don't wish to sound ungrateful, but I have been here for eight years, and I haven't done a day's work in that time. Back home, I was put to work on the farm from the age of twelve, then I worked in the distillery, and then I killed greenhides for a living in Jezra. I did all that by the time I was eighteen. I cannot help but feel that I am wasting my twenties doing nothing.'

Edgar glanced at her. 'Lord Elmhirst is in charge of all recruitment to the Doomed Worlds; I trust his judgement.'

Konna frowned. 'Can't you do something to help me, cousin?'

'I am not going to interfere,' said Kyra. 'It took me ten years to be accepted by Elmhirst, the gods and the dragons; you will have to be patient.'

'But I have been here eight years,' said Konna; 'why do you get special treatment?'

'You know why,' said Kyra. 'I am mortal. I cannot wait a century, not when the Dominion needs the powers I possess. I protect this city from the Sapphire Empire, and I am training my two sons to take over from me when I become too old to carry out my duties.'

Edgar looked away. 'I would rather not talk about this.'

Konna opened her mouth to speak, but Esher shot her a look, so she sipped from her wine glass instead.

'Perhaps we could travel around Inopei; you and I,' said Esher. 'There is much to see beyond the walls of Nom Karta. After that, we could sail to Aucteran, and visit the great cities on that continent. The harbour at Naeth is reportedly one of the great marvels of Athumia.'

Edgar got to his feet. 'Please excuse me,' he said. 'I have other matters to attend to.'

Kyra also stood. She glanced at Konna, then she followed Edgar out of the dining room.

'Did I miss something?' said Konna.

Esher lowered his gaze.

'Well?' said Konna.

'All of this is as new to me as it is to you,' said Esher. 'Eight years ago, I was a mortal draughtsman in Jezra, and then you and your brother came along and... Anyway, I am not going to pretend I understand the inner workings of Edgar's mind.'

'But you have noticed it, too?' said Konna. 'He seems... preoccupied. Gloomy.'

'A melancholy has settled upon his shoulders,' said Esher.

'Aye, but why?'

Esher gazed at her. 'Kyra is dying.'

'What? But... No. She seems healthy to me. What have you heard?'

'I don't mean that she is about to die right now,' said Esher, 'but I think Edgar is depressed about the inevitability of her death. Kyra is thirty-three; close to the traditional halfway point of a mortal's natural life.'

'She has decades left.'

'Yes, but Edgar has been alive for well over ten thousand years. What are a few decades to him? He loves her deeply, and every day that passes is one fewer he can spend by her side. Look – I don't understand it, either. I can accept that, yes – I am an Ascendant, but you and I are similar. My mind was scoured by Karalyn twenty-six years ago, when you were a baby. We both have memories that span the same amount of time. To gods like Edgar, Elmhirst and Bailey, we are indescribably young; to them, we shall always be young, even after a millennium has passed.'

Konna's spirits sagged. 'Do you ever regret what happened to you? Do you wish that my crazy brother had never given you salve and unblocked your self-healing?'

'I did,' said Esher. 'For at least two or three years I missed my old life, even though I was lonely and friendless in Jezra. I still cannot comprehend what it means to be an Ascendant. Edgar told me that I was once a mortal, thirty thousand years ago. I was one of those who *ascended* into immortality, back on the world that existed before Implacatus. For millennia, I was worshipped as an almighty god.' He laughed. 'Can you imagine? Part of me is glad that I cannot remember any of it. How many wars have I fought? How many civilisations have I seen come and go?' His smile faded. 'How many mortals have I killed? Millions? I am very glad I don't remember that part.'

'None of that helps us now,' she said.

'I know. Do you recall what Kelsey Holdfast said when Kyra suggested that I live among the gods on Inopei? She was worried that the Dominion would gain a great advantage over the Empire, because I was an Ascendant. If only she knew the truth. I am a liability, if anything. I have great power, but what use is power if I have no idea how to wield it? I am like a child who is in possession of one of the Empire's new destructive weapons – a danger to friend and foe alike.'

'Then what do we do?'

'We wait,' he said. 'I was serious about the two of us travelling. Edgar won't allow either of us to get our hands on a Quadrant, so we would have to do it the old-fashioned way, by carriage, on foot, and by ship. We could take years to make our way round Inopei and Aucteran; we could even sail to Zamata.'

Konna said nothing.

'What do you want to do?' said Esher.

'I want to feel useful,' she said. 'Failing that, I would like to visit my mother in Kell. Both are forbidden to me. I feel as out of place here as I did in the Sapphire Empire. I remember telling Maxwell that I wanted to live in the Dominion. Part of the reason for this was to perhaps meet someone. For the same reasons why Edgar is now feeling bad about Kyra, I didn't want to get involved with a mortal. I saw how my mother was after my father died, and I wanted to avoid that. But the gods here aren't interested in me, not beyond a short fling, or a casual affair. They have grown cynical about love and relationships, and so I am stuck between two worlds – the mortals who love but die too soon, and the gods who have forgotten what it is to be human.'

Esher nodded, then his gaze went to the balcony window, as a large pillar of smoke rose up from the streets that ran between the palaces. Moments later, the fierce cry of a dragon in pain reached Konna's ears. She and Esher got to their feet and walked out on to the balcony. The cries were coming from more than one dragon, as smoke billowed up into the clear blue sky.

The cries faded, then a bell started to ring, and Banner soldiers appeared on the nearest street. They were running towards the smoke, but Konna couldn't see what was burning.

'Let's get down there,' said Esher.

Konna powered her battle-vision, as Esher did the same. They leapt over the side of the balcony and landed on the smooth paving slabs by the street below them. Other gods were also rushing towards the scene, along with more soldiers and a few dragons. A large black and white dragon soared over Konna's head, then it circled above the source of the smoke.

'Betrayal!' cried the dragon. 'The Sapphire Empire has broken the peace!'

Konna and Esher ran the rest of the way. They turned a corner by another palace, and saw the smouldering bodies of three dragons. All were dead, their scales charred and blackened, while their flesh continued to burn. The smell was overwhelming, and Konna flinched from the sight. Two dragons landed close to the bodies. They sniffed the roasted remains, then they cried out in grief and rage.

Lord Elmhirst appeared via Quadrant, along with a cadre of armed gods. They pushed back the other humans and formed a cordon, then the black and white dragon landed.

'We have been surprised by the perfidious Holdfasts!' the dragon shouted.

'Please, Lord Konran,' said Elmhirst, 'let us take a moment to investigate. Mortal mages cannot burn dragons; neither can dragon fire. Summon Queen Famula, I beg you.'

Konran eyed Elmhirst with contempt, then he lifted his wings and soared away.

'Did anyone see what happened?' Elmhirst shouted.

'My squad and I were first to arrive, my lord,' said a Banner officer. 'There was no one else here.'

The air shimmered, and Edgar appeared by Kyra's side.

'Holdfasts?' said Edgar.

'I would hesitate to say so, my lord,' said Elmhirst. 'You know my feelings towards the Sapphire Empire, but I struggle to see how a mage or god with fire powers could have done this. Dragons are resistant to that form of attack.'

The gods moved closer to the still-burning bodies. Konna and Esher joined them, and they stared at the blue flames dancing over the flesh of the three dragons.

'It is as though they were burned from the inside,' said Esher. 'How is that possible? How could they still be burning?'

'I do not have an answer,' said Edgar, 'but I agree with Lord Elmhirst – no god or mage power could have done this.'

'A new weapon, my lord?' said Elmhirst. 'We know that the Sapphire Empire has been developing all kinds of abominable devices. Perhaps I spoke too soon; perhaps the Empire is responsible.'

'But why now?' said Kyra. 'We have been at peace with the Empire for fifteen years. If they were going to stage a surprise attack upon Nom

Karta with new weapons, it would have been on a far larger scale. I shall go at once to Zamata to speak to Lord Bailey.'

'Go with her, Elmhirst,' said Edgar. 'Protect my beloved.'

Elmhirst bowed, then both he and Kyra vanished. Several other dragons approached from the sky, including Queen Famula and Lady Abda. They circled overhead, then landed close by. Famula stretched out her long neck, her eyes cold, as she inspected the bodies.

'What could have done this?' she said.

Abda lowered her head. 'I fear I have the answer, my Queen,' she said; 'for I have seen this before.'

'You have?' said Famula. 'Where? Tell us.'

'Upon the battlefields of Gunst, my Queen,' said Abda. 'What we are witnessing are the effects of the Gift of Immolation. I was there, with King Naghad, and I saw what the Gifts could do. The Gifts of Pain, of Withering, of Immolation – all were used to destroy Naghad's invasion forces. We are under attack, but not from the Sapphire Empire.'

'Impossible,' said Famula. 'If it were Gunstians, then where are they? How did they cross the mighty ocean?'

Abda bowed. 'I have no answer to that, my Queen, but I recognise what I see. The Gift of Immolation burns from the inside out. I have seen soldiers burst into flames, though no fires were close by; and I saw dragons explode in the sky, falling to the ground ablaze, though no fires were sent in their direction.'

'Do the Gunstians have Quadrants?' said Konna.

'They do not,' said Edgar. 'The last time Nom Karta was attacked, Konna, your brother Cairney was responsible. Can we be sure that he remains safely in exile?'

'As sure as we can be,' said Konna; 'but my brother has no Gifts.'

'The Sapphire Empire will be to blame,' said Abda. 'They will have been negligent with their Quadrants, just as they were during Cairney's rampage.'

'The Empire has sworn to me on many occasions that they keep a tight grip on their Quadrants,' said Edgar. 'Arrosa Holdfast is responsible for ensuring none go astray. I cannot believe that they would allow the Gunstians to seize any.'

The air shimmered, and Kyra appeared with Elmhirst and Lord Bailey.

Bailey bowed low, then he stared at the smouldering bodies.

'Lady Abda believes that this was the work of the Gifted,' said Edgar.

Bailey frowned. 'But the Gunstians have no way to reach Nom Karta.'

'I know what I saw in Gunst,' cried Abda, 'and I know what lies before my eyes.'

Bailey raised his palms. 'I meant no offence, your noble grace.' He glanced at Kyra. 'Are there Gunstian agents hidden within this city?'

'I have no way of knowing,' said Kyra. 'My powers cannot detect Gifts; I would need to scan the minds of every mortal within the city to be sure.'

'Arrosa would know,' said Konna. 'She has the Gift of Kenning.'

'We shall not be asking the Empire for assistance,' said Famula; 'the humiliation would be too great. I shall consume the bodies of these slain dragons with real fire, to purify this desecration. You will all need to stand back.'

Edgar gestured to the other gods, and they withdrew from the street, pulling back to where the soldiers had formed their cordon.

'What are your orders, my lord?' said Elmhirst.

Edgar gazed at the bodies for a few moments. 'Bailey shall travel to the Star Continent without delay,' he said. 'If one of the Empire's Quadrants has gone missing, we need to know.'

Bailey bowed. 'I shall proceed to Plateau City immediately.'

'Today is Summer's Day in the Holdings calendar,' said Kyra. 'The imperial court might be in Colsbury Castle for the birthday of the Empress.'

'Duly noted, ma'am,' said Bailey.

'Might I go with Lord Bailey?' said Konna. 'Please? Let me help.'

Edgar frowned, then he inclined his head. 'You may go.'

A great burst of fire exploded from Queen Famula's open jaws as she flew over the bodies. The flames flooded the street, consuming the three slain dragons where they lay. Waves of heat rolled out in all directions, as the bodies were reduced to ash.

'If the Gunstians prove responsible,' said Edgar, 'they shall pay for this outrage. Lord Elmhirst, assemble a Quadrant death squad, and begin drills. Be ready to travel to Great Gunst at a moment's notice. And Kyra, contact your mother, and inform her that we are upon the brink of war.'

CHAPTER 2
TOLD OFF

Plateau City, The Plateau – Summer's Day 560

Cael Holdfast walked through the large open archway and on to the Dragon Bridge of the Blue Palace. The heat inside his apartment had been stifling, and he stood for a few moments in the cool breeze. He lit a cigarette and gazed at the view. Below him, Plateau City was basking in the sunlight. The capital of the Empire had outgrown its defensive walls, and the southern suburbs stretched out along the banks of the Inner Sea. Compared to Great Gunst, Plateau City remained small, and Cael knew the exact population, down to its last man, woman and child. He also knew how many people lived in every town and village over the entirety of the Plateau, and, for ten days, he had been supervising the election that had been taking place there.

It had taken eight years, but he had done it. The Plateau had been transformed into a functioning province of the Empire, with its own government based in the Ministry of the Plateau and, when the votes had been counted, it would have its first elected Lord Marshal. He should be feeling proud, but he was exhausted, having used his Quadrant hundreds of times during the previous days, visiting polling stations in the remotest villages, and talking to officials everywhere in the Plateau, from Rainsby to Westport, and from Stretton Sands to Bannerton.

'Good morning, Adjutant,' came a low voice.

'Good morning, Halfclaw,' said Cael. 'Are you ready to travel to Colsbury?'

The blue and green dragon lowered his head towards Cael. 'I am,' he said, 'but Frostback and I shall be flying, rather than appearing by Quadrant. Would you care to join us? It is but a four hour flight to Colsbury, and there can be few pleasures as fine as that of feeling the warm summer air rush over one's wings. Frostback shall be bearing Calpurnia upon her back, but there is room for you and your family.'

Cael smiled at the dragon. 'Thank you for the offer,' he said. 'I am sorely tempted to accept, but the Empress needs us on Colsbury as soon as we are ready, and I wouldn't want to disappoint her. It is Her Majesty's birthday after all.'

'Of course,' said Halfclaw; 'I understand.'

Cael eyed the dragon. He seemed disappointed by Cael's response, but was too proud to admit it.

'Arrosa and I have to be on Colsbury within the hour,' Cael said, 'but the children don't. Might Cowie be allowed to travel upon your back? The other two are too young for such a journey, but Cowie loves nothing more than flying upon a dragon.'

Halfclaw's eyes glowed. 'I would be honoured to carry your son, Adjutant Cael.'

'Then I had better tell him the good news,' said Cael. 'I will send him down to you as soon as he is ready.'

The dragon tilted his head. 'I shall be waiting.'

Cael stubbed out his cigarette, tilted his head at the dragon, and walked back into the Teal Garden of the palace. The waterfalls were glistening in the strong light coming through the long panes of glass, but the gardens had the feel of a greenhouse – hot and humid. Cael walked along the gravel paths, crossing two little bridges over the streams that wound their way through the gardens, then he climbed the steps to his apartment. Inside, Arrosa was trying to organise the three children and their luggage. Kelvin and Carrie were racing around the living room, ignoring their mother's instructions, while Cowie was sitting by the front door with a pack on his knee.

'Carrie, come here and get your shoes on,' said Arrosa; 'it's time to leave.'

Cael waited until the girl ran past him, then he scooped up the six-year-old in his arms. She laughed as Cael set her down on a chair. Arrosa passed him Carrie's shoes, and he crouched down and placed them onto her feet.

'Halfclaw wants to know if Cowie would like to fly to Colsbury,' Cael said, as he laced up the girl's shoes.

The ten-year-old boy sat up straight. 'Can I? Please?'

'You will need to take a flask of water with you,' said Arrosa. 'You will be in the air for four hours. Take some food as well, and a blanket; it can get cold in the mountains.'

The boy raced off into the kitchen.

'Can I go on Halfclaw's back?' said Carrie.

'Maybe next time,' said Cael.

The front door was knocked, and Cael glanced over to see Alva Longhold standing by the entrance.

'Is this a bad time?' said Alva.

'It's not the best time,' said Arrosa, as she pulled a coat over Kelvin's shoulders. 'If you are looking for Cole, he's gone to Colsbury.'

'I know, ma'am,' said Alva; 'I have just been there, and Cole told me you were here. There has been an… incident.'

'What kind of incident?' said Cael.

'I was doing my routine checks along the southern coast of the Inner Sea,' said Alva, 'but I received no response from our agent in Stretton Sands. I went there, but there was no sign of her.'

'Which agent is currently in Stretton Sands?' said Cael.

'Muriel of Hold Terras,' said Arrosa.

'Could she have travelled back to the Holdings for Summer's Day?' said Cael.

'Agent Muriel is reliable,' said Arrosa. 'She wouldn't have absconded like that without asking for permission.'

'She was scheduled to be on duty in Stretton Sands for the entire holiday, ma'am,' said Alva. 'There were signs of a struggle in her apartment – the door had been forced; chairs knocked over – and there was a full cup of tea sitting on a table.'

'When was this?' said Cael.

'I was there less than an hour ago,' said Alva, 'then I went to Colsbury. I told Herald Kelsey and Lord Saewa, and they told me to let you know right away.'

'Was anything taken from her apartment?' said Cael.

'Her Quadrant wasn't there, sir, if that's what you mean,' said Alva.

Cael and Arrosa glanced at each other.

'I had better visit her family home in the Holdings,' said Arrosa.

'Lord Saewa will take care of that, ma'am,' said Alva. 'He should be there by now.'

'How many people knew Muriel's address in Stretton Sands?' said Cael.

'Seven,' said Arrosa, 'and I have vetted each one of them. It's possible that someone might have overheard her talking about it, I suppose; though no agents are permitted to tell anyone what they do.'

'Muriel mentioned to me that she had started seeing someone,' said Alva.

Arrosa's eyes narrowed. 'She didn't tell me that. Who?'

'I don't know, ma'am.'

Cowie emerged from the kitchen carrying a second bag. 'I have got water and food for the journey,' he said.

'Good lad,' said Cael. 'Halfclaw is waiting for you on the bridge.'

Arrosa kissed her son on the cheek, then he swerved past Alva and ran out of the apartment. Cael walked out onto the balcony to watch Cowie race through the gardens, and he noticed two figures walking off the Dragon Bridge.

'Bailey and Konna are here,' he said.

Arrosa and Alva joined him on the balcony, and they watched as

Cowie passed the two gods by one of the little bridges. Bailey glanced up and raised a hand in greeting, then both he and Konna appeared on the balcony.

'Happy Summer's Day,' said Cael. 'What can we do for you?'

'I wasn't sure if you would still be here,' said Bailey.

'We were just about to leave,' said Arrosa.

Cael remained by the edge of the balcony, his gaze on Cowie as he ran up to the green and blue dragon. Halfclaw and the boy exchanged a few words, then Cowie clambered up onto the dragon's back. Halfclaw stretched out his wings, just as Frostback appeared through the archway leading to the Eastern Tower, with Calpurnia on her shoulders. The two dragons took off and ascended into the clear blue sky. They circled the palace once, then sped off towards the north.

Cael turned. 'I didn't think Edgar allowed you to leave Nom Karta, Konna.'

'Is that supposed to be a joke?' said the demigod.

'Just an observation,' said Cael. 'Did you know that the population of the Plateau has spent the last ten days voting for their new government? Ask my sister when she intends to allow the Aucterians to vote.'

'I am sure this is all very amusing to you, Adjutant,' said Bailey, 'but we are here with some bad news. A short time ago, Nom Karta was attacked, and three dragons were slain. We are here to ask if you know anything about this.'

'Why would we know about an attack on Athumia?' said Cael. 'Are you implying that we ordered it?'

'Certainly not,' said Bailey. 'However, previous lapses in imperial security have led to problems in the past; you would agree? The perpetrators used a Quadrant to assault Nom Karta. Are all of your Quadrants accounted for?'

'When did this attack occur?'

'Around two hours ago.'

Arrosa eyed Alva. 'When were you last in contact with Agent Muriel?'

'Yesterday evening, ma'am,' said Alva; 'but I spoke to one of her neighbours, who assured me that she was in her apartment this morning. The cup of tea on her table was still warm.'

'And who is Agent Muriel?' said Bailey.

'She's one of ours,' said Arrosa. 'She has gone missing, along with her Quadrant, but the times don't seem to match. The attack on Nom Karta appears to have taken place before Muriel's disappearance.'

'What else do you know?' said Cael. 'Were there any clues regarding the identity of the people who killed the dragons?'

Bailey eyed them. 'They were Gunstian.'

Arrosa frowned. 'How do you know that?'

'Lady Abda was part of King Naghad's invasion of Gunst,' said Bailey, 'and she has assured us that the dragons were killed by the Gift of Immolation. They were burned from the inside out. How else could fire destroy a dragon? That was a serious question, by the way. If you have an answer, I would like to hear it.'

'I didn't think any kind of fire could kill a dragon,' said Cael.

'The Gift of Immolation could,' said Arrosa. 'The assailant would need to be close, but it could certainly work. Have the Gunstians responsible been caught?'

'They have not,' said Bailey. 'They seemed to have used a Quadrant. Perhaps they used Agent Muriel's Quadrant? If that is the case, then the Empire has once again failed to adhere to the most basic precepts of security.'

'Her cup of tea was still warm,' said Alva. 'Muriel disappeared after this attack, not before.'

'So you say,' said Bailey. 'Tell me – if the device used was not the one owned by Muriel, then which other device could it have been? The Dominion certainly hasn't been leaving Quadrants lying around where any Gunstian could pick them up. Have you lost any others?'

'None,' said Arrosa. 'There are tight controls on the agents authorised to keep a Quadrant; it isn't like the old days, when they were handed out to all and sundry. I am responsible for every imperial Quadrant in existence.'

'And yet you have allowed Muriel to vanish with hers?' said Bailey.

'That is true,' said Arrosa.

'What are you going to do about it?'

'We learned of this minutes before you arrived, Bailey,' said Cael. 'We will take care of it.'

'How?'

'That's none of your damn business,' said Cael.

'I fear Queen Famula will not be satisfied with this response,' said Bailey. 'You have lost a Quadrant, but I am supposed to tell her that it wasn't used to kill three of her subjects? What other Quadrant could it have been?'

Cael cursed under his breath. He caught Arrosa's gaze.

Do you remember Archpriest Paltanai? he said in her mind.

Arrosa narrowed her eyes.

'What is going on?' said Bailey. 'I can tell when you are using your vision, Cael. What are you hiding from me?'

'We aren't hiding anything,' said Cael. He lit a cigarette. 'Eight years ago, Arrosa and I were in Great Gunst.'

'Yes, I recall,' said Bailey. 'You were supposed to be negotiating a trade deal and, instead, you obliterated the oldest temple in Gunst. Your diplomatic prowess is well known, Adjutant Cael.'

'I had good reasons for acting as I did,' said Cael. 'The Gunstians were lucky I didn't obliterate their entire city.'

Bailey rolled his eyes. 'Was there a point to this digression?'

'My Quadrant was taken while I was under arrest,' said Arrosa.

Bailey stared at her. 'What?'

'It was reported at the time, in full,' said Cael. 'A Gunstian priest took it, then he accidentally triggered it and disappeared.'

'I remember that,' said Konna.

'Thank you, cousin,' said Cael. 'We had all assumed that this priest was dead. He could have gone anywhere on Athumia, or even to another world. And he had no idea how to use it. It is possible – unlikely, but possible – that this priest somehow made it all the way back to Great Gunst.'

'Might the Gunstians have then used that device to steal Muriel's Quadrant?' said Alva. 'That would mean they now have two.'

'But how could they have learned how to operate a Quadrant?' said Arrosa. 'The design isn't intuitive; you need to be taught.'

'I can think of a few ways,' said Bailey. 'Your portals, for instance. The men and women who control the Calendar Pole Portals make no attempt to conceal their finger movements when they activate their devices. And, if we are talking about Gunstians, then perhaps a Death Reader could have taken the information from someone recently deceased.'

'That's pure speculation,' said Cael.

Carrie walked on to the balcony. 'When are we going to Colsbury?' she said. 'I am ready.'

'That's a fine idea, little miss,' said Bailey. 'Perhaps we should all go to see the Empress. I have a few things I would quite like to say to her.'

'You take them, Cael,' said Arrosa. 'Alva and I will visit Muriel's apartment. She might have returned, for all we know.'

'All right,' said Cael.

Arrosa kissed him, then she took out her Quadrant. She moved her fingers over its surface, then she and Alva disappeared. Cael stubbed out his cigarette and took hold of his own Quadrant.

'Let's move into the house,' he said. 'We have a lot of luggage to take along.'

They walked into the living room. Cael locked their front door, then he gathered Kelvin and Carrie, and stood next to their pile of baggage. Bailey and Konna joined them, and Cael activated the Quadrant.

The air shimmered, and they appeared in the wide forecourt on Colsbury, between the two keeps and the Summer Palace. Flags and pennants were flying from every tower, and were draped over the front of the palace, while the forecourt was busy with members of the imperial government who had arrived for the summer.

'Very festive,' said Bailey.

'It's the Empress's birthday,' said Konna.

'I am glad to see you remember,' said Cael.

Konna eyed him, then she turned to Bailey. 'I would rather not have to see the Empress or the Herald,' she said. 'I wouldn't want to make a scene.'

'Quite,' said Bailey. 'You can remain down here.'

'There is food and entertainment on offer in the gardens,' said Cael; 'or you could run away and hide, so you don't have to go back to the Dominion.'

Bailey raised an eyebrow. 'Yes, I am sure that Konna would wish to live in a place where terrorists can easily get their hands on a Quadrant.'

'It's the price of living in a free society,' said Cael.

'And yet it is the Dominion that keeps footing the bill,' said Bailey.

The god touched his Quadrant, and they appeared on the middle balcony of the Summer Palace, leaving Konna in the courtyard below them.

Cael caught the eye of a courtier. 'Could you please take Kelvin and Carrie to our quarters?'

'And your luggage, my lord?' said the courtier.

'Aye, that too.'

Cael watched as the courtier led the two children away, then he gestured for Bailey to follow him into the palace.

'If it transpires that the attack upon Nom Karta was carried out with the use of an imperial Quadrant,' said the Empress, 'then I can only apologise on behalf of the Empire. We believed Archpriest Paltanai had long since perished.'

'That might still be the case, Your Majesty,' said Kelsey. 'Lord Bailey has brought us no evidence regarding this attack.'

'Are you suggesting that I am being less than honest, Herald?' said Bailey.

'No one is suggesting that,' said the Empress.

'Forgive me, Your Majesty,' said Lucius Cardova, 'but might we all be missing the larger point? If Lady Abda's suspicions are correct, and if the Gunstians have carried out this attack; indeed, if they now possess two Quadrants and the knowledge of how to use them, then both the Empire and the Dominion are in danger. We might do better to work more closely together, in order to face this mutual enemy.'

'How is the Empire in any danger, Lord Constable?' said Bailey. 'The Dominion has been the Gunstian's enemy for over a thousand years.'

'And yet the Gunstian's three biggest enemies all reside within the Empire,' said Cardova: 'Lord Sigum, Lahnos Laimos, and Cael Holdfast. If the Gunstians have a list of targets, those three names will appear near the top.'

'Then perhaps we should retaliate first,' said Cael. 'I am not averse to the idea of going back to Great Gunst to finish off the job.'

Bailey shook his head. 'And who ever said that the Holdfasts were warmongers? You slaughtered over a hundred leading figures in the Gunstian army, navy, church and government, as well as reducing their most sacred temple to a pile of charred rubble – and for what? Because they arrested your wife?'

'Aye,' said Cael, 'and I would do it again. Let me do it again, Your Majesty.'

'Calm down,' said Kelsey. 'We are going to need to see some evidence before we send anyone to Gunst. The Empire has had no official word from the Gunstians since you destroyed the Temple of the Martyrs, but we can be sure that they have spies on Zamata.'

'If they have Paltanai's Quadrant,' said Bailey, 'they might also have spies on the Star Continent. I like the Lord Constable's thinking, however; perhaps we should see if the next attack occurs on imperial soil.'

Kelsey laughed. 'They hate you more than they hate Cael or Lahnos, Bailey. If anyone is next on the list, it will be you.'

'I would like to come to an agreement with the Dominion,' said Cardova. 'We could share intelligence, and coordinate our efforts. There is no reason for us to work in isolation.'

'I would be open to that,' said the Empress.

Bailey shook his head. 'I will relay this to Lord Edgar and Queen Famula, Your Majesty, but I can guess their response. Unfortunately for the Empire, your past record of assaulting Nom Karta does not inspire us with confidence. If Karalyn hadn't stopped you, the entire royal family would have been annihilated. Dragons rarely forget such slights; gods never do.'

'That was fifteen years ago,' said Kelsey, 'and we were at war.'

Bailey smiled. 'I love how mortals think. Fifteen years must seem like a terribly long time to you, Herald. What was it? – a thousand dragons in one day? Quite the achievement; worthy of the gods, one would think.'

'You have crossed a line, Bailey,' said Cael.

'Of course,' said the god, 'you were there, too, weren't you, Adjutant Holdfast; along with Sable and Cole. And you call the gods bloodthirsty?'

'This is getting us nowhere,' said the Empress. 'I care nothing for your petty gibes, Lord Bailey; and if you have nothing productive to add, then you may return to the Dominion.'

Bailey bowed low. 'You are too gracious, Your Majesty. I shall return forthwith, as soon as I have recovered Konna from the gardens of Colsbury.'

He swiped his Quadrant and vanished. The members of the Imperial Court eyed each other.

'That could have gone better,' said Kelsey.

'It was all an act,' said Cael. 'Bailey doesn't care that we killed a thousand Wystian dragons fifteen years ago. We rescued him from a dungeon in Nom Karta that day, after Ward, Allura and Belfar had placed a restrainer mask onto his face. It was an act, so that he can go back to Edgar and Famula and tell them that he gave us all a proper telling off.'

'I do not doubt your words, Adjutant,' said the Empress, 'but I regret a missed opportunity to work closer with the Dominion. We have far more in common with the Dominion than either of us does with the

Gunstians. If our suspicions are correct, and they are in possession of two Quadrants, what will they do next?'

'If I had to guess, Your Majesty,' said Kelsey, 'they want three things – to neutralise the Dominion as an enemy capable of destroying them; to gain revenge over the Empire for what Cael did to them eight years ago; and to eliminate those we have already mentioned – Bailey, Lahnos, Sigum and, aye, our own Cael Holdfast. Arrosa, too, if they get the chance.'

'Their armed forces are extremely numerous,' said Claudian, 'but they pose no serious danger to the Empire.'

'Maybe so, Chief of Staff,' said the Empress, 'but I am not worried about their army. It is the combination of Gifts and Quadrants that concerns me. If they have the ability to project small teams of elite Gifted to anywhere within the bounds of the Empire and Dominion, they could cause tremendous damage. To my mind, our priority must be to recover any Quadrants in their possession, and to ensure that no more go missing. On that subject, where is my Postmaster?'

'Arrosa is investigating the apartment of the missing agent, Your Majesty,' said Cael; 'and another agent has been dispatched to her family home in the Holdings. Until now, Arrosa has kept a very tight grip on the Empire's Quadrants, but she couldn't have foreseen Paltanai's return, if that is what has happened.'

'No one is blaming your wife for this, Cael,' said the Empress, 'but I need answers. We need to know how many Quadrants are in the hands of the Gunstians, and we need a plan to get them back, or to destroy them. See to it, Adjutant.'

Cael bowed, then he turned and began to walk out of the large audience chamber. He caught Cole's gaze, and gestured for his cousin to join him, and they both left the hall.

'It was nice to hear your opinion in there, cousin,' said Cael.

'You know me,' said Cole. 'I prefer to listen.'

'And what did you conclude?'

'That your life is in danger,' said Cole. 'The Gunstians will never forget what you did to them, cousin. Did you have to go so far? Couldn't you have executed a couple of priests and left it at that? Of course you couldn't, because you are the mighty Cael Holdfast, and you have a reputation to uphold. *Arrest my wife? In return, I will slaughter hundreds and demolish the most holy temple in all of Gunst.*'

'I had to teach them a lesson,' said Cael.

'Maybe, but that was a lesson from the Sable school of thought.'

'What would you have done?'

Cole looked thoughtful for a moment. 'I think I would have taken Arrosa out of there and left no trace behind; that would have rattled them. They wouldn't have been able to understand what had happened; it would have looked to them as though she had just vanished.'

They walked out on to the middle balcony, and found Arrosa and Alva standing there, talking to Lord Saewa.

'Did you find anything?' said Cael.

'The man Muriel was seeing has also seemingly vanished,' said Arrosa. 'We questioned several neighbours, who saw him arrive at Muriel's apartment this morning.'

'I thought her door had been forced open?' said Cael.

'It had,' said Arrosa. 'Maybe she didn't want to let him in, or maybe he wanted it to look like a robbery. The house had been turned over, but the cup of tea is still sitting on the table.'

'There was no sign of her on the Hold Terras estate, sir,' said Saewa; 'and they had never heard of any boyfriend.'

'So, what are we thinking?' said Cael. 'That Muriel was taken in by a smooth-talking Gunstian agent, even though she has vision powers? And then that agent stole her Quadrant and vanished with her?'

'Muriel couldn't speak Gunstian,' said Arrosa. 'She wouldn't have been able to read his thoughts.'

'And she didn't think that was suspicious?' said Cael.

'She was only twenty,' said Alva. 'She could be dead by now.'

'If I were that Gunstian agent,' said Saewa, 'and I was ruthless enough, I would have taken Muriel to a Death Reader. If that's the case, then the Gunstians will now know everything she knew.'

Cael leaned on the balcony railings and lit a cigarette. 'Is it any wonder the Dominion is angry with us? A twenty-year-old agent gets tricked by the Gunstians, and now they have her Quadrant and her knowledge of the inner workings of the Empire.'

'Muriel did not know very much,' said Arrosa. 'I am very careful about the information given out to individual agents. She didn't know the names or locations of any other agents, for example; apart from Alva, and she only knew her name.'

'Did she know that the Imperial Court moves to Colsbury every summer?' said Cael.

'Everyone in the Empire knows that,' said Arrosa

'Let's try to think like the Gunstians,' said Saewa. 'They will be expecting the Dominion to retaliate; and they will foresee a time when the Empire might have to take action against them. We could imagine that they have formed a tight group – Gifted warriors, and those able to operate a Quadrant. I wouldn't place a group like that in Great Gunst – I would put them somewhere remote, and allow them to operate as a closed unit. Give them a list of targets, and let them get on with it. They know we can read minds, so they are likely to have withheld any detailed information from the bulk of the government in their capital city. Perhaps no one in Great Gunst knows where they are. Perhaps they aren't even based in Gunst. That's what I would do.'

'They could be right under our noses,' said Cael.

'Precisely,' said Saewa. 'To counter them, we shall have to anticipate their next move. Am I correct in saying that the location of Lord Lahnos Laimos and Lord Sigum is a secret known to very few in the Imperial Court?'

'You are,' said Cael.

'Then you or Lord Bailey would appear to be the most likely targets, my lord,' said Saewa.

'There is another option,' said Cole. 'The attack on Nom Karta and Muriel's disappearance could be unrelated. All we have to go on is the testimony of Lady Abda, who claims that the three dragons were killed by the Gift of Immolation. We might be jumping to the wrong conclusion. There might be a rogue Gunstian living on Inopei, who is acting without orders. They might not have a Quadrant.'

'I agree,' said Cael, 'but we should behave as though the threat is real. If I am a target, then I am happy to act as bait.'

Arrosa frowned. 'I don't like that line of thought. You have a wife and three children, Cael. I have no desire to be a widow.'

'I am not going to hide away,' said Cael. 'If the Gunstians want me, they can come and get me.'

CHAPTER 3
ANOTHER TIME AND PLACE

Unnamed World – No Calendar (Summer's Day 560)

Karalyn placed her hand onto the flat surface of the Sextant.

What is your desire, Karalyn?

'Show me the Star Continent,' said Karalyn.

Her vision blurred, then it re-focussed into sharp detail. Karalyn gazed down at the vast continent spread out below her. She preferred looking at the world of her birth from a great height; it looked peaceful and quiet. She stared at the world for a long time, almost forgetting why she had chosen to look at it, then she remembered – she was checking that the peace still held. She couldn't recall how many years had passed since her brother Corthie had died, but it had been at that point that she had forced the Empire and the Dominion to agree to a peace treaty. It wasn't just that she had lost track of time; the world where she lived – a world that she had created for herself – had no calendar or seasons. Every day lasted twelve hours, and the nights that followed were the same. The weather followed a regular pattern: cool in the mornings, warm and sunny in the afternoons, with clear skies each night, and an hour or two of rain before dawn. She had created no moon for her world, but she could gaze up at the stars before going to sleep.

Her next world would have a moon, if she could work out the best way to make one. On a previous attempt, her moon had collided with her newly-created world, obliterating both, and killing all of the plants and animals that had populated the land and seas. That had been heartbreaking. She would need to do better.

She frowned. What was she supposed to be doing?

The Star Continent. Aye. She was checking that the world was at peace.

'Move closer to Plateau City,' she said to the Sextant.

Her vision centred on the sea in the middle of the continent, then homed in on its northern shores. Karalyn rolled her eyes at the first thing she could make out in the city – the damnable Blue Palace; a great edifice that, to Karalyn, proved beyond doubt the hubris and arrogance of Thorn of Greyfalls Deepen. Thorn stayed at the very top of one of the two horn-like towers – a ridiculous place to live. Did she believe herself to be a god? It was pathetic.

On the first few occasions when Karalyn had attempted to penetrate Thorn's living quarters, she had been rebuffed by the ingenious architecture, which had clearly been designed to prevent vision mages and Quadrant-owners from seeing what was going on inside, but, after practice, she had mastered the tower's complexities. She pushed her vision into the gardens that covered all three floors of Thorn's residence. She liked the gardens, and had to admit they were a nice touch that humanised the place, but her contempt towards Thorn remained undiminished.

Karalyn had developed a list of the most dangerous people to watch, and Thorn sat at the very top. Before the massacre of the Wystian dragons, she had been more ambivalent towards Thorn, but that event had tarnished her forever in Karalyn's eyes. To her great regret, her own son Cael was second on the list. He had been eager to assist Thorn on that day on Na Sun Ka, and had he not also been moments away from hammering nails into the eyes of his cousin Cairney? Cael was arrogant and over-confident, and Karalyn hated the way that he reminded her of her own mother Daphne. She had been just as bad, in her own way, and her grandson had inherited many of her traits. Cael was as ruthless as Sable, but Karalyn's aunt had no place on her list. Lara and her two children had seen to that, and Sable had remained peaceful for well over a decade.

Karalyn gazed around the garden, but it was deserted. She peered into the quarters of Kelsey and Thorn, but no one was there. Where was everyone?

'Show me Colsbury,' she said.

Her view panned out, then it raced to the north, covering two hundred miles in a few seconds. The view refocused on the small island where Karalyn had lived for many years, while she had been caring for her children, and while Lucius Cardova had been her husband. She should probably loathe Lucius for going off with her sister Kelsey. Most women would, she guessed, but, in truth, she didn't care what he did. At least he made Kelsey happy, and Karalyn was content with that. She scanned the people crowding the large forecourt at the heart of the isle. It was summer on the Star Continent, and a huge number of people were there for the endless parties and festivities that ran until Autumn's Day. Karalyn had hated that time of year, when her tranquillity would be disturbed by hordes of visitors attending the imperial court.

Karalyn frowned. What was Bailey doing on Colsbury? The god was wandering through the forecourt as though he was looking for someone.

She entered his mind.

What are you doing here, Bailey? she said.

The god jumped, his eyes widening in fear.

Answer me, she said. *Why are you on Colsbury? Has the peace been broken?*

Karalyn? he said. *Is that you?*

Who else would it be?

Well, I don't know. Um... No. The peace is intact, but there is a little local trouble with the Gunstians. It seems that the Empire's incompetence has allowed them to get their hands on a Quadrant, and they killed three dragons. I was sent here to...

I don't care. As long as the peace remains, I will stay out of human affairs. Goodbye.

She withdrew from his mind, and turned her attention to the Summer Palace. Standing on the middle balcony were several people she knew – Cael, Arrosa and Cole. They were with a Holdings woman, and an older man... Was that Saewa from the Serpent Isle? Odd. Karalyn moved her vision away from the balcony and entered the palace. She went to the grand audience hall, where a giant curved window was letting in the summer sunshine. It was mostly empty, but sitting by a table were Kelsey and Lucius Cardova. They were whispering together, then Kelsey laughed. Lucius started to laugh too, and Karalyn began to feel jealous. He had rarely laughed like that when he had been married to her, she thought. She gazed at them. They seemed happy. They seemed right for each other, and, for the first time in years, Karalyn felt a slight pang of loneliness. She rebuked herself. She had craved peace and quiet, and she had found it; in fact, she had created her own world precisely so that she could live alone, unencumbered by the demands of others.

She left the hall, and found Thorn climbing the stairs to her private quarters, accompanied by a large group of sycophantic courtiers. Karalyn watched the Empress for a few moments, resisting the temptation to pry into her mind. How had such a vain and shallow woman become the anointed ruler of an entire empire? Karalyn had never been able to understand it. What seemed to make it worse was that so few others saw what she saw – Lucius Cardova, for example, held Thorn to be a great and noble leader, and his loyalty to her had always rankled with Karalyn. Kelsey also loved her deeply, and respected her; and Kelsey did not respect many people. Sable was the same – she admired Thorn, though she was also aware of her faults. Cael, too, was devoted to the Empress; the list went on. What did they see in Thorn that Karalyn didn't? Only Kyra and Keir had rejected Thorn's callow charms, while Bridget had loathed her from the very beginning. Now, there was a fine Empress. Bridget may have had her difficulties with alcohol and a rash temper, but she had loved the people of the Empire above all else. If only she hadn't tried to place her son on the throne – that one act of folly had allowed Daphne to engineer Thorn's coronation.

'Show me Nom Karta on Athumia,' she said, as Thorn disappeared into her quarters.

Her vision went black for a moment, then the great city of dragon palaces emerged in front of her. It was far cleaner than it had been when Karalyn had been there while in Lyla's body, and the palaces had been restored to their former grandeur. Most of the Bullan had gone, replaced by Banner soldiers in shiny Tempest breastplates, and the sky was filled with dragons circling and wheeling over the city.

Karalyn made for the palace of Naghad, and entered the residence where her daughter lived with Edgar. Kyra had been a source of great joy and an equal measure of frustration to Karalyn over the years, but she had matured into a principled woman; and she still abhorred violence in all its forms. It was strange how the pendulum swung. At times, Karalyn had been closer to Cael, and then Kyra, and then Cael again; but for the previous few years since Corthie's death, Karalyn had preferred her daughter. While Cael had tried to drive nails into Cairney's head, Kyra had taken pity on Esher and Konna, and had allowed them both to live in peace on Athumia.

She saw no sign of her daughter in the residence, and took her hand off the Sextant, her scan complete. The Empire and the Dominion remained at peace, and there was nothing more to see. Karalyn frowned, as though she was missing something, then it struck her – she had overlooked her other two children. She had seen Cael, and had looked for Kyra, but neither Caitlyn nor Carden had entered her thoughts.

Karalyn closed her eyes, cursing her selfishness. How could she have forgotten the two children she and Lucius had made together? Were her earlier children more important because they had been fathered by Lennox? No – that was too simplistic. Caitlyn and Carden were both immortal, and that had given Karalyn a warped view of their relationship. While Cael and Kyra's time was short, the other two would be around forever, and Karalyn's assumption was that she would be able to resume her relationship with them at any point in the future.

She remembered promising Caitlyn and Carden that she would pay them more attention as soon as they developed their god powers, whatever those powers happened to be. Had that occurred? What year was it? How old were they? She couldn't recall. She hovered her hand over the Sextant, then hesitated. She knew she should look for them, but something was making her feel awkward and foolish. The longer she left it, the worse it would be, and yet she couldn't bring herself to touch the Sextant. What if they hated her? Had her neglect of them made them bitter? There were too many questions, and Karalyn had no desire to have them answered.

Another time, she told herself, as she pulled her hand away. Another time.

She walked out of the Sextant chamber, and onto a balcony that ran along the entire front of her large house. The word *house* was wrong. The rooms had been dug out of the side of a cliff, tunnelled backwards into the bedrock, and her balcony overlooked the most beautiful view on the whole world – mountains, valleys, rivers, meadows. She had retained the trees and shrubs that had clung onto the side of the cliff, and birds would nest there all year long; though how long each year lasted was a mystery to her. It all rolled into one. She sat down and gazed at the view. Her view. No other human eyes had ever looked upon it, and none ever would.

She should give her world a name. She laughed. It was a recurring thought – what should she call her world? – but she had never found an answer. She had made it for only two reasons – as somewhere to hide the Sextant, and as a place where she could rest and find peace. Were it not for the fact that she had to travel into more civilised places to purchase food, clothes and everything else she needed, she would never leave it. There was a large market in Naeth on Aucteran that sold all the things she required. She would disguise herself as a little old lady, and wander through the streets, listening to the sound of the gulls flying over the vast, circular harbour. Anonymous, she could buy whatever caught her eye, before retreating back to her home. The people living in Plateau City liked to think that they were the epitome of civilisation, but Karalyn found Naeth to be a better city in many ways. It was dirty and bustling, but it was also full of life; and it was far more similar to cities in the Empire than anyone on either side of the divide would care to admit. It was the same with Teros City. In fact, Aucteran seemed almost like the Holdings at times, or the Plateau.

Karalyn started to grow restless. She should go back to the Sextant, to continue her long labours on the creation of a world suitable for the Rakanese to inhabit. She required vast continents filled with low-lying wetlands, and her first few attempts had been dismal failures. Some had been too salty, others too dry, others too rocky; but she would need to carry on. If she didn't, then, some day in the future, the Rakanese population would overwhelm the Star Continent, which would lead to a whole set of new problems that everyone would expect her to fix. People always expected her to fix their problems.

She had been made aware of a terrible rumour, one that filled her with disgust. She had read it from Lucius Cardova's head the last time they had spoken. She hadn't thought much of it at the time, as she had been preoccupied with his feelings for Kelsey, and it had only been later that she had remembered the details of what she had seen. There was a temple in Plateau City – a new temple, whose congregation worshipped her as the one true god. Apparently, they prayed to her, invoking her name as they begged her for whatever it was they wanted. She hadn't answered any of their prayers; instead, she had stayed well clear of the building, never once going to see if the rumours were true. No one could be that gullible, could they? If they were behaving rationally, they should have disbanded as soon as they had realised that she was never going to respond to their pleas; but Karalyn suspected that human nature didn't work that way.

She got to her feet, then sat down again. She needed to learn how to relax.

She got back to her feet and walked into the third floor of her home. She went into the Sextant chamber, and listened to the gentle noise it made. The Weathervane was always embedded into its flank; with no one knowing how to find her unnamed world, there was little point in separating the sword from the device. She lifted her right hand, and placed her palm on the surface of the Sextant.

What is your desire, Karalyn?

She thought of her Rakanese swamps, and changed her mind.

'Show me Cairney's world,' she said.

Her vision went dark, then she saw the small, forested continent upon the world where she had placed her nephew. Dark clouds were covering the sky, and great mountain peaks were rearing their barren heads above the shadowy lands. Karalyn searched until she found a wide river she recognised, then she followed it away from the ocean. She reached the caves where she had deposited Cairney, and saw the remains of many fires that had blackened the stony ground. She peered into the caves. Animal bones were piled up in one corner, along with several homemade spears and a small stone-bladed axe. In another cave was a bed formed from thick piles of moss and leaves, covered with furs and skins; and in a long alcove were the books that Karalyn had brought when she had last visited. The volumes of history, languages and politics had clearly been well-read, and they were all present, apart from one – her sister's *History of the Star Continent*. Karalyn smiled to herself. Cairney had most likely burned Kelsey's book; but she wondered if he had read it first.

She withdrew from the caves, and gazed around the harsh landscape. Cairney was sitting on the brow of a low, rocky ridge, staring out at the deep valley that ran below him. He was still wearing a few tattered pieces of his original clothes, but thick furs were draped over his broad shoulders, and his right hand was grasping a stone-tipped spear. Sympathy welled within Karalyn for a brief moment, as she gazed at the young god sitting alone. He was the only human on the entire world, and she felt a sudden longing to speak to him in person. She took her hand off the Sextant, and walked into a side room, where her small library of books was stored. She selected a few volumes at random, then she went into her kitchen and packed a large bag with items Cairney would be unable to find on his world – cheese, bread, olives, jam, and a bottle of wine. She placed the books into the bag, and pulled the strap over her shoulder.

The ridge where Cairney sits. Go.

The air shimmered, and she appeared a few feet from where Cairney was sitting. The young god eyed her without flinching, then he went back to gazing over the valley.

'Hello, Cairney,' she said.

'Have you come to release me?' he said.

'Do you deserve to be released?'

Cairney laughed. 'Read my mind, ya mad witch, and you'll find out.'

'Do you regret what you did?'

'Which bit? No. I don't regret any of it. I made a lot of mistakes; stupid mistakes – but what's the point of feeling regret?'

Karalyn pulled the bag from her shoulder. 'I have brought you some things.'

She placed the bag next to him, but he ignored it.

'How is my family?' he said.

'They are all well,' she said. 'Killop is working on the Hold Fast estate. He has taken over from Celine, who has finally been allowed to retire. They are getting along well. Konna is still on Athumia, living with Kyra and the gods from the Doomed Worlds.'

Cairney said nothing.

'Your other siblings are all living in Clackenbaird,' Karalyn went on. 'Carter and Clova both have jobs in Marchbrae; but Carron will be eighteen soon, and he is getting ready to leave.'

'Where is he going?'

'To the Holdings, to help Killop on the estate,' said Karalyn. 'Your youngest sisters Ceres and Carla are still at school.'

'If Carron is going to be eighteen soon,' he said, 'then I have been here for nearly eight years.'

'Is that right?' she said. 'I find it hard to keep track of time.'

'Do you know why that is, Karalyn?' he said.

'Why?'

'Because you're a fucking idiot. You have more power than anyone who's ever been born, but you live in your own wee dream world. I hate your mortal children, but they know how to act – one of them is running the Dominion, the other is next in line to become the fucking Emperor – but you? What do you do, Karalyn?'

'I keep the peace.'

He laughed again, then he opened the bag. 'Books? I can't eat books.'

'There is food under the books.'

Cairney raked around in the bag, then he took out a wrapped block of cheese. His eyes lit up, and he took a large bite out of it.

'Fucking cheese,' he said; 'come to Cairney. Is there any booze?'

'Some wine.'

Cairney snorted. 'Well, that was a waste. I won't be drinking any of that shite. Next time, bring me whisky. You know what, Karalyn – one day, I am going to kill you.'

'You can try,' she said. 'I am unkillable. You may succeed in destroying this body, but my spirit will never die.'

'So you say,' he said. 'I'm going to put that theory to the test.'

'I shall not release you until you are repentant.'

'Then I guess I'm going to be stuck on this world for a while longer,' he said. 'It makes no difference to me. Naxor always told us to be patient, but I didn't appreciate what he meant. I was too headstrong; too eager for revenge, and that was my mistake. This world has taught me patience. When I'm out hunting, I sometimes have to wait for hours, still and silent in the darkness of the forest, stalking prey. Without patience, I would never be able to eat meat, and Cairney can't survive on fruit and berries alone.' He gazed up at her. 'The same applies to you. I'm going to stalk you, as if you were just another beast, and then I'm going to cut your fucking head off.' He laughed. 'I won't eat you, though. I'll throw you to wild dogs, and they can have you. It's funny – when I was growing up in Kell, it was the Empress and Kelsey I hated. I wanted to kill them both; but now? I don't think I give a shit about them any more. They're only mortal; they're beneath my contempt. It's you I hate, Karalyn.'

'I saved you from execution,' she said, 'and I saved you from a restrainer mask.'

'All that proves is that the great Karalyn also makes mistakes,' he said. 'If you were smart, you'd kill me now.'

'I am not going to kill you, nephew.'

Cairney turned his gaze back to the valley. 'How is my mother?'

'The same,' she said. 'I rarely check on Aila. She hates me almost as much as you do.'

'I'm glad she hates you. Will you do something for me, but? Will you tell her that I love her? Will you tell her that I'm trying hard to be patient?'

'I will do this.'

Cairney nodded. 'You can go now.'

Karalyn eyed the young god, then she turned away.

The Sextant Chamber. Go.

Karalyn appeared back in her cliffside home, a yard from the Sextant. Rather than dwell on what Cairney had said to her, she stepped forward, and placed her hand onto the device.

What is your desire, Karalyn?

'Show me Clackenbaird Farm.'

Her vision swept to the peninsula on the far south-western corner of the Star Continent, and she saw the large farmhouse on the top of the hill. On the next summit along stood Corthie's cairn; and the buildings of Marchbrae Distillery were spread out between the two peaks. Karalyn focussed on the farmhouse, and entered through a window. The house was quiet. The older children were out at work, while the youngest were at school, and Aila was standing alone in the kitchen. She had a faraway look in her eyes as she waited for the kettle to come to the boil on the stove, and Karalyn almost turned back. She took a slow breath, and entered the mind of the demigod. Rather than talk to her like that, she projected an image of herself standing a few yards away from Aila.

The demigod turned her head. 'Are you really here?' she said.

'No,' said Karalyn.

'What do you want from me, Karalyn?'

'I have visited Cairney,' she said.

Aila folded her arms over her chest. 'You don't want to talk to me, do you?' she said. 'You hate being here. You would rather be building your little worlds and ignoring what goes on among us mere humans.'

'Cairney is well,' she said. 'He asked me to tell you that he loves you; and that he is trying hard to be patient.'

'Can I see him?'

'No.'

'Is he being released?'

'No.'

'Then I have nothing more to say to you.'

'Cairney deserved to be punished; I was merciful.'

'I am grateful you didn't kill him,' said Aila; 'and I am grateful that you stopped Cael from hammering nails into his eyes – but don't imagine for a moment that I forgive you. You had the power to stop the war that killed Corthie, but you were too wrapped up in your own life to do anything. You are a grave disappointment, Karalyn. With all that power, you could have been so much more; you could have done great things.'

'How long has it been?' said Karalyn.

Aila frowned. 'Since what?'

'Since Corthie died?'

'Fourteen years, ten months and thirty days.'

'Is it that long?'

'It will soon be longer than the time I knew him,' said Aila. 'Corthie was eighteen when we met, and thirty-three when he died. Fifteen years – that's all I had with him. Are you now going to tell me how sorry you are?'

'I *am* sorry.'

'Yes, of course you are. But for what? I don't think you know. You have moved beyond normal emotions. I have heard people say that you have changed because you are immortal, but I am immortal, and I have never behaved as callously as you do. You were always detached from the rest of us – mortals and immortals alike. It would have been better if you had stayed dead.'

'Aye, maybe.'

Karalyn lifted her hand from the Sextant, and the vision connection to Aila was cut. She walked out on to her balcony and sat down.

Did she care what Aila thought of her? She remembered telling the demigod that no good would ever come of her relationship with Corthie, but she hadn't listened; and eight immortal children had been the result. It should have been twelve – that had been Aila's plan, but Dragon Eyre had seen to that.

She felt a slight niggle in the back of her mind, which could mean only one thing – Kyra was trying to get in contact. Karalyn brushed the attempt aside, and sealed off her mind to her daughter.

Kyra could wait.

Karalyn stared out at the beautiful view, and tried to think of a suitable name for her world.

CHAPTER 4
HER MOTHER'S DAUGHTER

Udall, Ulna, Eastern Rim – 20th Tradinch 5281 (18th Gylean Year 32)

Lindi Holdfast powered her battle-vision and vaulted the railings of the ship. She fell forty feet, and landed on the quayside of Udall harbour, her self-healing repairing the strain to her legs and ankles.

'Get back here, Alindi'osso,' Lara shouted from the deck of the ship.

Lindi laughed, then she put her head down and sprinted through the crowds of dock workers and sailors on the quayside. She almost collided with a cart carrying crates of fish, but she swerved past it just in time. She glanced over her shoulder. Lara was still standing on the railings of their great new dragon carrier – the *Mischief Maker*.

Lindi turned her head, and managed to scramble to a halt as a dragon descended right in front of her.

'Your mother is calling you, Lindi,' said the green dragon.

'Lara isn't my mother,' said Lindi. 'You know that, Seamoss; or if you don't, you should.'

'I am aware that Sable is your birth mother, girl,' said the dragon, 'but we also call Alara'osso your mother, out of respect. She is calling you, and yet you run in the opposite direction. Have you once again found yourself in trouble? What have you done this time?'

'I don't know what you're talking about, lizard,' said Lindi; 'I am never in trouble.'

'Lies,' said the dragon.

'So what? Get out of my way, or I'll make you believe that your wings have fallen off.'

The dragon's eyes burned like emeralds. 'You are not as powerful as you believe yourself to be, child.'

Lindi put a hand on her hip. 'Should we test that? I could be in your mind right now, and you would never know. I have more powers than you can imagine, you fat ugly lizard; shall I try a few out on you?'

You cannot see me.

Seamoss blinked, then he gazed around, looking for her. Lindi suppressed a laugh, and went into the mind of the dragon. He was strong, but Lindi's powers were already more than a match for most dragons.

You have forgotten why you landed on the quayside. You will forget seeing me here today.

The dragon looked confused for a moment, then he stretched out his wings and ascended into the air. Lindi remained invisible, and carried on her way, walking towards the riverside entrance to Queen Blackrose's palace. A drunk sailor staggered out of a nearby tavern and blinked in the sunshine, then he almost walked into Lindi. She stuck out her unseen foot and tripped him up, and he sprawled to the ground.

'Watch where you're going, you stupid mortal,' she said, her disembodied voice bewildering the sailor, who gazed around, his eyes wide.

Lindi stepped round him and reached the entrance to the River Palace. Next came the part she hated – the hundreds of steps that led all the way up to the part of the palace where the dragons lived. If only she had a Quadrant, but her mother had forbidden her from even touching one, and her mother was the only being on any of the known worlds that Lindi feared. Even so, Sable's grip on her was loosening over time, as it fought a losing battle against Lindi's determination to break free.

She powered her battle-vision again, and ran up the steps, taking two at a time until she reached the top. She turned for the queen's cavernous audience chamber, not because she had any desire to see the scaly old black dragon, but because she suspected that Amy Jackdaw might be there. Amy had the kind of naïve mind that Lindi found ridiculously easy to manipulate, but, at the same time, she was also Lindi's only friend on Ulna. No one at the local school trusted Lindi, especially not the teachers, and the sailors crewing the *Mischief Maker* had long since learned to stay out of her way. They all said that the great ship had been named after her, which Lindi took as a compliment.

She walked into the hall, and saw Blackrose speaking to several other dragons about farming, or some other tedious mortal nonsense. She ignored the dragons, and glanced at the low podium, where the humans usually gathered. There was no sign of Legate Bedig or Maddie Jackdaw, which gave Lindi a sense of relief, as neither could stop talking once they had started. Maddie's two daughters were there – Beth and Amy – and Lindi walked up to them. Beth was five years older than her, and she and Lindi were no longer the friends they had once been. When Lindi had been younger, Beth had always watched out for her, but, at some indiscernible point when Lindi had been around twelve, Beth had finally tired of being tricked and manipulated by her. After that, Lindi had turned to Beth's sister Amy. She was two years younger than Lindi, and possessed not a single malicious bone in her body. So sweet and innocent was she, that no one could believe that she would ever do anything to hurt anyone else. In other words, she was perfect for Lindi. If she needed to teach someone a lesson, all she had to do was implant the idea into Amy's head, and then erase her memory once it had been done. Lindi would always have an alibi, and no one ever suspected Amy. It was ingenious.

You can see me.

Lindi appeared before the two Jackdaw sisters.

'Hello, Lindi,' said Amy. 'I thought you were working on the *Maker* today.'

'Lara told me to take a break,' said Lindi.

Beth eyed her.

'It's true,' said Lindi; 'I don't care if you don't believe me.'

'What are you planning for your birthday?' said Amy.

'Nothing much,' said Lindi; 'nothing but my freedom. My mother promised that I would be able to travel when I turned seventeen, and I intend to hold her to that. I want to visit my immortal cousins on the Star Continent. I might be gone for months.'

'You're dreaming,' said Beth. 'There is no way that Sable and Lara will allow you to go off on your own.'

'My brother left home years ago.'

'That's completely different,' said Beth. 'Joss was a master's mate on a ship when he left Udall – he wasn't on his own.'

'I have self-healing,' said Lindi. 'I can survive just about anything. And I have god powers – death, fire, flow, vision – I think I can look after myself. What does my brother have? Sure, he's as tall as a Kellach, and he has battle-vision; but that's it. He's over-rated.'

Beth rolled her eyes. 'I remember when you were such a cute little girl, Lindi. Try not to become a typical god, always showing off.'

'I am the only god on Dragon Eyre,' she said, 'and I'm a Holdfast. My mother is a fucking legend. Can you give me a reason not to show off?'

'How about trying to stop people from disliking you?' said Beth. 'No one likes arrogant know-it-alls.'

'Why would I care what mortals think of me?' she said. 'You'll all be dead soon.'

Blackrose broke away from her conversation and turned her gaze upon Lindi and the Jackdaw sisters. Lindi looked up at the dragon, as a slight sense of guilt and regret for her unkind words passed through her mind.

'Alindi'osso,' said the queen, 'I fervently hope that this is merely a phase you are going through. You are sixteen years old, and yet you speak as though you were an Ascendant of old. The more powerful one becomes, the more humility is required.'

'Is my mother humble?' said Lindi.

'She is not,' said Blackrose, 'but, with Sable, there is a difference – she has proved herself many times over; and she has also suffered great loss. Sable is entitled to boast, because all of her boasts are based upon the truth. What have you done that you can boast about?'

'Nothing,' cried Lindi, 'because Lara and my mother won't let me do anything. But have no doubt – I will be great. I will be more powerful than my mother ever was. I can do everything she can do, and more. I will live forever.'

'Perhaps,' said Blackrose, 'but for now, you are a distraction. Beth, please remain here; Lindi and Amy, amuse yourselves elsewhere while I am conducting business.'

Amy got to her feet and curtsied before the queen, then she and Lindi walked out of the vast hall.

'What will we do?' said Amy.

'Do you want to get drunk?' said Lindi.

'I don't think that's a good idea,' said Amy. 'I have never been drunk, but I see the sailors when they come out of the taverns; they can hardly walk.'

Unbeknown to Amy, she had been drunk on several occasions, much to Lindi's amusement, but her memory had been wiped clean of the incidents, leaving Amy with the impression that she sometimes suffered from inexplicable headaches.

'We could walk down by the docks,' said Lindi.

Amy shook her head. 'I don't want to run into Atoni'enna, and he is working on his father's ship just now. I wish he would leave me alone.'

'Toni isn't too bad,' said Lindi.

'He is rude, and a thug. I really dislike him.'

Lindi suppressed a laugh. Sixteen-year-old Atoni'enna was one of Lindi's longest running jokes. Several months before, Amy had made an innocent comment about how little she thought of him, and so, for a laugh, Lindi had gone into his mind and made him fall obsessively in love with her. He would follow Amy around like a little dog, begging her to go out with him; it was hilarious. The manipulation of Toni's thoughts required constant maintenance, and Lindi would return to his mind every month or so, when her powers were starting to fade, and reinforce his devotion towards Amy. She would plant visions into his mind of them kissing, or getting married, and the poor boy was almost demented with longing. His reputation for being a thug had developed as an unforeseen consequence, due to his regrettable habit of punching anyone who dared question the purity of his love for Amy Jackdaw.

But what else was Lindi to do with her time? Lara had tried to mould her into a sailor, and Lindi had been to sea more than once as a junior officer, but she hadn't taken to it, not like Joss, who adored life on the ocean. Her brother was quite simple, in some respects. He loved ships and drinking beer with his friends, and had an eye for the good-looking girls of Udall, who worshipped him in return. Lindi loved him, but he was so popular that it could be quite annoying at times. Worse, he was as strong as a bull and as quick as a fox – and his Kellach build combined with his battle-vision meant that no one ever wanted to get into a fight with him. Some of the sailors had started to call him the new Corthie, but his mother had dampened that down as soon as she had heard about it.

There was only one Corthie, Sable had said, and the sailors had understood.

'Why are we going down the stairs?' said Amy. 'I thought we weren't going to the quayside.'

'It will be fine,' said Lindi. 'If Toni says anything stupid, I'll throw him into the harbour, and we'll see if he can swim.'

'What if he drowns?'

'Then I will bring him back from the dead,' said Lindi. 'I can do that, you know; I can resuscitate corpses. Maybe with Toni, I will give it a few minutes, though, and turn him into our mindless slave.'

They emerged from the dark stairwell and into the bright sunshine.

'Damn that idiot Simon,' Lindi muttered. 'Occasionally, I would actually like some rain to fall from the sky. Why does it always have to be sunny?'

Amy frowned as Lindi opened her cigarette case. 'Your parents have told you not to smoke cigarettes until you're eighteen.'

Lindi lit a stick of dreamweed. 'This isn't a cigarette,' she said. 'Do you want some?'

'No, thank you.'

Lindi inhaled deeply, and clamped down on her self-healing so that she could feel the effects.

'My cousin Killop grows this on the Hold Fast estate,' she said, as her mind grew hazy. 'I have never been there. I'm a Holdfast, but I have never set foot in our ancestral home. It's next to a desert; did you know that?'

'Then it will be even warmer there than it is here,' said Amy.

'Yeah. Udall is such a dump.'

'It is not,' said Amy. 'I love it here; the sunshine, the sea, the palm trees. Simon was definitely not an idiot, no matter what you say.'

'He was a homicidal maniac,' said Lindi.

'Maybe, but he did a good job with Dragon Eyre.'

Lindi started to laugh hysterically. 'Does that make him all right?' she cried. 'He was a murderous psychopath, but all is forgiven, because he knew how to make a decent coconut tree?

Amy frowned. 'You know what I mean.'

You want some dreamweed.

'Maybe I might have some of that dreamweed, after all,' said Amy.

'Are you sure?' said Lindi. 'I don't want anyone accusing me of corrupting the youth of Udall.'

One puff won't hurt.

'One puff won't hurt me,' said Amy.

Lindi passed her the weedstick, as they walked by the banks of the wide, brown river. Amy placed it to her lips, inhaled, then coughed, her cheeks flushing red. She dropped the weedstick, and Lindi's hand shot out to catch it. Amy swayed, then she started to giggle. A group of dock workers eyed them as they passed, and Lindi received a few disapproving looks. One of the workers, who clearly didn't know who she was, eyed her with a different emotion, then he whistled at her.

'Hello, little darling,' he said. 'Could I have some of that weed?'

Two of his friends pulled him away before Lindi could respond.

'Don't be messing with her, you stupid twat,' said one. 'That's Sable's daughter.'

Lindi smiled at the workers, but the exchange had made her angry. It wasn't the unwanted advances that annoyed her; she could easily handle herself even against the most brutish of sailors or workers; it was the fact that only the most stupid or foolhardy of boys weren't put off by her name and her abilities. Not that she was interested in going with a mortal, but it would be nice to have the chance to turn them down.

'I could walk down here naked,' she said, 'and no man would look at me.'

Amy gave her an appalled look. 'Why would you do such a thing?'

'I wouldn't,' said Lindi. 'I'm just saying that my mother has frightened off every man in Udall.'

Amy rolled her eyes. 'You're sixteen, Lindi; no man should be looking at you.'

'I wish time would hurry up; I wish I was eighteen, so that I could lead my own life.'

'But you said that your parents promised to let you travel when you were seventeen.'

'I know I said that, but I don't believe it. Lara thinks I should be locked in my cabin until my eighteenth birthday. She doesn't trust me.'

'Well, sometimes you can be quite rebellious,' said Amy. 'My head feels funny. Is it supposed to?'

'It's just the dreamweed,' said Lindi. 'You'll be fine.'

Lindi finished the last of the weedstick and tossed the butt into the river. They were approaching the harbour, and she gazed at the large selection of ships that were tied up. The fishing fleet was out plying the coastal waters of Ulna, but over a dozen merchant vessels were docked, along with a variety of smaller boats. Towering above them all was the *Mischief Maker*, its long, wide dragon deck rising into the air to a level taller than many of the other ships' masts.

'Oh no,' Amy whispered. 'Look who has seen us.'

Lindi glanced up, and saw Atoni'enna up on the deck of a narrow sloop, a tub of bitumen in one hand, and a paintbrush in the other. His father was also on the deck, along with a few other workers, but Toni's gaze was directed at Amy.

'Just ignore him,' said Lindi.

'He is staring at me,' said Amy.

'Are you sure you haven't been leading him on?' said Lindi.

'Of course I haven't. You know I haven't. I have told him countless times that I'm not interested. Can we go back? Please?'

'You have to face your fears,' said Lindi.

Toni set the tub and the brush onto the wooden deck of the sloop, then he began to clamber over the side.

'Atoni,' called out his father. 'Get back up here.'

The sixteen-year-old boy ignored him, and jumped down to the quayside. Lindi tried not to laugh as he approached. He looked so forlorn and pathetic.

'Amy,' he said. 'You are looking beautiful today.'

'Please leave me alone,' said Amy.

'My heart stops whenever I see you,' he said. 'If you would just give me a chance, just one chance, then I could show you how much you mean to me.' He smiled. 'I dreamed about you last night.'

His father leaned over the sloop's railings. 'Leave the girl be, son,' he said. 'You have to stop this.'

Toni's demeanour altered in an instant, and rage was on his face as he turned to his father. 'Go fuck yourself!' he shouted.

His father eyed the other men on deck, and they made for the gangway.

'I think your dad wants a quiet word with you, Toni,' said Lindi.

'Piss off, Lindi,' said Toni. He turned back to Amy. 'I love you; why can't you see that? I would die for you.'

The men approached Toni from behind, and his father placed a hand onto his son's shoulder. Toni clenched his fist and swung it as he turned, cracking his father on the jaw. Two of the other men reached out to grab Toni, but the boy continued to lash out, and a stray fist connected with the side of Amy's head, sending her flying to the ground.

'No!' cried Toni. 'I'm sorry, Amy; I didn't mean it.'

Lindi powered her battle-vision and hit Toni so hard that his face exploded in blood, then he tottered on the edge of the quay, and fell into the water. His father stared at Amy, then at Lindi, then he dived into the harbour. Toni was sinking, unconscious from the blow to his face, and two other men also jumped into the water. Lindi crouched by Amy as a crowd began to gather. Amy's left temple was bleeding, and a bruise was forming by her eye.

'What happened?' she groaned.

'Nothing; you'll be all right,' said Lindi. She pressed a finger to Amy's brow, and sent a wave of healing into her body. Amy spasmed, and the injury to her face healed.

Sable barged through the crowd. She knelt by Lindi and Amy.

'She's fine,' said Lindi. 'I healed her.'

'Who hit her?' said Sable.

'Atoni'enna,' said Lindi. 'He was aiming for his father at the time. It was an accident.'

Sable turned her head, and she and Lindi watched as the three men dragged Toni out of the water and up onto the quay.

'He's not breathing,' shouted his father. He caught sight of Sable. 'Your daughter punched him; look at his face. His jaw, his nose. His skull is broken, Sable.'

'I can't feel a pulse, boss,' said one of the other men.

Sable got to her feet, a hand going into a pocket at the same time. She took out a small vial, opened it, and emptied its contents into Toni's open mouth.

The boy shuddered as the men held him down, then his features reformed. He spluttered and coughed up blood, then his eyes opened. His father clutched his hand, and wept.

'Who started the fight?' said Sable.

'It was the boy,' said someone in the crowd. 'I saw the whole thing. The boy was chatting up Maddie's girl. She didn't like it, and the boy's father tried to get him to stop. That's when he started throwing punches.'

'I don't understand,' said Toni's father. 'My son has never behaved like this.' He gazed at Amy. 'I am sorry, young lady. I have told him to stop harassing you, but he doesn't listen.'

'I love her,' gasped Toni. 'We are meant to be together.'

Sable frowned, her eyes narrowing, then she leaned over and gazed into Toni's eyes.

'Oh shit,' muttered Lindi.

Toni stared at Sable, then he blinked. He gazed around. He saw his father, then he looked over at Amy, who was sitting on the ground. He looked confused, then his face flushed with embarrassment.

'I... What happened to me? Amy? I... I'm sorry. Father, I don't know what I was thinking. I don't even like Amy Jackdaw.'

'I don't understand,' said his father.

'I do,' said Sable. 'Your son will be fine from now on. Lindi – you are coming with me.'

Sable put a hand into her pocket, the air shimmered, then she, Lindi and Amy appeared in Blackrose's audience chamber.

'Fetch your mother, Beth,' said Sable. 'I will be back in a moment.'

Sable vanished again.

'From the look on your mother's face, Alindi'osso,' said Blackrose, 'I fear that you may be in store for a reprimand. Have you done something egregious?'

'It wouldn't be the first time,' said Beth, as she walked out of the hall.

'What did you do?' said Amy. 'Is it because you punched Atoni'enna? But he punched me first; you could argue that you were defending me.'

'A boy struck you?' said Blackrose.

'He was trying to hit his father,' said Lindi. 'He missed.'

'You do not look very concerned,' said Blackrose.

'It's all a misunderstanding,' said Lindi. 'I think my mother is a little more confused than normal.'

The air shimmered, and Sable appeared with Lara and Oto'pazzi. Sable had clearly told Lara what she had seen inside Toni's mind, as she marched up to Lindi and started wagging a finger in her face.

'How could you?' Lara shouted. 'What a disgusting thing to do.'

Lindi rolled her eyes.

'What did she do?' said Maddie, as she walked into the hall with Beth.

'Nothing,' said Lindi. 'I protected your daughter. You're welcome.'

'Do you know that boy who has been pestering Amy for months?' said Sable.

'Toni?' said Maddie. 'Of course I know him. I have spoken to his parents several times, and they always promise that they will deal with their son's behaviour, but they never do. I was starting to wonder if...'

'It wasn't Toni's fault,' said Sable. 'Lindi went into his mind, and forced him to follow Amy around. Lindi made him think he was in love with her.'

There was a moment of silence, as Maddie, Beth and Amy all stared at Lindi.

'I thought it was funny,' said Lindi.

'It was you?' said Amy, looking heartbroken. 'You did that to him? I thought you were my friend.'

'I tried to warn you about Lindi,' said Beth. 'This is not the first time she has done something like this.'

'But this occasion nearly resulted in a boy drowning,' said Sable. 'Lindi punched him so hard that his skull fractured. I had to dose him with an entire vial of salve.'

Lindi shrugged. 'I could have used my healing powers to fix him.'

'You should keep your mouth bleeding well shut, Alindi,' said Lara. 'We have already heard enough from you. Oh Sable, what are we going to do with her?'

'You had best think of something quick,' said Maddie; 'because I have a few ideas of my own. This *little madam* has gone too far. That boy could have died, and what about all of the nights when Topaz and I have found Amy crying in her bed – crying because Toni wouldn't leave her alone? We thought the boy was mad; and his poor parents thought they had raised a brute.'

'I remember thinking how strange it all was,' said Topaz. 'Toni seemed like a decent enough young man, up until he developed his... crush on Amy.'

'It was more than a crush,' said Sable. 'Lindi made him obsessed with your daughter. It could have been dangerous.'

'I wouldn't have let anything terrible happen to her,' said Lindi. 'It was just a joke. Have none of you got a sense of humour?'

Sable narrowed her eyes. 'We will take her to sea, for a very long voyage. I want to apologise to everyone for Lindi's behaviour. I have clearly failed as a mother. Lara, how long will it take to get the *Maker* ready to sail?'

'Four or five days,' said Lara. 'I agree; a long voyage to the other end of Dragon Eyre might do the trick. We could do the whole circuit; Alef to Gyle to Haurn and back. Topaz, you can stay here; I'll pinch Vitz from Tilly's ship, and he can be our master.'

'No,' said Lindi.

'What was that?' said Lara.

'You heard me, Lara,' said Lindi. 'I am not going on a ship for months. I'll be seventeen soon, and you promised me that I would be able to travel.'

Lara smiled. 'Travelling is exactly what you'll be doing; only with me and Sable, and the crew of the *Mischief Maker*.'

'You can't treat me like this,' cried Lindi. 'I am a god.'

'Young dragons often misbehave,' said Blackrose. 'They then have to take their punishment bravely, without complaint.'

'I'm not a bleeding lizard!' shouted Lindi.

Blackrose's eyes flared red.

'Apologise to the queen. Now,' said Sable.

'She needs to apologise to Amy and Toni as well,' said Maddie. 'In fact, she should apologise to everyone.'

Lindi placed a hand on her hip. 'Gods never say sorry.'

Legate Bedig walked into the hall. 'Is everything all right? I couldn't help but hear shouting.'

'Sable's daughter has been caught using her powers to play hurtful tricks on the children of Udall,' said Blackrose. 'It is a personal, family matter; not something that should concern the Empire's representative.'

Bedig raised his palms. 'Understood, Your Majesty.'

'You should know that we'll be taking the *Mischief Maker* out in a few days,' said Sable. 'Lara and I will be taking Lindi with us, and we'll be going to the Western Rim and back. We feel that some hard work on an open deck might do her some good.'

'Right you are, Sable,' said Bedig. 'If you like, I could talk to the dragons of the Western Rim who are currently on Ulna, and ask them if they would like to try out your new dragon carrier. How many does it fit?'

'Five at a push,' said Lara, 'but three is a better number for such a long voyage.'

Bedig inclined his head, and Lindi sprang at him. She powered her battle-vision, and knocked the Kellach man to the floor before anyone else could react. She reached into an inside pocket of his coat, and took out his Quadrant.

'Stay where you are,' shouted Sable.

Lindi winked at her mother, the very person who had shown her how to operate a Quadrant, then she activated the device, and vanished.

CHAPTER 5
PARENTAL DUTIES

Colsbury Castle, Republic of the Holdings – 2nd Day, First Third Summer 560

Cael waited as Arrosa gave her instructions to the small army of nannies, servants and tutors who looked after their three children when they stayed in the Summer Palace on Colsbury. While he listened to Arrosa speak, he recalled his own childhood, when he had been passed from his mother to Thorn and back again, twice over. His earliest memories were of Thorn caring for him and his sister on the Hold Fast estate, but there had always been staff around to help. When his mother had returned from Lostwell, they had moved to Colsbury, where almost no one had lived at that time. Shorn of servants, Karalyn had spent every moment with the twins. When she had died in Clackenbaird, Cael and Kyra had gone back to live with Thorn, who was, by that time, the Empress; and dozens of servants were again employed to care for them. Their shuttling between Plateau City and Colsbury had come to an end with Karalyn's second return, and they had settled into the Great Keep with Lucius Cardova. That was when Arrosa had also appeared.

Two mothers – Karalyn and Thorn. As a boy, Cael had always preferred Karalyn and, had it not been for his insistence that she was alive, she might never have come back from Athumia. Unlike Kyra, Cael had never viewed Thorn as his real mother, though he had loved her; but, as time had gone on, he had found himself siding with Thorn more and more. While Kyra had irrevocably broken with the Empress, Cael was her favoured successor. In the process, he had damaged his relationship with his birth mother, but none of Karalyn's relationships had survived her transformation unscathed.

He knew he had earned his mother's disapproval. He knew she saw him as over-aggressive and over-confident, stubborn and arrogant; and he also knew that there was some truth to her judgement of him. He cared about his mother's opinion, but not enough to force himself to change. He was what he was, and he would rather be honest to himself than try to live up to his mother's unrealistic expectations.

Arrosa understood that; she understood him, and accepted him as he was. She, too, had been reared by Karalyn, and their relationship had also suffered when Cael's mother had started to distance herself from the rest of the family. Arrosa was an orphan, while Cael only felt like one. Instead of parents, he had a dead father he had never met; a mother who had retreated from the world of mere mortals; a stepfather who was living with his aunt; and an adopted mother who was the ruler of the largest Empire in existence.

'What do you think?' said Arrosa.

Cael blinked.

Arrosa frowned. 'Were you listening to what I just said?'

'Sorry, I was dreaming,' he said. He glanced up, and saw that the children were being led out of the apartment by the servants and tutors, ready to begin that day's lessons.

'I was asking if you thought we needed to replace Kelvin's language tutor,' said Arrosa. 'I don't care for her, and Kelvin certainly doesn't like her. Should I hire someone new?'

'I don't know,' he said. 'Kelvin can be a handful, and I respect anyone who can maintain their patience with him. Give her another third.'

Arrosa eyed him.

'I miss the dogs,' he said. 'It might be time to get some puppies.'

'It's too soon,' said Arrosa. 'My heart couldn't take it. Having them was wonderful, but the pain that comes from them passing was almost too much to bear. I still cry when I see the space where their bed used to be.'

He put his arms round her. 'I know. We can wait for a bit longer, but I think the children would benefit; and I like the idea of big fierce dogs guarding the children when we're not here.'

Arrosa gazed up at him. 'Is this more about you? You are a good father, Cael.'

'I wish I were here more,' he said.

'Compared to the way we were brought up,' she said, 'we are a bastion of stability. We are both in the Imperial Court, and yet we manage to spend most mornings and evenings here. I was never going to be a housewife; you knew that.'

'I'm not criticising you as a mother,' he said; 'but I am admitting that it's difficult to balance being parents while working for the Empire. I guess Lucius is my model; he was able to run the army while looking after me and Kyra.'

'If you become Emperor,' she said, 'then let us hope that the children will have grown up by then. I will think about getting more dogs; perhaps when we return to Plateau City at the beginning of autumn, certainly not before then.'

'Three again; one for each child.'

'Maybe. We had better go.'

'We still have time. I need to speak to Lucius, though, as I still don't know where Lahnos actually lives.'

'You could have read it out of his mind.'

He smiled. 'Would I do such a thing? The Empress told me not to pry.'

'And do you always obey orders, Cael Holdfast?'

'Usually,' he said. 'It depends on the order.' He kissed her. 'I'll be back soon.'

He left their apartment in the Summer Palace, and walked up the steps to the rooms where Lucius was staying with Kelsey. Caelius Logos was outside their front door, sitting by a small balcony with a cup of tea, just as he did when they were in the Blue Palace in the city.

'Morning, Caelius,' said Cael.

'Good morning, lad,' said Caelius. 'If it's Kelsey you're after, you're too late. She's gone upstairs to see the Empress.'

'It's Lucius I'm here to see,' said Cael. 'Is he in?'

'He is.'

Cael tilted his head, and walked into the apartment. As Lucius and Kelsey's children had decided not to accompany them to Colsbury that summer, the apartment was quiet, but Cael heard voices coming from one of the rooms, so he knocked and entered.

Lucius was sitting by a dining table with Rosie Jackdaw, who had moved on from the Imperial Court to become the director of the Empire's entire weapons programme. She had a wooden box sitting in front of her, and it was lying open.

'Good morning, Cael,' said Lucius. 'Rosie was just showing me her new toy.'

Cael glanced into the box. Inside was a metal tube, around a foot and a half in length. It had leather wound round one end as a grip, and there was a small lever where the user's thumb would sit.

'What does it do?' he said.

'It's a miniaturised Battanara,' said Rosie. 'You load it, hold it in one hand, aim it, and press the lever. It has a Tempest-lined, rifled barrel, and it takes about six seconds to reload. It uses a small piece of flint on the underside of the lever to spark the Ectus powder, so there is no need for matches and fuses.'

'May I?' said Cael.

Rosie nodded.

Cael picked it up. It felt like one of the batons the militia used to keep order in the city.

'How are you supposed to aim it if you have to hold it like a spear?' he said.

'You hold it out and look down the sights,' said Rosie.

'I'm not denying that it's a very fine piece of engineering,' he said, 'but it could do with a handle; like a crossbow.'

Rosie frowned. 'That's what Lucius was saying. I might have spent too much time on the reloading mechanism and the barrel. All right; I will rethink the handle.'

'The barrel is the important part,' said Lucius; 'keep that exactly as it is. Have you got a name for it?'

'I'm not sure,' said Rosie. 'I have been calling it the *firestick*, but that's a bit crap.'

'Let's call it the Jackdaw,' said Lucius. 'The Mark One Jackdaw. After all, if Ravi can get away with naming a weapon the Battanara, why shouldn't you do the same?'

Rosie pursed her lips. 'I don't think my big sister would appreciate a weapon being named after our family.'

'Your sister didn't design it; you did,' said Lucius. He turned to Cael. 'Were you wanting me for anything in particular?'

'I have been ordered to warn Lahnos about the possibility that the Gunstians have Quadrants,' he said.

'And you don't know where he lives?' said Lucius.

'That's right.'

Lucius narrowed his eyes. 'You haven't read it from my head?'

'I was told not to.'

'Fair enough. All right – I am thinking of the location.'

Cael went into his mind, and saw what he needed.

'I wasn't expecting him to live there,' he said. 'The location itself might be a Gunstian target.'

'Lahnos needs to be told that he may have to defend it, as well as defending himself,' said Lucius. 'When are you leaving?'

'In a few minutes; I will be taking Arrosa with me.'

'Let me know how it goes; we may need to reinforce his position.'

'Aye, sir.'

Cael nodded to Rosie, then he left Lucius's apartment and went back down the stairs to his own quarters. Arrosa was waiting by the door for him.

'Do I need to bring anything?' she said.

'I don't think so,' said Cael. 'It's summer where we are going, but it shouldn't be too warm.'

He took out his Quadrant.

'Aren't you going to tell me where we are going first?' said Arrosa.

'It will be a surprise. I don't think you have ever been there before, and I haven't been for years; which is a little strange, as I'm the damn Adjutant, and it's one of the most important locations in the Empire. The Herald has always looked after it personally.'

Arrosa rolled her eyes. 'Get on with it, Cael.'

He smiled, then he swept his fingers over the Quadrant. The air crackled, and they appeared in a small valley under a sky of pinks and reds. Two large dragons were stretching out on the grass by the banks of a little stream, while a third, much smaller dragon was playing in the pool next to a waterfall, where a series of caves lay. In the far corner of the valley, to the right of the waterfall, a stone cottage stood, almost surrounded by trees.

'Do you know where we are?' said Cael.

'No,' said Arrosa; 'but I can guess. 'If we are on the world of the City of Salve, then this must be the salve mine. But where are the miners and the soldiers who guard the mine?'

'They are now based on the far side of that ridge,' said Cael. 'The seam of salve that starts in this valley has been exhausted, and all mining operations have moved to a location a couple of miles away. We should now think of this as Jade's valley, not the actual salve mine. I think that's why Lahnos is able to stay here without too many people knowing.'

The two large dragons lifted their heads from the grass.

'Arrosa,' said the silvery-green male; 'how good to see you again; and you, Cael.'

'I am glad to see you looking so well, Sigum,' said Arrosa.

'Greetings, Lord Sigum,' said Cael; 'and Lady Dawnflame.'

'I am not a *lady*,' said the purple female. 'I am a dragon. Spare me your human titles, little Holdfast insect.'

'Certainly, ma'am,' said Cael.

Sigum turned his gaze towards the cottage. 'Lahnos,' he called out; 'we have visitors.'

Dawnflame also turned her head, but in the direction of the caves. 'Jade,' she said; 'insects.'

Cael and Arrosa walked along the bank of the stream towards the pool. Arrosa eyed the young dragon splashing in the deep water, and slowed her pace.

'Firestone will almost certainly not eat you, girl,' said Dawnflame. 'He may chew upon your leg, but he does not care for the taste of human flesh.'

'It disturbs me slightly that you are telling the truth,' said Arrosa.

'I never lie,' said Dawnflame. 'Do you take me for a dragon from Athumia?'

'Have I ever lied to you?' said Sigum.

'No, but that is why you are an exile from your world, Sigum,' said Dawnflame. 'You are the exception.'

Jade emerged from one of the cave entrances wearing a dark green dress.

'Who is it?' she said.

'Two of the younger Holdfasts,' said Dawnflame. 'I forget their names.'

Jade narrowed her eyes. 'I recognise Kyra's brother,' she said. 'Where is Kyra? I like her. She was a very sweet little girl.'

'Kyra is on Athumia,' said Cael.

'Why?' said Jade. 'Does she like dragons who tell lies?'

'I'm not sure, but she likes a god by the name of Edgar,' said Cael. 'They are married with two badly-named children.'

'Kyra has children?' said Jade. 'Why hasn't she been to visit me? It is the same with Rosie Jackdaw; she never visits any more. Why are mortals like this?'

'I saw Rosie this morning,' said Cael.

'Did she mention me?' said Jade.

'She didn't know I was coming here. And you do happen to live in a place that is not only very remote, but which is also a heavily-guarded imperial secret. Very few people now know how to get here, and fewer know that Lahnos lives in this valley.'

Jade came to a halt in front of them. 'Naxor knows how to get here.'

'Aye, I suppose he does.'

'Is he still alive?'

'He is.'

Jade shook her head. 'When will you foolish mortals learn? You would be wise to cut his head off before he betrays you.' She eyed Arrosa up and down. 'Who is this?'

'This is Arrosa, my wife,' said Cael.

'She is a friend,' said Sigum. 'She is Gifted.'

Jade raised an eyebrow. 'In what? Painting? Singing? Can she dance?'

'It means she's a Gunstian with Gifts,' said Cael. 'Mortal powers.'

'Eh?' said Jade.

'In the way that Lahnos has Gifts, Jade,' said Sigum. 'The Gift of Pain, for example.'

'Oh, right,' said Jade. 'What Gifts do you have, Arrosa?'

'I can sense when someone is lying,' she said.

Jade raised an eyebrow. 'Any dragon can do that.'

'I suppose so,' said Arrosa. 'By the way, it is very nice to meet you at last, Jade.'

'Is it?' said Jade. 'Why?'

'I have heard a lot about you.'

'Really?' said Jade. 'I doubt that.'

The front door of the cottage opened, and a woman came out into the little valley. She was holding on to the hand of a girl, while a teenage boy walked behind them.

Arrosa's eyes widened. 'Dermot has horns.'

'What's wrong with having horns?' said Jade. 'Don't you insult my dear little Dermot; I am very fond of him.'

'I wasn't insulting him,' said Arrosa. 'He looks like his father.'

The woman and the two children stopped by the pool, in front of the others. Firestone reached out with a forelimb, and pulled the teenage boy into the water with a splash.

'Should we help him?' said Cael.

'They are only playing,' said Dawnflame. 'Firestone is also fond of little Dermot.'

'He's not so little any more,' said the woman.

'It is good to see you, Ora'lya,' said Cael. 'How old is he now?'

'Fourteen,' said Ora'lya, 'and Lana'lya is nine.'

'Hello, Lana,' said Cael.

'Who are you?' said the girl.

'I am Cael Holdfast, and this is Arrosa. We are friends of your father, and of Lord Sigum.'

'Lahnos won't be a minute,' said Ora'lya.

'Here he comes,' said Sigum.

Cael glanced at the cottage as Lahnos walked out on to the grass.

Cael smiled and shook his head. 'You haven't aged a day, Lahnos.'

'I was eight when I met him,' said Arrosa, 'and he looks the same now as he did then.'

'Tell me about it,' said Ora'lya. 'While the rest of us age, Lahnos stays the same.'

'I don't age,' said Jade.

Ora'lya laughed. 'But people don't expect you to age, Jade – you are a demigod. Lahnos was born a mortal.'

Lahnos stopped by his wife, as Dermot continued to play in the pool with the young dragon.

'The Holdfasts are here,' said Ora'lya.

Lahnos narrowed his eyes. 'Arrosa is always welcome to visit,' he said; 'but, and don't take this the wrong way, Cael, but I always feel a sense of dread whenever I see you. I assume you have some news to share?'

'The Empress asked me to come here,' said Cael. 'It might be nothing, but Her Majesty thought you should know. It seems that the Gunstians may have got their hands on a couple of Quadrants. They attacked Nom Karta a few days ago, and killed three dragons.'

'Didn't you say that Arrosa was a Gunstian?' said Jade.

'I am a Zamatan Gunstian,' said Arrosa. 'I am not from Gunst itself.'

Jade raised an eyebrow.

'It means she comes from the same little island as I do,' said Lahnos. 'Are you certain it was Gunstians who killed the dragons?'

'Personally, no,' said Cael, 'but Lady Abda swears that they were killed by the Gift of Immolation.'

'I am more frightened of Abda than the Gunstians, to be honest,' said Lahnos. 'She despised me. She tried to have me executed when I returned from Gunst.'

'Is Abda a dragon?' said Dawnflame.

'She is,' said Sigum; 'a most disagreeable dragon. She loathed me as much as she loathed Lahnos.'

'She is now one of Queen Famula's advisors,' said Cael; 'but I don't think she likes me, either. Regardless, if it turns out that the Gunstians are embarking upon offensive operations, then they might have a list of targets. You and I will be on that list, Lahnos.'

'I understand why I would be on their list,' said Lahnos, 'but what have you done to anger the Gunstians?'

Cael hesitated for a moment. 'I killed a few of them. I also obliterated the most sacred temple in Great Gunst – the Temple of the Martyrs. I created three hundred new martyrs that day, along with a smoking pile of rubble.'

Lahnos stared at him. 'Why?'

'I was angry.'

'The Gunstians arrested me,' said Arrosa. 'They charged me with treason and apostasy. Cael released me, then he decided that Gunstians required to be taught a lesson.'

Dawnflame raised her head and laughed. 'I am starting to like you, Holdfast insect,' she cried. 'You acted as a dragon would – they hurt your mate, and you took terrible revenge upon them. I applaud your actions – you are indeed a worthy member of the Holdfast clan.'

'Thank you,' said Cael, 'but not everyone sees it that way. Some think I went too far.'

'What does the Empress think?' said Jade.

'She was fine with it,' said Cael. 'Her Majesty possesses her own ruthless streak.'

'Let us sit by the pool,' said Lahnos.

The humans arranged themselves on the grassy banks of the small pool. Dermot had climbed out of the water, his clothes and hair dripping wet, while Firestone was basking in the warm sunlight.

'Are you still the Lord Marshall, Cael?' said Lahnos.

'I'm Adjutant now,' he said.

'What happened to Claudian?'

'He said he was getting too old for active operations, so he moved to become Chief of Staff instead. There is no current Lord Marshal. A new one will be selected by the government of the Plateau, once all of the votes have been counted.'

'Votes?' said Jade. 'Has the Empire succumbed to the same affliction that has taken over the City under the inane rule of the Aurelians? Are they allowing mortals to pick their rulers?'

'Not the entire Empire, not yet,' said Cael, 'but the Plateau is now a democracy.'

'Cael was working on it for eight years,' said Arrosa. 'To be honest, I'm glad it's over.'

'I thought you like the Aurelians, Jade,' said Cael.

'Oh, I like them as people – Daniel and Emily have always been kind to me,' she said, 'but that doesn't mean I like mortals running the City. But, who else is there nowadays? Lydia? Doria? That imbecile Maxwell? There are no gods of any calibre left in the City.' She lowered her voice. 'Aila is probably the most qualified, but I hope she doesn't come back. She was quite rude to me.'

'Aila seems settled in Kell with her family,' said Cael, 'not that she would say that to me. The Marchbrae Holdfasts... well, let's just say that I am not their favourite person.'

'Is that because of Corthie?' said Jade.

'Aye. They blame us for his death.'

Lahnos shook his head. 'That's bollocks. You were by Corthie's side when he died, Cael – how can they hold you responsible?'

'They blame the Empress, my mother, Herald Kelsey, and then me, in that order,' said Cael; 'but they don't blame Cole, for some reason.'

'It's because you are the Empress's chosen successor,' said Arrosa. 'They hate you because you are so close to Her Majesty.'

'Aye, that's probably it,' said Cael. 'Anyway, Aila doesn't speak to me.'

'It will be Naxor's fault,' said Jade. 'If he lives with Aila, he will have poisoned her mind against you, and he will be doing the same with Corthie's children. You need to have him executed, Cael. If you don't, you will regret it.'

'I have looked into Naxor's mind,' said Cael. 'He has a plan, but it spans centuries. A future generation can deal with him.'

'Me, in other words?' said Jade.

Cael smiled. 'Maybe.'

'There was another reason Cael asked me to come along today,' said Arrosa. 'This concerns your children, Lahnos. If you like, I can test them for Gifts.'

'Can you do that?' said Ora'lya.

'I have the Gift of Kenning,' said Arrosa. 'In adults, I can usually tell if they have any Gifts as soon as I'm a few yards from them. With children, it's a little more difficult, and, of course, you might not want to know.'

'I would like to know,' said Dermot.

Lahnos said nothing.

'Would it have helped you,' said Arrosa, 'if you had known about your Gifts when you were younger?'

'I don't know,' said Lahnos. 'Growing horns came as a complete shock to me; I'm not sure I could have handled knowing I had Gifts at the same age.'

'But we prepared Dermot for the possibility of having horns,' said Ora'lya.

'I love my horns,' said Dermot.

'And so you should,' said Lahnos. 'All right; if Ora'lya agrees, you can test both children, Arrosa.'

'Will I grow horns?' said Lana'lya.

'You might,' said her mother.

'If you are very lucky,' said Jade. 'I wish I had horns.'

'Please remember that there is a good chance that neither child will have any Gifts,' said Arrosa. 'It often skips a generation.'

'Do your children have Gifts?' said Ora'lya.

'Just one,' said Cael. 'Kelvin has the Gift of Truth, as well as a few dream vision abilities.'

'Why are you not as powerful as your mother?' said Jade.

'I have come to believe that my mother truly is an aberration – a one-off,' said Cael. 'Neither I nor Kyra have the full set of powers that she possesses, and our own children's abilities are weaker still.'

'Yes, but why?'

'I don't know, Jade.'

'Go ahead and test them, Arrosa,' said Ora'lya.

Arrosa nodded, then she moved a little closer to the two children, as the two adult dragons stooped their heads to watch.

'You first, Dermot,' said Arrosa. 'Hold out your hand.'

The boy did so, and Arrosa took it.

'No,' she said. 'No Gifts.'

Dermot narrowed his eyes, but said nothing.

'You next, Lana'lya,' said Arrosa.

The girl reached out with her hand, and Arrosa pressed her own around it.

Arrosa closed her eyes. 'Death Reading. Death Seeing.'

Lahnos stared at his daughter. 'Lana's a Death Seer?'

'Yes,' said Arrosa. 'Just like you, Lahnos.'

'Wait,' said Ora'lya. 'That's the Gift that turned Lahnos into an immortal. Are you telling me that if my daughter uses that Gift on a god, she will become a god?'

Arrosa's eyes widened. 'Uh, yes. I suppose so. When Chadura

created Athumia and the Gifted, there were no gods on that world. The two powers were never supposed to meet.'

'But this is a way to ensure that she lives forever?' said Ora'lya. A tear rolled down her cheek. 'Lahnos would never have to see her grow old and die.'

'What happens to the god that this Gift is used on?' said Jade.

'They die,' said Arrosa.

'Then I recommend using Naxor, Ora'lya. Not only would that vile beast be dead, but I would have Lana'lya for company for centuries to come. I like this idea. Please arrange it, Cael.'

'I'm not sure I agree with this notion,' said Lahnos. 'I view what happened to me as a curse, not a blessing. I am fated to lose everyone I love; and I don't want the same thing to happen to my daughter.'

'Let's talk about it later,' said Ora'lya. 'Our guests might be hungry, and we are their hosts.'

Lahnos eyed his wife for a long moment. 'All right. Shall we put together some lunch?'

'That sounds great,' said Cael.

Ora'lya got to her feet. 'Dermot, Lana – you can help me. Come on.'

'I saw the glint in her eyes, Lahnos,' said Sigum, as Ora'lya led the children away. 'I doubt your wife will forget what she has discovered any time soon. Are you not tempted? Your daughter would ascend into godhood.'

'She would never get sick,' said Jade; 'and she would be able to heal any injury. Why wouldn't you want that for her?'

Lahnos gazed into the deep waters of the pool, and said nothing.

Three hours later, Cael and Arrosa returned to Colsbury in a shimmer of air. They had arrived on the middle balcony of the Summer Palace, and Claudian got to his feet as soon as he saw them.

'Cole has been waiting for you,' he said. 'It seems that the Gunstians have violated imperial territory.'

'Where?' said Cael.

'Just outside Plateau City,' said Claudian. 'Their intelligence is good, Cael. They knew what lay within a certain warehouse that sits upon the shores of the Inner Sea.'

'Shit,' said Cael. 'I know the place you mean. Is Cole there now?'

'He is. He asked me to tell you to appear by the jetty. He will have someone there to greet you.'

'Thank you, Claudian,' said Cael. He turned to Arrosa. 'Could you tell Lucius about our visit to Lahnos? I shouldn't be too long.'

Arrosa nodded, then she kissed him. 'I will see you when you get back.'

Cael glanced down at his Quadrant, then activated it. A moment later, he arrived on a long stone jetty that protruded out into the Inner Sea. To the north, the two peaks of the Blue Palace in Plateau City were visible on the horizon, while a few old warehouses were arranged along the shore. A squad of imperial soldiers were standing by the base of the jetty, and they gestured for Cael to approach.

'Lord Adjutant,' said a lieutenant; 'would you please follow us?'

They set off towards the nearest warehouse. They reached the tall entrance doors, and Cael saw two rows of bodies laid out on the ground. On the left, seven men and women in imperial uniforms were lying, their withered limbs twisted, and their skin leathery and desiccated. On the right were five men. Four were young, and in Gunstian uniforms, while the fifth was an older man in dark robes. Each had signs of injuries, ranging from crossbow bolt wounds, to slashes inflicted by swords.

Cole emerged from the building.

'Adjutant,' he said; 'we were lucky and unlucky, it seems.'

Cael frowned.

'The Gunstians made a complete mess of this raid,' Cole went on. 'First, they arrived in the wrong building. This warehouse was almost empty, and there were no mortars or Battanaras being stored here. They were clumsy, and the soldiers on duty were able to surround them quickly.'

'Wait,' said Cael. 'Go back a bit. Did they definitely have a Quadrant?'

'I saw it, sir,' said a Kellach soldier. 'One of the Gunstians was holding onto it when the survivors escaped.'

'That's the unlucky part,' said Cole. 'Two managed to flee. One had the Quadrant, the other was clutching onto a crate of Forty-Eighters. The soldiers killed the other five, including their Gifted agent. That old man had the Gift of Withering.'

'How many Forty-Eighters are kept in each crate?' said Cael.

'Forty-eight, appropriately enough,' said Cole. 'We should imagine that they will waste a few testing them out, but the others will be usable.' He gestured to the bodies of the five slain Gunstians. 'And now we have definitive proof that Gunst is attacking both the Dominion and the Empire; as well as proof that they have at least one Quadrant.'

'But how the fuck did they know how to find these warehouses?' said Cael.

Cole's eyes darkened. 'Agent Muriel knew their location, sir.'

'Why didn't I know that?'

'We only discovered it a short time ago,' said Cole, 'when Lord Saewa was here. He has been working on a list of everything Muriel knew, in case she has been subjected to a Death Reader. I will make sure you are given a copy of that list, sir.'

Cael felt his temper rise. 'The Dominion is going to hold us responsible if those Forty-Eighters are used against them,' he said. 'I want everything moved by this time tomorrow. I want every warehouse emptied, and the munitions stored elsewhere; preferably somewhere that Muriel didn't know about. Is there anything else of vital importance that she knew?'

'Not that I am aware of, sir.'

'Praise Pyre for small mercies,' said Cael. 'I had better report this to the Empress; and then I'll have to go on bended knee to Lord Bailey, to warn the Dominion of what might be coming.' He sensed the eyes of the soldiers on him. 'Good work, everyone,' he went on, 'you stopped a setback from turning into a complete catastrophe, and I am grateful that you prevented the Gunstians from getting their hands on a few Mark Seven Battanaras. I will mention your service to the Empress.'

He activated the Quadrant, and vanished.

CHAPTER 6
PRESERVING HUMANITY

Nom Karta, Inopei – 5th Abrinch 1613

Konna relaxed on the wide terrace as she gazed at the sun setting over Nom Karta's gleaming palaces. Servants were clearing away the plates and bowls from the dining table that had been set up on the roof terrace, and the small party of diners were drinking coffee and whisky as they talked.

'The Empire is a far graver threat to the security of the Dominion than Gunst could ever be,' said Achan.

Konna glanced at the mortal. As far as she could tell, he was old and embittered, and held myriad grudges. He claimed to have been good friends with Konna's father, and with Queen Emily of the City of Salve, but he had nothing but contempt for Empress Thorn and the Empire of the Sapphire Throne.

'The Empire is peaceful,' said Kyra. 'They have reached their natural limits but, even if they became hostile, my mother would put them back in their place.'

'Praise all that is holy for Karalyn,' said Achan; 'for I truly believe that, without her, the Empire would have invaded Aucteran and Inopei by now.'

Konna snorted. 'Bullshit.'

Achan smiled. 'How so, daughter of Corthie? Let me elaborate – the Empire has three immutable attributes; each of which has been proved beyond doubt – aggression, complacency and decadence. Aggression – for did they not conquer Rakana, Rahain and the Eastern Rim of Dragon Eyre? They also held the Tempest mine in Inopei for many years before it was liberated. Complacency – consider the grievous lapses in security that have allowed rogue elements to obtain Quadrants; Quadrants that have invariably been used to attack the Dominion. And decadence – for has the Empress not built a gigantic and monstrous monument to her vanity and hubris, the disgusting Blue Palace? At the very summit of this celebration of folly lives Empress Thorn, isolated from the people she purports to rule, while her two chief advisors are more interested in lying together in debauchery than trying to govern with any moderation.'

Konna laughed.

'Please point out exactly where I err,' said Achan.

'I hardly think that Kelsey and Lucius Cardova are leading lives of debauchery,' she said.

'I always had a feeling they would get together,' said Kyra.

'If I may continue?' said Achan. 'These three attributes that I have been describing – aggressiveness, criminal complacency, and a laxity of moral standards – find themselves ideally personified in one man – a notorious murderer and brigand, a terrorist and warmonger – namely Cael Holdfast, the heir to the Sapphire Throne.'

Kyra rolled her eyes.

'You doubt me, my lady?' said Achan. 'Were it not for Cael's recklessness, the Gunstians would have neither a Quadrant nor a motive to lash out in their understandable fury; for did not Cael mercilessly wipe out three hundred of the leaders of Gunst, and obliterate their most sacred and holy temple? And for what – because the Gunstians were faithfully following their own laws? They had not tortured or executed Arrosa of Zamata; they had merely brought her in for questioning. She was suspected of breaking two of the most important laws in Gunst – treason and apostasy, and, in this case, we have the perfect example of the arrogance of the Holdfasts. Does Cael appeal to the Gunstian authorities? Does he attempt to negotiate, to find a reasonable and peaceful conclusion to these criminal proceedings? Does he show any respect whatsoever for the laws of a sovereign nation? No. He murders three hundred priests, government officials and military commanders. And worse, he brutally defiles the most sacred place in Gunst. Is it any wonder that the Gunstians are angered beyond all sense of restraint? It is clear to me that Cael Holdfast wishes to weaken the Dominion, making it easier for the Empire to control us, but how does he do this without breaking Karalyn's treaty? He provokes Gunst, knowing full well that they will attack Nom Karta.'

'I don't like Cael,' said Konna, 'but I cannot believe that he was planning years ahead like that. He was reckless and impetuous when he attacked that temple in Gunst, but I doubt this was all deliberate.'

'Achan sees patterns where none exist,' said Kyra. 'He finds a coincidence, and calls it a conspiracy.'

Achan smiled. 'I merely evaluate the evidence, ladies,' he said. 'Tell me – who was the great conscience of the Empire? Which Holdfast always worked to the highest moral standards? Who was so pure of heart that he became a threat that needed to be eliminated? None other than Konna's father, the great and beloved Corthie. The Empire viewed him as a liability, and so they sent him to his death. And then, in a display of the most wanton cruelty and savagery, the Empire used his death to massacre a thousand dragons in one day. Empress Thorn bathed in the blood of the Wystians; she revelled in it, and, of course, Cael was by her side, urging her on. And what were they going to do after they had carried out that appalling atrocity? They were going to exterminate the dragons and gods of Nom Karta. They were a whisker away from absorbing the Dominion into their Empire; and again I say – praise all that is holy for Karalyn.'

Konna sipped from her whisky glass. She didn't enjoy hearing Achan speak about her father, but some of his points made sense to her. Had the Empire seen Corthie as an obstacle that needed to be removed? Was a martyred Corthie, killed fighting for the Empire, a safer and more useful figure than a living Corthie who might have opposed the Empire's greed?

The air on the terrace shimmered, and Edgar appeared with Elmhirst.

'May we join you?' said Edgar.

'Please do,' said Kyra. 'There is plenty of whisky left.'

Edgar and Elmhirst took seats next to the others, and Achan filled their glasses.

'The squads are ready,' said Edgar.

'Aye?' said Kyra.

Edgar nodded. 'Elmhirst, let the others know what we have been doing.'

'Yes, my lord,' said the Ancient. 'We have four spare Quadrants, and so I have formed four teams, each with two gods and ten Banner soldiers. The teams will be flexible; in other words, they will be carrying out reprisal attacks on their own, and they will also be coming together to form two portal teams. The raids will be simple. Arrive, strike, depart. I have had a list of military targets around the city of Great Gunst drawn up – army assets, naval assets, fortifications and suchlike. The Gunstians are new to this way of fighting, but I have millennia of experience of organising such attacks. Every time they hit us, we shall answer with overwhelming force. They will soon learn that any attack upon the Dominion will cost them dearly.'

'Will you be leaving the ordinary citizens of Gunst unharmed?' said Kyra.

'That is certainly our plan, ma'am,' said Elmhirst; 'however, if the Gunstians turn their raids onto the civilians of the Dominion, then we shall escalate our own reprisals accordingly. In each squad shall be at least one god with death or flow powers, and if the Gunstians wish to target our people, we shall be forced to do the same.'

'What will happen if the Gunstians simply keep going?' said Konna. 'How will it end?'

'There will never be an invasion of Gunst, if that is what you are implying,' said Edgar. 'The Dominion cannot occupy a land containing millions of people who hate us.'

'Would it not perhaps be wise, my lord,' said Achan, 'to investigate the possibility of stealing some of the Empire's weapons technology? There are only eighty-six gods in the entire Dominion, and sending them to Gunst on these raids might result in casualties from the Gifted. If we used the explosive devices of the Empire, then Banner soldiers could conduct the raids without any immortals being risked.'

'Absolutely not,' said Edgar. 'In fact, I view the scientific advances of the Empire to be our greatest long term threat. Believe me – I have seen this happen before. The spread of knowledge among the mortals tends to imbue them with an attitude of invincibility; and if they can construct weapons that can easily kill gods, they will one day use those weapons against us.'

Kyra frowned, but Konna found herself nodding along in agreement.

'I have been saying that for a while, my lord,' said Konna. 'Why are we waiting for the Empire to build bombs big enough to destroy us? In the old days, the only people the gods had to fear were exceptional Holdfasts like Sable or my father, but now a teenage mortal with a Battanara could remove the head of a god with the press of a lever. Cael has no battle-vision, but he has already killed many gods and dragons.'

'That is a question we shall be pondering as the decades unfold,' said Edgar. 'My immediate priority is to encourage the production of more immortals. We lack many divine children, due to the fact that those posted to the Doomed Worlds by Implacatus were all experienced governors who travelled without their families. Now that the remaining gods have been resettled on Athumia, I hope that more family units will form, and then children shall start to flow from those unions. Out of the eighty-six immortals we now have, over fifty are pure gods, which means that they can have demigod children with mortals.'

Elmhirst raised an eyebrow. 'Does that mean, my lord, that you are prepared to reconsider my application to form a harem of mortals?

Grant me that, and I will soon be producing immortal children for the Dominion.'

Kyra narrowed her eyes at the Ancient.

Konna laughed. 'You might have to wait until Kyra dies before you get your harem, Lord Elmhirst.'

'If Corthie was the conscience of the Empire,' said Achan, 'then I feel that Lady Kyra fulfils that role for the Dominion.'

'By all means find yourself a mortal woman, Elmhirst,' said Edgar, 'but there will be no harems in Nom Karta.' He turned to Konna. 'And I would ask that you never speak those words again, daughter of Corthie. I do not wish to hear about my wife's mortality.'

'It's fine,' said Kyra. 'I am only thirty-three; I have plenty of time left.'

'It is far from fine, my beloved,' said Edgar. 'The thought of you being taken by old age fills me with grief and horror. I would do anything to have you by my side for evermore.'

'I look at your situation, my lord,' said Elmhirst, 'and I feel reluctant to take a mortal woman to wife. That is why harems are better, in my opinion. They are more... impersonal. I would not fall in love with any of the girls I selected, and so I would not suffer, as you do.'

'Why don't you choose a woman from among the gods?' said Konna.

Elmhirst smiled. 'Only a child-god could say such a thing. I am an Ancient, and I have known all eighty-six of the surviving gods for thousands of years. I have already been with every woman among them, some several times over. I had a relationship with Lady Ambrosia that spanned eight centuries. Do you think I wish to rekindle a flame that died out long ago?'

Konna frowned. 'You have been with every female god on Athumia?'

'Yes. I have been alive for twelve thousand years, Konna; only Lord Edgar and Lord Bailey among us are older than I. Eventually, boredom and curiosity forces together gods who may have even loathed each other for centuries. I would bet that it is the same for Bailey; not so much for Edgar, though.'

'I was always viewed as overly prudish,' said Edgar, 'but even I have had a few dalliances with some of the female gods on Athumia; some of which took place thousands of years ago; so long ago that I can barely remember any details.'

'I don't want to hear about this,' said Kyra.

'Is this what I have to look forward to?' said Konna. 'An endless shuffle of the gods sleeping with each other? What about the great romances of the past, such as Belinda and Nathaniel, or Theodora and Edmond?'

Edgar raised an eyebrow. 'Edmond murdered Theodora because he wanted to be with Belinda, and Belinda herself had been with most of the other Ascendants at one time or another. So had Nathaniel, for that matter, and Simon. They were all doing it. The great romance, as you say, of Belinda and Nathaniel happened when both were elderly; there was no salve back then, if you recall. We were all elderly by that point.'

'What was Esher like back then?' said Konna.

Elmhirst laughed. 'He was as bad as the others,' he said. 'I remember he once owned a harem on Solitudus that numbered five thousand – girls and boys. He would disappear into it for months at a time. And now I look at him, and marvel that he is the same man.'

'This is not what I had imagined that being a god was all about,' said Konna.

Elmhirst shrugged. 'One requires distractions to get one through the eons. You will learn this simple truth as you get older. You are a demigod, yes? If you have children with a mortal, they will be mortal. You need to find a god, if you are to assist with the repopulation of this world with the immortals that Lord Edgar desires. I would not be averse to impregnating you. Any offspring of ours would be full gods, and you wouldn't have to worry about me falling in love with you. We could keep it straightforward and practical.'

Konna narrowed her eyes. 'No, thank you.'

Elmhirst laughed again. 'I shall keep the invitation open. You may change your mind a thousand years from now.'

'What about love?' said Konna.

'Love can be sweet,' said Elmhirst, 'but it invariably leads to bitterness and grief when one lives forever. This, too, you will learn.'

The air shimmered next to them, and Cael Holdfast appeared on the darkening terrace. Elmhirst leapt to his feet and drew his Tempest sword, and Cael raised his empty palms.

'I have warned you about this before,' cried Edgar, as he got to his feet; 'and yet you have once again disregarded the most basic tenets of the treaty.'

'I had not wished to come directly to Nom Karta,' said Cael; 'I had no choice. Sister, read my mind. We need to go to Zamata, now.'

Kyra frowned at her brother, then she peered into her eyes. Her face paled, and she stood.

'Edgar,' she said, 'hold your temper; my brother is telling the truth. He had to come here. We should go to Zamata immediately.'

'Why?' said Edgar.

'You will see,' said Kyra.

'Do we need to bring soldiers?' said Elmhirst.

'Soldiers will not be required,' said Cael. He lowered a hand, and withdrew a Quadrant from a pocket. 'May I?'

Edgar eyed him. 'Very well.'

'Stand, Konna,' said Cael. 'You, too, Achan, if you also wish to come.'

Konna and Achan stood, and Cael activated the Quadrant. The air shimmered, and they appeared on the slopes next to the monastery of Zamata Gataza. Konna turned, then her mouth fell open. The monastery was a smoking pile of rubble. The thousand-year-old structure was lying in a great heap of smouldering timber beams and charred rock. To the left of that, over a hundred bodies were lying next to the road that wound down the hillside towards the Hansarta. Each body was that of a monk, and they had been mutilated, their corpses desecrated. Konna heard a cry leave Edgar's lips, and she turned. Hanging from the exterior wall of the monastery's courtyard was another body, its limbs splayed out, and its head missing. A hole in the body's chest had been gouged out, and blood was soaking the man's clothes. By the base of the wall lay the head – Bailey's head, into which his heart had been stuffed.

Further down the hillside was a crowd of Zamatan militia soldiers, who were guarding the perimeter of the monastery from the local inhabitants.

'What the fuck happened here?' said Konna.

'The Gunstians came for Bailey,' said Cael. 'They opened a portal.'

'How do you know this?' said Elmhirst.

Cael gestured to the militia. 'They were already here when I arrived to speak to Bailey,' he said. 'Some of them saw the Gunstians leave through the portal when they had finished slaughtering the monks.'

Edgar fell to his knees by the body hanging from the wall, his eyes closed, as tears flowed down his cheeks. Kyra put a hand onto his shoulder.

'Why didn't the militia lend Lord Bailey aid if they were here?' cried Elmhirst.

'They were subdued by the Gift of Pain,' said Cael. 'No Zamatan civilians were killed; just Bailey and the monks. The Gunstians also raided the supply of Serpent Eye jewels that Bailey was keeping. They were careful to remove them all before evacuating.'

'How do I know you are telling us the truth, Holdfast?' said Elmhirst.

'I have read my brother's thoughts,' said Kyra. 'He is not lying.'

'But he has not told us everything,' said Elmhirst. 'Why did you wish to speak to Lord Bailey this day, Holdfast?'

'To inform him that the Empire was raided by Gunstians yesterday,' said Cael.

'What kind of raid?' said Konna.

'Our missing agent Muriel of Hold Terras did not know too much about the secrets of the Empire,' said Cael, 'but she was aware of one of the locations along the shores of the Inner Sea where certain munitions were being stored. We now believe that her memories have been examined by a Gunstian with the Gift of Death Reading, for the raiders knew exactly where to strike.'

'Munitions?' said Elmhirst.

'Aye. Five of their number, including the Gifted agent, were killed by our soldiers, but two survivors used a Quadrant to escape with a crate of Forty-Eighters. I was here to warn Bailey.'

Edgar turned his head, his eyes full of rage. 'You allowed Gunstians to steal your vile explosives?'

'We have taken steps to secure all remaining munitions,' said Cael. 'Muriel's memories will do them no more good.' He gestured to the ruins of the monastery. 'And, judging by the damage to Zamata Gataza, the Gunstians have already used most of what they stole.'

Edgar got to his feet. 'How could the Empire be so complacent?' he cried. 'You let thieves steal your Quadrants, and now your bombs? Bailey is dead because of your negligence, Adjutant Holdfast. He was my friend for countless years, stretching back to the earliest days of Implacatus; and look what those barbarians did to him!'

'I understand,' said Cael. 'I also mourn the loss of Lord Bailey.'

'How could you possibly understand, mortal?' said Edgar. 'Who do you love the most? Your wife and children? Your sister? Your cousin Cole? Your mother? You have not known any of them for more than three short decades; I knew Bailey for over ten thousand years. How dare you compare your grief to mine?'

'Perhaps Cael Holdfast is happy to allow the Gunstians to hurt the Dominion, my lord,' said Achan; 'for doesn't the Empire stand to benefit from our pain?'

'Fuck off, Achan,' said Cael. 'You are as full of shit as you always were.'

Achan nodded. 'Aggression, complacency; just as I was saying.'

'The Empire will hunt down and kill every Gunstian who attacks us,' said Cael. 'I don't care if that sounds aggressive. If the Dominion is going to do the same, then I suggest that we coordinate our efforts. We wouldn't want to get in each other's way.'

The air shimmered, and Cole appeared. He eyed Edgar and the others, then he turned to Cael.

'I have informed the Imperial Court of what has taken place here,' he said.

'Thank you, Cole,' said Cael. 'What were Her Majesty's orders?'

'She wants us to offer the Dominion any help they require,' said Cole. 'She also requests that Lady Kyra tells Karalyn that the official arbiter of the peace has been killed.' He glanced at Edgar. 'Her Majesty expresses her deepest sympathies for your loss, my lord,' he went on. 'She would like to establish a new way for the Empire to communicate with the Dominion.'

'I care nothing for her sympathy,' said Edgar, 'and I have no desire to continue this dialogue. There is but one thing I require from the Empire – that it leaves us in peace.'

Cole inclined his head. 'I will pass on your words, my lord.'

'Wait a moment,' said Cael. 'How will we contact you if we have information to share? I know you hate us turning up in Nom Karta unannounced; but what else can we do?'

'The decapitated body of my oldest friend is displayed on a wall just yards from where you stand, Holdfast,' said Edgar, 'and you wish to negotiate? Be gone with you. Let me mourn without your presence by my shoulder.'

Cael eyed Cole, then he took out his Quadrant.

'Wait,' said Kyra. 'Tell the Empress that I will talk to our mother, Cael. I will tell her what has happened.'

Cael bowed his head, then he swiped the Quadrant, and both he and Cole vanished.

Konna stood a little back from the others as Edgar wept on his knees before the body of Bailey. After a few moments, Elmhirst began to cut the body down from the wall. He sliced through the cords holding Bailey's limbs to the wooden posts, and lowered him to the ground.

'I want revenge,' said Edgar, as he got to his feet. 'I want the temples of Gunst to burn for this outrage. I want the Gunstian fallen to be piled high in the streets of their capital city. One death for every year Bailey lived.'

Kyra stared at him, but Elmhirst inclined his head.

'It shall be done, my lord,' said the Ancient. 'Should I order the squads to move out right away?'

Edgar eyed the ruined remains of Zamata Gataza. 'Search the mines below the monastery first,' he said. 'Look for any Serpent Eyes that the Gunstians may have missed. Konna can help you. I will take the body of Bailey back to Nom Karta.'

'As you will, my lord,' said Elmhirst.

Edgar took out a Quadrant, then he Kyra, Achan and the body of Bailey disappeared.

A few militia soldiers approached.

'Might we gather the slain monks, sir?' said one.

'You may,' said Elmhirst, 'but stay out of the ruins for now while we investigate.'

He gestured to Konna, and they entered the monastery compound. They scrambled over the heaps of smoking rubble, then Elmhirst used his battle-vision to move huge blocks of masonry.

'What are we looking for?' said Konna.

'A way down into the basements and mines that lie below,' said Elmhirst.

Konna helped the Ancient lift a great section of wall. They heaved it to their left and set it down again, revealing stairs that descended into the gloom. Elmhirst led the way down the steps, and Konna followed. They passed empty alcoves and storerooms and came into a vast cavern.

'This is where Lord Malum and Lady Macsin were killed,' said Elmhirst; 'and, if the legends are true, it is where the spirit of Karalyn Holdfast was placed into the body of an Aucterian woman.'

'You hated Bailey, didn't you?' said Konna.

Elmhirst eyed her. 'Why would you say that at such a time?'

'It's true, isn't it?' she said. 'None of the gods I have spoken to in Nom Karta liked Bailey. Only Lord Edgar was his friend.'

'Yes, but their bond was strong, and I would not recommend saying any of this to Edgar. He is liable to lash out in his grief.'

'How long was Bailey alive for?'

'Around fifteen thousand years, I think.'

'Then you are going to have to massacre fifteen thousand Gunstians?'

'More or less. I am not actually going to count them all.'

'And that doesn't bother you?'

'Of course not. They deserve to be punished for assassinating a god of the Dominion.'

They kept walking, and went down more steps. Elmhirst lit a lantern, and they examined the caverns. Elmhirst stopped by an alcove, where two bronze plaques had been fixed to the stone wall.

'What's that?' said Konna.

'The tombs of two Ascendants,' said Elmhirst; 'the First and the Fourth – Theodora and Nathaniel. Two of the mightiest beings to have ever existed, and this dark, squalid cave is their final resting place. The Gunstians, in their haste, must have walked right by this alcove, for they would have desecrated the graves had they known who lay here.'

They carried on, and came to a large cavern were several crates were lying smashed on the ground.

Elmhirst knelt by them. 'The Serpent Eyes were stored in here,' he said. 'Search the cavern; let us see if they missed any.'

Konna got down on her hands and knees next to Elmhirst, and they combed through the straw that had cushioned the jewels inside the crates.

Elmhirst smiled, and held up a red Serpent Eye. 'Cael was rather negligent, it seems. He should have searched down here before summoning us from Nom Karta.'

'Why are we doing this?' said Konna. 'No one in the Dominion knows how to make Quadrants.'

'It is to prevent the Empire from being able to construct any more,' he said. 'They have enough, I think.'

'Here's another one,' said Konna, as she picked up a green jewel. 'The Gunstians must have been in a hurry. Can I come along on one of the raids?'

'You are much too young.'

'Aye, but I can change my appearance. As far as I know, I am the only god on Athumia who can do that. I could disguise myself as a Gunstian priest, or even as Bailey, to make them think he had risen from the dead.'

Elmhirst eyed her. 'And you have death powers also?'

'And vision; the entire range of vision.'

'Would you be prepared to slaughter hundreds of Gunstians at a time?' he said. 'Killing fifteen thousand is harder than it sounds. Many young gods baulk at the sight of so many bodies. How many people have you killed, Konna?'

'I have killed greenhides, but never a human.'

'And you wish to begin by taking part in a great and terrible massacre?' he said. 'I think not. Preserve your humanity while you still have it, for it will be gone soon enough. The long centuries will see to that.'

Konna picked up another jewel from the ground. 'Have you ever known a god who didn't become cynical and jaded? One who retained their sense of humanity right until the end?'

'Only one,' said Elmhirst.

'Who?'

'Can't you guess?' he said.

She frowned. 'Bailey?'

'Exactly,' said Elmhirst. 'Bailey was the only one who still thought like a mortal, and he was despised for it. With his death, I fear that the final vestiges of Lord Edgar's humanity shall swiftly turn to dust. Konna, we are about to witness the full wrath of the gods, and it will be a fearsome sight to behold.'

CHAPTER 7
PLEASING NO ONE

Unnamed World – No Calendar (6th Day, First Third Summer 560)

The marshes spread out in every direction for hundreds of miles. Long-limbed wading birds were picking through the wetlands with their beaks, trying to catch fish, while others were flying overhead. The marshes were fed by a network of rivers that flowed down from a range of mountains two hundred miles to the north, creating a vast area that Karalyn believed would be a suitable environment for the Rakanese of the future to settle. She had ensured that thick banks of clay were plentiful, to provide the raw material for bricks, and there were numerous woodlands in areas that sat just above the waterline.

Karalyn gazed down at her handiwork, and was pleased. It had taken her many attempts to get right, but her latest version of a Rakanese world seemed perfect. She had yet to align its time with that of the Sextant, which meant that she could leave it for centuries, and it would be exactly the same when she next visited. That was the secret to creating worlds. The creator could spend years within their new world, without any time passing upon the aligned worlds, but, as soon as its time was aligned, the seconds would begin to pass in the same way they passed everywhere else. From that point onwards, the world would be *set*, and unchangeable.

There were dozens of partly-finished worlds stored by the Sextant in which the time had not been aligned, and Karalyn had visited many of them. For some, it was obvious why the work had been abandoned. Several of Theodora's earliest works were nothing but volcanic wastelands, the air a poisonous brew of toxins, while others had been obliterated by their own moons, or by other massive objects that had struck it. There were fewer failed worlds that had been made by either Simon or Nathaniel, but they had been in possession of the Sextant for a far shorter time than Theodora, and both had been trained by her in the arts of world-building. Karalyn could have added many unfinished worlds to the others, but her sense of order and neatness had seen her systematically destroying them utterly, leaving no trace of them behind.

There were also dozens of finished worlds in existence that had lost contact with the others for millennia. Some were lifeless, but others teemed with civilisations. As the owner of the Sextant, Karalyn was the only person capable of reaching out to those worlds, but she had deliberately neglected to do so. She had observed them from a distance, but had not intervened. Again, most had been made by Theodora, and several had oddities that made them unique in some way. Karalyn wondered if Athumia would have been one of those lost worlds, had Theodora not died while finishing it. Her work had been completed by Simon, who had then ignored the world, as he was eager to move on to creating Dragon Eyre, and it had been Nathaniel's later intervention that had allowed Gahad and a large number of humans from Lostwell to settle upon Inopei and Aucteran. It was strange to imagine it, but that one act meant that Athumia contained by far the largest number of *original* humans left in existence. The Lostwell humans had come from Implacatus, and, before that, from the first world, the one that had been destroyed in the endless wars between mortals and immortals. The City of Salve had a few thousand *originals*, who mostly lived in Jezra as exiles from Lostwell. Dragon Eyre also had a few thousand – the remnants of the settlers from Implacatus; and the

Star Continent had those who had been rescued from Dragon Eyre to form the Banner of the Sapphire Throne – but these thousands were dwarfed by the millions who lived on Aucteran and Inopei. Every other human alive was sub-created by Theodora, Simon or Nathaniel. Were the humans of Aucteran and Inopei aware of their heritage? Did it matter?

Karalyn felt a niggle in the back of her mind. She frowned. Was Kyra trying to interrupt her again? She pushed the attempt aside, and went back to gazing down at her new world. She had yet to name it, but she knew that the Rakanese tradition was to name their cities and nations after a founding member, so the name could wait until the first Rakanese settled there, which could be centuries in the future. She hoped they would like it.

The niggle came again, and Karalyn's temper surged.

What do you want, daughter? she said. *I am busy.*

I have been trying to contact you for days, said Kyra.

Aye, I know. If it's about the Gunstians, I'm not interested. Leave me.

I cannot, said Kyra. *The situation has deteriorated. Wait – how did you know about the Gunstians?*

I spoke to Bailey a while ago, she said. *This is not something I care about. The Dominion and the Empire can handle a few rogue attacks; you don't need my help.*

Bailey is dead.

Karalyn fell silent.

The Gunstians killed him, Mother, Kyra went on, *and both sides want you to appoint a new arbiter of the peace.*

That's not true, is it? said Karalyn. *I can see your thoughts, daughter. The Empress wants a new arbiter, but Lord Edgar is too grief-stricken to care.*

Aye, that's right, said Kyra. *Edgar is oscillating between grief and anger. He wants revenge. Bailey was... well, he was the only real friend Edgar had. There is going to be terrible carnage; both sides are putting together death squads armed with gods, explosives and Quadrants. They won't work together, but both intend to massacre Gunstians.*

Karalyn went deeper into Kyra's thoughts, and saw the scene she had witnessed at Zamata Gataza. Her gaze went over the dead monks, then the mutilated body of Bailey, and then to Edgar shouting at Cael.

How dare you compare your grief to mine? Edgar was telling her son.

I do not wish to get involved in this, said Karalyn. *This is not my problem.*

But you need someone to act as a conduit between the Dominion and the Empire, said Kyra. *It is clear to me that you are not paying attention to what is happening upon the Known Worlds, and you need to find a new arbiter. That, Mother, is certainly your problem.*

Where are you?

Nom Karta. On the roof of the Palace of Naghad.

Karalyn pushed Kyra out of her thoughts, and took her hand off the Sextant. She gazed around at her quarters on her unnamed world, then she walked out onto her long balcony. She sat, and stared at her view.

Kyra was right. Karalyn had no intention of spending her every waking hour monitoring the peace, and she had been happy to allow Bailey to act as her representative. Unless she wished to get more involved in the lives of the Empire and the Dominion, she would have to appoint someone else. An immortal would be better; someone who could remain in post for a few centuries – but who? Bailey had been perfect. He had been a god, but not one too closely connected to the immortals of the Doomed Worlds; and he had been respected by both sides.

Aila would be suitable, but she was a Holdfast who loathed the Empress, and she might allow her personal feelings to warp her judgement. Esher was also suitable, as he had yet to settle into his life as an Ascendant, but he was too young for such a responsibility.

She stood.

The roof of the Palace of Naghad. Nom Karta. Go.

The air crackled, and Karalyn appeared on the roof terrace of the grand palace. A few people were seated by a long table, and Karalyn walked over to them.

Kyra stood. 'Thank you for coming, Mother.'

'I had no choice,' said Karalyn. She eyed the others. 'Elmhirst, Esher, Konna and Achan; greetings. Where is Edgar?'

'He is watching over Bailey's body as he is prepared for burial,' said Kyra.

'Your children?'

'With their tutor,' said Kyra. 'Do you want to see them?'

'Maybe when they are older. What does Queen Famula have to say about Bailey's murder?'

'Her Majesty views it as an attack on the Dominion as a whole,' said Elmhirst; 'and she has approved Lord Edgar's plan to strike back at certain Gunstian targets.'

Karalyn eyed the Ancient. 'I assume that you will be closely involved with these strikes? It is what you used to do for Lord Edmond the Second Ascendant, is it not?'

'That is correct,' said Elmhirst.

'You led dozens of raids on the Star Continent during the Ascendants' invasion of my home world.'

'I did,' said Elmhirst. 'We eliminated several bands of fleeing Banner soldiers and members of the imperial army. I was good at what I did; I still am.'

'I don't like you.'

Elmhirst shrugged. 'If you are a god, Karalyn,' he said, 'you are a frightfully young one. How long have you been immortal? Twenty-five years? Twenty-six? Come back with your ignorant criticisms of my methods after a millennium or two. I will be interested to see if you have changed your mind by then.'

Konna's eyes widened. 'I didn't think any god would speak to Karalyn like that.'

'I am not afraid of her,' said Elmhirst. 'She could kill me with a click of her fingers, but that doesn't scare me. She is like a child who has happened upon a very sharp knife.'

Karalyn smiled and sat down next to them. Her gaze went to a bottle of whisky.

'Where did you get that?' she said.

'Zamata,' said Kyra. 'We didn't steal it from the Marchbrae Holdfasts. Bailey used to buy it in Plateau City for us.' She gestured towards Konna. 'It was your niece's idea.'

'What can I say?' said Konna. 'I like a few comforts that remind me of home.'

'We need a new arbiter,' said Karalyn.

'Lord Edgar might disagree,' said Elmhirst. 'Let's face facts – Bailey didn't actually arbitrate much, did he? He was a conduit, used to pass messages between the two sides.'

'Was Bailey's Quadrant taken?'

'It was,' said Kyra. 'That means the Gunstians now have three.'

'Any arbiter will need a Quadrant.'

'The Dominion has none to spare,' said Elmhirst.

'I will get one from Arrosa,' said Karalyn. 'Elmhirst, I think you would be a good choice as arbiter.'

The Ancient began to laugh, and Karalyn raised an eyebrow.

'Were you being serious?' he said.

'Aye.'

'But I am a member of Lord Edgar's government,' said Elmhirst. 'What possibly makes you think I would be unbiased? I loathe the mortal Empire, and, present company excepted, I hate the bloody Holdfasts.'

'You say what you think, and you aren't afraid to contradict me,' said Karalyn. 'I don't need someone who passively agrees to every idea I have. You are now the last Ancient left, aye?'

'Well, apart from Lord Edgar himself,' he said. 'What's in it for me?'

'I would gift you enough gold to build yourself a palace on Zamata,' said Karalyn, 'and I would present you with a new Quadrant, so that the Dominion doesn't lose one. You would have to behave yourself on Zamata; and that means not antagonising the local administration. And you would have to be available to pass on messages between the Dominion and the Empire.'

'Then I respectfully decline,' said Elmhirst. 'Such a role holds no interest for me.'

'Perhaps I could do it,' said Esher.

Karalyn eyed him.

'I have been looking for something to do,' Esher went on, 'but everyone here says I am too young. Gods bow when they see me, but none of them will give me any responsibility.'

'For obvious reasons,' said Elmhirst. 'When the same thing happened to Queen Belinda, the other gods made the mistake of assuming that she was still, at heart, the same person she had always been. Many believed that her memories would return eventually. Arete and Leksandr tried to reason with her and, of course, Edmond wanted to marry her. We were all wrong. Belinda was a new person, with a new personality, and she had decided to side with the Holdfasts.' He eyed Esher. 'We still have no idea what form your new personality will take. You are an Ascendant, but you are not the same Esher you once were.'

Karalyn got to her feet. 'I am going to speak to Edgar.'

'Be gentle,' said Kyra. 'He is in pain.'

Karalyn reached out for Edgar's god powers, using her vision to sense his self-healing. She found him.

Next to Edgar. Go.

She appeared in a lamplit hall, where a body was being cleaned and prepared for burial by several servants. Standing next to the table was Lord Edgar, his gaze on the body of Bailey. He caught sight of Karalyn, but said nothing.

'You have my sympathies, Edgar,' she said. 'When shall the funeral take place?'

'Three days from now,' said Edgar. 'We were thinking of burying him next to the graves of the two Ascendants beneath Zamata Gataza, but with the destruction of the monastery, I am not so sure.'

'The monastery can be rebuilt,' said Karalyn.

'The Gunstians could attack it again.'

'They could strike anywhere.'

'I suppose they could. Will you be attending the funeral? I would like you to be there.'

'Aye. I'll be there.'

Edgar nodded.

'I hear you are seeking vengeance,' she said.

'That is correct. Are you going to try to stop me?'

'I have decided not to interfere,' she said.

'That pleases me greatly. No – *pleases* is the wrong word. I am aware that revenge will not make me feel any better about the loss of Bailey; but justice demands a response. The Gunstians butchered my friend over a religious disagreement, and they need to be shown that such acts of barbarity come with a heavy price.'

'Perhaps.'

'Bailey's death has taught me a hard truth,' he said; 'a truth I had always known, and yet it was one I had refused to admit – even gods die. I will die. My death might not occur for another ten millennia but, in time, it will come. It is inevitable. The Ascendants believed they would live forever, and look at them now. When we talk of mortals and immortals, we are really talking about two different types of mortals, distinguished only by the lengths of their life spans.'

Karalyn said nothing.

'There is but one exception to this rule, Karalyn,' he said: 'you. Only you are capable of truly living forever. One body dies, you take another. At some point, Albany's body will be destroyed, and you will have to find a different host in which to dwell.'

'I try not to think about it,' she said.

'Why is that? Is it not the greatest blessing one could imagine?'

'I see it as a curse, not a blessing,' she said. 'I did not plan to be forced into the body of Lyla the Aucterian.'

'But you did choose Albany? That's what Bailey told me – you chose to kill her in order to take control of her body.'

'Only after she had killed Lyla,' she said. 'Albany was not innocent.'

'I know; I wasn't criticising. How did it happen, though? Not Albany, nor Lyla, but the first time? What happened when your original body was destroyed? Do you remember?'

'Only vaguely,' she said. 'I was in the farmhouse in Clackenbaird, but I was using my vision powers to watch the advance of the Ascendants and their armies. I was linked to the Sextant, and I wasn't paying attention to what was happening next to my resting body. Bastion and Edmond were already in the farmhouse, and they were waiting for me to return to my physical form.'

'I see,' said Edgar. 'They were worried that, if they killed you, the Sextant would become unusable.'

'That's right. Bastion attacked me as soon as I opened my eyes. As my body was being cut to pieces, I released my vision powers again. I fled to the Sextant, as if I might somehow be safe inside that device. I cannot recall the exact moment it happened, but when my body died, my consciousness remained within the Sextant. The Sextant then told me that I would be trapped there forever, but that wasn't true. Sable deactivated the Sextant, and my consciousness remained free; it wasn't tied to the Sextant; it was free. I had no body, of course, and it didn't occur to me at the time that I would be able to take another one.'

'But the Sextant was key to this process?'

'Aye. Well, I think so. I had been spending too much time with the Sextant, and I had become obsessed with creating a new world. The Sextant was displeased that I abandoned this work to return to the real world.'

'How could a machine be *displeased*? How could it form opinions about you being trapped within it?'

Karalyn smiled. 'I wish I had an answer to that. I have always heard the inner voice of the Tempest held within both the Sextant and Quadrants. I think that was important. You could always blame Nathaniel, I suppose; he created dream mages.'

'I doubt even the great Nathaniel had a clear idea of what he had done when he created dream mages.'

'It was a mistake, or so I have been told. He had assumed that his creation of dream mages had failed, so he moved on and forgot about it. He then went on to create mages with more traditional god powers – flow, death, and so on.'

'Did you retain any powers while you were without a body?'

'Some, though not all. I could use my vision to travel anywhere, and

I could read the thoughts of anyone I came across, but only if I understood their language. My power to persuade still functioned, but it wasn't as strong as before.'

'And in Lyla's body?'

'I was then at my weakest,' she said. 'Lyla had not only been killed and raised from the dead a minute too late, she had no powers of her own. I was barely able to use any of my abilities at first, but I slowly learned how to do a few things – like persuade with the power of my voice; but I could only vision while I was sleeping.'

'Why didn't you simply destroy that body and take a better one?'

Karalyn raised an eyebrow. 'It never crossed my mind. For a long time, I believed I was both Lyla and Karalyn. Lyla was... dear to me. Is there a reason for these questions?'

Edgar eyed her. 'I apologise if I seemed to be intruding. Bailey's death has left me questioning the purpose of existence, and you are unique in that regard.'

'I will leave you now,' said Karalyn, 'but I shall return before the funeral.' She gazed at Bailey. 'Sleep well, my friend.'

Colsbury Castle. Go.

Karalyn appeared on the middle balcony of the Summer Palace on Colsbury. Around her, several people were eating lunch at a series of tables, and all conversations ceased the moment they saw who had arrived.

Kelsey got to her feet. 'Sister,' she said. 'This is a surprise.'

Karalyn swept her gaze over the table where Kelsey had been sitting. Lucius Cardova was there, along with Rosie Jackdaw and her husband.

'I am looking for Arrosa,' she said.

'Do you know about Bailey?' said Kelsey.

'Aye. Edgar is preparing the body for burial. We need a new arbiter, and that arbiter shall require a Quadrant.'

'Do you have any candidates?'

'A few. I will announce who it is in due course. You can inform the

Rakanese that I have finished their new world. It is ready whenever they need it.'

'A new world?' said Lucius.

'That's right – for the Rakanese when their population starts to overwhelm the rest of the Star Continent. I have tried to make it perfect for them – freshwater marshes, plenty of clay and wood. Many millions could live there. Hundreds of millions. I haven't named it, though; I think that should be their choice. It's very beautiful, if you like wetlands, and it's teeming with birds and fish...' She realised that everyone was staring at her, and knew that she had allowed her natural enthusiasm for her creations to make her appear wide-eyed and over-excited. She flattened her demeanour. 'Do you know where I might find Arrosa?'

'She will be with Cael and their children,' said Kelsey. 'It's good to see you. It has been a while.'

'Caitlyn and Carden have remained in Plateau City this summer,' said Lucius. 'We felt they were old enough to fend for themselves. Caelius is also there; he will look after them.'

Karalyn nodded. She sent out her powers to find Cael, and located him on an upper floor of the Summer Palace.

Next to Cael. Go.

She arrived on a much smaller balcony, where Cael, Arrosa and their three children were enjoying a private lunch. Cowie stared up at her, and Carrie blinked in surprise and started to cry.

'It's all right,' said Arrosa. 'It's only Granny Karalyn, come to visit us.'

'Why is she crying?' said Karalyn.

'You gave her a little fright, appearing like that,' said Arrosa.

'She isn't used to it,' said Cael. 'Are you hungry? Take a seat, Mother.'

The young girl calmed down as Arrosa stroked her hair, and Karalyn sat down.

'Are you really our *Granny*?' said Cowie.

'Aye,' said Karalyn. 'I am your father's mother.'

'But you look younger than Father,' said the boy.

'I know. I am a god now. Do you not remember me?'

'I think he was four when you last spoke to him,' said Arrosa.

'How old is he now?' said Karalyn.

'Ten,' said Cael.

'He has dream powers,' she said. 'Weak, but there. Arrosa, I need a Quadrant to give to the new arbiter. Please get one for me.'

Arrosa eyed her for a moment, then she wiped her lips with a napkin and stood.

'I will be back shortly,' she said.

Cael watched her leave the balcony, then he glanced at his mother. 'What is Edgar planning?'

'Bloody retribution,' said Karalyn. 'I will not stand in his way.'

Cael shook his head. 'You stopped us from killing the leadership of the Dominion, but you won't stop Edgar from slaughtering the Gunstians. Interesting.'

'Is it? The two situations are not the same.'

'Aren't they? We were also embarked upon a campaign of bloody retribution. Edgar wishes to avenge Bailey; we were avenging Corthie.'

Karalyn gazed at her son. 'I guess I hold the Holdfasts to a higher standard. We should be better. We need to do better.'

'How is Cairney?'

'Truculent. Defiant. I will not be releasing him any time soon.'

Arrosa emerged from their quarters with a Quadrant in her right hand. She sat, and placed it on to the table.

'Thank you,' said Karalyn. 'This is one of Elbannon's Quadrants.'

'Yes,' said Arrosa. 'We don't have any originals to spare.'

Karalyn slipped it into a pocket.

'Who will be the new arbiter between the Dominion and the Empire?' said Arrosa.

Karalyn eyed her. 'Esher.'

'The Ascendant?'

'Aye. He is genuinely neutral when it comes to politics, and he needs something to do.'

'I had imagined that the gods on Athumia would be worshipping him,' said Arrosa.

'They have learned from what I did to Belinda that Esher is not the same as he was before,' said Karalyn. 'They respect his status as an Ascendant, but they do not trust him with any responsibilities. They are treating him as a young god, in the same way as they are treating Konna.'

She got to her feet.

'How did Esher react when you told him?' said Cael.

Karalyn smiled. 'He doesn't know yet.'

The roof of the Palace of Naghad. Nom Karta. Go.

She appeared back on the roof terrace, where Kyra, Achan, Konna, Elmhirst and Esher were still sitting.

'How was Edgar?' said Kyra.

'Surprisingly calm and rational,' said Karalyn. 'I will return for the funeral.'

'You are welcome to stay here until then,' said Kyra. 'You could spend some time with Edward and Alfred.'

Karalyn frowned. 'Who?'

Anger passed over Kyra's face for a moment, then she composed herself. 'My two sons, Mother.'

'Oh. It's their names, Kyra; I can't get used to them.'

Kyra rolled her eyes.

'She forgets her own children exist,' said Konna. 'Why are you surprised that she forgets her grandchildren?'

'That isn't true,' said Karalyn. 'I have just seen Cael's three children.'

Konna caught her gaze. 'When did you last see Caitlyn and Carden?'

'I can't recall; but Caitlyn and Carden are immortal. I have centuries to get to know them.'

'You are slipping away from us, Mother,' said Kyra. 'You spend so much time alone with the Sextant, that you are forgetting who you are.'

Karalyn looked away. She hated moments like those, when she felt exposed to the barbs of others. She knew there was some truth to what

Kyra and Konna had said, but she refused to dwell on it. She took the Quadrant from her pocket and held it out towards Esher.

'This is for you,' she said.

Esher raised an eyebrow. 'For me?'

'That's what I said. Take it.'

'I don't know how to use it.'

'I will teach you. I have decided that you shall become the new arbiter of the peace. I am going to take you to Zamata. Do you need to pack?'

Esher stared at her, then he smiled and took the Quadrant.

Elmhirst frowned. 'Has Lord Edgar agreed to this?'

'I haven't asked him,' said Karalyn.

'Don't you think you should?' said the Ancient.

'Why?' said Karalyn. 'Edgar doesn't own Esher.'

The Ascendant stood, the Quadrant in his hand. 'Show me how to use this, and we can go to Zamata now. I can come back for my things later.'

'Is that it?' said Konna. 'Are you leaving us?'

Esher smiled. 'I will be travelling back and forth; you will still see me every few days. This is what I need, Konna – a purpose; a way to feel useful.'

'I shall return for the funeral,' said Karalyn.

The gold room. Home, with Esher. Go.

The air shimmered, then she and Esher appeared in her cliffside home on her unnamed world, within a deep cavern where she kept a vast quantity of gold and silver. She walked over to crates of Athumian coins that were legal tender on Zamata, as Esher stared with wide eyes at the great wealth on display.

'Where are we?' he said.

Karalyn said nothing.

The Dragon Palace, Zamata; with Esher and these crates. Go.

The air shimmered again, then she, Esher, and the crates of coins appeared on the neat lawn in front of the white, marble palace in Igatz.

'You might consider living here, in the palace,' said Karalyn, 'at least until you can use the gold to build a new home for yourself. I recommend constructing a fortified building on the site of Zamata Gataza, but that will take a few years to complete. Until then, I am sure that President Bauchlie will allow you to live here.'

Esher eyed her. 'You aren't going to just leave me to sort it all out on my own, are you?'

'I will stay with you here for a few days,' she said. 'I will teach you how to use the Quadrant, and I will tell you how to act as the arbiter of the peace. This is what you wanted, aye?'

Esher grinned. 'Yes. Thank you, Karalyn; this is exactly what I wanted.'

Karalyn smiled back at him. At least she had made someone happy.

CHAPTER 8
MEETING THE COUSINS (PART ONE)

Plateau City, The Plateau – 6th Day, First Third Summer 560

Lindi walked through the busy streets of the Kellach Quarter in Plateau City. The area where the Kellach lived was larger than the whole of Udall on Ulna, and the Quarter bustled with life. Tall wooden and stone tenements towered over the streets, and taverns were on every corner, while, above the rooftops, the towers of the Blue Palace dominated the city.

Lindi passed a large blacksmith's forge, and felt the heat from the furnaces as the sound of iron being hammered pounded at her ears. She had left the hostelry where she had been sleeping that morning, as soon as she realised that her mother had departed the city. Sable had been looking for her, using her Quadrant to travel among the worlds to search for her daughter; but Lindi had been prepared. She had guessed that her mother would look in Plateau City, so she had waited until she had arrived, and had then waited until she had left again. She wondered if her mother knew that she was able to sense her presence. It was Sable's unique mixture of vision and dream powers that made her so recognisable to Lindi; though it was Lindi's own dream powers that were required to sense her. When she had awoken that morning, she had scanned the city. Sable had visited the Blue Palace and the

Holdfast townhouse on the previous days, but all traces of her had gone, and so Lindi had emerged from hiding.

She relaxed as she walked through the busy streets, keeping the Blue Palace to her right. She had been to Plateau City before, but never on her own, and she was exhilarated by the sights, sounds and smells. Not all of the smells. Something rancid and noxious lay somewhere to the south. She had asked about it in the tavern where she had been staying, and had been told that the source of the odour was a nearby tannery. The barman had then proceeded to tell her why it smelled so bad, and Lindi had asked him to stop talking. At least she no longer had to wonder what the city did with all of the dragon shit produced by the Blue Palace – she had her answer.

She gazed at a group of Kellach men who were erecting some scaffolding around an old tenement. All of them were around the size of her brother Joss. It was the stature of the Kellach women that had surprised her. There were none in Udall, and she hadn't realised that they were almost the same size as the Kellach men. In truth, she had been expecting something more like the Sanang, where the men were far larger than their womenfolk, but among the Kellach, there was little difference between the sexes. She guessed that was why so many of them served in the army. Among them, Lindi felt short and slight, and her dark skin made her look like a young woman from the Holdings.

She glanced up as two dragons soared over the streets. Her gaze tracked them as they sped north, then they were lost from view. Lindi lowered her gaze, and saw a bronze statue on a stone plinth ahead of her. Groups of Kellach were loitering close to it, and Lindi approached. She had been told about the statue, but had never seen it. As she got closer, she gazed up. The two figures on the plinth were twice life-size, and depicted a Kellach woman with her arm outstretched, and a young girl huddled by her knees.

Lindi gazed at the plaque.

Keira – Fire Mage and Saviour d.507

Lindi smiled. Fifty-three years had passed since Keira had killed Nathaniel the Creator. She had sacrificed her life to save the Star Continent, but the little girl by her legs was still alive. The little girl by her legs would never die. Karalyn Holdfast was a true immortal, and when Sable spoke of her, it was usually in a tone of reverence. Lindi had no opinion about Karalyn. She didn't seem like a real person to her, as though she was already little more than a myth. Some referred to her as the only genuine god, which Lindi found to be insulting. She had found some trick to cheat death, but that did not make her special; just lucky. As for being all-powerful, how could that be true if she had needed the help of Lindi's mother to escape from Athumia?

'Did ye come to see the statue, lass?' an old Kellach man said to her.

'I was just passing,' said Lindi.

'Do ye know who the wee girl is meant to be?'

Lindi said nothing.

'Back when the statue was first put up,' the old man went on, 'everyone thought the wee lassie was meant to represent the people of the city; but that isnae true. It's Karalyn Holdfast, that's who it is.'

'Do you remember the statue being built? Are you that old?'

The man laughed. 'I'm seventy-five, hen. I remember fleeing Lach when the Rahain invaded. I was here when Bridget became Empress. I remember everything.'

Lindi smiled. 'You should write it all down before you become senile, which might not be too far away. That's assuming you can write, of course.'

The old man laughed even louder, and Lindi walked away, slightly annoyed that he hadn't taken offence at her words.

She passed out of the Kellach Quarter, and entered an area where folk from the Holdings predominated. She kept the Blue Palace to her right, and entered the Old Town of the city. The streets immediately narrowed, and Lindi almost got lost as she navigated her way to the north. She spotted the three tall spires of the university over the walls of the Old Town, and headed in that direction. She passed groups of Rakanese sailors, Holdings merchants, and even a few Sanang and Kellach labourers, and her stomach growled at the sight of so much hot food being sold from stalls and the backs of carts. She reached an open gate in the walls, and entered the New Town, the Blue Palace still on her right. She turned left by the university, and walked along the elegant streets of the city's aristocratic district. Lara and her mother had often mentioned Plateau City University as a possible option for her future, but Lindi regarded the idea of spending several more years in education as a waste of time. She had centuries in which to learn how the worlds worked, and she would rather pick up the knowledge she required from experience. Who needed to hear some old mortals lecture from dusty books on subjects that were tedious beyond belief? Joss had certainly not desired to go to university, and he seemed happy enough with his life.

She took a right, and walked up a street that ran by the great sea wall. She eyed the large townhouses on her left, and stopped at one. She glanced up and down the road, and walked to the front door.

She knocked.

The door opened, and a middle-aged Holdings man peered out at her.

'Can I help you, miss?' he said.

'I am here to see Caitlyn Holdfast,' she said.

'Is Miss Holdfast expecting you?'

'Possibly.'

Let me in; I am no threat.

'Please come in,' said the man.

Lindi beamed at him. 'Thank you.'

She crossed the threshold and gazed at the narrow hallway, seeing stairs at the end of the corridor that went up.

'Please wait here for a moment, miss,' said the man, as he closed the door.

Lindi stood by the entrance as the man went up the stairs, then she sent her vision after him. The house was narrow, but had many floors, as well as a cellar beneath the kitchen. She saw the man knock upon another door, then a young woman answered it. The woman's eyes widened slightly, then she nodded, and followed the man down the stairs.

Lindi cut her vision powers and smiled. 'Hello.'

Caitlyn Holdfast gestured to the butler, who bowed his head and went into the kitchen.

'Lindi?' said Caitlyn.

'That's me.'

'Your mother was here yesterday,' Caitlyn went on. 'She is looking for you.'

'I know; that's why I came here today – my mother is no longer in Plateau City. Could I have some coffee? What about breakfast?'

'Of course,' said Caitlyn; 'but... well, I wouldn't want to cross your mother.'

'I am here to visit my immortal cousins,' said Lindi. 'If you tell my mother that I have arrived, then I guess we won't be friends, Caitlyn. I would rather be friends.'

Caitlyn said nothing for a while, and Lindi knew she was debating what to do. She also knew that she could go into her cousin's mind and persuade her to say nothing to Sable, but that seemed like cheating, and she wanted to give Caitlyn a chance to come to the correct conclusion on her own.

'I won't tell your mother,' said Caitlyn, 'but I can't speak for Carden or Caelius.'

'What about the butler?'

'He may complain, but he will do as he's told; he's a good man. Are you planning to stay for long?'

'Coffee first,' said Lindi; 'explanations to follow.'

Caitlyn smiled. 'Very well. Come in.'

'I might have to borrow some of your clothes while I'm here,' Lindi said, as she walked with Caitlyn into the kitchen. 'As you can see, I have no luggage.'

The butler eyed her.

'This is Alindi'osso,' said Caitlyn.

'I prefer Lindi Holdfast,' said Lindi.

'We are not planning to inform her mother of her whereabouts,' Caitlyn went on.

'Might I counsel the opposite approach, ma'am?' said the butler. 'Lindi is only sixteen, and her mother deserves to know that she is safe and well.'

'I'm seventeen in seventeen days,' said Lindi.

'That may be so, miss,' he said, 'but you are under your mother's authority.'

'Even so,' said Caitlyn, 'we shall not be informing her; not yet, at any rate. Let us show Lindi a proper Holdfast welcome.'

The butler bowed his head. 'Very well, ma'am; I am at your service. Did I overhear a request for coffee and breakfast?'

'Yes, please,' said Lindi.

'And should I summon your brother and cousin, ma'am?' he said.

Caitlyn inclined her head. 'We shall be on the balcony.'

'Very good, ma'am.'

Caitlyn and Lindi left the kitchen and walked up a flight of stairs.

'You can browse through my wardrobes,' said Caitlyn, 'and see what fits you.'

'I like what you're wearing now,' said Lindi. 'Do you have other dresses like it?'

'A few.'

'I had to hand wash these clothes in a bathtub last night,' Lindi went on.

Caitlyn eyed her. 'Do you know how to do that?'

'Of course I know,' snapped Lindi. 'How else can you wash clothes on a damn ship?'

'I wasn't meaning it like that,' said her cousin. 'I would have no idea how to wash my own clothes; that's why I was asking.'

A bell sounded as they walked out on to the balcony by Caitlyn's bedroom, and Lindi narrowed her eyes.

'That bell was to awaken Carden and Caelius,' said Caitlyn. 'They always sleep in when they haven't got classes, and, well, it's the summer holidays, so they stay up for half the night.'

'Doing what?' said Lindi.

'Drinking and smoking weed, mostly,' said Caitlyn. 'They go out to the taverns as well, but I am too young to get served.'

Lindi sat down and gazed over the Inner Sea. 'You are older than me,' she said.

'Only by a few thirds,' said Caitlyn. 'I turned seventeen back in spring. Carden is almost eighteen, but he looks older, and Caelius is twenty.'

'But he's mortal, isn't he? Caelius?'

'Yes, he's mortal.'

'I really came here to see my immortal cousins. You and Carden. I want to know how you are living with being gods.'

'I seldom dwell on it.'

'What powers do you have?'

'Vision, death and fire.'

'Any dream abilities?'

'None.'

'That's weird, isn't it? Your mother is the most powerful dream mage who has ever lived, and yet her children have no dream powers.'

'Cael and Kyra do, but my mother...' She sighed. 'My mother was in a different body when she gave birth to me and Carden. That's what makes the difference. We got Albany's powers, not Karalyn Holdfast's.'

A well-built young man walked on to the balcony, and Lindi sensed his self-healing.

'Cousin Carden,' she said.

He eyed her.

'Yes, it's Lindi,' said Caitlyn. 'Let's not tell anyone she is here.'

He sat down between them. 'Do we want to piss off Sable? Is that wise?'

'Who gives a fuck about being wise?' said Lindi. 'Let's have some fun for a few days. Do you have any cigarettes?'

Carden took a packet from a pocket and set it onto the balcony's table, along with a box of matches.

'Will you keep your mouth shut, brother?' said Caitlyn.

'Aye, all right,' said Carden.

The butler appeared with a tray. He set down a silver coffee pot, milk, sugar, and four cups.

'Breakfast shall be another ten minutes,' he said, bowing.

'Thank you,' said Caitlyn, as the butler walked back into the house.

'Do you all go to the university?' said Lindi.

'I have just finished school,' said Caitlyn, 'and, after summer, I shall be going to the Cavalry Academy in Holdings City. I am being commissioned as a junior lieutenant.'

'Oh,' said Lindi. 'The cavalry, eh? Do you like horses?'

Caitlyn smiled. 'Yes.'

'And I'll be going to Pebble Strand,' said Carden, 'as an ensign.'

Lindi lit a cigarette. 'What's Pebble Strand?'

'It's the training camp for the Imperial Marines,' said Carden. He shrugged. 'I have battle-vision, so I'm joining the marines.'

'All of us sitting here have battle-vision, brother,' said Caitlyn, as she filled three cups with coffee.

'So, you are both joining the military?' said Lindi. 'Why?'

Carden laughed. 'Do you know who our father is?' he said. 'Constable Cardova would very much like his children to attain a military education. We each have to serve for a few years, and then we can change our minds if we don't like it. Personally, though, I can't wait to join the marines.'

'What powers do you have?'

'Death and vision.'

A slighter man walked on to the balcony and yawned. 'Why was the bell rung?'

'Look who's here, Caelius,' said Carden.

Caelius squinted at Lindi. 'Who?'

Caitlyn rolled her eyes. 'It's Lindi; our cousin from Dragon Eyre.'

'Does Sable know?'

'No, and we're not going to tell her,' said Caitlyn.

Caelius eyed Carden, who shrugged.

'Greetings, mortal,' said Lindi.

'Greetings, smartarse,' said Caelius, as he sat and poured himself a coffee. 'I heard you ran away, taking nothing with you but a Quadrant. Do you ever think things through?'

'Occasionally,' she said. 'Right now, I'm thinking through the consequences of punching you in the face.'

Caelius laughed.

'I will lend her some clothes,' said Caitlyn.

'Are you also joining the army?' said Lindi.

'Not a chance,' said Caelius. 'I have just completed my second year studying law at the university.'

'Law? How indescribably dull.'

'I love it,' he said. 'It tells me, for example, that as the only one of us over the age of eighteen, I will be held criminally responsible if we do not inform your parents of your whereabouts. I might even be charged with child abduction.'

'That would be funny,' said Lindi. 'But here's the trick – you could just tell them that I went into your head and forced you to let me stay here for a few days. That will get you off.'

Caelius eyed her. 'Can you do that?'

Lindi smiled. 'There is a very good chance that you will get your answer over the course of the next few days.'

'Can you do everything Sable can do?' said Carden.

'Everything, and more,' said Lindi. 'Flow, fire, vision and death, all mixed with a good sprinkling of dream powers, and with battle-vision that could beat the arse off a greenhide. Are you jealous?'

Her cousins glanced at each other.

'That begs a question,' said Caelius.

'I'm all ears.'

Caelius leaned in a little closer. 'Who was your father?'

Lindi scowled at him.

'That was quite rude, Caelius,' said Caitlyn.

'She can handle it,' said Caelius. 'Anyone so loose with delivering insults should be able to take a few; that's what my mother always says.'

Lindi decided that the time had come to teach Caelius a lesson. It wasn't so much that he had been rude to her; she didn't mind that at all, but she wanted to provide him with some evidence of her powers. She shot out her dream vision to enter his mind. Her eyes widened. Caelius's mind was impenetrable. She tried again, but there was no way through his defences. It was as though he wasn't even there.

'Did you enjoy that?' said Caelius. 'I did.'

'But...'

'You do know who my mother is, don't you?' he said. 'I might be a pathetic mortal with no powers, but you will never be able to get inside my head, Lindi. Are you jealous?'

'But I used my vision powers to look into this house,' said Lindi.

'I don't block the local area,' said Caelius; 'only my mother can do that. But I can block myself.'

'Fair enough,' said Lindi. 'Consider me chastised. That's a good trick, for a pathetic mortal.' She gazed back at the sunlight reflecting off the Inner Sea. 'I don't know who my father is. My mother's mind is also sealed to me, and she won't tell me.'

'Why not?' said Caitlyn.

'She says she doesn't want me to know. I've looked into Lara's mind, but she doesn't know, either.'

'It was clearly a very powerful god,' said Carden. 'That should narrow it down.'

'Perhaps it was one of Edgar's gods,' said Caitlyn. She frowned. 'It wasn't Edgar, was it?'

'My mother insists it wasn't him,' said Lindi; 'but that is the only clue she has given me.'

'Why hasn't your father come looking for you?' said Carden.

Lindi felt her spirits sink. 'I suppose there are several possible answers to that. He might know about me, but not care. He might be dead. Or, my mother might have made him forget.'

'You have a brother, don't you?' said Caitlyn. 'Joss?'

'Yeah. His father was definitely a Kellach Brigdomin, though, not a god. I love my Joss.' She gazed up at the blue sky. 'Do you know what else I miss? Dragons flying about. I saw two earlier, for only a few seconds, and then they were gone. In Ulna, there are always dragons flying overhead; the sky is full of them. I didn't think I would miss that, but there you go.'

'Three dragons live in the city,' said Carden. 'They stayed here when everyone else went up to Colsbury for the summer with the Empress and the Imperial Court. You often see them flying over the Inner Sea.'

'Why didn't you three go to Colsbury?' said Lindi.

'My sister and I wanted to spend our last summer as civilians here,' said Carden.

'And I was roped into staying to supervise them,' said Caelius. He laughed. 'I am the responsible adult, if you can believe that.'

'You look hungover,' said Lindi.

'I am hungover.'

Lindi reached out with a hand to heal him, then stopped. 'That won't work, will it?' she said. 'You cannot be healed.'

He shook his head. 'Unless you have some salve, I am destined to suffer.'

'Where is your sister, Caelius?' said Lindi. 'She's older than you, isn't she? Why isn't she here?'

'Calpurnia cares about one thing, and one thing alone,' said Caelius: 'a large, scaly, silver dragon. Now that she has finished university, she and Frostback are inseparable. Where Frostback goes, she goes; so they are both staying in the Blue Palace.'

'Is she the dragon's rider?'

'She is. My mother and Calpurnia officially swapped places a couple of years ago. It's better for everyone, I suppose. My mother is so busy with being the Herald that she didn't have much time to spare for Frostback, while my sister is utterly devoted to the dragon. I used to be quite jealous. I used to nag Halfclaw about becoming his rider, but I'm past all that now. Well, that's what I tell everyone.'

'It is irritating not being able to tell if you are joking or not,' said Lindi.

Caelius smiled. 'Good.'

The butler made another appearance, wheeling a trolley to the balcony door. He eyed the four young Holdfasts by the table, and unloaded the plates and bowls from the trolley.

'I hope this is to your satisfaction,' he said.

'You are very kind,' said Caitlyn. 'Thank you.'

'Take the rest of the day off,' said Carden. 'We shall amuse ourselves, I think.'

The butler bowed, and departed.

Carden eyed Lindi. 'He'll be here if we need him,' he said. 'He never takes any time off, even when we insist.'

Lindi reached for a fork and got stuck into the plentiful supply of food the butler had brought. She didn't know what some of the items were, but as they tasted good, she didn't care.

'Do we have anything on for today?' said Caelius, as he sipped his coffee.

'Nothing,' said Caitlyn. 'Another lazy summer day.'

'What are you suggesting?' said Carden.

'Well, we can't take Caitlyn and Lindi out to the taverns,' said Caelius; 'they are too strict nowadays with checking ages. But who needs a tavern when the house is full of booze and weed?'

'I like your thinking, mortal,' said Lindi.

Caitlyn frowned. 'This *idea* is the same idea Caelius and Carden have every day,' she said. 'It's as though they have decided to spend the entire summer drunk.'

'What's wrong with that?' said Lindi. 'I'm up for it.'

'Let's face it,' said Caelius, 'it's what our parents on Colsbury expect us to be doing. Well, my mother and Caitlyn and Carden's father.'

'Who are living together, yeah?' said Lindi. 'Now, that's fucking weird. Lucius Cardova, who was married to Karalyn, and Kelsey Holdfast, who was married to... um... what was his name?'

'Van Logos,' said Caelius. 'Did you know that he is now on his fourth wife? My mother was his first, and he has had three others since then. It's like he dumps them when they reach their mid-twenties.'

'What a charmer,' said Lindi.

'Indeed,' said Caelius. 'My mother fucking hates him.' He got to his feet. 'Hold that thought – I'll be back in a minute.'

Caelius disappeared through the balcony door, and Lindi put down her fork.

'Maybe you shouldn't refer to Caelius as a *mortal* all the time, Lindi,' said Caitlyn.

'Why not? He is a mortal.'

'But it could sound quite insulting. Don't you like him?'

'No, I like him enough,' said Lindi; 'that's why I'm teasing him. He can take it. He knows I'm only having a laugh with him. You need to lighten up a bit, Caitlyn.'

Carden laughed, and his sister shot him a look.

Caelius returned with a large bag. He sat down, and unpacked sealed jugs of wine, bottles of whisky, and a very large bundle of weedsticks.

'Let's get to know each other,' he said. 'We are all cousins, after all; let's get hammered before Sable turns up to kick our arses.'

Lindi and Carden smiled, as Caitlyn frowned and turned away.

Three hours later, Lindi was drunker than she had ever been. Carden was well on his way, but Caelius seemed able to handle the drink better than most. Caitlyn joined in, but Lindi could sense her using her self-healing to keep herself sober, which was no fun at all.

'That's not right,' Caelius was saying; 'my mother helped to kill two Ascendants. It wasn't all Sable, Karalyn and Corthie.'

Lindi shook her head. 'Dragons killed those two Ascendants, not your mother.'

'Yes, but the dragons were only able to kill them because my mother was blocking the Ascendants' powers. She was necessary, but not sufficient.'

'Is that a legal term, you know-it-all twat?'

'All right; what about when your mother forced Lennox to burn down a fucking hospital?'

'What about it?' said Lindi. 'My mother is a fucking legend.'

A gull swooped down and stole a piece of bread from the table.

'You cheeky little bastard,' Lindi cried.

She raised her finger as the gull soared away, and the bird exploded into a thousand pieces, sending blood and feathers flying through the air. Carden started to laugh, then couldn't stop.

'That was horrible,' said Caitlyn. 'Please don't do that.'

Caelius patted Carden on the back. 'Sip some water before you choke.'

'Fuck that,' said Lindi. 'Pour more whisky down his throat.'

'It's barely noon,' said Caitlyn, 'and the three of you are behaving like beasts.'

'Oh shut up, Caitlyn,' said Lindi. 'Do you get your prudishness from your mother? I heard she was absolutely no fun at all. Does she even remember that you exist?'

Caitlyn stared at Lindi. 'At least I see her more than you see your father.'

'Is that right?' said Lindi. 'When was the last time you saw her?'

Caitlyn said nothing.

'Answer me,' said Lindi.

Carden stopped laughing. He eyed Lindi. 'We last saw her about eight years ago. There. Are you happy now?'

Lindi narrowed her eyes. 'Karalyn Holdfast; the great and mighty Karalyn fucking Holdfast hasn't visited her children in eight years? What a bitch.'

'I don't want to talk about it,' said Caitlyn.

'I'm sorry, but that makes me angry,' said Lindi. 'Why did she bother having you, if she was going to ignore you? That's fucking terrible. Where does she live?'

'No one knows,' said Caelius; 'not even the Empress.'

'She's making worlds, apparently,' said Carden.

'Every time she turns up,' said Caelius, 'which is rarely, Lucius Cardova and my mother try to convince her to visit. Do you know what she always says? She says that Caitlyn and Carden are immortal, so she has centuries to get to know them.'

Lindi winced. 'That's harsh.'

Caitlyn started to cry. Lindi felt Carden power up his self-healing, and he sobered himself in an instant. He passed his sister a handkerchief, then he and Caitlyn walked off the balcony.

Lindi frowned. 'Was it something I said?'

'Karalyn is a sore topic in this house,' said Caelius. The people on the Known Worlds might regard her as an almighty god, but Caitlyn and Carden don't see it that way. They know that she fought long and hard to be reunited with Cael and Kyra, and they wonder what they did wrong.'

'They haven't done anything wrong.'

'I know that, and you know that; but look at it from their point of view. Sable is a legend, just like you said. Can you imagine how you would feel if she had no interest in ever seeing you, or talking to you, but everyone else thought she was wonderful? I was passed back and forth between my mother and father for years, but at least both actually cared enough to look after me. And your father probably had no choice – if I had to guess, then your mother likely wiped his memories. In other words, he isn't deliberately neglecting you, because he has no idea you exist. It's worse for Caitlyn and Carden; much worse. Their mother has *forgotten* that they exist.'

Lindi puffed out her cheeks. 'If you put it like that, what can I say? Pass me another weedstick.'

CHAPTER 9
RETRIBUTION

Colsbury Castle, Republic of the Holdings – 10th Day, First Third Summer 560

'We haven't taken the decision lightly,' said Saewa, 'but, from now on, every imperial agent will be accompanied at all times by two marines, who will be dressed as civilians. They will live with them, eat with them, and guard them while they sleep. Their job will be to protect the agents, and to prevent their Quadrants from falling into the hands of the Gunstians.'

'Won't that interfere with their jobs?' said Cael.

'You are quite correct,' said Saewa, 'but we must ensure that no more Quadrants fall into the hands of the Gunstians. I understand that the constant presence of marines will limit the types of activities they will be able to undertake, but the Gunstians now have three Quadrants, and two of them were lost by the Empire. We must lose no more. I have also informed our agents that if they are attacked by a Gunstian squad, they should defend themselves with all vigour, but they should flee rather than be captured; for if they are taken alive, they will be executed by a Gunstian with the Gift of Death Reading, and every secret they hold will become known to the enemy.'

'This is a disaster for intelligence gathering,' said Arrosa. 'Most agents will not be able to carry out their duties if marines are following them wherever they go. Their anonymity will also suffer, and some will be exposed.'

'I understand,' said Cael, 'but the Empress has made it clear that we cannot afford to lose another Quadrant.'

'But there is a risk that agents unknown to the Gunstians will become known,' she said, 'simply because two marines will be following them around. They might as well wear signs around their necks saying, *I am an imperial agent.*'

'It appears,' said Saewa, 'that a cold calculation has been made – namely, that our agents are expendable, while the Quadrants they carry are not.'

'As soon as the University uses up its last remaining Serpent Eye jewel,' said Cael, 'that's it. There will be no new Quadrants being made. We have plenty of Tempest, but no more jewels. A few years ago, we were acting as though the supply of Quadrants was unlimited, but it's not, and every Quadrant we have needs to be protected. Without them, there would be no Empire.'

'How many Quadrants do we have?' said Alva.

'Forty-seven,' said Arrosa, 'not including the one I gave to Karalyn for Lord Esher, but including the one currently being held by Lindi Holdfast, who remains at large. It sounds a lot, but the portal and courier systems require ten, and the members of the Imperial court and their staff have a dozen between them. The military bases on Yearning, Na Sun Ka and so on need eight; and the agents fifteen. That comes to forty-five, and of the two remaining, one has been loaned to Legate Bedig on Ulna to replace the device he lost to Sable's daughter, and the other is safely in my possession. In an emergency, we also know that Quadrants are being held by Sable on Dragon Eyre, and Naxor in Kell, though it would be a brave agent who tried to separate either of them from their devices.'

'We have but one spare left?' said Saewa.

Arrosa nodded, her eyes dark. 'If our stocks continue to be depleted, we shall have to cut back. Does the City of Salve really require four, for example? Currently, we have one in Pella for the portal, one by the salve mine, one for the personal use of the King and Queen, and another in Jezra, which is used by Lord Maxwell when he is fighting the greenhides on the Western Bank.'

'There is a solution to this,' said Cael. 'I have asked the Empress if I might be permitted to conduct a series of raids within Gunst. One of our objectives would be to locate and seize the Serpent Eye jewels that they have stolen from Zamata. Not only did they clear out the mine when they assassinated Lord Bailey, but, according to Zamatan history, the Gunstians systematically looted hundreds of jewels during an earlier occupation. If we could get our hands on them, our problems would be over.'

'I find it hard to believe that Lord Bailey wasn't channelling some of the jewels he found under Zamata Gataza to the Dominion,' said Saewa. 'It is possible that the government there might be amenable to selling them to the Empire.'

'The price would be high,' said Cael. 'The Dominion has been trying to work out how to construct their own Quadrants for some time – they have Tempest, and they have jewels, but they do not understand the function or design of the Zamatan coils within. I would imagine that they would demand we give them this knowledge for any deal.'

'Then we should give it to them,' said Arrosa. 'Do we care if the Dominion can build their own Quadrants?'

'That is a decision for the Empress, the Herald and the Constable.'

'This might seem like a stupid question,' said Alva, 'but why doesn't the Dominion just open up one of their own Quadrants to discover the truth?'

'The original Quadrants are extremely fragile,' said Arrosa. 'Opening them destroys the insides, making it impossible to work out how they were put together. We learned that ourselves the hard way.'

'What about the Elbannon Quadrants?'

'They are designed to break in a certain way if opened or otherwise tampered with,' said Arrosa; 'as a security measure. The result is the same as the original Quadrants. The Dominion could dismantle as many as they liked, but they won't discover the truth that way.'

The door opened, and a nanny led in Cael and Arrosa's three children.

'Is it time?' said Arrosa.

'Yes, ma'am,' said the nanny.

'I will travel down to Plateau City, ma'am,' said Saewa, 'to speak to the portal and courier staff about increasing their security. Enjoy the festivities.'

'Thank you, Saewa,' said Arrosa.

The Zamatan man took out his Quadrant and vanished.

Cael gestured towards the door, and then he and Arrosa left the room, with Alva, the nanny and the children close behind. They were in the Great Keep on Colsbury, and they descended the steps to the castle forecourt, then took the tunnel that led to the gardens. They passed among the apple trees, and came to the large clearing that was used each summer to host the plays and other entertainments put on by the Empress. Tables were flanking the rows of chairs, and Kelsey was standing by Cole and Sable next to one of them.

Cael led the others over. 'Good morning,' he said.

'Good morning, nephew,' said Sable. She smiled at the children. 'And good morning to you.'

'I presume you haven't found her?' said Cael.

Sable eyed him. 'I know exactly where she is,' she said. 'She's in the Holdfast townhouse in Plateau City, but she doesn't know that I know. I'm keeping an eye on her from a distance; if I get too close, she can sense me, and she's liable to bolt.'

'What is she doing in the townhouse?' said Cael.

'Getting drunk with her cousins Caelius, Carden and Caitlyn.'

Cael laughed. 'I am glad she's safe.'

'How did you find her?' said Arrosa.

'I had some assistance from the butler who lives there,' said Sable. 'He let me know when I checked in with him. There are three gods in the townhouse who, if they bothered to read his memory, would know this. Caelius knows, as I asked the butler to tell him, but Karalyn's children are still in the dark.'

'Caelius has been told to stop the others getting into too much trouble,' said Kelsey. 'He will keep them contained within the townhouse.'

'Lara thinks I should bring Lindi back immediately,' said Sable, 'but I want to give her a few days of freedom first. Her punishment has been delayed, not cancelled.' She frowned. 'I was in the townhouse before Lindi arrived,' she went on. 'Caitlyn and Carden are almost adults, and it pisses me off that their mother never visits them.'

'I think it pisses everyone off,' said Kelsey. 'I keep telling Karalyn to see them; well, I do whenever my sister makes one of her increasingly rare appearances; but she keeps putting it off.'

'The next time I see her,' said Sable, 'I will be forthright with my opinion.'

'If you want to speak to my mother,' said Cael, 'I think she might be on Zamata just now.'

Sable frowned. 'What is she doing there?'

'Our agent on Zamata saw her a few days ago,' said Arrosa. 'It looked as though she was training Esher to be her new arbiter. I don't know if she is still there, though.'

'She will be going to Bailey's funeral tomorrow,' said Cael; 'that's what Kyra told me.'

'And that is taking place where?' said Sable.

'The funeral is in Nom Karta, but Bailey is being buried next to Nathaniel and Theodora under the ruins of Zamata Gataza.'

'Thanks, Cael,' said Sable. 'I think I might pay Zamata a quick visit. You don't mind if I shout at your mother, do you?'

'Feel free,' said Cael. 'Her neglect of Caitlyn and Carden angers me as much as it angers you.'

'But be careful,' said Arrosa. 'I love Karalyn dearly, but she can be unpredictable.'

Sable smiled. 'I know how to handle my errant niece, Arrosa.' She glanced at the chairs, which were rapidly being filled with spectators. 'It looks as though the play is about to begin, so I had best be off.'

'It's not a play,' said Kelsey; 'it's the recital of a long historical poem – an epic.'

Sable rolled her eyes. 'Then I definitely should be going. I will see you all soon.'

She placed a hand into a pocket and vanished.

Cael frowned. 'An epic poem? I thought we were getting a comedy. We brought the children.'

'It's a cultural milestone,' said Kelsey; 'the children will love it. Well, they probably won't, but it will be good for them. It's the five-hundredth-year anniversary of its publication, and it's all about the unification of the Realm of the Holdings. It was written by a contemporary eye witness.'

Cael sighed. 'How long is it?'

'About three hours, give or take,' said Kelsey. 'I used it as source material when I was writing my book.' She raised an eyebrow. 'Why are you all looking at me like that? It will be fun.'

Arrosa eyed her husband. 'She isn't lying,' she said. 'She really believes that.'

'I think it sounds interesting,' said Cole.

'You would,' said Cael. 'Maybe I can go and get a drink, and you can summarise it for me later.'

'Do we have to go?' said Cowie.

Kelsey gazed down at the boy. 'The Holdfasts are in it,' she said. 'In fact, they are the villains of the story. Hold Fast was the last to join the realm, and even when all of the other Holds were attacking it, they refused to bow before the new king. We didn't want to lose our independence, so we fought to the bitter end.'

'Did we win?' said Cowie.

'No, Cowie,' said Kelsey. 'We got our arses kicked.'

Arrosa rolled her eyes. 'Let's find our seats.'

They started walking towards the crowd spread out in front of the wooden stage. Cole and Alva peeled away from them, and took seats in the middle of the crowd, while Kelsey led the others closer to the stage.

'Have any results from the voting in the Plateau come in yet?' said Kelsey.

'The counting won't start until every ballot box has been returned to Plateau City,' said Cael, 'and some of the more remote villages are hard to reach.'

'I want this to run smoothly, Cael.'

'Then you will have to be patient, Aunty.'

They were halfway to the stage when a black void opened up in the midst of the apple orchard, on the far side of the crowd. The portal focussed in on a landscape of fields and snow-capped mountains. Five robed figures were standing by the portal's edge, and they raised their hands.

'Gifted!' shouted a soldier.

Screams filled the air as the Gift of Pain swept over the crowd, then random people burst into flames as though they had been soaked in oil. Hundreds fell to the grass, knocking over chairs and other people, and they writhed in agony. Cael pulled his children behind him, as the Gift of Pain slammed into his body. Kelsey fell, her voice choked in pain, then Arrosa. Cael dropped to his knees, torment flaying his nerves. A woman crouching a few yards in front of him burst into flames, and thick black smoke billowed up from her burning flesh as she screamed.

A great cry echoed out from the area by the portal, and dozens of armoured soldiers charged through from the Gunstian side, slashing out at the prostrate people in the crowd, and killing them where they lay.

Cael managed to keep his gaze on the portal, but the Gift of Pain was stopping him from moving. The five robed figures each took a step back, departing the gardens of Colsbury, and the portal vanished, leaving behind over two hundred Gunstian soldiers. Cael panted as the Pain ceased. All around him, people were starting to recover, but the Gunstian soldiers were rampaging through them. Cael checked that his children were all right. His body had shielded them from most of the agony, but both Carrie and Kelvin were crying, and Cowie looked in shock.

He turned to Arrosa.

'I'm fine,' she said.

'Protect the Empress, Cael,' cried Kelsey from his left. 'I'll get your children out of here.'

Imperial soldiers began pouring into the gardens from the direction of the gatehouse, as Cael got to his feet, then a company of Imperial Marines entered the gardens from the direction of the harbour. In the centre of the gardens, the Gunstians were still cutting down the civilians who had been seated to hear the epic poem, though those who could were fleeing. The marines crashed into the right flank of the Gunstians, and started to push them back. The ranks of Gunstians broke under the onslaught, and they fled into the path of the soldiers of the Imperial Guard coming from the other direction.

Cael raced towards the place where the Empress had been, and saw her surrounded by a wall of Kellach marines. From the look on her face, it was clear that she had been subjected to the Gift of Pain, but she was otherwise unharmed. Cael turned back to the battle. It was nearly over. The Gunstians were caught between the marines and the army, and were being annihilated in the centre. Even with no hope of success, the Gunstians were refusing to surrender.

Cael ran towards the front lines, jumping over the butchered bodies of the spectators.

'Take some prisoners!' he shouted. 'Don't kill them all.'

A group of marines dragged several Gunstians to the ground, disarmed them, and pulled their arms behind their backs. The last few Gunstians on their feet raised their swords and charged at the front line of army soldiers, and they were cut down to the last man.

The gardens fell into silence, broken only the cries of the wounded. Cael gazed at the carnage. Barely any marines or imperial soldiers had been killed, but the ground was littered with bodies. Over a dozen had been immolated, their charred bodies smouldering with low, blue flames, while the others had been cut down with sword and axe blades. Chairs lay scattered and smeared with blood, then Cael saw the body of a child. He put a hand to his face, then he pulled off his coat, and crouched down to spread it out over the murdered boy.

'Fucking savages,' said a woman next to him.

Cael looked up, and saw Shella staring at the ruins of the garden.

She turned to the soldiers. 'Get every surviving civilian out of the gardens, and take the injured to the Summer Palace. Marines, secure the members of the Imperial Court, and get the prisoners to the Lesser Keep.'

The Empress, Cardova and Claudian joined them.

'The Gifted abandoned their own soldiers,' said Claudian.

'I think that was their intention,' said Cael. 'The Gifted were only there to subdue the crowd, then the soldiers were unleashed. They knew they were going to die.'

'Not all of them died,' said the Empress, as she watched several Gunstians being bundled away by the marines.

'I asked the marines to spare a few for questioning, Your Majesty,' said Cael.

'Might I be present at the interrogations?' said Arrosa. 'I will help quicken things.'

The Empress eyed her. 'Cael and Arrosa – you shall lead the questioning of the prisoners. After that, all of them are to be executed. I want the body of every Gunstian gathered and sent back to the centre of Great Gunst by Quadrant. Let their people know what happens to those who dare attack us.' Her gaze went down to the body of the boy that Cael had covered, and her eyes darkened. 'Adjutant Cael,' she said, 'you are hereby commanded to plan and carry out punitive raids upon Gunst. For every civilian massacred here today, I want ten Gunstians killed in retribution.'

Cael bowed his head. 'Aye, Your Majesty.'

He glanced at Arrosa, and they both turned away from the gardens.

'Kelsey took the children into the palace,' said Arrosa.

'Have you seen Cole and Alva? Are they all right?'

'They were on the edge of the crowd,' said Arrosa. 'They were knocked over by the Gift of Pain, but the Gunstians didn't get close to them.'

Cael eyed her. 'If the Gunstians had opened the portal on our side of the gardens…'

'I know,' she said. 'How do we fight this, Cael?'

'There is only one way I can think of,' he said. 'We teach Gunst that we can hurt them more than they can hurt us.'

'But we are dealing with people who are prepared to martyr themselves for their religion.'

Cael said nothing as they left the gardens. They followed the marines to the Lesser Keep, and entered a large room on the ground floor, where the six Gunstian prisoners were being kept. Each one was sitting on the floor with their hands behind their heads, as the marines aimed loaded crossbows at them.

Cael and Arrosa came to a halt in front of them.

'Chadura is dead,' Cael said in Gunstian.

The prisoners began to shout curses at him.

'Do you know who I am?' Cael went on, continuing to speak in the language of the prisoners. 'I am the man who destroyed the Temple of the Martyrs. My name is Cael Holdfast, son of the Demon Witch.'

One of the prisoners jumped to his feet, his eyes blazing with rage.

Cael pointed at him. *Sleep.*

The other prisoners cried out as the man collapsed to the ground.

He pointed at another prisoner. *You will tell us why you did this.*

'Glory to Chadura!' shouted the prisoner. 'The news of our great success has spread all over Gunst. The faithful rejoiced in the death of the arch-hypocrite and blasphemer Bailey of Zamata, and now every pious man in Gunst wishes to volunteer as martyrs against the unbelievers.'

'Did you know the portal would close, leaving you here?' said Cael.

'Of course we knew,' said the prisoner. 'The blessed Gifted cleared the way for us to bathe in the blood of the wicked Empire. Every Gunstian who died is now celebrating in paradise with Chadura – praise be her name!'

Some of the other prisoners lifted their arms and began to pray aloud.

'Are more attacks coming?'

'If Chadura wills it,' cried the prisoner.

'Where?'

'Everywhere! There are millions of the faithful in Gunst, and they shall punish the demons of the Dominion, and the betrayers of the Empire. You, Cael Holdfast, are to blame for this. You murdered our leaders eight years ago, and destroyed our most sacred place; and now you shall pay.'

Cael said nothing for a moment, then he gestured to the marines. 'Hand them over to the Imperial Guards for execution,' he said. 'I have all I need from them.'

He turned and walked out of the room, as Arrosa hurried after him.

'Are you all right?' she said.

'Did you hear what he said to me?'

'I heard him,' she said. 'Their next target could be anywhere, and...'

'I meant the part about me; that it was my fault.'

She eyed him as they walked out into the castle forecourt.

'Did I bring the Gunstians down upon us?' Cael went on.

Arrosa fell silent as they crossed the forecourt and entered the Summer Palace. Injured men, women and children from the gardens were being brought into the large dining room on the ground floor, and the Empress was already there, tending to their wounds. Amid the bustle, Cael caught sight of Kelsey and his three children. He and Arrosa walked over, and they embraced Cowie, Kelvin and Carrie.

'It's all over,' said Cael. 'The Gunstians have gone.' He glanced up. 'Thank you, Aunty, for getting them clear of the gardens.'

'It was the least I could do,' Kelsey said. 'I'm no good with a sword, and I can't block Gifts.'

'Could I... could I have a word in private with you?'

'Aye. Sure,' she said.

Cael turned to his wife as he got to his feet. 'Could you look after the children while I speak to Kelsey?'

Arrosa nodded, but said nothing, then Cael and Kelsey walked back out of the dining room. Cael lit a cigarette as they came out into the sunlight. Soldiers and marines were protecting large groups of uninjured civilians throughout the forecourt, and cries of mourning and weeping could be heard coming from the vicinity of the gardens.

'I spoke to a captured Gunstian,' Cael said.

Kelsey kept her gaze on him.

'He said that I was to blame for this attack,' Cael went on. 'It was revenge for what I did to the Temple of the Martyrs eight years ago.'

Kelsey remained silent.

'Should I resign as Adjutant?' said Cael. 'I will resign if you think I should. I will take responsibility for this disaster. I went too far on Gunst.'

'You did go too far,' said Kelsey.

'I wanted to deter an attack, not encourage one,' Cael said, 'but I... I don't know. Am I flawed in some way, Aunty? I felt no pity for the Gunstians in the temple when I was slaughtering them; that can't be right.'

'What you did in Great Gunst was reckless and, aye, it was cruel,' she said. 'As for your resignation, I can tell you now that the Empress would not accept it. She has invested far too much in you, nephew, to have you thrown out of the Imperial Court for a mistake you made eight years ago.'

'But it was a mistake. Perhaps I am unsuitable to be her chosen successor.'

'That judgement isn't up to you,' she said. 'When a new Emperor or Empress is selected, they will be chosen by the Succession Council, the membership of which is clearly defined. They will decide if you are suitable.'

'All the same, should the Empire be governed by someone capable of slaughtering people without remorse?'

She held his gaze. 'Tell me this, Cael – do you want to be Emperor?'

'I don't know.'

'What do you want, nephew? What does Cael Holdfast actually want from life?'

'I want to... be like your mother; like Granny Daphne. I want to protect the Holdfasts; I want the Holdfasts to be strong and united. I love this damn family. For my first eighteen years, I was passed between my mother and the Empress, and I stopped believing in things like stability. I thought that I would never be settled, never truly at peace with myself, but Arrosa changed that. We have been married for fifteen years, and it's taught me that a secure family life is possible. I don't want to lose that. My wife and my children are the most important people in my life, and part of me just wants to live out a quiet and peaceful existence with them. I want to see my children grow up, and I want to see them have children of their own. But, Aunty, my heart is split down the middle, because I also want to lead the Holdfasts, and the Empire, to eternal glory. I want our family to shine like a star in the sky. I cannot fight like Corthie or Sable, but I can lead. The question is – should I lead? What if I am too flawed to be a good Emperor?'

'Tell me honestly,' she said; 'why did you slaughter so many in Great Gunst?'

His eyes tightened. 'Because they laid hands on my wife. That's it – that's what it was. How dare they fucking touch my wife? I needed to show them what happens if you harm a Holdfast.'

'The Empress does not believe that you are flawed,' said Kelsey. 'She and I have disagreed over what you did that day in Great Gunst. I think you went too far, but Her Majesty supports your actions. I think she was proud of what you did. She can hardly disavow you now, not after she gave you her backing at the time. You remind me of my mother, Cael, but you are not Daphne Holdfast. For one thing, she wouldn't be harbouring the doubts you are currently feeling. She would be telling all and sundry that what she had done in Gunst was perfectly appropriate, and anyone who disagreed could go jump in the ocean. All the same, you are certainly her grandson. Out of every Holdfast of your generation, you are the most like her, but you possess something she didn't – a conscience. I don't think that's a bad thing.'

Cael wrenched his gaze from Kelsey and watched as the first bodies were carried into the forecourt by soldiers of the Imperial Guard. He felt sick. Was he the cause of their deaths? He tried to push away his feelings of regret. Kelsey was right – Daphne would have felt no regret; instead, she would be planning her revenge.

'I should get back to work,' he said. 'The Empress wants me to lead raids on Gunst to avenge this atrocity. I might have a conscience, but I also have a duty to the Empire.'

'You could be a great Emperor, Cael,' said Kelsey, 'whether you want it or not. Bridget didn't want it, and she was a great Empress. Now, don't get me wrong – I love Thorn deeply, and would do anything for her – but Bridget loved the people of the Empire, while Thorn wants to be loved by the people of the Empire. There is a difference, nephew. Which model will you follow, or will you create a new model of your own?'

'I wish I knew.'

'When you strike at the Gunstians,' said Kelsey, 'will you be doing it to attack those you hate, or to defend those you love? Only you can work out the answer to that question.'

Cael stubbed out his cigarette. He straightened his spine, and composed himself.

'Thank you for talking to me, Aunty,' he said. 'I have work to do.'

CHAPTER 10
GONE SOFT

Nom Karta, Inopei – 13th Abrinch 1613

'And so, my friend, my dearest and most beloved friend,' said Edgar from the podium as he gazed at the coffin of Bailey, 'I must now say goodbye, for the final time. Often in the past, when we were parted, we each knew that we might not see each other again for a very long time. Sometimes, centuries would pass before we were reunited, sometimes, it turned out to be millennia; but we always knew that, one day, our paths would cross again.' A tear rolled down his cheek. 'It is hard to accept that, this time, there will be no reunion. Were it not for you, my friend, I would still be imprisoned within a restrainer mask inside the Palace of the Almighty, and it seems unfair that I am the one left alive.' He gazed out over the crowd of humans and dragons packed into the cavernous hall. 'I will avenge you, Bailey. I will make of Gunst a desert of ash and blood, tears and bones, where widows weep and orphans wail; and yet, it will never be enough.'

Kyra took his hand, and he gazed down at her, his eyes darkened by a mountain of pent-up rage.

Lord Elmhirst stepped up onto the podium. 'Ladies and gentlemen,' he said, 'noble dragons of Nom Karta, the funeral service is now at an end. There will be a break of three hours, and then we shall be travelling to the island of Zamata, in order to bury Lord Bailey next to his sister Theodora. A portal shall be opened to facilitate travel, and it shall be established in the road outside this, the palace of the Mighty King Gahad. Thank you all for coming.'

The people watching started to get to their feet, and Konna did the same. Over to her right, the contingent from the Empire of the Sapphire Throne also rose to their feet. Cole caught her gaze, and bowed his head a little in her direction, but Konna ignored him, her full attention on Cael, Karalyn and Lucius Cardova. Her old anger stirred at the sight of them, then she noticed Sable a little further along, and she frowned.

The crowd began to disperse. Several dragons made for the huge entranceway, while groups of humans either left the hall, or stood around talking.

'What did you think of the service, Konna?' said a voice.

She turned, and saw Esher standing next to her.

'You're back,' she said.

'I have a Quadrant,' he said; 'I can come and go as I please, or so Karalyn has told me.'

'Are you living on Zamata now?'

'I have rooms in the Dragon Palace in Igatz,' he said. 'It was my job this morning to inform President Bauchlie that a large number of gods and dragons will be arriving at the ruins of Zamata Gataza this afternoon. He wasn't particularly pleased by the news, I have to say, but he quickly realised that he had no choice. You didn't answer my question, though.'

'I didn't much care for the service, if I'm being honest,' she said. 'There was too much emphasis on revenge.'

'I think that might be a characteristic of the gods.'

'I'm not so sure,' she said. 'When Cael spoke, he also went on about vengeance.'

'But hundreds of innocent civilians were massacred only yesterday on Colsbury,' said Esher. 'Cael's emotions must still be raw.'

'Aye, but how many innocent Gunstians are going to die to avenge

Bailey's death and the massacre on Colsbury? And where will it end? Edgar has said many times that an invasion of Gunst would be impossible to manage. We cannot rule millions of folk who hate us. Are we on a path towards their complete annihilation? Is that the plan – to kill them all?'

Esher frowned. 'I don't know how to answer that.'

'If we raid them, they will use that as an excuse to raid us, and so on, forever, unless we put an end to them. I don't like it. Is there no one able to work out a way we could live together in peace?'

Esher gazed at the dispersing crowds. 'The Gunstians are driven by their religion, and the gods and the Holdfasts are driven by their passions. But, I cannot believe that Karalyn would allow either side to annihilate the other.'

Konna snorted. 'Karalyn is a fool,' she said. 'She has no idea how to behave as an all-powerful god.'

'I am starting to like her,' said Esher.

'Why, because you have just spent a few days with her on Zamata?'

'She is very lonely; did you know that? She has sacrificed everything to try to do the right thing.'

'Pyre's tits, Esher; are you out of your mind? She doesn't intervene when she should, and she intervenes when no one wants her to. And look at the way she has treated her own family. She brushed her husband aside, almost as though she had forgotten they were married, and he's ended up in the arms of Kelsey, of all people. And what about her children? She's a terrible mother, a terrible sister, and a terrible wife.'

'She has difficulties understanding how others think and feel,' said Esher. 'That isn't her fault. If you spent time with her, you might realise that she isn't as bad as you think.'

Konna rolled her eyes, then she noticed that Cael, Cole and Cardova from the Empire's contingent were walking towards them.

'What the fuck do they want?' she muttered.

'Good morning, Konna,' said Lucius Cardova. 'I am glad to see that you are well. How is life in Nom Karta?'

'Why are you speaking to me?' said Konna. 'What makes you think I have anything to say to any of you?'

'We came over to talk to Lord Esher, cousin,' said Cael. 'You happened to be standing next to him, and Lucius Cardova was just being polite. But, couldn't we try to coexist without rancour? None of the Colsbury Holdfasts bear you any ill will, Konna.'

Konna folded her arms over her chest. 'You murdered my father.'

'I've had it with this shite,' said Cael. 'Ward killed your father. I was there; I saw him do it. Cole and I tried our best to fight by your father's side. Corthie saved Blackrose; he saved the entire fucking Eastern Rim, and yet you carry on as though it was I who had stuck a knife into his back. How long is this bullshit going to last?'

'That's enough, Cael,' said Cardova. 'We are at a funeral; control your temper.'

Cael lowered his gaze. 'You're right. I apologise, Konna. Yesterday's events on Colsbury have torn at my heart, and I am not myself.'

Konna glared at him, but said nothing.

'I hear that you are the new arbiter of the peace, Lord Esher,' said Cardova. 'I look forward to working with you. Might you be able to spare some time later today, so that we could go over a few protocols?'

'Perhaps when we have returned from Zamata, Lord Constable?' said Esher.

Cardova inclined his head. 'That would be wonderful. Do you require any assistance in rebuilding Zamata Gataza?'

'Queen Famula has already decreed that the Dominion will pay for it,' said Esher, 'but thank you for the offer.'

Cardova bowed again, then he gestured to Cael, and they walked away.

Cole stayed where he was. 'If only you knew how much Cael loved your father, cousin,' he said, 'then I believe that you wouldn't say such things. Why do you hate him, but not me?'

'Maybe I do hate you, Cole,' said Konna.

He smiled. 'Maybe you do. I will never hate you, though. I guess you will have to live with that.'

Konna narrowed her eyes as Cole walked away to join Cael and Cardova.

'Why do you do that?' said Esher.

She eyed him. 'Will you take me to Kell, Esher? I don't want to go to Zamata, and no one will miss my presence in Zamata Gataza. It's my brother Carron's eighteenth birthday today, and I would like to see him.'

Esher chewed his lip for a moment. 'How would you get back to Nom Karta? I can't wait for you in Kell; I need to be at the burial.'

'I could ask Naxor to bring me here.'

'I had better inform Kyra first,' he said.

'Why?'

'So that they don't think you have run off, Konna,' he said. 'I'll just be a minute.'

Konna stayed standing as Esher walked off in the direction of Edgar, Kyra and Elmhirst. She thought over the words she had said to Cardova and Cael. Did she still believe them? For her entire childhood, she had been fed the same line – that the death of her father had been a direct result of the Empire's greed and warmongering. Perhaps her anger at the Empress was justified, but were Cael and Cole worthy of her hatred? Even her mother had told her that Cole was blameless, and her mother was the angriest person she knew. Aila's loathing for those responsible for Corthie's death had never wavered. She missed her mother, she realised. She missed the certainties of her youth, even if those certainties had been based upon anger and resentment.

She paused for a moment, wondering if any of her mother's anger and resentment would be aimed at her if she turned up in Clackenbaird uninvited. There had been a vague fear in the back of her mind for years – that her mother loathed her because she had helped Cael and Cole capture Cairney on Dragon Eyre. It was worth the risk, she told herself.

Esher returned, his Quadrant in his hand.

'Kyra and Edgar have granted their permission,' he said. 'Are you ready?'

She nodded, and Esher swiped his fingers over the copper device. The air crackled, and they appeared on the path leading up to Clackenbaird farmhouse. The sun was out, and a pleasantly warm breeze was drifting over the green hillside.

Konna smiled as she breathed in the air of Kell, then she started to cry.

'What's wrong?' said Esher.

'Nothing,' she said. 'I'm being stupid. I haven't been here in eight years, and... I'll be fine.' She wiped her eyes. 'You can go if you like; I know my way around.'

'All right,' said Esher. 'I will see you later, yes?'

Konna watched as Esher disappeared, then she gazed up at her father's cairn on the summit opposite the farmhouse.

Fifteen years. She turned away from the cairn, and walked up the slope towards the farmhouse. She opened the front door without knocking, and removed her shoes. Clova peered into the hallway, then her eyes widened and she ran towards Konna. She threw her arms round her older sister.

'Konna,' she cried. 'I missed ye so much.' She turned her head. 'Ma! Konna's home.'

Aila came into the hallway wearing an apron. Konna embraced her, then all three women wept for a few moments as they held each other.

'Why are you here, daughter?' said Aila. 'Can you stay?'

'Maybe,' she said. 'It was unplanned. I was at a funeral, and I just knew I had to see you all. Esher brought me.'

'Whose funeral were you at?' said Clova.

'Lord Bailey's,' said Konna. 'Who else is here?'

'Ceres and Carla are at school in Marchside,' said Aila; 'can you stay until they get home so they can see you? Carron's here, of course – we've been celebrating his birthday. Carter and Naxor are also here – they've taken time off from working. Come into the dining room.'

Aila took Konna's hand, and they walked into the large front room of the farmhouse, where Naxor, Carron and Carter got to their feet. Konna embraced each in turn.

'Happy birthday, Carron,' said Konna. She smiled at her siblings. 'You have all grown up.'

'We all look the same age now,' said Carter. 'Are ye back for good? Are ye looking for a job in the distillery?'

Konna laughed. 'Maybe. Life with the gods of Nom Karta is not what I imagined it would be. The other gods treat me as though I were a child. I do like living there; I mean, I have an enormous apartment in a palace, and I have my own servants, but I miss my family.'

'And we have missed you,' said Aila.

Konna smiled. 'It is great to see you all.'

'What in Pyre's name has happened to yer accent, sister?' said Carron. 'Ye sound like a Colsbury Holdfast.'

Konna winced. 'Shit. Do I?' She gazed at her mother. 'I need to ask you something, Ma. Are you angry with me?'

Aila eyed her. 'Why would I be angry?'

'You must know that I helped the Empire to catch Cairney,' she said. 'He was going insane; he forced me, Maxwell and Esher to do some terrible things, and I couldn't bear it. I'm sorry, Ma; I'm sorry I let it happen.'

Aila said nothing for a long moment, then she nodded. 'You did the right thing, Konna. Cairney's heart was devoted to hate and revenge, and Karalyn was correct to exile him. He killed many innocent people. I know that he believed he was doing the right thing, but he was mistaken.'

Konna took a step back, her eyes widening.

'Your mother's rage may have cooled a little over the last few years, Konna,' said Naxor.

Carter's eyes darkened. 'Ma's gone soft on the Colsbury Holdfasts, sister.'

'No,' said Konna. 'I don't believe it.'

Aila took a seat, as everyone else in the room gazed at her.

'For over a decade, my grief and anger were all I knew,' she said. 'I blamed everyone but myself for what happened to your father. I blamed the Empress for starting the war; Karalyn for not ending it;

Kelsey for resigning as Herald when the Empire needed her most; Cardova for being in command of the army when Corthie was posted to Na Sun Ka; and Cael for... you know, I don't remember exactly why I reserved such contempt for Cael.' She broke down in tears. 'Cael held Corthie's hand as he died. He was with your father in his last moments, and perhaps I was jealous that he got to share that time with him. For over a decade, I carried all of that hatred within my heart as though it was my most precious possession, when I knew the truth. I had known it all along. Karalyn begged Corthie not to go to Dragon Eyre; I heard her do it. Kelsey tried to have Corthie reassigned, but he wouldn't listen.' She gazed up at Konna. 'Do you know why he didn't listen to his sisters? Because I, his wife, told him to hunt down Ward and to not stop until he had killed him. It was me, Konna. I told Corthie to fight.'

Carter strode from the dining room, slamming the door behind him on the way out. Konna stood frozen to the floor, her eyes wide in shock. Next to her, Clova was also weeping, while Carron and Naxor were standing in silence, their heads bowed.

'But what about all of our plans for revenge,' said Konna; 'our plans to take over the Empire and rule it as gods?'

'My plan hasn't changed one jot,' said Naxor. 'I was never in favour of exacting bloody revenge, if you recall, nor was I ever in favour of eliminating those mortals among the Holdfasts we perceived to be our enemies. That does not mean I like them; but such mortals should be beneath our contempt. Instead, my plan calls for patience; a slow and careful build up of our wealth and strength. A campaign of consolidation that would span several centuries, until the Empire fell into our laps without the need for violence or bloodshed. We shall rule the Empire, Konna; indeed we shall, but not through Cairney's crude methods.'

'I think Naxor suspected that I would eventually see the truth,' said Aila. 'He knew, and so he waited.'

'Gods mourn differently from mortals,' said Naxor. 'For us, the pain of loss can be so much deeper, for we have lost so much more time with those we love compared to those whose lives twinkle out over a few short decades. This is yet another reason to avoid involving ourselves emotionally with mortals.'

'Does Kelsey know about your change of heart, Ma?' said Konna.

'None of the Colsbury Holdfasts have visited Kell for a long time,' said Naxor. 'I think they have decided that we are irredeemably hostile. To be honest, that suits me. We should not concern ourselves with their opinions.'

'It isn't quite true that none of them have visited,' said Aila. 'Karalyn was here a few days ago.'

'Was she?' said Naxor.

'She wanted to tell me that she had visited Cairney; that he is well,' said Aila, 'but I told her that she was nothing but a disappointment, and then I showed her the door.'

'Good for you, Ma,' said Carron.

Konna took a seat next to her mother. 'Cael was at Lord Bailey's funeral,' she said, 'and I practically accused him of murdering my father.'

'How did he take it?' said Clova.

'Badly,' said Konna. 'He got angry with me, but then he apologised. After that, I had to listen to a telling off from Cole.'

'I have never understood why we were supposed to hate Cael,' said Clova. 'All I remember of him as a girl was when he and Lahnos rescued me and Arrosa from Solitudus. He was kind to me.'

'If you see Cael again,' said Aila, 'tell him I am sorry.'

'I don't think that's a good idea, Ma,' said Carron. 'We'd be better off ignoring them. We don't want to draw attention to what we're doing on the Hold Fast estate. Maybe Uncle Naxor is right – it's better that they think we're hostile and unapproachable.'

'Let me intercede for a quick moment, Carron,' said Naxor. 'What you said is mostly true, but Killop would not have succeeded on the Hold Fast estate if Kelsey and the others had believed him to be hostile. You, too, may have to ingratiate yourself with the Colsbury Holdfasts, even if you find the thought distasteful.'

Konna frowned. 'What the fuck am I missing here?'

Naxor smiled. 'Possibly a fair bit, Konna. Firstly, Carron will this very day be travelling to the Hold Fast estate. Killop is doing well as the estate manager, but he wishes to have one of his siblings join him there to lend assistance. And secondly, Killop's attitude towards the Colsbury Holdfasts might not be perfectly aligned with your conception of it.'

'What exactly is that supposed to mean?' said Konna.

Clova frowned. 'It means that Killop was playing a trick on us all. He has been pretending to like Kelsey and the others, when all he wanted was to gain control of the Hold Fast estate.'

Konna turned to Aila. 'Ma, is this true?'

'It was your Uncle Naxor's idea,' she said.

'And it was an exceedingly good idea,' said Naxor. 'When it comes to the great wealth of the Holdfasts, there are two main centres – Marchbrae and the estate in the Holdings. Of course, there are a myriad other sources of income, such as the shipping companies that plough the Inner Sea, and the mines in Northern Kell, and so on; but Marchbrae and the estate are the real centres of financial power. If we are to one day rule this Empire, having both under our control is essential. And so, to that end, we sent Killop to the estate several years ago. In order for him to be accepted by the others, he had necessarily to pretend he had a greater affection towards them than is actually the case. And, I must say, he has done a marvellous job.'

Anger surged through Konna. 'I can barely believe what I am hearing,' she said. 'All those times we teased Killop about his feelings towards Kelsey and the others – and he was lying to us? What about that book he bought me for my eighteenth birthday – Kelsey's *History*? Was he deceiving me? I feel like you and Killop have been laughing at us behind our backs.'

'I am sorry you feel that way,' said Naxor, 'but Killop's act had to be convincing. As for the book, I genuinely think he enjoyed it. For all her grievous faults, Kelsey is quite the writer.'

'But why couldn't you tell us the truth?'

'One word,' said Naxor; 'Cairney. That boy simply couldn't be trusted with the truth. With a mouth as wide as the Great Tunnel under the Grey Mountains, he was bound to reveal our secrets to those we were trying to deceive. Look at his plan to provoke a war between the Empire and the Dominion; a plan you were heavily involved with, Konna. Was it well thought out? Did it consider the consequences of certain actions? Had Cairney killed the Empress, then Karalyn's wrath would have taken a very different shape. Can you honestly tell me that he could have been trusted with such a secret?'

Konna lowered her gaze.

'The plan does have one major drawback,' Naxor went on. 'If Cael or Kyra were to read our minds, they would discover the truth about what Killop has been doing. However, the good news is that I am an expert in hiding my true feelings from prying minds. I must have had my thoughts read a hundred times since I moved to Clackenbaird. I keep my main plan foremost in my mind – the plan that spans centuries, and so I am considered to be harmless to the current crop of mortal Holdfasts. If Cairney had known the truth, it would have been discovered when he was arrested.'

'But now Kyra could read it out of my head,' said Konna. 'I see her every day.'

'Give her no reason to read your mind,' said Naxor. 'Kyra isn't interested in the politics of the Empire, and, if you have settled into Dominion society, she will not suspect your motives. Now tell me this – you have heard the plan, so what do you think of it?'

'Is Killop the estate manager?' she said.

'He is.'

'But he could be removed from that position at any time by Kelsey, aye?'

'For the moment, yes.'

'Unless he becomes Holder Fast.'

Naxor smiled broadly. 'Indeed. That is the next step; that is precisely what we are now working towards. For now, there are several possible candidates to succeed Kelsey in that prized role – her own children, of course, as well as Cael, Cole, and Killop. In theory, Karalyn should be Holder Fast, but she rejected that role. Because of that, it does not necessarily follow that Calpurnia should inherit, for the principle of inheritance through the direct line has already been broken. And then we have the politics of the Holdings to consider. The aristocrats dislike the idea of absentee Holders, so having Killop based in the Holdings gives him a strong advantage. It is Killop, after all, who has to deal with the other Holders, not Cael or Cole. There will be an outcry if Kelsey nominates someone who doesn't live in the Holdings.'

'But Kelsey doesn't live in the Holdings.'

'And the other Holders hate that,' said Naxor. 'As Holder Fast, she has a seat in the Holdings parliament, but is she ever there? No, she is not. Daphne was meticulous in ensuring that she regularly attended parliamentary sessions, but Kelsey is notorious by her absence. Being Herald gives her some leeway, but the other Holders will be watching with great interest when she decides to appoint her successor. Killop's bid to become Holder Fast will be based on his commitment to playing a full role in the Holdings government, including the possibility of becoming First Holder. Such a role would be an excellent stepping stone to becoming Emperor.'

Aila raised an eyebrow. 'Holdings politics has become Naxor's latest obsession, as you can see.'

'It is all for the good of our family, cousin,' said Naxor. 'One day, we, the descendants of Amalia and Malik, shall sit astride the greatest Empire in existence – surely, that requires a little in the way of planning. Anyway, I have talked enough; I should be taking Carron to the estate.'

'Are you leaving now, Carron?' said Konna. 'I only just got here.'

'He was supposed to leave a little while ago,' said Aila. 'I have a thought; why don't you go with them, Konna? It would be good to see your oldest brother again, especially now that you know why he is in the Holdings. Naxor can take you there and bring you back.'

'I would be delighted to take Konna,' said Naxor. 'Carron, fetch your luggage from your room, and we shall depart.'

Carron hurried out of the room, and Konna got to her feet.

'Should I assume,' Konna said, 'that Carter is still opposed to the Colsbury Holdfasts? I saw the way he stormed out.'

'Carter feels much the same way as Cairney did,' said Aila, 'and his hatred of the mortal Holdfasts remains undiminished. You heard him – he thinks I have gone soft.'

'I still don't know how I feel about your change of heart,' said Konna. 'In fact, I have a suspicion about it, but I am a little hesitant to say it out loud.'

'Don't keep it to yourself,' said Aila.

'All right. What if Cairney was partly responsible for your unceasing hatred towards the Colsbury Holdfasts? We now know that he can manipulate people's thoughts and emotions through the power of his voice, and we also know that he was altering your memories, Ma. Was his hatred keeping your hatred going?'

Aila lowered her gaze. 'It's possible. My feelings did start to change after Cairney was exiled, but how would I know for sure?'

'There was so much anger in this house after Da's death when I was growing up,' said Konna. 'I am glad that has changed. As Naxor said, maybe the mortal Holdfasts are not worthy of our contempt.'

Carron came back into the dining room, his strong arms carrying a great heap of baggage. He set it down, and Naxor withdrew his Quadrant. Carron embraced his mother and Clova, then he stood by Naxor.

'Enjoy yourself, son,' said Aila, 'and remember how hot it gets in the Holdings.'

'I'll be fine, Ma,' said Carron.

Naxor inclined his head towards his cousin, then he activated the copper device. The air shimmered, then he, Konna, Carron and the pile of luggage appeared on a patch of dry and brown grass next to the Holdfast mansion in the estate. The sun was blazing down from the clear blue sky, and the heat was strong and oppressive.

Carron staggered, as though he had run into a brick wall. 'This heat,' he cried. 'How can anyone bear it?'

The sound of laughter came from the rear porch of the mansion, and Killop walked out of its shade into the sunshine.

'You get used to it, Carron,' he said, then he gazed at his sister. 'Konna, this is a surprise.'

'I am the reason Carron is late,' she said.

'That's no problem,' he said embracing her. 'I've missed you, sister.'

'I missed you, too.'

Killop glanced at Naxor.

'She knows,' said Naxor.

Killop nodded. 'I'm glad,' he said. He quietened his voice to a whisper. 'Aunty Celine is on the porch, though, so let's talk about it later.'

Killop helped Carron carry the luggage into the shade of the rear porch, where an old woman was sitting on a comfortable couch. She smiled up at the arrivals.

'This is Carron, Aunty,' said Killop. 'He is going to be helping out on the estate.'

Celine smiled. 'It is lovely to meet you, Carron,' she said. 'If you are as good as Killop, you will settle in fine.'

'And this is my sister Konna,' Killop went on, 'but she is just visiting.'

'This is just wonderful,' said Celine. 'Can you all stay for iced tea?'

Naxor smiled. 'Iced tea sounds marvellous, Celine. Thank you so much.'

'Everyone, sit yourselves down,' said Celine, as she pulled on a cord that rang a bell. 'I want to hear all the news.'

CHAPTER 11
THE FUNERAL

Nom Karta, Inopei – 13th Abrinch 1613

Karalyn remained in her seat, wishing she was elsewhere. She had liked Bailey, and would miss him, but the crowds at the funeral had made her feel uncomfortable; or perhaps it wasn't the crowds, but the way that many had been staring at her. The gods from the Doomed Worlds had known Albany well, and Karalyn understood that it would be strange for them to see her body inhabited by a Holdfast. As for the dragons of Queen Famula's court, they loathed the Demon Witch, seeing her as the cause of every disaster to befall the Dominion.

She had listened in silence to Edgar's eulogy for his friend, but his call for vengeance had left her feeling nauseous. Even so, she had sat quietly, and had done her best to fit in with the others. Edgar was the only reason she was there – he had asked her to attend the funeral, but her mind was already on the creation of her wetlands world. She had noticed a problem in certain areas with saltwater leaching into what were supposed to be freshwater marshes. If left unchecked, the salinity could ruin entire stretches of coastline on the world's largest continent.

She caught Lucius Cardova glancing in her direction. He had been seated a few rows away next to Cael and Cole, and he tilted his head at her when he noticed her glancing back at him. She looked away before he could say or do anything else. She wanted to speak to Cael, but not while Lucius was standing next to him; it would be too awkward, too uncomfortable. Lucius knew her better than anyone else; the only other person who knew her almost as well was her sister, and the thought of her and Lucius together was not something Karalyn wished to dwell upon. She had given her blessing to the relationship, but that didn't mean she liked it. She wanted Kelsey to be happy, but she would prefer never to think about how she had attained that happiness. Part of her still loved Lucius, but separating had been the right thing to do, not only for Lucius, but also for her own peace of mind. Without any ties to Lucius, she no longer had to feel guilty about how she had neglected him during the latter half of their marriage.

She glanced over at him, but he was talking to Kyra and a few gods. A few yards from them, Esher was with Konna, then both vanished. Karalyn wondered if anyone would notice if she also disappeared. There were still three hours of waiting to get through before the funeral party travelled to Zamata – would anyone care if Karalyn discreetly absented herself? Edgar had requested her attendance, but he hadn't spoken to her since she had arrived that morning. Karalyn gazed at the crowd. Should she mingle among them, trying to make small talk with people about whom she cared nothing; or should she confront her anxieties, and talk to Cael, even if Lucius was there? Or, maybe she should sit in silence for the full three hours, ignoring all attempts at conversation. She eyed her son, who looked over at her. Cael's gaze went to her right, then back to her, and Karalyn turned her head to see Sable walking towards her.

Karalyn frowned. What was Sable doing at Bailey's funeral?

Her aunt took the empty seat next to Karalyn.

'Did you know Bailey well?' said Karalyn.

'Not really,' said Sable. 'I notice that you haven't spoken to Cael or Kyra since you got here; or Lucius Cardova, for that matter. The two of you are still married, aren't you? Your divorce has never been completed.'

'What business is it of yours?' said Karalyn.

'We're family, and it's family business,' said Sable. She eyed her. 'Do you recall what the word *family* means?'

'I intend to speak to both Cael and Kyra today,' said Karalyn. 'There is plenty of time.'

Sable nodded, then she lit a cigarette.

'You shouldn't still be smoking,' said Karalyn. 'It is bad for your health, and you are... how old are you, Sable?'

Sable said nothing.

Karalyn narrowed her eyes. 'You don't look your age.'

'Neither do you, to be fair,' said Sable.

'Are you getting regular healings?' said Karalyn. 'Or are you using salve?'

'A bit of both,' said Sable. 'I'm not as quick as I used to be, but I look after myself. Apart from the smoking. How have you been? We haven't talked in years.'

'I am fine.'

'Are you? When did you last see your other children?'

Karalyn looked away, her temper rising. 'Is that why you are here – to chastise me?'

'You deserve to be chastised, niece. The way you have treated Caitlyn and Carden is appalling.'

'I am not going to have this argument with you, Aunty,' said Karalyn. 'What I do is of no concern to you.'

'You're wrong. The way you behave affects everyone in this family.'

'You live on Dragon Eyre with Lara and your own children. I fail to see how it affects you in any way.'

'Caitlyn and Carden are my sister's grandchildren,' said Sable. 'Of course their welfare affects me. Right now, my own daughter is spending time with them. They have seen more of Lindi in the last few days than they have seen their mother over the last decade. Do you know how that makes them feel?'

'I'm sure you are about to tell me.'

'I would be more interested in hearing your reasons. Everyone in the family has noticed. Everyone is saying – *why does Karalyn not care about Caitlyn and Carden? Why did she fight for Cael and Kyra, and then neglect her other children?*'

'You know the reason,' said Karalyn. 'I refused to get involved in the war on Dragon Eyre and, as a consequence, my brother was killed. I promised then that I would guard the peace; that I would watch over the worlds. Isn't that what everyone was telling me to do? You, Sable, were one of those people who were nagging me about doing more. And, now that I am doing more, you have found another way to criticise me.'

'That's horseshit, Karalyn. What are you doing right now? Are you watching over the worlds? If you can spare a few hours to attend a funeral, you can put some time aside to visit your children.'

'You make it sound simple.'

'It *is* simple. You can travel anywhere you like with a thought. You know where they are. What's difficult about it? I am aware that Daphne sent you away more than once when you were a child. You were packed off after you hurt Keir; then you went to Kellach Brigdomin with your father, and then you had to live in the desert with Laodoc.'

'That was different,' said Karalyn. 'I was a danger to others.'

'But how did it make you feel at the time?'

'As though I was unloved.'

'Do you want Caitlyn and Carden to think you don't love them? Visit them, niece; talk to them.'

Karalyn stared directly ahead. 'And what would I say?'

'You could start with *sorry*.'

'What if it is already too late?'

Sable shook her head. 'How can you say that? All three of you are immortal – how could it ever be too late? It will be worse the longer you leave it, but it will never be too late.'

'Do they hate me?'

Sable fell silent for a moment. 'They are angry,' she said, after a long pause. 'Angry and hurt. They don't understand what they have done to deserve being abandoned by their mother.'

'They didn't do anything wrong. It's me, Sable – I'm the problem.

When I first left them with Lucius, I got so absorbed in creating new worlds with the Sextant that I lost track of time. I don't even know what year it is. Being with the Sextant, building my worlds... it seems more real to me than reality. I don't get lonely. I don't miss company; I don't miss anyone. When I look at people, I think – *when they die, they will stay dead*, but when Albany's body finally dies, as it will at some point, I will linger on. Nothing lasts forever, except me. This knowledge has changed the way I think about everything, and I can feel my humanity slipping away. I know people think I'm strange. I try to act normally, but I recognise that others see through the act. People also think that I am uncaring, and the more I think about it, the more I realise that it's starting to come true. I am being hollowed out. People say I am the most powerful being to ever exist, but I just feel... empty.'

'You need to stay away from the Sextant for a while,' said Sable. 'Spend time with your family; bring your children to Dragon Eyre, and we'll take the *Mischief Maker* out on a long voyage. You could relax in the sunshine, and forget about the treaty and the worlds you have been making, and just *be Karalyn*. Caitlyn and Carden have the entire summer with nothing to do. If left to their own devices, they will spend the whole season having one continuous party. This is your opportunity, Karalyn. Seize it. Spend the summer with them, and when they leave at the beginning of autumn, you will be glad you did.'

Karalyn frowned. 'Where are they going in the autumn?'

'Caitlyn is enrolling in the Cavalry Academy in Holdings City, and Carden will be going to Pebble Strand to train as a marine.'

'What? But I didn't give my permission for them to join the armed forces. I don't like it. I should stop it from happening. Lucius had no right to map out their futures like this.'

'Lucius had every damn right,' said Sable. 'He has been looking after them on his own for over a decade. What was he supposed to do? Should he have waited for you to show some interest? You were lucky Lucius was there. You were lucky that Caitlyn and Carden had one parent who cared.'

Karalyn turned away in anger. She should leave. She should

imagine herself sitting on her balcony on her unnamed world; one thought, and she would be there.

'Why don't you and I go to Plateau City after the funeral?' Sable went on. 'I will come with you to the townhouse, so that you don't have to do this on your own. What do you say, Karalyn? It's time to make this right.'

'Leave me alone.'

'I will not. I am going to keep needling you about this.'

'I could make you leave me alone.'

'Just think about what you said – you are threatening me because I am trying to persuade you to do the right thing. Where is the Karalyn I used to know?'

'She's gone, Sable. I am all that remains.'

Karalyn got to her feet and started to walk away, but Sable rose and followed her.

'After the funeral,' Sable said; 'I will take you. You will apologise to your children, and you will promise to do better.'

Karalyn ignored her. She saw Cael, and approached him, but Sable remained by her side.

'Mother,' said Cael.

'Tell her to visit her other children,' said Sable.

Cael's gaze went from Karalyn to Sable and back again. 'Aunty Sable's right,' he said. 'You need to visit Caitlyn and Carden. You've missed their entire teenage years.'

Cole and Cardova saw them and walked over.

Karalyn's eyes narrowed. 'Why are you sending the children into the armed forces?'

Cardova raised an eyebrow. 'Was that addressed to me?'

'Who else am I speaking to right now?'

'All right,' said Cardova; 'I felt that a little structure would be good for them. Both have battle-vision, so they should be able to cope physically, and I allowed them to select which branch of the services they wanted to join. Both are being commissioned as junior officers, so they will learn how to lead, and...'

'I don't want them to become soldiers.'

'Neither will be soldiers,' said Cardova. 'Caitlyn will be a cavalry trooper, and Carden will be a marine.'

Karalyn's temper boiled over. 'Don't do that!' she cried. 'You know exactly what I mean, Lucius. How dare you assume that I would be happy with them learning how to fight and kill?'

'How am I supposed to know what you want?' he said. 'I haven't seen you for years, Karalyn.'

'But you knew I hated the armed forces. Are you doing this to spite me?'

'Of course not. I came to a decision based on what I thought was best for them both. Caitlyn loves horses, and Carden likes boats; and they only have to serve for a few years. If they hate it, they can apply for a discharge. But, you know what? – I think they will love the experience. It will help them in so many ways, and...'

'I want you to withdraw their applications.'

Cardova's eyes tightened. 'Let's think this over,' he said. 'Why don't we sit down with them – just the four of us? We could ask Caitlyn and Carden what they want to do. I am open to that. If either or both insist that they don't want to be commissioned, I will withdraw their applications. But I will not do it simply because you demand it, Karalyn.'

'That seems reasonable, Mother,' said Cael. 'You should find out what they want before you try to interfere.'

'You could go to Plateau City after the funeral,' said Sable.

Karalyn took a step back.

'How about it, Karalyn?' said Cardova. 'Shall we go to the townhouse after we have been to Zamata for the burial? I can make time to see the children. Let them see that we are both invested in their futures.'

'No,' said Karalyn.

Sable frowned. 'I am not taking *no* for an answer.'

'Tough shit, Sable.'

Home. Go.

The air shimmered, and Karalyn appeared on her long balcony. She clutched the iron railing to stop her hands shaking and stared out at her beautiful view. She tried to calm her thoughts. She would never have to leave her unnamed world again, not if she didn't want to. She could stay there forever, watching the centuries roll by, with just the Sextant for company. She could build dozens of new worlds; and she could make her own sub-created humans to populate them, just as Nathaniel had created the Holdings and Kellach Brigdomin from whom she was descended. Wait; that wasn't right. She was in Albany's body, so did that mean she was now an original human with a sub-created consciousness?

She lowered her gaze. If she remained hidden on her world for centuries then Sable, Cael and Kyra would be dead, if and when she emerged from her self-imposed exile. Kelsey, too. Every mortal she knew would have died, but Caitlyn and Carden would still exist. She closed her eyes and, probably because Sable had mentioned her, an image of her mother appeared in her mind. Daphne Holdfast would have been extremely displeased with her daughter's behaviour, and Karalyn knew it. In some ways, Sable had been saying the things her mother would have said, had she still been alive. She tried to picture herself walking into the Holdfast townhouse with Lucius – how would her children react? There would be raised voices, and possibly tears of anger and recrimination. It would be painful, uncomfortable and awkward, and Karalyn would have to resist the urge to flee.

Were those her options – to hide as a recluse until everyone had died, or to face her children? Maybe Sable was right; maybe it wasn't too late.

Karalyn cursed under her breath.

Back to Nom Karta. Go.

She appeared inside the cavernous hall in exactly the same place where she had been standing. Cael, Cole, Sable and Cardova had been joined by Kyra, and they fell silent as soon as they saw her.

'I will do it,' said Karalyn. 'After the burial, if you agree, Lucius, we shall go to the townhouse in Plateau City.'

Cardova smiled. 'I would be more than happy to go with you, Karalyn. Cael, can you let Kelsey know when you get back to Colsbury?'

'I can do that,' said Cael.

'Thank you, Karalyn,' said Sable.

Karalyn eyed her. 'You are more like my mother than you realise.'

'I will take that as a compliment,' she said.

'I am pleased by this,' said Kyra, 'but might I change the subject for a moment?'

The others turned to her.

'I have felt Quadrants being used,' Kyra went on. 'One of them was Esher's, when he took Konna to Kell, and then when he returned; but I have sensed others, and I wonder if it is sensible for us all to be gathered here like this. The Gunstians have been to Nom Karta before. If they have spies in the city, then they will know about the funeral. I have spoken to Edgar about this, but he seems unconcerned.'

'Edgar is right,' said Karalyn. 'The Gunstians would be insane to attack us; we have dragons, Holdfasts, soldiers, gods; and we have me.'

'That's the problem, Mother,' said Kyra. 'The Gunstians' faith makes them do things that we might consider to be insane. The prisoners Cael interrogated were overjoyed to be able to martyr themselves.'

'What do you advise?' said Cael.

'We should disperse this crowd,' said Kyra. She frowned. 'There – I felt it again. A Quadrant.'

'I sensed it, too,' said Karalyn. 'Hold on.'

The roof of the palace, with Kyra. Go.

The air shimmered, then she and her daughter appeared on the flat roof of the gargantuan palace of Gahad. They gazed down at the streets of Nom Karta. Several of those who had been attending the funeral were gathered by the main gates of the palace, and soldiers were out in numbers, patrolling the streets and guarding the palace. In the sky above them, six dragons were also patrolling, their keen gazes on the streets below.

'It was coming from somewhere to our right,' said Kyra.

'I didn't know you could sense Quadrants,' said Karalyn.

'It must be because I hear them speak whenever I touch them,' said Kyra. 'I don't think Cael can do it.'

Karalyn gazed down the street to their right, then she felt it again.

'Three figures have just appeared on the roof of a palace,' she said.

'I see them, on the palace of Macsin,' said Kyra. 'We should let Edgar know.'

'Why? By the time we do that, they will have gone, and we don't even know who they are. We should act now, before they have a chance to open a portal.'

The three figures disappeared.

'Damn it,' said Karalyn. 'Wait here.'

The roof of the palace of Macsin. Go.

Karalyn appeared on the other roof, a few yards from where the three figures had been standing. She gazed back at the view of the great palace of Gahad, and saw Kyra in the distance. Karalyn looked over the roof she was on, but the three figures had left nothing behind. As far as she could recall, two of them had been men, and the other a woman, but they had vanished before Karalyn had been able to use her vision to see them more closely.

The air shimmered, and Kyra appeared next to her.

'What were you hoping to find?' said Kyra. 'They've gone.'

Karalyn felt it again – the faint sensation of a Quadrant being used.

'That came from inside the palace of Gahad,' said Kyra. 'I will take us there.'

The air moved, and Karalyn appeared next to Kyra inside the great, cavernous hall where the funeral had taken place. By one wall, a portal had opened up, and five robed figures were standing at its edge, as hundreds of Gunstians soldiers formed up behind them.

'Portal!' shouted a soldier.

Four of the figures raised their hands, and swept the hall with the Gifts of Pain and Despair, while the fifth – an old woman, pointed at a huge dragon. The dragon screamed as he started to burn from the inside. He thrashed around, crushing gods and soldiers, as smoke drifted up from his eyes and mouth. The Gunstian soldiers charged through the portal, just as the Gift of Pain knocked Karalyn off her feet. Agony gripped her, an agony she hadn't experienced since Lahnos had struck her with the Gift of Pain on Zamata. She noticed Cael by her side, crouching behind an over-turned bench.

'This is what they did on Colsbury,' he shouted. 'Gifts first, then the Gifted withdrew, closing the portal and leaving the soldiers behind. We have to stop them before they escape.'

Karalyn managed to lift her gaze, and saw the soldiers moving through the crowd, decapitating gods, while the old woman was aiming her Gift of Immolation at the dragons. Three were already dead, their enormous bodies smouldering with a low blue flame. Karalyn raised her hand, and summoned her death powers, but the agony was too pervasive, and she couldn't focus. She tried to concentrate, but the Gift of Despair was sapping her courage, telling her that all was lost, and she almost collapsed in tears. Karalyn was incredulous – wasn't she the most powerful being in existence? And yet, all it took were the Gifts of Pain and Despair, and she was helpless. Cael staggered up, then he moved in front of her, taking the brunt of the Gifts to shield his mother. He knelt on the floor, shuddering in agony, as Karalyn's pain receded.

'Get them, Mother,' Cael gasped.

The edge of the portal. Go.

Karalyn appeared next to the five robed figures. Most of the Gunstian soldiers had already passed into the hall, and Karalyn lifted her hand and aimed it at their backs. Over two dozen Gunstians fell, their hearts stopped, then Karalyn pointed her hand at two of the robed men, and the flesh melted from their skulls. Another man reached for his Quadrant. Karalyn pointed at him, and he died just as his fingers swept over the copper surface.

The air crackled, the portal collapsed, and Karalyn found herself in a large field near a range of tall, snow-capped mountains. The entire area was full of armed Gunstians, and lines of tents had been pitched next to a little stream. Karalyn pulled on her battle-vision as the first soldiers charged at her.

Sleep, she commanded, and dozens fell.

She dodged a crossbow bolt, and switched back to death powers, felling dozens more. As much as she hated killing, she knew she had no choice. She had unwittingly discovered the base from where the Gunstian raids were being sent out, and she knew what she had to do. She raised her hand again, then felt despair surge through her, followed by a pain unlike any she had ever felt. She fell to her knees, and saw the old woman and the last surviving Gifted man pointing at her.

'Burn, Demon Witch!' the Gunstian woman cried.

Karalyn tried to move, but her insides were burning, and her heart was telling her to give up. Lie down and surrender to the pain, said the voice of despair in her mind, and it was so powerful that she was paralysed. A sword was rammed through her side by a soldier, and she fell to the ground. She powered her self-healing to confront the Gift of Immolation, and a terrible equilibrium was established. Her self-healing was keeping her alive, but the agony was unbearable, as healed flesh arose in flames again and again. Despite the Despair echoing through her, Karalyn managed to stagger to her feet, as the Gunstians around her stared in stunned amazement. She pulled the sword out of her side.

'Kill her!' cried a Gunstian officer.

'I am trying,' the old woman shouted back. 'She is a god; she is fighting my Gift.'

Karalyn swung the sword, and its blade slashed across the agent with the Gift of Despair. As he screamed and fell, Karalyn felt the heavy presence of his Gift start to lift from her mind, then she was struck in the back with a crossbow bolt, followed by another two in quick succession. Soldiers charged at her, their hands gripping her smouldering clothes. Despite the pain to their scalded fingers, there were so many of them that Karalyn was weighed down, unable to move. A knife jabbed into her stomach, and Karalyn was pulled to the ground.

'Take her head,' shouted someone.

Karalyn lashed out with death powers, and every soldier touching her fell to the ground; but the old woman was still there, her hand pointed at Karalyn. Karalyn raised her own hand towards her, just as a sword swiped at her throat. The blow wasn't strong enough to remove her head, but the blade bit deep into her neck, and Karalyn felt the flow of blood spill onto the ground as she collapsed next to those she had killed.

Nom Karta. Go.

Nothing happened. It was too late; she was too weakened by the Gift and the wounds, and her self-healing was close to failing. She rolled onto her back, and saw the sword come down at her again.

She closed her eyes. The sword made contact with her neck, cleaving through all that had remained after the first blow, and, for the third time, Karalyn knew what it meant to die.

Her consciousness rose up from the grisly scene, as hundreds of Gunstians began celebrating, and, at once, all of Karalyn's pain ceased. The old woman was being embraced by the soldiers as a hero, along with the young officer who had delivered the fatal blow. Karalyn gazed down at the body of Albany. The head had been picked up by a soldier, who was holding it aloft, while the charred body was still smouldering, as the Gift off Immolation incinerated it from the inside.

Karalyn's shock turned to anger. She had loved being in Albany's body. Compared to Lyla, Albany had possessed great reserves of power; the heritage of a granddaughter of an Ascendant – and Karalyn had lost it. She eyed the old Gunstian woman, who was beaming with pride, and laughing at the sight of Albany's head being passed around. No one in the field seemed remotely concerned with the fate of the soldiers who had been abandoned in Nom Karta, or of their comrades whom Karalyn had killed in the field – all they cared about was that they had slain the Demon Witch.

Karalyn would show them how wrong they were. Bathed in raw fury, she drove her consciousness deep into the mind of the old Gifted woman, determined to use her Gift of Immolation against the other Gunstians. She felt herself take control of the woman's mind and body but, when she looked for the Gift, she couldn't find it. She had been expecting the Gifts to work in the same manner as god and mage powers, but she was mistaken. She searched through the woman's mind, using her knowledge of Gunstian to locate her name, as well as her thoughts and memories, but saw no way to access the Gift. Frustration gripped her, and she turned her anger on to the old Gunstian woman.

I am inside your mind, Galina, Karalyn said; *and you are about to die.*

Karalyn scoured the old woman's mind, obliterating every last vestige of her personality and memories, then her own consciousness inserted itself into the empty space. At once, the woman's body became Karalyn's, and she felt all of the aches and pains Galina had been living with. Her knees hurt, and she was exhausted after the exertions of fighting the Demon Witch. Karalyn grimaced. She had been so used to being in Albany's body that she had forgotten what it felt like to be mortal; then she panicked. She hadn't intended to take over the woman's body, but now that she was in it, there was no way out, except through death.

Karalyn cried out in impotent rage, and a few of the soldiers eyed her with alarm. Karalyn took a breath, then she forced a smile on to her face, and they relaxed.

'We shall take the body of the witch to Great Gunst,' said an officer. 'Chadura has blessed us this day; she has blessed you, Lady Galina.'

'Praise Chadura,' said Karalyn.

The crowd cheered, but Karalyn felt numb. She had made a terrible mistake, perhaps one of the worst mistakes of her life. She had killed the old woman in anger, and now she was stuck inside her body – a body with no self-healing, and no god powers. She tried to use her vision, but nothing happened.

Nom Karta. Go.

Nothing.

She was trapped, and on her way to Great Gunst.

CHAPTER 12
MEETING THE COUSINS (PART TWO)

Plateau City, The Plateau – 12th Day, First Third Summer 560

'I don't care,' said Lindi, as she sat on the townhouse balcony with Caelius. 'I want to go out tonight.'

'But everything we need is here,' said Caelius.

'Yes, but we've been doing exactly the same thing for six days and nights. It's been a laugh, but I want to drink whisky in a Kellach garden-tavern, and then eat at one of the Rakanese restaurants.'

Caelius raised an eyebrow. 'Insects appeal to you, do they?'

'They also eat fish, dipshit,' said Lindi. 'It's not just insects. I like fish. After the restaurant, we could go to a dodgy tavern in the Old Town and smoke dreamweed.'

Caelius produced a weedstick from a cigarette case. 'We have weed here,' he said, as he lit it.

'So you keep saying,' said Lindi. 'I am starting to suspect that you want to keep me in the townhouse. Do I embarrass you? Is that it? You don't want to be seen out in the city with your cousin from Dragon Eyre?'

Caelius laughed. 'I have gone over this a hundred times – you won't get served in any of the taverns. The council currently running Plateau City has cracked down on children drinking.'

'I am not a fucking child!'

'Steady on, o mighty god,' he said. 'I didn't say that – but you are under the legal age. You can't buy booze in a tavern until you're eighteen. I didn't make the damn rules, but we all have to abide by them.'

'You're a fucking idiot,' she said. 'All I'll have to do is *persuade* the bartenders that I am eighteen, and I'll get served no problem. And anyway, how do they actually check your age?'

'Voting cards,' said Caelius. 'Everyone eighteen and over was given a card that allowed them to vote in the Plateau elections. No card, no booze. Before that, they had no way to check.'

'But I'm from Dragon Eyre!' she cried. 'How could I have a bleeding voting card? What about visitors to the city – do they have to go without? I smell bullshit, Caelius. You have an ulterior motive, and it's driving me crazy that I can't read it out of your head.'

'I'm not responsible for your craziness,' he said; 'you've managed that on your own.'

Lindi narrowed her eyes as she stared out at the Inner Sea. She was suspicious of more than just Caelius's reluctance to take her out into the city; she was also starting to wonder why her mother hadn't arrived to look for her. Six days – and not even the slightest hint that Sable had been in the near vicinity. Her mother wouldn't have given up her search, so why hadn't she been back to Plateau City? Something didn't add up.

'I'm going for a piss,' she said, as she got to her feet.

'*That* is why we aren't going out,' Caelius said. 'You're too vulgar to be seen in my exalted company.'

Lindi ignored him, and walked through the large sitting room to the main stairs. Caitlyn and Carden were out for the morning, buying things they would need for their new lives in the autumn. They had asked Lindi if she had wanted to accompany them, but shopping was far from Lindi's idea of fun, and so she had refused. Caelius had seemed almost relieved, which led Lindi to suspect that Karalyn's two children were not part of whatever scheme Caelius had cooked up. She passed the butler on the stairs without a second thought, then she paused. What if Caelius had confided in the old man? It seemed unlikely, but Lindi was out of ideas.

'Hey,' she said.

The butler turned on the stairs and inclined his head. 'How can I help you, ma'am?'

'Why doesn't Caelius want to take me out to a tavern?'

'You are too young to be served in a tavern, ma'am,' he said.

'That is not what I asked,' she said, as she entered his mind. 'Are you part of his little conspiracy to keep me indoors?'

You will tell me the truth.

The butler blinked.

Lindi's frowned deepened. The butler seemed to be resisting her powers – not completely, but enough to send Lindi's suspicions soaring. She examined the man's mind in closer detail, and discovered that certain blocks had been placed there – blocks designed to protect him from Lindi's powers. She ripped them to pieces, and pain passed over the butler's face.

You are commanded to speak only the truth, she said, battering her orders into his head.

The butler groaned, and put a hand to his head.

'Why doesn't Caelius want to take me out to a tavern?' she said.

'He has been asked to keep you contained within the townhouse,' gasped the butler.

'Asked? By whom?'

'By Kelsey Holdfast, ma'am; his mother.'

'How the fuck does Kelsey know that I am here?'

'She was informed by your mother, ma'am,' he said. 'Sable Holdfast has known your location since you arrived.'

Rage made Lindi bare her teeth. 'Does Caelius know that my mother knows I'm here?'

'Yes, ma'am. I reported your arrival to Sable, and she asked me to let Caelius know.'

'Treachery!' Lindi cried. She stormed back into the sitting room to confront Caelius, then she saw him turn on the balcony to glance at her. She growled at him, then hurried back to the stairs. She ascended two flights, and went into the guest room where she had been sleeping. She began to throw the clothes Caitlyn had lent her into a travelling bag, then she heard low voices on the stairs. Two minutes later, Caelius appeared at the door.

'I knew you'd find out eventually,' he said. 'No hard feelings, eh?'

'Fuck off.'

'Come on; what was I supposed to do? And you were right before – it has been a good laugh having you here; but I was told to keep you in the townhouse.'

'Do you always do what your mummy tells you to do?'

'You are sixteen years old, Lindi,' he said. 'I was keeping you safe.'

'I am a fucking god!' she shouted. 'I don't need to be kept safe.'

'All right; then I was keeping the city safe from you. Your mother could have whisked you back to Dragon Eyre at any point, but did she? No, she trusted that you would be all right here, and she allowed you to have fun.'

'Controlled fun is not fun,' she said. 'I want to be free, Caelius, and you kept me corralled in this building as though I was a dangerous animal. Worse, you colluded with my damn mother.'

'Your powers and age don't mix well with alcohol and weed, Lindi,' he said. 'I didn't obey my mother because I'm a good little boy; I did it because I knew it was the right thing to do. Come back when you're a couple of years older, and we can go out drinking all night.'

She pushed the last of the clothes into the bag, and tied the cords to close it.

'Are you going home?' said Caelius.

'Tell Caitlyn that I will be borrowing her clothes for a while,' she said. 'I don't know when I'll be back.'

Caelius frowned. 'Are you returning to Dragon Eyre?'

'You have proved you can't be trusted, Caelius,' she said, as she took her Quadrant out of a pocket.

'Fair enough,' he said. 'I hope you realise that I was trying to help you.'

'You were trying to control me, and I don't like that.'

'Put yourself into my position – that is all I ask.'

She eyed him. Caelius was a hard man to hate, but she would try her best. She activated the Quadrant, arrived in Clackenbaird, and immediately wished that she had put on a raincoat. She glanced up at the grey sky as she got soaked in a Kell downpour, then she ran under the shelter of some trees.

'What happened to the fucking summer?' she muttered to herself, as she slipped the Quadrant back into a pocket. She glanced up to her left, and saw a small cairn sitting on the summit of a low hill. That must be Corthie's cairn, she thought. Her mother had often spoken about it. She turned to the right, and saw the farmhouse of Clackenbaird upon the brow of another low hill. The rain stopped, the clouds broke apart in the breeze, and the sun came out. Sheets of mist started to rise from the paths as the sun began the long process of drying out the land, and Lindi edged out from under the branches of the tree. She gazed at the hills and valleys to the north. They were completely transformed in the sunshine, from grey and forbidding to resplendent greens, and her spirits lifted. She saw the large collection of stone buildings that she imagined comprised the famous distillery, then she wondered if Aila would let her drink whisky.

First things first, she told herself. She gazed up at the farmhouse, and sent out her vision. She tried to sense her mother's powers, but felt nothing. She looked into the farmhouse, gliding her vision through the hallway and into the kitchen. No one was there, but signs of a meal having been prepared were evident all around. Lindi pushed her vision into the dining room, and saw Aila and four of her Marchbrae cousins sitting eating dinner by a long table. She tried to remember their names. She knew that there were eight cousins in the Marchbrae branch of the family, and that one of them was a wicked renegade who had been exiled for trying to assassinate the Empress. That was Cairney, and he sounded interesting. Three of the cousins at the table were girls, and two of them looked younger than Lindi, despite their Kellach stature. The other girl, and the sole boy, looked older. Was the boy Carter, perhaps? Lindi wasn't sure. She saw no sign of Naxor, about whom she had heard much, and none of it good. He was not to be trusted, or so her mother had often told her.

She wondered how long it would take for her mother to discover that she had left Plateau City. Lindi cursed, her anger still simmering. How humiliating, to find out that Sable had known all along where her daughter was. She felt disappointed in Caelius. He had seemed set to become Lindi's favourite cousin, but he had taken her mother's side, and had helped to *contain* Lindi in the townhouse. That was the word the butler had used. Lindi needed to be *contained*, as though she was a venomous snake that had been found on board a ship. Lindi had imagined that she had outwitted her mother, and she felt foolish. She had been tricked; worse, she had been treated like a child.

She glanced up at the sky. More dark clouds were coming in from the west, and if she didn't come to a decision, she was liable to get soaked again. She gripped her bag, and set off up the hill towards the farmhouse. The rain was starting again when she reached the front door. She thought about knocking, but opened the door instead, and peered inside. She saw a small entrance hall, where coats were hanging from pegs, while pairs of shoes and boots were in a neat line by the wall. Lindi walked into the house, and closed the door. It made a loud creaking noise, and Lindi frowned.

A moment later, the older girl appeared in the hallway. She eyed Lindi, who eyed her back.

'Ma,' shouted the girl; 'we have a visitor.'

'Who is it?' came Aila's voice from the dining room.

'I'm not sure, Ma. She looks Holdings.'

Lindi put a hand on her hip. 'I'm your cousin. I'm Lindi Holdfast.'

The girl kept her gaze on her. 'Yer Ma's looking for ye, but I guess ye probably know that already. Before ye take one more step into the house, but, ye'll need to take yer shoes off. My Ma doesnae have many rules, but yer not allowed shoes in the house. Oh, and I'm Clova, by the way.'

Lindi raised an eyebrow, then she crouched down and began to unlace her boots.

'Who is it?' said another voice, and Lindi glanced up to see the only boy in the house. He was more of a man, now that she could get a better look at him – a young man of the same build as her brother Joss. In fact, from a distance, they were quite similar in appearance.

'It's Lindi,' said Clova. 'Our cousin.'

'I thought it might be,' said the man.

'Are you Carter?' said Lindi, as she slid one boot off.

'Aye, that's me,' he said. 'Have ye run away from home?'

'I am... on holiday,' Lindi said. 'I'm visiting the cousins; well, the immortal cousins. I'm not overly enthusiastic about meeting the mortal ones; I mean, they'll all be dead soon, so what's the point?'

Carter laughed.

'Yer Ma was here a few days ago, Lindi,' said Clova.

'Are you going to rat me out?'

Clova frowned. 'What?'

Lindi slid off her other boot and stood. 'Are you going to tell my mother that I'm here?'

'How the fuck would we do that?' said Carter. 'Uncle Naxor has the Quadrant, and he's not here.'

'He could be back soon, but,' said Clova; 'along with Konna. Are ye hungry, Lindi? Do ye want something to eat?'

'I could eat,' she said.

Clova gestured towards the hallway, and Lindi followed her two cousins into the dining room.

'Ma,' said Carter, 'this is...'

'I could hear what you were saying, son,' said Aila, as she peered up at Lindi.

'Good evening, Lady Aila,' said Lindi. 'I hope I'm not interrupting anything; well, I am clearly interrupting dinner, but it's raining outside, and I...'

'Sit down, Lindi,' said Aila. 'Carla, fetch a plate and cutlery for our guest.'

The youngest of the girls got to her feet and walked to a sideboard, as Lindi sat down.

'It is nice to meet you, Lindi,' said Aila. 'Any child of your mother's is welcome here. I should warn you, however, that Sable has been looking all over the worlds for you. She is concerned for your safety. There is a good chance that she will visit the farm again, to see if you have found your way here.'

'Where have ye been?' said Clova, as she retook her seat.

'I was in Plateau City,' said Lindi, 'staying with Caitlyn, Carden and Caelius.'

Carter rolled his eyes. 'The Colsbury Holdfasts, eh? Ye visited them before ye visited us?'

Aila shot her son a look. 'How are they doing, Lindi? It has been a while since I saw the children of Karalyn and Kelsey.'

Lindi chewed her lip. 'They, uh... well, they don't have anything to do all summer, so they spend a lot of time sitting on their balcony smoking weed.'

Carla returned to the table, and set down a plate, a knife and a fork next to Lindi, along with two glasses.

'Help yerself,' the girl said; 'that's what we do here.'

Lindi nodded, then she started to heap food onto her plate from the various bowls on the table. She picked up a flagon, assuming it was water, and filled a glass. It was ale.

'Am I allowed to drink this?' she said.

Carter laughed. 'Why else would it be on the table?'

'Yes, you can drink it,' said Aila. 'It's only ale. For whisky, you have to be over sixteen.'

'I'm nearly seventeen,' said Lindi. 'There's a lot of meat in these bowls. What is it?'

'Beef and lamb,' said Clova; 'from the farm.'

'I thought you made whisky.'

'We do,' said Aila, 'but Clackenbaird is also a large farm. We grow barley in most of the fields, but we also have cattle and sheep. Carter is the farm manager.'

'You run the farm?' she said.

Carter nodded. 'If ye hear someone moving about the house before dawn, it'll be me,' he said. 'Are ye planning on staying?'

'I... don't have a plan,' said Lindi. 'I would like to stay. I want to get to know my cousins.'

'You can stay,' said Aila. 'In fact, I insist.'

Lindi beamed. 'Thanks.'

'You can take Carron's old room for now,' Aila went on. 'He has gone up to the Hold Fast estate in the Holdings, to help Killop, my eldest.'

'Why are our cousins in Plateau City not working?' said Carla. 'We all have to work. I have about a dozen chores I have to do each afternoon after I get home from school.'

'Me, too,' said the other girl.

'And I work in the distillery,' said Clova. 'I'm an apprentice. Today, I was helping out at the copperworks; I did a twelve-hour shift.'

'Well,' said Lindi, 'they are all waiting for autumn. Caelius is at university, Caitlyn is joining the cavalry, and Carden is going to become a marine. This is their last summer together.'

'That's bloody typical,' said Carter. 'While we work our arses off, our Colsbury cousins get to sit about all day, doing fuck all. Caelius is mortal, aye?'

Lindi nodded.

'The other two are gods, but,' said Clova. 'Proper gods, not demigods; that's what I heard.'

'Like me,' said Lindi. 'I am a full god, but, before any of you ask – the answer is no. I have no idea who my father is. My mother refuses to tell me, and I think she's the only person who knows. Well, my father might know, but I reckon she wiped his memories; otherwise, why hasn't he visited me?'

'I think you are probably right,' said Aila. 'I was quite surprised when your mother announced that she was going to have children. I had never seen Sable as particularly maternal, but she proved me wrong. I recall hearing that she was going to choose the father or fathers with great care.'

'My brother has a different father,' said Lindi. 'A Kellach father. He has battle-vision.'

'A Kellach with battle-vision?' said Aila. 'I think I can guess where your mother got that idea from.'

'Do you mean Corthie?' said Lindi. 'My mother talks about him a lot. I've caught her crying about him a few times.'

The dining room fell into silence.

'Sorry,' said Lindi. 'But, you know, it's been fifteen years. Is that right?'

'Aye,' said Clova. 'Fifteen years without Da.'

'I never got the chance to meet him,' said Carla. 'He died before I was born.'

'I remember him,' said Carter. 'I was six when he was killed. The Empress sent him to die on Dragon Eyre. They abandoned him, and he had to fight gods and hundreds of dragons on his own. When he died, the Empress used it as an excuse to slaughter the dragons – she killed over a thousand in one day; so, tell me – why didn't she help Da when he most needed it, eh? Why did the bitch wait until he was already dead before getting up off her fat arse to help?'

'That's enough,' said Aila.

Carter's expression darkened. 'Ma's changed her mind about it. She used to blame the Empress and Kelsey; she used to blame all of the Colsbury Holdfasts, but now she's gone soft on them. It's like, she's gone through the anger bit, and now she just feels guilty.'

Lindi eyed Aila, but the demigod remained silent.

'I think it's more complicated than that,' said Clova.

'Cairney had the right idea,' said Carter. 'He came so close, Lindi; so fucking close.'

'Close to what?' she said.

'Close to hacking off the Empress's head,' said Carter. 'He had the Empress and Kelsey at his mercy, but those bawbags Cael and Cole stopped him. It took both of them to bring Cairney down, even though he was only sixteen at the time.'

'Cairney is in exile, isn't he?' she said.

'Aye. Punished by Karalyn for being a rebel. Have ye met Karalyn?'

'I saw her when I was younger, but I don't remember it,' said Lindi.

'She's out of her fucking mind,' said Carter. 'A crazy old witch who can't die, and now she has Cairney stashed away somewhere. If we could get Cairney back, then everything would change.'

'I am calling a halt to this discussion,' said Aila. 'You can talk about this with Lindi later, Carter; I have no desire to hear it. Cairney was let off lightly, and that's the truth. Had he not been a Holdfast, he would have been executed. He was saved because Karalyn would not kill her brother's son.'

'And she stopped Cael from hammering nails into his eyes,' said Carla.

Lindi frowned. 'What?'

'Cael was making a restrainer mask for Cairney,' said Carter. 'Can you imagine? I'd like to hammer a fucking nail into that bastard's head – see how he likes it.'

'What did I just say?' said Aila, her tone hardening. 'You can talk about this later, when I don't have to hear it.'

The room fell silent again. Lindi glanced at her cousins, then she tried to enter their minds. She sent her vision to Carter first, but it was rebuffed. It wasn't like Caelius, though; Lindi knew that if she pushed hard, she would probably be able to break through the protections shielding Carter's mind, but there was no way to enter his thoughts without him understanding what she was doing. She tried to read the minds of the other cousins, but found the same result. She eyed Aila, and was able to enter her mind with ease. Unlike the cousins, Aila had no natural dream mage abilities, and Lindi saw how easy it would be to manipulate her thoughts.

You are happy to let me stay for as long as I like.

'Do ye always do that when you meet new folk?' said Clova.

'What was that?' said Lindi.

'I said, do ye always try to read folks' minds when ye meet them?'

Lindi smiled. 'Yes, but I haven't met many gods, so I wanted to see where we all stood. You can try to read my mind, if you like.'

'None of us have that type of vision,' said Carter. 'We've all got battle-vision, but; and some of us have death powers or healing, and a few other wee tricks.'

'Your mother used to read minds without permission,' said Aila. 'I would ask you not to do that here, Lindi.'

'All right,' she said.

A sound came from the hallway, then a man and a woman entered. Both were immortal – Lindi sensed it as soon as they entered the dining room.

'Good evening, all,' said the man.

'Evening, Uncle Naxor,' said Carter. 'I see ye brought Konna back in one piece.'

'Are ye disappointed?' said Konna.

Aila got to her feet and embraced Konna. 'How is Killop?'

'He's doing all right,' said Konna. She glanced at Lindi.

'Hello,' said Lindi.

'Ah,' said Naxor. 'Miss Alindi'osso is here, I see.'

'I prefer Lindi Holdfast,' she said.

Naxor smiled. 'Does Sable know?'

'How could we have possibly told her?' said Aila. 'She arrived less than an hour ago, and you have the Quadrant.'

'I was wildly hoping that Sable herself might have brought her here,' said Naxor.

'Are you going to tell her?' said Lindi.

'The answer to that is a resounding *yes*, Miss Holdfast,' he said. 'Don't take it personally, but I try to remain on your mother's right side; she and I have not always seen eye to eye, and I have no desire to anger her.' He took out his Quadrant.

'Sable was attending the funeral in Nom Karta, the last I saw her,' said Konna. 'She might still be there.'

'The funeral was yesterday, yes?'

Konna nodded.

'I shall try Ulna first,' said Naxor, 'as I am a little wary of travelling to Nom Karta unannounced. I shall return as soon as I am able.'

Lindi frowned as Naxor vanished. Part of her wished she had persuaded him to keep her arrival a secret, but after what had happened in Plateau City, she knew it was only a matter of time before her mother found her. She went back into Aila's mind, and carefully removed all traces of her earlier manipulation, as she was sure her mother would check. She glanced at Clova after she had finished, but the young woman hadn't noticed. She must have detected Lindi's attempt on her own mind, she reasoned, not the attack on her mother's thoughts. That was something to note for the future.

Konna sat down next to her.

'So,' said Lindi, 'you are Konna? No one has actually introduced us.'

'This is my eldest daughter,' said Aila. 'She lives in Nom Karta.'

'With the Dominion dragons?' said Lindi. 'The dragons of Dragon Eyre don't like them very much. They say that they are all liars who dishonour the good name of dragons.'

Konna narrowed her eyes a little. 'I went there for the gods, not the dragons.'

'I was the only god on Dragon Eyre,' said Lindi. 'That's one of the reasons I'm here – I wanted to meet other immortals. I find it hard to take mortals seriously.'

'We heard ye were always getting yerself into trouble,' said Carter. 'Yer Ma told us that.'

Lindi smiled her most charming smile. 'I am a free spirit,' she said, 'and I don't like being told what to do.'

'Can ye fight?'

'Do you want to find out, Carter?' she said.

He laughed.

'I have the full range of vision,' she went on, 'from battle to inner; as well as death, flow, fire and plenty of dream powers. I'm like my mother, only better.'

Aila rolled her eyes.

'It's true,' said Lindi. 'It's not as though I can do anything about it. My father, whoever he is or was, must have been a very powerful god.'

'There aren't many of them left,' said Konna. 'I wonder if it was

Bailey? It won't have been Edgar; I'm sure about that. Maybe Elmhirst, although he doesn't have flow powers.'

'It might have been Edgar,' said Carter. 'What if Sable wiped his mind after they had done the business?'

'It isn't Edgar,' said Lindi. 'Why don't you ask my mother when she gets here?'

'There's another god it might have been,' said Konna.

'Who?' said Clova.

The air shimmered, and Naxor appeared in the dining room with Sable.

Lindi's face paled. 'Mother.'

Sable eyed her, then she smiled. 'Did you get fed up with Plateau City, Lindi?'

Lindi scowled at her. 'I know that you knew I was there.'

'Work it out, did you?' Sable said. She glanced at the others. 'I am forgetting my manners – it is very nice to see you all again.'

'Were you in Nom Karta?' said Konna.

'I had just returned from there,' said Sable. 'Naxor found me in Udall. Listen – there has been another attack by the Gunstians. As if Colsbury wasn't bad enough, and Bailey before that – the Gunstians assaulted the funeral party in Nom Karta. They killed three more dragons, and several gods lost their heads. They used the same tactics as Colsbury, and...'

'We didn't know about any attack on Colsbury,' said Aila.

'Oh. Right. That was two days ago, and the attack on Nom Karta was yesterday. These are their tactics – they open up a portal, then agents with Gifts subdue whoever is there, and then soldiers charge forward. The portal closes, stranding the soldiers at their destination, where they kill until they are killed. These operations are designed to end in the death of every soldier who crosses through the portal. They are all martyrs, as the Gunstians see things. Crude, but very effective. Anyway, this time, in Nom Karta, Karalyn was waiting for them.'

'Karalyn was there?' said Clova.

Sable nodded. 'She was attending the funeral. I confess that I didn't see too much of the attack, as I was hit with the Gift of Pain. It's not a pleasant experience; let me tell you. By the time I got to my feet, Karalyn had already killed at least two of the Gifted agents but, when the portal collapsed, Karalyn disappeared with the others. We then had to kill all of the soldiers who had come through, but that was the easy part, as there were no more Gifts to contend with. Queen Famula killed about twenty of them on her own, and Edgar was also in action.'

'Has Karalyn returned?' said Aila.

'She hadn't when I left Nom Karta.'

'And she disappeared yesterday?'

'Yes. The general assumption is that she has decided to teach the Gunstians a lesson. She might be slaughtering them all as we speak. Cael and Kyra will look for her if she doesn't come back soon.'

'Thank you for letting us know,' said Aila. 'Now, what shall we do about Lindi?'

'Do you mind if I sit?' said Sable.

'Please do.'

Sable took a seat and poured herself a glass of ale. She took a sip. 'This is very nice. Do you make it yourself?'

'We do,' said Aila. 'I am hardly going to buy ale when we make thousands of gallons of the stuff every third.'

'I might have to go into the whisky shop before I leave,' said Sable.

'You never have to pay for whisky, Sable,' said Aila.

Sable smiled. 'Thank you.' She turned to her daughter. 'The holiday is over, I'm afraid. It's time to go back to Ulna.'

'No,' cried Lindi. 'Please let me stay, just for a few days? Lady Aila said it was all right. I want to get to know my cousins. Please? I'm sorry I ran away like that; can I please stay?'

Sable frowned.

'Is there any harm in allowing her a few more days, Sable?' said Aila. 'I will keep an eye on her.'

'Lara is growing impatient,' said Sable.

'But I've only just got here,' said Lindi. 'Just two more days? Or maybe three? Please, Mother.'

'And what would you be doing, if I let you stay?'

'I don't know.'

Sable glanced at Aila. 'Would you put her to work? If she stays, I think she should work, either on the farm, or in Marchbrae Distillery. Could you find something for her to do?'

'Of course,' said Aila. 'She can help Carter on the farm.'

'Work?' said Lindi. 'I'll have to work?'

'That's the deal,' said Sable. 'If you want to stay, you'll have to work.'

Lindi frowned.

'Workshy, are you?' said Carter.

'I've worked on ships for half my life, you cheeky bastard,' said Lindi. 'I'm not frightened of hard work.'

Sable smiled. 'Then it's settled. Thank you very much, Aila, and thank you, Naxor.'

'I am delighted to be of service, Sable,' said Naxor, bowing. 'Shall I accompany you to the shop? I will ensure that you are not charged for anything you take.'

Sable eyed him. 'You always make me suspicious when you are being helpful, Naxor.' She got to her feet, then she kissed Lindi on the forehead. 'Behave yourself while you are here, daughter,' she said. 'These people are my friends but, more importantly, they are family. Holdfasts. Do not let them down.'

'Thank you for letting me stay, Mother.'

'Don't make me regret it,' said Sable. 'Come on, Naxor; let's walk to the shop.'

Lindi watched as Naxor led her mother out of the room, then she slowly exhaled.

'Can I have some whisky now?' she said.

Carter laughed. 'Aye, but remember that you'll be up before dawn tomorrow, cousin. We have a lot to do on the farm.'

'That's why it so wonderful to be a god,' said Lindi; 'no hangovers.'

CHAPTER 13
A RECORD OF ANNIHILATION

Colsbury Castle, Republic of the Holdings – 12th Day, First Third Summer 560

Cael and Arrosa walked down the grand staircase within the Summer Palace on Colsbury. Arrosa had issued strict instructions to the nannies and tutors who were looking after their three children that day, and Kelsey, Cardova and Cole were already waiting for them by the main entrance that led to the castle forecourt. A small group of lawyers and well-armed marines were also waiting, and Kelsey had her Quadrant ready.

'Sorry we're late,' said Arrosa. 'Carrie did not want us to leave.'

'It's fine,' said Kelsey; 'it's only the most important meeting between the Empire and the Dominion to take place for over a decade; I'm sure the government in Nom Karta doesn't mind waiting.'

'Pay her no attention,' said Cardova. 'Kelsey has clearly forgotten what it's like to have small children.'

'I am well used to her barbs, Lucius,' said Arrosa.

'Before we go,' said Kelsey, 'I assume there has been no word from Karalyn?'

'Not that I'm aware of,' said Cael. 'She could have gone back to her own world after annihilating the Gunstians; you know what she's like.'

'I'm getting worried about her,' said Cole. 'Even Karalyn cannot withstand the Gifts.'

'I'm sure she's fine,' said Kelsey. 'What's the worst that can happen? Even if she gets herself killed, she can just choose a new body to take over.'

'If she doesn't return by the end of the meeting,' said Cael, 'then Kyra and I will look for her.'

'How?' said Kelsey. 'How exactly does Kyra make contact with your mother?'

'I'm not sure of the precise process,' said Cael, 'but Kyra sends out a dream vision message and my mother can hear it. The problem is that I would imagine she's already tried that.'

'Can't you do it?' said Kelsey.

'I would need the Sextant for that,' said Cael. 'I can speak through it to find Mother; but we would have to be right next to it.'

A flicker of anxiety passed over Kelsey's features.

'Kyra and I will sort it out,' said Cael.

'Before I forget,' said Cole, 'word has arrived from the Ministry of the Plateau. All voting has stopped as of today, the ballot boxes are in the city, and the counting has begun. The election is over. If the initial counts are accurate, then Holder Smith appears to have won, and he will be the first elected Lord Marshal of the Plateau.'

'I will have to send him our congratulations,' said Cael.

Kelsey frowned. 'I wish the damn Holders would stick to Holdings politics.'

'Like you, Aunty?' said Cole. 'You are a Holder, so when was the last time you were in the Holdings parliament?'

'All right, smartarse,' said Kelsey. 'That's a touchy point with the Holders. Did you know I got a letter from Holder Terras, demanding that the next Holder Fast is based in the Holdings? What a bloody cheek.'

'Does that mean you still haven't chosen your successor?' said Cael.

'Why, do you want the job?'

Cael smiled. 'Aye. I'd take it. To be Holder Fast would be a greater honour than becoming Emperor.'

'Well, I have my favourite candidate, but it's not you,' said Kelsey. 'You are my second favourite, though, if that's any consolation. Regardless, the next Holder will have to wait until I am dead. I'm not giving it up before then.'

Arrosa raised an eyebrow. 'I thought you said we were going to be late?'

Kelsey gave her a look. 'I am so dreadfully sorry, Lady Arrosa,' she said. 'Right; let's go.'

She stared at the surface of the Quadrant for a moment, then she swiped her fingers over it. The air crackled, and the imperial party appeared in the wide boulevard outside the palaces of Nom Karta. A full company of Banner soldiers were waiting to greet them, along with a black and white dragon.

Kelsey bowed her head. 'Greetings, Lord Konran Mon Gahad,' she said.

'And greetings to you, Herald of Sapphire,' said the dragon. 'I see you have brought soldiers; there was no need.'

'These men and women are members of the Imperial Marines,' said Kelsey. 'We felt it prudent to bring them, in case the Gunstians try anything.'

'The Demon Witch will have disposed of the Gunstians by now, I would think,' said Konran. 'She has a long and distinguished record of annihilating her enemies.'

'We also brought our lawyers,' said Kelsey, as she gestured to the other small group who had accompanied them from Colsbury. 'I hope the lawyers are needed more than I hope the marines are needed.'

'Shall we enter the palace of King Gahad?' said Konran. 'Her Majesty Queen Famula awaits us there.'

The dragon turned, and the imperial party was escorted by the company of Banner soldiers through the vast entranceway of the huge palace. More Banner soldiers were inside, along with gods in full armour wielding massive battle axes or broadswords.

'Every god with battle-vision has been assigned to the defence of this palace,' said Konran, as he led them through the wide hallways; 'and every Banner soldier in the city is on duty.'

'Does the Banner mostly consist of Aucterians these days, my lord?' said Cardova.

'Indeed,' said the dragon, 'though many veterans and officers from the Doomed Worlds remain in their posts. They are all the same people, or so I am told – the Aucterians and the humans of the Doomed Worlds are descended from the same stock.'

'I am also from that line of humans,' said Cardova; 'we all originated on Implacatus.'

'Edgar disagrees,' said Konran. 'He says you all come from a world that existed before Implacatus; a world that he is the last being alive to remember.' He eyed Kelsey. 'Be warned, Herald – the loss of Bailey, who was as old as he, has struck Edgar deeply. You were not at the funeral; you did not hear his call for vengeance.'

'Thank you for the warning,' said Kelsey.

They came to the entrance of a vast hall lined in streaks of coloured marble, where Esher and Sable were waiting.

Esher bowed. 'Welcome to Nom Karta, Herald Kelsey,' he said. 'I shall be chairing today's meeting, as Karalyn's arbiter.'

'And I'll be helping him,' said Sable, a sly smile on her lips.

'I thought you'd gone back to Dragon Eyre, Aunty,' said Cael.

'I did, then Naxor fetched me. Lindi is in Clackenbaird. She gave me a sweet smile, and I buckled, so I am allowing her to stay with Aila for a few days. Lara was not happy, so I decided to avoid her wrath by coming here.' She glanced at Esher. 'Take everyone else inside; I want to speak to Cael and Kelsey for a moment.'

Esher bowed again, then he led the others through the entrance and into the hall.

'I discovered something that might interest you,' Sable said.

'Aye?' said Kelsey.

'Aila's anger has melted away,' said Sable. 'It seems she needed a good decade of rage to get through her grief, but she no longer hates either of you.'

'Thank Pyre for that,' said Cael.

'Some of her children remain a little confused by her change of heart,' Sable went on, 'but I think that, if you give it some more time, a reconciliation might be possible.'

'How do you know this?' said Kelsey.

'Naxor dropped a few hints,' she said, 'then I read Aila's mind when I got to Kell. That was only an hour ago. It's evening in Kell; it's strange to find it's only noon here.'

'How does Aila feel about the Empress?' said Kelsey. 'And has she softened on Karalyn?'

'That's not quite as simple. She still holds some bitterness towards Thorn for starting the war in the first place, and towards Karalyn for not intervening sooner; but her anger has lost its bite. Anyway, I thought you should know.'

They turned for the entrance.

'The other reason I'm in Nom Karta is to speak to Karalyn, if and when she gets here,' said Sable. 'Right before the Gunstians attacked yesterday, we had just got her to promise to visit Caitlyn and Carden.'

'Lucius told me how persistent you were,' said Kelsey.

'I don't want her forgetting about it,' Sable went on. 'As soon as she arrives, I will be reminding her of what she said.'

They came into the grand hall. Queen Famula, Lady Abda and Lord Konran were the only dragons present, but the Dominion had gathered a large number of gods, soldiers and officials. A horseshoe-shaped table had been set up, and Esher was standing by its head. One side of the table was empty, and awaiting the five delegates from the Empire, while Edgar, Kyra and Elmhirst were sitting on the opposite side, next to government officials and senior Banner officers. Esher gestured towards the empty seats, and Cardova led the way to them. Kelsey sat closest to Esher, followed by Cardova, Cael, Arrosa and Cole.

Esher remained on his feet, and Sable moved to stand next to him.

'Renowned dragons, ladies and gentlemen,' Esher said, 'we are ready to begin this first official convention between the Dominion and the Empire of the Sapphire Throne. As the new arbiter of the peace, I shall act as Karalyn's representative but, as you all know, I am inexperienced in such gatherings; so I would like to thank Sable Holdfast for offering to help me.'

'I object to this woman's presence,' said Lady Abda. 'Sable Holdfast has assaulted Nom Karta twice and, on both occasions, she tried to murder our beloved queen.'

'My lady,' said Cael, 'Cole and I were present on one of those attacks.'

'You were,' said Abda, 'but you have proved by your later actions to be a human we can trust. Sable has not.'

'I understand,' said Sable; 'but we were at war. I have not raised a finger against the Dominion since Karalyn forged the Peace of Corthie.'

'She may stay,' said Queen Famula. 'If we analysed the pasts of everyone present, we would indubitably find fault with each one of us.'

'Thank you, Your Majesty,' said Sable.

'Might I begin by passing on the Empire's sympathy for yesterday's attack by the Gunstians?' said Kelsey. 'Just as the heart of our government was struck not two days ago, so it was the turn of Nom Karta yesterday. The Empress wishes it to be known that she commiserates with the losses suffered by the Dominion.'

'Thank you, Herald,' said Famula. 'So, what is to be done? A strange turn this is, to find the Dominion and the Empire facing the same pitiless foe. Lord Edgar, please inform the Empire of our intentions.'

'Yes, Your Majesty,' said Edgar. He gazed down at the documents in front of him on the table, and Cael could see that he was struggling to retain his composure.

'The Dominion has formed four Quadrant teams,' Edgar said, 'each with two gods and ten Banner soldiers. Under the leadership of Lord Elmhirst, these teams will begin striking the Gunstian Empire tomorrow. Lord Elmhirst has already sent out scouts to select targets, and we have a list we shall work through. The raids will be short but brutal, and death powers will be deployed. We... we feel it would be useful to share this list with the Empire, so that we do not attack the same place at the same time.'

He slid a sheet of paper across the table, and Cardova picked it up.

'The Empire greatly appreciates this gesture,' said Cardova, as he gazed at the list. 'This all seems sensible. Military depots, army bases, naval dockyards and so on.'

'It was compiled before yesterday's attack,' said Elmhirst. 'Had I to write it again, I would be sorely tempted to include civilian targets.'

'Aye,' said Kelsey. 'I have the same temptation after what they did on Colsbury; but can we agree for now that we shall limit our raids to military targets?'

'For now, that shall be our policy,' said Edgar.

'We also have a list of targets,' said Cardova, as he passed over a document to Edgar and Elmhirst. 'They are of a similar nature to yours. Cael Holdfast will be leading the imperial response.' He glanced at Kelsey, who nodded. 'The Empire,' Cardova went on, 'is also willing to lend the Dominion a further four Quadrants, to facilitate your raids. Postmaster?'

Arrosa placed her bag onto the table and withdrew four Elbannon Quadrants, which she laid down in front of her.

'This is very generous,' said Queen Famula; 'what do you want in return?'

'Military cooperation,' said Cardova. 'The sharing of intelligence. It is in the interests of the Empire that the Dominion raids are successful, and it is in the interests of the Dominion that our raids are equally successful. I propose that we establish a quick and efficient means by which we can pass each other vital intelligence. After each raid, both sides should come together to discuss what went right, and what went wrong. Let us learn from each other's mistakes, if any are made. To this end, I propose that Lord Elmhirst and Adjutant Cael Holdfast meet on a regular basis, to coordinate our efforts. I also want us to think about how this ends. What counts as victory?'

No one spoke for a while, then Lady Abda's eyes gleamed. 'You all know what I think,' she said. 'The Gunstians should be annihilated. They cannot attack us if they are no more.'

'If I may, my lady?' said Elmhirst; 'let us deal with the practicalities first. I accept the proposal to meet with Cael Holdfast, but he has an advantage over me – he can read my mind, but I cannot read his. How will I know that he is being honest?'

'I can sit at these meetings,' said Kyra. 'I will ensure that they are conducted properly.'

'That's fine with me,' said Cael.

'As for victory,' said Elmhirst, 'I would be supportive of a more limited campaign. Our priority, as I see it, is to retrieve every Quadrant currently in the possession of the Gunstians. If we can achieve that, our mutual enemy will once again be confined to their homeland, and the threat from them will evaporate. That is what I see as victory.'

'To do that,' said Cael, 'we would need to find the location of the Gifted raiding parties. If the Gunstians were being clever about it, these groups will not be situated near Great Gunst, or close to any known military base. Were any prisoners taken from yesterday's attack?'

'A few,' said Edgar. 'They have been interrogated by dragons using the truth spell, but not a single one of them knew from where they had been sent. They volunteered in Great Gunst, but then they were taken to a different location by Quadrant. They described this place as being inland and rural, and close to a range of large mountains. Unfortunately, that could be anywhere. It does seem, though, that this is their only base, as they saw several Gifted agents gathered there, along with hundreds of soldiers.'

'We need to capture one of their officers, or a Gifted agent,' said Kelsey. 'They are bound to know where their base is located.'

'All of this may be moot,' said Lord Konran. 'For all we know, the Demon Witch may have already slaughtered our Gunstian enemies. She could be knee-deep in their blood.'

'While I hope that is the case,' said Famula, 'we should be prepared for a long conflict. Raids alone will not find their base.'

'Why don't we set down what we have agreed to paper?' said

Cardova. 'I think we have the makings of a mutually beneficial pact, and I would like to go over the details.'

'I am not required for that,' said Kyra. 'I want to look for my mother, and I will need Cael to help me.'

Both sides glanced at Esher.

'That's fine,' said Sable. 'Why don't Kyra and Cael start their search for Karalyn, while the rest of us draft the agreement?'

'Very well,' said Famula. 'You are both excused.'

Cael got to his feet. He glanced down at Arrosa, then he walked over to where his sister was getting up. Kyra met his gaze, then the air shimmered, and he found himself in his sister's apartment. The moment they arrived, Kyra's calm expression dissolved, and Cael saw fear in her eyes.

'I have already tried to contact Mother,' she said. 'I have been trying ever since she vanished yesterday. Usually, even when she doesn't want to speak to me, I can still sense her, but, Cael, this time, I can't.'

Cael frowned. 'Should we be worried?'

'I am already worried,' she said. 'Everyone seems so confident that our mother is destroying the Gunstians that no one has thought of the alternative. None of us can withstand the Gifts, brother; they aren't like god powers that can be blocked.'

'I know,' he said. 'I saw Mother when she was first struck by the Gift of Pain yesterday. She felt it as much as anyone else.'

'And I saw what you did, though you haven't told anyone.'

'I did what I had to do.'

'You took the Pain that was meant for her, brother,' she said. 'You shielded her.'

'What are we going to do? What's the plan?'

Kyra walked over to a drawer in a cabinet and opened it. She rooted through piles of clothes, then she took out a small metal object.

'The Compass,' she said.

'How will the Compass find her?'

'It won't, but it will find the Sextant,' said Kyra, 'and then you can find her.'

'She's going to be pissed off if she discovers that we've visited her secret world.'

'At this point, I couldn't care any less, Cael. If she's so offended by this breach of her privacy, then she can make herself a new world.'

'Wait a minute,' said Cael. 'That thing finds Tempest, aye? The Gunstian raiding parties have three Quadrants – couldn't it locate them?'

'In theory,' said Kyra, 'but it would take forever to scan all of the worlds for the tiny amount of Tempest contained inside a Quadrant. Compared to that, finding the Sextant will be easy. Look; if this attempt fails, then I will start combing over the continents of Athumia, looking for the Gunstians' Quadrants, but the Sextant is a far better bet. Shall we?'

'What do I do?'

She smiled at him. 'You do nothing. I will activate the Compass, and you will have to wait.'

Kyra pressed her thumb onto the surface of the Compass, and her eyes glazed over. Cael walked over to a large bay window, and gazed out at the palaces of Nom Karta. It was a city he had never liked. There were no shops or taverns, and very few human-sized buildings, and it seemed to be a city that lacked a centre. Instead, two dozen enormous palaces stood in rows, each designed for the comfort and use of dragons.

'I've found it,' said Kyra.

Cael turned back to her. 'That was quick.'

'There is an awful lot of Tempest within the Sextant,' she said.

'Can I try the Compass?'

Kyra narrowed her eyes a little, then she handed him the small device.

'Put your thumb onto the circular part,' she said.

Cael did so. 'Now what?'

'Do you sense anything?'

'Like what?'

'Tempest, brother. Do you sense the presence of Tempest?'

'I can't sense anything.'

'Then it doesn't work for you,' she said; 'just as Quadrants do not speak to you. But you can use the Sextant, and I can't, so I suppose it balances itself out.'

'Are you happy in Nom Karta, sister?' he said.

'Why would you ask that?'

'I was just gazing out of the window,' he said. 'It's not my favourite city.'

'Try to think of each palace as a separate little town,' she said. 'And aye; I'm happy here. I have Edgar and the two boys, and I have a small measure of influence over the politics of the Dominion.'

'Some say that you are controlling the Dominion from behind the scenes,' said Cael. 'I have heard others say that Karalyn's twins secretly control both the Empire and the Dominion.'

'You are in line to become Emperor one day, brother; so perhaps that's not too far from the truth.'

'I am glad we have moved past our earlier arguments,' he said. 'We could work well together; we could bring the Empire and the Dominion into a closer relationship.'

Kyra eyed him. 'Share with us the secret of how to make a Quadrant, and destroy your advanced weapons – and then we can talk.'

Cael laughed. 'Didn't you attend university?' he said. 'Maybe you should have paid more attention in Professor Elbannon's class.'

'Elbannon kept much of the inner workings of Quadrants from his students,' said Kyra. 'It's like asking you to build a Battanara just because you have used one a few times. Anyway, we are wasting time.'

The air crackled, and Cael found himself in a room with rough stone walls. In front of him was a glass door that led on to a long balcony, and Cael stepped out into the fresh air. He gazed at the mountains, rivers and forests spread out before him.

'Pyre's arse,' he said. 'What a view. No wonder Mother likes it here. What world are we on?'

'I have no idea,' said Kyra, 'but the Sextant is in here.'

Cael turned, and walked back into the chamber. He stared at the Sextant, then he shook his head.

'This thing used to obsess me,' he said.

'I know; I can remember.'

'I wonder how World Three is doing.'

'You can check, after you have found Mother. Are you ready?'

Cael nodded. He took a step forward, and heard the low hum being emitted by the large device, then he reached out with his right hand, and pressed his palm to the Sextant's smooth surface.

What is your desire, Cael?

'Show me Karalyn Holdfast.'

Karalyn's connection has been broken.

'What is that supposed to mean?'

Karalyn's connection has been broken.

'Upon which world is Karalyn?'

Karalyn's connection has been broken.

'What is it, Cael?' said Kyra. 'What is it saying to you?'

'It's saying that Mother's connection has been broken.'

'Connection to what – the Sextant?'

'I guess so; the Sextant can be vague at times. It said something else that was obscure when I was looking for Mother on Athumia. Wait; let me try again. Sextant, is Karalyn Holdfast alive?'

Karalyn's connection has been broken.

'Fucking stupid machine,' Cael muttered. 'Sorry, Kyra, but this isn't going to help us. Something has happened to Mother, but the Sextant doesn't know how to find her.'

'But if she was dead... I mean, if... if Albany's body has been destroyed, then Mother's spirit would be free, aye? Is that how it works? And, if that was the case, then the Sextant would be able to communicate with her.'

'Therefore,' said Cael, 'she cannot be in spirit form. But if she's not a ghost, then where is she?'

'Let's think back to what happened. I saw Mother kill two of the

Gifted agents, and then she went to kill another one, but that one already had the Quadrant in his hands. Then the portal collapsed and they all vanished. Where could they have gone that the Sextant couldn't see?'

'Nowhere,' said Cael. 'The Sextant can see every world in existence. Even if she was in the void, the Sextant would be able to contact her.'

'The void?'

'It's like the place that exists before a world has been created within it. At least, it's something like that; it's hard to explain. But she isn't there, because I once called to her when she was in the void, and she heard my voice. Let me try something else.'

He pressed his hand to the Sextant again.

What is your desire, Cael?

'Mother, can you hear me?' he said. 'Mother, it's Cael, and Kyra is standing right next to me. We are looking for you. Can you hear me?'

Cael closed his eyes and concentrated, but heard no response come through the Sextant.

'Let's check that this thing is actually working,' he said. 'Sextant, show me one of Karalyn's creations that has one immortal living upon it, but no mortals.'

Cael's vision blurred, then it re-focussed on a forested landscape of spruce and pine.

'What are you doing?' said Kyra.

'I'm checking that Cairney is still safely in exile,' he said. 'Sextant, show me the one immortal.'

The view of the forested landscape changed, and Cael saw the figure of a man running among the trees, a long, stone-tipped spear in his right hand.

'Can you see him?' said Kyra.

'Aye. I can see him.'

'What's he doing?'

'Hunting.' Cael lifted his hand from the Sextant, and his vision ceased.

'What now?' said Kyra. 'Is it possible that Mother has created some kind of barrier, like she did over Marchside during the war? – a barrier that could block the Sextant from seeing her?'

'Anything is possible with Mother,' he said. He eyed his sister. 'What if she was killed, and has taken the body of someone else already? Her second body didn't work properly for a long time. Arrosa remembers Lyla's early days well. Mother couldn't speak, and she had to relearn how to read and write; and her powers were useless. She was fine when she went into Albany, though; I don't think there were any problems that time.'

'But Albany had vision and other powers,' said Kyra. 'Lyla had nothing like that. You might be right, Cael. If Mother has gone into a body with no powers, then that might explain it. But why would she do such a thing? If her body was destroyed, then the logical next step would be to return to us, to let us know.'

'What, and then we'd find her another god-body to inhabit?'

Kyra shrugged. 'We should go back to Nom Karta. I have no choice now; I am going to have to begin a great sweep of Athumia with the Compass, in the hope that I can find the Quadrant that was used to take our Mother away. This could take a very long time, brother.'

'Maybe not,' he said. 'After all, she's only been gone one day, and we've already located the Sextant.'

'The Sextant is like a giant beacon of light when seen through the Compass. Quadrants are like tiny pinpricks in comparison. Unless I look very closely, I will miss them. Where should I start?'

'Gunst.'

'Which is enormous,' she said. 'This is bad, Cael. Everyone believes Karalyn is fine, that she's fighting the Gunstians. How will they react when they discover that she has vanished from the sight of the Sextant?'

'Should we keep it quiet for a couple of days?' he said. 'If asked, I can tell people most of the truth – that you are searching for her with the Compass. We don't need to go into details.'

'The truth will come out eventually.'

'Then you had better begin your search, sister.'

Kyra nodded. She glanced at her brother, the air crackled, and they both disappeared.

CHAPTER 14
AN OFFER OF SERVICE

Marchside, Kell – 14th Day, First Third Summer 560

Konna walked out of the whisky shop, her bag bulging with bottles. The rain that had swept over the hills and fields of Southern Kell that morning had petered out, though more dark clouds were coming in from the west. It was bad luck, she told herself, that it had rained every day during her short stay in Clackenbaird, but one could never count on the weather in Kell, not even in the First Third of Summer.

'Did ye get everything ye needed?' said Clova, who had been waiting for her under the shelter of some trees.

'Aye,' said Konna; 'nothing fancy; a couple of twelve-year-olds and a fourteen-year-old. I got the Strathlanach for a change; I think the others will like it.'

'When is Naxor taking ye back to Nom Karta?'

'Soon, I think; when he stops for lunch.'

Clova nodded. 'Do ye have to go?' she said. 'The reason ye left in the first place was because ye were worried that Ma would hate ye. And ye might have been right eight years ago, but ye've seen Ma now – she doesnae bear a grudge about what ye did.'

'Carter does,' said Konna. 'He still blames me for Cairney getting caught.'

'Carter's a numpty,' said Clova.

'He's not,' said Konna. 'He wouldn't be able to run the farm if he was stupid. I've seen him – he knows what he's doing; he might be the most capable out of us all.'

'All right; but he's a numpty when it comes to Cairney,' said Clova. 'He still believes that the Empire is to blame for everything bad that's happened, and he ignores all the good it's done. It's the Empire that allows us to sell whisky all over the Known Worlds; it's the Empire that's made us rich.'

'And it was the Empire that got Da killed,' said Konna.

'I've never believed that,' said Clova. 'Even when the rest of us were calling for vengeance, I didnae agree. Da got Da killed, Konna. Da wanted to fight, because the gods attacked Clackenbaird. If he had any doubts about what he was doing, then Ma buried them – she told him to fight.'

'Are you blaming Ma?'

'I'm not blaming anyone, Konna. It just happened.'

Konna shook her head. 'Ceres and Carla seem to agree with Carter on this.'

'I know, but neither of them can actually remember Da – one was a bairn, the other wasnae even born when he died. All they know is what Carter tells them; and Carter thinks Da was murdered by the Empire, and that Cairney was a fucking hero. You know the truth, Konna; if ye stayed, ye could talk some sense into them.'

Konna gazed up at the hill where the farmhouse stood. 'I can't stay.'

'Why not? Ye could get a job in the distillery tomorrow, if ye wanted it. Yer old room's sitting empty; you could move back in. I heard ye saying that the gods of Nom Karta treat ye like a child; that wouldnae happen here. I know ye want to meet other gods, but maybe ye went too soon. Maybe ye should try again when yer older.'

Konna said nothing.

'What is it ye actually do in Nom Karta, sister?' said Clova. 'Do ye have a job?'

'It doesn't work like that,' said Konna. 'The gods don't work; they have mortals to do that for them. Soldiers, servants, cooks – whatever ye want, someone will do it for ye. The gods give the orders, and the mortals obey. I have servants who do everything for me, Clova.'

'That doesnae sound like a healthy way to live,' said Clova.

'The problem I have with Nom Karta,' Konna went on, 'is that the gods judge each other by their ages – so Edgar is on top, because he's the oldest. Elmhirst comes next, because he's the only other Ancient, and so on. I'm twenty-five years old, so ye can guess where I sit in the hierarchy.'

Clova put a hand on her arm. 'Then stay here. Wait a century or two, and try again. Who knows – I might even come with ye.'

'But I need to prove myself to the other gods,' said Konna. 'I need to show them that I'm not a child, that I can be trusted with more responsibility.'

'How many close friends have ye made?'

'Esher was probably my best friend,' she said, 'because even though he's an Ascendant, the other gods treated him as though he was too young to know anything. But he's moved to Zamata. I know plenty of the other gods, but I wouldn't say we were close. The older they are, the more walls they put up around themselves. Each one of them has been hurt, betrayed and deceived countless times throughout the centuries, and they are all wary of lowering their guard. Paranoid, even. Among everyone else in Nom Karta, I am probably closest to Kyra.'

'Kyra?' said Clova. 'Pyre's tits, sister – Kyra is the one Holdfast I cannae stand. Do ye not remember how she hurt us when she ran away from Colsbury? She drained the life out of Ma, and Killop, Cairney, and you, too. I saw it. I thought ye were all gonnae die.'

'Aye, but Kyra regrets that,' said Konna. 'She was only eighteen at the time, and she knew we would all recover. Folk do stupid things when they're eighteen, Clova.'

Clova frowned, then she turned at the sound of voices coming up from the lower fields to the west of the distillery. Konna glanced down the path, and saw Carter and Lindi walking towards them. Both had clearly been out in the rain, and their clothes and hair were soaked through. Despite that, Lindi was laughing and smiling, as Carter kept her entertained with a story he was telling her.

'What do ye think of Lindi?' Clova whispered.

'I like her,' said Konna, 'but she's fucking trouble.'

'Aye. The kind of lassie who would burn down the world for a laugh.'

They waited until Lindi and Carter had reached them.

'Are ye going up to the house for lunch, girls?' said Carter.

'Aye,' said Clova. 'This is Konna's last morning in Clackenbaird. Uncle Naxor is taking her back to Nom Karta.'

Carter's smiled faded. 'Aye? Bollocks. I was hoping ye'd be here for longer. A third, at the very least. Ye've only been here a couple of days, Konna – what's the matter? Don't ye like us any more?'

'Sable told us about the attack,' said Konna. 'I need to go back so I can help defend the Dominion against the Gunstians.'

Lindi raised an eyebrow. 'Is that right? Will you be fighting? Do you work for the Dominion?'

'I don't have an official position within the Dominion,' said Konna, 'but I intend to offer my services. The Gunstians have been on a rampage since summer began; we have to stop them.'

'Uncle Naxor told me the real reason the Gunstians are sending out raiding parties,' said Carter. 'It's because Cael Holdfast slaughtered hundreds of them a few years ago – and he completely destroyed their most sacred temple – can ye believe that? He used explosives to level the entire building, with hundreds of innocent Gunstians trapped inside. That's why they're pissed off. That's what started this.'

'I don't remember much about Cael,' said Lindi, 'but he sounds like a dick.'

'Basically,' said Carter, 'the Gunstians are trying to avenge what Cael did, but it's the Dominion that's suffering. What's fucking new, eh? Once again, the Empire fucks over everyone else.'

'Uncle Naxor has told you some of the truth, brother,' said Konna, 'but he left out a few things. Did you know that the Dominion invaded Gunst a few decades ago, for example? That's why they're pissed off with Nom Karta.'

'Aye, but where did they get their Quadrants from, eh?' said Carter.

Konna frowned. 'The Empire lost them.'

'Exactly.'

Konna and Carter glared at each other, then Clova coughed.

'We should go up to the house before the rain starts again,' she said.

'I don't mind the rain any more,' said Lindi, as they set off up the hill. 'It makes a change from the endless sunshine on Dragon Eyre. Every day is the same there – blue skies, nice and warm, but not too hot. Gentle breezes coming off the sea, palm trees swaying by the golden sands. It's awful.'

Clova laughed. 'Now yer making me jealous.'

'And I'm so glad I came to Kell in the summer,' Lindi went on. 'If this is the best of the weather, then winter must be a fucking nightmare.'

'It's dark all the time,' said Clova. 'There's only six hours of daylight on Winter's Day. And it's freezing. Sometimes, the snow comes up to yer chest.'

'Why does Lady Aila not move you all to a sunnier place?' said Lindi. 'You are rich enough to build a palace anywhere you like.'

'We stay here because this is where our Da was from,' said Carter.

'Bullshit,' said Konna. 'Da moved here in his twenties, after he got back from killing greenhides in the City of Salve. I was born in Threeways, but Killop was born in Colsbury Castle. Da was brought up on the Hold Fast estate.'

Carter narrowed his eyes. 'But his ancestors came from Kell; that's what I meant, ya pedantic cow. Anyway, I fucking love living down here.'

They reached the farmhouse, and trooped inside. They each removed their outer coats, then they pulled off their boots and set them down in a neat line by the front door. Konna hung her bag up on a hook next to the row of coats, and they walked through the house to the kitchen. Her mother was there, along with the cook, and they were preparing food.

'Sit down,' said Aila; 'lunch will just be a few minutes.'

The four young gods sat by the table, and Carter filled their glasses with ale from a covered jug.

'Konna was telling me, Ma,' said Clova, 'that the gods of Nom Karta don't do any work; and here you are – a demigod chopping up vegetables.'

Aila smiled. 'I do it because I want to,' she said. 'I know exactly what Konna means – that's how I used to live as a demigod in the City. We had palaces and servants, and would never dream of making our own lunch. Instead, we would order some mortals to do it for us, and shout at them if they made a mistake. I made a conscious choice that I didn't want my own children to grow up like that.' She nodded at Lindi. 'And your mother did something similar, by getting you to help out on her ship. Did you have servants running around after you all day, Lindi?'

'Not if I'm with my mother,' said Lindi, 'but there is a big difference between here and Ulna, Lady Aila. If I want to have servants looking after me, I can go up to the Bridge Palace. Blackrose has hundreds of servants up there. I work hard on some days, especially when we are at sea, but on others I can, if I want, have people cooking and cleaning for me. I live in both worlds. I am a hard-working sailor, *and* a pampered goddess.'

Aila laughed. 'At least Sable understands the need for hard work. I want my children to earn what they have, not have it handed to them on a plate.'

Carter rolled his eyes. 'I must be the only god alive who has to get up before dawn each morning to milk cows in the rain and wind.'

Lindi nudged him with an elbow. 'You said you loved it.'

'I do love it,' said Carter, 'but some luxury now and again wouldnae go amiss.'

'Well, you are sitting on your arse while your mother makes you lunch,' said Lindi, 'so it's not all bad.'

They quietened as food was served, and Konna started to feel a sense of dread about returning to Nom Karta. What if Clova had been right – should she wait until she was older before trying to compete with the gods of the Doomed Worlds? She glanced at Clova and Carter. They were very different from each other, but she would miss them both.

Naxor came into the kitchen just as the lunch was ending.

'Apologies for my tardiness,' he said, 'but I had to deal with several large orders that have come in – one of them was from the Royal Palace in Pella; and I would hate to disappoint the beloved Aurelians.' He eyed Konna. 'Are you ready?'

'I am having second thoughts about going back to Nom Karta,' she said.

The kitchen fell silent.

'I see,' said Naxor. 'The decision is yours, Konna.'

'You are very welcome to stay,' said her mother, her eyes lighting up. 'You can stay as long as you want. We can find you a job, if you like.'

'Or,' said Naxor, 'I could take you back to Nom Karta, and you could think about it. It might be a simple case of homesickness; after all, you haven't been here for eight years, so it is perfectly understandable that you would feel emotional about leaving.'

Aila glared at her cousin. 'Are you trying to persuade my daughter to go?'

'Come now, Aila,' said Naxor; 'you must be able to see the utility of having one of the Marchbrae Holdfasts nestled within the bosom of the Dominion. When the day finally comes – the day when we take control of the Empire, think how essential it will be to have sound contacts among the gods and dragons that rule the Dominion.'

Aila's features hardened. 'That might be decades away. Why can't Konna stay here for the summer? That would hardly ruin your carefully-woven plans.'

Lindi raised a hand. 'Excuse me,' she said. 'Could I, uh... could we go back to the part where Naxor said that *we* are going to take over the Empire? Who are you talking about?'

Naxor beamed. 'I am talking about us, Lindi – the gods among the Holdfasts, of which you are one. We are the sole inheritors of a dual ancestry – the immortals, and the Holdfasts. Well, I am not personally a Holdfast, but you get the general idea, yes? When the Kelseys and Caels and Thorns of this world are dead and buried, we shall all still be here.'

Lindi's eyes narrowed. 'That sounds a teeny, tiny bit like treason, Naxor.'

'Not at all,' said Naxor. 'It is merely the natural operation of things. Mortals die, immortals consolidate. If it were treason, I would be clapped in chains, for my mind has been read by Cael and the others on numerous occasions.'

'So, I am being included in this?' said Lindi.

'You are possibly the most powerful Holdfast god of all, Lindi,' said Naxor; 'it would be rather imprudent to exclude you.'

'There is no *possibly* about it,' said Lindi. 'In this plan of yours, do I get to be Empress? Think before you answer, Naxor; much could depend upon what you say next.'

Konna got to her feet. 'Take me to Nom Karta, Uncle Naxor,' she said, 'if only to spare me Lindi's megalomania.'

Aila's face fell. 'But...'

'I will think about my future when I am back in the Dominion, Ma,' said Konna. 'I honestly don't know what I am going to do, but I will say this – if I can't find my place in Nom Karta, I will come home.'

'Could you not at least stay until Ceres and Carla get home from school?'

'I said goodbye to them this morning, Ma,' said Konna.

Aila held out her arms, and Konna embraced her.

'Take care, daughter,' Aila said.

Konna glanced at her brother and sister. 'Work hard, you two, and don't let Lindi lead you astray.'

Lindi cackled with laughter.

Naxor took out his Quadrant.

'Wait,' said Konna. 'I have a bag by the front door.'

Naxor followed her out into the hallway, where she put on her coat and boots. She pulled her bag over her shoulder, and nodded to Naxor.

'Where should we arrive?' he said. 'I confess that I am not overly familiar with Nom Karta.'

Konna took the Quadrant from him, and showed him the correct finger movements.

'That will take us into the entrance hall of the Palace of Naghad,' said Konna, as she gave it back to him.

'Excellent, thank you,' said Naxor.

He moved his hand over the device, the air crackled, and they appeared in a cavernous chamber inside the grand palace.

'This is nice,' said Naxor, as he gazed around.

Konna eyed him. 'Is this your first time in Nom Karta, Uncle?'

'Apart from a few short trips to the Tempest mine,' he said, 'this is my first time on Athumia. You must recall that, since my resignation from the Imperial Court fifteen years ago, I have rarely left Kell. Your mother needed me, and I was loath to leave her.'

'I know,' she said. 'You were always there for us after Da died. I will never forget that; none of us will.'

'You are family, Konna; you come first. But, now that you live here, I would be eager to see a little more of the Dominion. As I said before, making contacts among the gods of the Doomed Worlds will help us in the future. What I would really like is an open invitation to come and go as I please. Would such a thing be possible?'

'I could ask Kyra, I suppose.'

Naxor frowned. 'No, not Kyra. She knows me too well.' He pointed at an approaching dragon with teal-coloured scales. 'Who is that fine dragon, for instance? She has a regal bearing.'

'That's Lady Abda,' said Konna; 'the Queen's sister. She doesn't like humans.'

Naxor smiled. 'We shall see about that. Introduce me, if you would.'

Konna rolled her eyes, then they waited for the massive dragon to get closer.

Konna bowed. 'Lady Abda Min Gahad, greetings,' she said. 'I have returned from my mother's home thanks to my uncle, Lord Naxor of Port Sanders and Marchbrae.'

Naxor stepped forward and bowed low with a flourish. 'O mighty dragon of the Dominion, I am humbled and honoured to be in the presence of such a magnificent scion of the house of the great King Gahad, blessed be his name for all eternity. Although I am but a feeble demigod, I stand in awe of your greatness, blinded by your splendour as I cower before your strength. Please allow me to express my horror and disgust at the recent actions of those most vile criminals – the Gunstians. I curse them all; may their flesh wither from their bones, and may their deaths come through great agony. Tell me, I pray – how might I be of service to you?'

Abda gazed down at him, her eyes amused. 'You are practised, I see,' she said, 'in the arts of flattery. Most of the gods and demigods now living here rarely speak such words to me, as though they see themselves as the equals of the children of Gahad, or perhaps they view themselves as better than us.'

'Such an attitude seems incomprehensible to me,' said Naxor, 'for you are as beautiful as the stars in the night sky, as mighty as the ocean that crashes upon the shores, and as fine as the most brilliant diamond. I offer you my skills as a vision demigod of the highest calibre.'

Abda's eyes narrowed. 'Do you dwell amid the Empire, demigod?'

'I do, Your Great and Noble Highness,' he said, 'but I do not serve the Empire. I belong to the Marchbrae Holdfasts, and we live apart from the other, mortal Holdfasts.'

Abda said nothing for a long while, then she gazed down at Konna.

'You were not here when the Gunstians attacked,' she said. 'The Demon Witch vanished.'

'Sable told me what happened,' said Konna.

'That disgusting witch should not be allowed to set foot within the palaces of this city,' said Abda.

'I completely agree,' said Naxor. 'Sable's crimes are legion; she is a disgraceful woman.'

Abda eyed Naxor, then she turned back to Konna. 'The Demon

Witch is yet to return; perhaps she is dead, or perhaps the slaughter of the Gunstians is taking her longer than she anticipated. I care not. If she is dead, I shall rejoice; if she has annihilated the Gunstians, I shall rejoice. I cannot lose.'

'For such is your great wisdom and foresight,' said Naxor. 'It would be a privilege of the highest order to be allowed to serve you.'

'I will take your offer into due consideration, demigod,' said Abda, then she walked away, and departed down the hallway.

Naxor clapped his hands with joy. 'I think that went splendidly,' he said. 'Dragons cannot resist a bit of flattery. Now that I have planted the seed in her mind, I feel it is only a matter of time before my efforts bear fruit.'

Konna eyed him. 'What exactly are you after, Uncle? Why would you want to offer your services to Abda?'

'To get a foot in the door, Konna,' he said; 'and I already know my way in. Abda thinks that the gods and demigods of the Doomed Worlds don't give her the respect she feels she deserves, and she doesn't like the mortal Holdfasts. And she is the sister of Queen Famula, yes? This gives me much to ponder. Now it is your turn to be of service to me and your family, Konna. Ask if I may be permitted to visit you again, to see how my niece is getting along; that sounds reasonable, does it not? If the replies are favourable, let me know through Lord Esher the next time you see him. Will you do this for me?'

'Fine,' said Konna. 'I will ask.'

Naxor beamed, then he swiped his Quadrant and vanished.

Konna walked all the way to her apartment and let herself in. As she had not announced the date of her return, none of her usual servants were in the vicinity, and she went from room to room, gazing at the luxury and splendour, as a sense of loneliness settled upon her. Was it merely homesickness, as Naxor had suggested; or was she in the wrong place at the wrong time? She decided to visit Kyra, so she left her apartment and walked along wide hallways to where her cousin lived with Lord Edgar and their two children.

She knocked on the front door and entered, passing several servants who bowed low. She was escorted to a grand drawing room, where Edgar and Elmhirst were sitting by a low table drinking brandy.

'Lady Konna is here to see you, my lords,' said the servant.

Edgar glanced up, but said nothing, his eyes dark and brooding.

Elmhirst stood. 'I wasn't sure if you would come back, Konna,' he said. 'I am glad you decided to return, we have need of every immortal with powers such as yours. Take a seat.'

Konna walked over and sat down by the table. Elmhirst retook his seat and poured her a drink.

'I was reviewing yesterday's raid with Lord Edgar,' Elmhirst went on. 'We destroyed seven Gunstian warships, and killed several hundred of their sailors. Best of all, their dockyard facilities were burnt to the ground. Their navy will not be troubling Zamata any time soon.'

'That sounds promising,' said Konna.

'It is just the beginning,' said Elmhirst. 'Now, should I assume that you know what occurred during the attack which took place here three days ago?'

'Sable told me about it,' said Konna. 'Were three dragons killed?'

'Three dragons and four gods,' said Elmhirst; 'along with around fifty mortal soldiers and courtiers.' His eyes glimmered with anger. 'I am about to say something I never thought I would, but we are indebted to the Demon Witch. Had she not killed some of the Gifted agents, the toll would have been far higher.'

'Lady Abda told me that she still hasn't returned,' said Konna.

'Indeed,' said Elmhirst. 'Lady Kyra is spending every waking moment trying to locate her.'

Edgar bowed his head, as though he was struggling to keep his composure.

Konna frowned. 'Are you all right, my lord?'

'No,' said Edgar. 'Karalyn was my last hope.'

Elmhirst sat back, his arms folded across his chest, and Konna wondered what they had been talking about before she had arrived.

'I don't know what you mean, my lord,' said Konna.

Edgar faced her, and she could see that he had been crying.

'Karalyn was the only one who understood the truth,' he cried, 'and she is lost to us.'

'What truth?'

'Let us discuss this another time, my lord,' said Elmhirst.

Edgar ignored the Ancient. 'The truth, Konna, about the nature of genuine immortality,' he said. 'Karalyn ascended – she was a mortal, and now she cannot die. She changed her very being, and became a god.'

'Aye, I know that, but…?'

'I want the same for Kyra,' said Edgar. 'Don't you understand? Kyra is dying before my eyes, and I cannot bear it. I will not bear it. Whatever was done to Karalyn, I want the same for Kyra. I want her to be by my side for millennia, not decades. But how am I to accomplish this, if Karalyn has gone?'

'Might I remind you, my lord,' said Elmhirst, 'that, just as you claim, Karalyn cannot die. Therefore, at some point, she will return. We have not lost her permanently.'

'And what if she returns a century from now?' said Edgar. 'By then, it will be too late. Time is running out. Kyra's life is slipping through my fingers like sand.'

'Perhaps you are still in a state of grief over Lord Bailey, my lord,' said Elmhirst.

'Bailey's death has crushed me, it is true,' said Edgar. 'I loved him as a brother, and his loss has made me realise how precious Kyra is to me. I cannot lose her, too, Elmhirst. I must find the secret. I must discover how Karalyn was able to cheat death. What do you know of it, Konna? You were there, were you not, the day Karalyn ascended?'

'I was a baby at the time,' said Konna. 'I don't remember any of it. All I know is that it had something to do with the Sextant.'

Edgar snapped his fingers. 'Yes. The Sextant. If I could find the Sextant, then perhaps its secrets would be revealed to me. But how, if Karalyn has gone? Kyra possesses a device that can locate the Sextant; did you know that?'

'I don't think we should be talking about this topic, my lord,' said Elmhirst.

'Shut up, Elmhirst,' said Edgar, as he stared into Konna's eyes. 'A device,' he went on, 'called the Compass. Kyra is in our bedroom right now, using it to look for the Quadrant that took Karalyn away. But, Konna, I cannot use it. I have tried; it does not respond to my touch, and I cannot ask Kyra to use it on my behalf. She refuses to discuss this with me. She says that she does not wish to become immortal.' A tear rolled down his cheek. 'She would rather that I suffer for all eternity.'

Konna thought about telling Edgar to snap out of his self-pity, but then she recalled how her mother had been after Corthie's death. Was such the fate of all gods who fell in love with mortals?

'I believe,' Edgar went on, 'that anyone who can hear the voice of the Sextant, or hear the voice of a Quadrant, might be able to operate the Compass. Do you know of anyone who can do this?'

'Cael can operate the Sextant,' said Konna; 'Sable, too. Apart from Karalyn herself, I know of no others.'

'What about Esher?' said Edgar. 'The Sextant was designed for the Ascendants, so it stands to reason that Esher would be able to operate it.'

'It's possible,' said Konna.

Edgar got to his feet. 'I am going to Zamata, to ask him.'

'But, my lord,' said Elmhirst, 'we have yet to discuss tomorrow's raid, and the meeting with Cael Holdfast that is scheduled for this evening.'

'You can deal with it,' said Edgar, as he withdrew his Quadrant.

He swiped his fingers over the device and disappeared.

Elmhirst exhaled, then he sipped from his glass of brandy. 'Konna,' he said, 'I would politely ask that you refrain from encouraging Lord Edgar's... delusions regarding this subject. He is clearly in a fragile state of mind.'

'I wasn't trying to encourage him,' said Konna. 'I think his plan is insane.'

Elmhirst eyed her. 'Then we are agreed. Poor old Esher is about to be bombarded with questions to which he will have no answer. His memories are gone, so how could he possibly know if he can operate the Sextant? At least Kyra is approaching it sensibly; as Edgar said, she understands that she is mortal and, as such, that she will die a mortal death. When that happens, we should prepare ourselves for a long and possibly violent period of mourning.'

'I think I understand what you mean,' said Konna.

His eyes pierced her. 'Of course you do; for your own immortal mother suffered greatly when your mortal father died at the hands of Lord Ward. What would Lady Aila have done to have Corthie transformed into an ever-living god?'

Konna kept her gaze on him. 'Anything. She would have done anything.'

CHAPTER 15
BEING GALINA

Unknown Location in Aucteran – 13th Abrinch 1613
Karalyn sat shivering from the cold by the entrance to her small tent. The morning prayers to Chadura had finished, and the young Gunstian soldiers filling the large field were preparing their breakfast rations. Karalyn pulled her blanket over her shoulders, but the cold had been so bad that she had barely slept in days. It was her third morning in the field encampment since she had taken over the painfully-mortal and frail body of Lady Galina, the hero who had helped to kill the foul Demon Witch, and she was swamped in misery and regret.

It had occurred to her on her second day in the field encampment that others believed that she knew exactly where they were; it was obvious – of course the Gifted agents would have been given more information than the ill-equipped soldiers who had volunteered to die as martyrs for Chadura. Karalyn had been forced to pretend that she knew their location, but the truth was that she had utterly destroyed the old woman's memories in her anger, leaving nothing behind. Had she not had a good grasp of the Gunstian language, her real identity would have become clear to everyone, but she had muddled through. She had seemed a little absent-minded at times; a little hesitant in her answers to the many questions she had received, but the others were putting that down to her old age, and were assuming that her recent actions had exhausted her.

A young soldier handed her a cup of hot Gunstian green tea, which she hated, but which she nevertheless drank several cups of every day. She was doing everything she could to fit in with the Gunstians – joining in with the daily prayers at dawn and dusk, and trying to seem cheerful about their great victory over the Demon Witch.

They had slain the monster that had killed King Gahad, the Gunstians were saying, and that meant Chadura had blessed them; that she was looking upon their heroic endeavours with approval; that she valued the sacrifice made by the hundreds of soldiers who had already martyred themselves against the Empire and the Dominion. For a group of men and women who knew they were going to die, they were surprisingly cheerful. It was their faith; they each believed that to die for Chadura would guarantee them a place by her side in the Gunstian afterlife. What was a little pain and suffering, when set against the rewards to come?

Another raid had been sent out on the second day, but Karalyn had been told to rest by her superior officers. They could see that she was too tired to be of much use, they had told her; and they wanted to preserve her life for a coming victory parade in Great Gunst. And so four Gifted agents had departed the field encampment, along with three hundred soldiers. Less than five minutes later, the four Gifted had returned with the two Quadrants they had used to open the portal, but every one of the soldiers had been left behind – to kill until they fell, just as they had been commanded to do. None of the remaining soldiers seemed disturbed by this; if anything, they were slightly envious that their fallen comrades would already be in Chadura's presence.

The raid had been on a military base on Aucteran; the focus switching to that continent in order to preserve an element of surprise. It had been then that Karalyn had learned that the Gunstian encampment itself was also on Aucteran, though in a remote, uninhabited corner of that land. The Gunstians found this amusing, that they were based so close to their great enemy, without the Aucterians having the slightest notion of where they had pitched their tents.

If Kyra was searching for her, as Karalyn desperately hoped she was, then how long would it take before she decided to look on Aucteran? It was so unlikely that Karalyn had given up hope of being found quickly. She was due to be transported to Great Gunst at some point, and that represented a far greater hope of being found, for Kyra was bound to concentrate her efforts there.

One of the other Gifted agents, a man by the name of Aitan, approached and sat down on the cold grass next to her.

'How are you feeling, Galina?' he said.

Karalyn smiled. 'I am well, thank you; very well.'

'You don't look it,' he said. 'A few of us have been speaking to the officers about your health. We're worried about you. It's too cold and damp for a woman of your age to be camping and sleeping outside.'

'Chadura will preserve me,' said Karalyn.

'No doubt,' said Aitan, 'but let us not test her. After we gave the colonel our concerns, he has decided to transfer you back to Great Gunst today. By this evening, you will be in a nice warm apartment, drinking wine and eating lavish dinners.'

'Today?' said Karalyn. 'I am going to Great Gunst today?'

'Indeed. The victory parade is being prepared, and will take place tomorrow. The Demon Witch's body has already been taken to Great Gunst, to the Temple of the Holy Mother.'

Karalyn wanted to ask who had done this, and when, but to do so would only show her ignorance of matters they all assumed she understood.

'The officers want to know,' Aitan went on, 'if you will be able to participate in the parade. You were the Gifted agent who immolated the body of the Demon Witch, Galina; were it not for you, she might have escaped. The government is expecting you to take a leading role in the celebrations, but the officers here are concerned that it might be too much for you.'

'I will be fine,' she said. 'Tell the officers that I will be proud to play my part.'

Aitan smiled. 'That's excellent news; thank you. Is there anything you need?'

'Another blanket?' she said.

Aitan laughed as he got to his feet. 'I will see to it, Galina.'

She watched as he walked away to a sergeant's tent. He held a quick conversation with a few soldiers, then one of them hurried over with a thick, dry blanket for her. The soldier bowed low, his gaze averted, as he handed the blanket to her.

'Thank you,' she said.

'It's an honour to serve you, Lady Galina,' said the soldier; 'a true honour.'

Karalyn smiled, then she placed the blanket over her knees. She sipped from the cup of green tea, relieved that she would soon be leaving the damp and miserable environment of the encampment, but also anxious about what would happen to her in Great Gunst. It had been very fortunate that none of the other Gifted agents had known Galina very well prior to the raids being launched, but there would be people in Great Gunst who would view her as a close friend; and there might also be family there waiting for her. What if Galina had adult children? What if she had a husband? Anyone who knew her well would realise that she had changed, and she again cursed the fact that she had obliterated the old woman's memories.

The rest of the day passed quietly. The soldiers did some drills, and trained with loosing crossbows in formation, while a few officers came and went, using their Quadrants to travel to wherever they were going. Karalyn spent the time trying to unravel the mystery of how her Gift worked. Or was it Gifts? She had only seen Galina use the Gift of Immolation, but could she have had others? Karalyn had sat in silent meditation for hours, focussing all of her thoughts on to the mind she was now inhabiting. Most things seemed to be in the correct place. Her normal human senses were the same, as was the part of her mind used to store memories. The difference lay in where she would have expected to see mage powers. She assumed that Nathaniel had simply copied the powers of the gods when he had first created mortal mages – that was the sensible thing to do; but Theodora had done something else when she had made mortal humans with Gifts.

Ever since Karalyn had been studying with Elbannon in Tell Hoard, she had presumed that Theodora had created Athumia for the sole purpose of allowing the gods to build an unceasing supply of Quadrants – Tempest, the Zamatan Coil, the Serpent Eye jewels – all of them were available for those who knew how to find them; but the Thirteen Gifts seemed even more remarkable. She recalled reading a book in Igatz about the Gifts but, at the time, she had been in Lyla's body, and she had forgotten almost everything she had learned. She had seen no need to remember anything about the Gifts; what use were they to her when she had been using the Sextant to create new worlds?

She ate her lunch and her dinner in a large catering tent, where cooks dished out lumps of bread and bowls of thick broth to the hundreds of soldiers. As a Gifted agent, Karalyn had wondered if she would receive special rations, but she had been served the same food as everyone else. When dinner was over, she was making her way back to her tent when she was approached by a group of the senior military officers in command of the encampment. Karalyn wasn't sure of their names, but she knew which one was the colonel.

'Good evening, my lady,' said one of the officers.

'Good evening,' said Karalyn.

'I trust that you have been told about your imminent return to Great Gunst,' he went on. 'We are ready to take you now.'

'I am looking forward to recovering my strength,' she said, 'so that I can take part in more raids.'

The colonel smiled. 'We understand that this has been a great strain for you, my lady,' he said. 'You could have been killed by the Demon Witch.'

'I would not have minded that,' she said. 'There is no greater honour than to die for the blessed Chadura.'

'Of course, my lady,' the colonel said; 'however, you are a very valuable asset to the Gunstian Empire, and Chadura would not wish you to throw your life away. She gave you a Gift for a reason, and so your life must be protected.'

Another officer produced a Quadrant from a pocket. Karalyn gazed at it. She saw the symbols etched onto its copper surface and, at once, realised that she could remember how to use it. But would it speak to her while she was in Galina's body? She longed to know the truth; she longed to reach out to touch it, but knew she couldn't.

'Where in Great Gunst shall we be going?' she said.

'To the Temple of the Great Mother, my lady,' said the officer with the Quadrant. 'You have been assigned a suite of rooms there. I will take you now.'

'Farewell, my lady,' said the colonel. 'I hope you are feeling better soon.'

Karalyn inclined her head at the colonel, then the other officer activated the Quadrant. The air shimmered, and they appeared on a long, wide loggia overlooking the main square in the centre of Great Gunst. In the middle of the square, a massive pyre had been constructed from timber beams, and it was being guarded on all four sides by soldiers. To the right of the unlit pyre, a great queue of Gunstian youths had formed – a queue so long that it stretched around the entire perimeter of the square. The queue terminated in a row of desks, where officers and clerks sat, and those who had reached the front were then led away along another street. Beyond the queue, down a street to the right, lay a large blackened heap of rubble, partly overgrown with bushes. It was the Temple of the Martyrs; the temple Cael had obliterated. She turned her attention back to the square.

'Is the pyre for the Demon Witch's body?' she asked the officer.

'Yes, my lady,' he said; 'and this is where you will be standing for the majority of tomorrow's ceremony. I thought I would bring you here first, so that you could see the preparations.'

'Why are all those people queuing?' she said.

He gave her a strange look. 'My lady, they are volunteering for martyr operations; do you not recall seeing them a few days ago before we left for the encampment?'

'I think the last little while has become mixed up in my mind,' she said. 'I am trying to pretend that I am fine, but I feel as though I am in a daze.'

He nodded, his expression becoming more sympathetic. 'We shall ensure that you are fully rested tonight, my lady. Perhaps a good night's sleep is what you need.'

'Thank you,' she said, her gaze remaining on the long queue of young people volunteering to die for Chadura.

'I have something to show you, my lady,' he said; 'would you follow me?'

He gestured to the arched openings behind them in the outer wall of the temple, and they passed through one. Priests, soldiers and officials were lining the walls, and they applauded Karalyn as she passed between them.

'Praise Chadura,' said Karalyn, 'for she guided my Gift.'

She was led into a small prayer hall, where more priests were waiting. They had gathered around a table, and were inspecting something.

'Your Excellencies,' said the officer, 'I have brought Lady Galina to view our newest relic.'

The robed priests moved aside to allow Karalyn to get close to the table.

'It has not long been finished,' said a priest. 'The goldsmiths have done a fabulous job.'

Karalyn glanced down. Upon a cushion of purple velvet sat a golden skull, perfectly gilt and encrusted with jewels, some of which seemed to shine with their own light.

'Behold, Lady Galina,' said a priest, 'the gilded skull of the Demon Witch.'

Karalyn's eyes widened. Was she gazing at the gold-plated skull of the head that had been hers only a few days before? Albany's head? The thought made her feel sick, and she struggled to maintain her sense of composure.

'If her accursed son ever returns to Gunst,' said another priest, 'I pray that he sees this and despairs.'

'On our next raid upon the Empire, Your Excellencies,' said the army officer, 'we intend to let the benighted people there know that we have slain their champion.'

'That lifts my heart,' said a priest, 'but say no more, I beg you – the less we know about the raids, the better. Knowing that we are being avenged is reward enough.'

The officer tilted his head. 'I shall now escort Lady Galina to her rooms for the night, Your Excellencies.'

'Rest well, Lady Galina,' said a priest. 'Tomorrow shall be a busy day.'

'Thank you, Your Excellencies,' said Karalyn.

She followed the officer out of the prayer hall, and they ascended a flight of stairs to a part of the great temple where guests were quartered. The officer opened the door, and gave her a tour. She had her own bathroom, though there was no running water, and her own small chapel for private prayer; but far more importantly, she had a large, comfortable-looking bed.

'There is fresh fruit and chilled water on the table for you, my lady,' said the officer. 'Is there anything else you require?'

'Not just now, thank you,' she said.

The officer bowed low. 'Then I shall see you in the morning, my lady; good night.'

Karalyn remained still, with her hands clasped by her waist, as the officer left her rooms; then her shoulder sagged, and her composure almost crumbled. She walked over to the bed and sat down on the thick mattress. The room was being lit by two wall lamps, and she knew she should blow them out and undress before going to bed, but she was so tired that she stretched out on to the blanket fully clothed, and was asleep within seconds.

. . .

Her dreams were incoherent and jumbled, full of unknown terrors and the threat of imminent violence; then they stilled and went quiet. Her dream vision arose from the silence, and Karalyn broke down in relief. She gazed at the body of the old woman sleeping on the bed.

That was her, she told herself; that was who she was now.

But she was still Karalyn, and she knew what she had to do. Her vision soared upwards, leaving the massive Temple of the Great Mother, until she was looking down on the urban sprawl of Great Gunst, by far the largest city on Athumia. Its suburbs stretched out for miles, having outgrown the city walls years before. The river that had once wound by its western flank had a new, rapidly-growing suburb on its opposite bank, and the battlefield where King Naghad had been executed was covered in brick houses. Millions resided in the great city of Gunst, and Karalyn remembered the long, winding queue of young men and women who were volunteering to fight and die for Chadura. The city held almost inexhaustible supplies of such volunteers; and then there were the millions more who lived all over the territory of the Gunstian Empire. Their faith united them, along with their hatred of the Dominion and the Sapphire Empire, and their willingness to die for their god.

Karalyn turned to the east, and her vision shot out, speeding above the land until everything became a blur. She broke over the coast, and across the great expanse of the ocean, then she reached Inopei. She passed over the lands of the Dominion, then the rebuilt city of Sat Orma, and her vision slowed when she saw the palaces of Nom Karta.

She looked for her daughter, and found her sitting upon her own bed, her legs crossed under her, and the Compass held within her hands.

She entered Kyra's mind.

I am here, daughter; I am alive.

Kyra blinked. *Mother?*

Aye, it's me. Albany is dead.

And you took another body?

How did you know?

Cael could not see you with the Sextant.

Cael should not have been anywhere near the Sextant. Why did you allow him to...

Please be quiet, Mother, said Kyra. *I took him to the Sextant; it was my idea. What else were we supposed to do? You vanished days ago.*

Karalyn fell silent. Her daughter was right – it was churlish of her to get angry over her son's use of the Sextant, and all that implied. Her unnamed home had been trespassed upon, and the view that had been meant only for her had been seen by others. Did any of that matter? She had lost all of Albany's powers, and she needed her daughter's help.

Will you come for me? she said.

Where are you, Mother?

Great Gunst.

But I have already looked there.

I arrived a short time ago. I am in the Temple of the Great Mother, in the guest quarters on an upper floor.

I will find you.

Please be careful, daughter, she said. *I will be unable to help you. I have lost every power but dream vision, and I can only do this because I am sleeping.*

Then wake yourself up, and be ready.

Kyra broke off the connection, something she wouldn't have been able to do had Karalyn still been in Albany's body, and Karalyn stirred on the bed. Her eyes opened, and she sat up, feeling groggy and terrible. One of her wall lamps had gone out, but the other was still flickering its light in the bedroom. Karalyn sat on the bed, and waited.

As the minutes passed, Karalyn thought she felt a presence come and go in her mind – was that Kyra checking it was really her? – then the air shimmered in the room, and her daughter appeared.

'Kyra,' said Karalyn.

'Mother. At least you look older than me now; the way it should be. But why did you choose this body?'

'I didn't intend to make it my new home,' she said. 'It was as though I created a space for my consciousness, and it moved in.'

Kyra narrowed her eyes. 'Stand up, Mother.'

Karalyn eased herself off the bed and placed her feet onto the floor, her knees and back aching. The air shimmered, and she appeared inside another bedroom, the one where she had found her daughter.

'We are in Nom Karta,' said Kyra. 'Are you Gifted? Are you in the body of the woman by the portal? She had the Gift of Immolation, if I recall what happened correctly.'

'Aye; I'm her,' said Karalyn. 'Her name was Galina. I have tried to access her Gift, but I have not been successful.'

'Maybe Arrosa can help with that,' said Kyra. 'Unless...'

'Unless what?

'There is one solution to this problem, Mother,' she said; 'an obvious solution. If this body were to be destroyed, your spirit would once again be free.'

'And then what – I live as a ghost?'

'Would that be better or worse than living in a body that does not respond to your powers?'

'I am mortal again, Kyra, and this body is old. I see no need to hurry up the process of death; it will come in its own time.'

'But...'

'This body is better than no body, daughter. I will not kill myself. I need time to rest and think.'

'Then I have one question for you, Mother – if you remain in this body, will you be able to keep the peace between the worlds?'

'I will not kill myself, Kyra,' she repeated. 'Everything else is just details.'

'Very well,' said Kyra. 'Let us inform Edgar of your change in... circumstances.'

She walked to the door, and Karalyn set off after her, but her steps were slow, and her knees ached with each movement.

Kyra turned back to gaze at her, and frowned.

'Stay behind me at first,' she said; 'and try to remain out of sight. I might need a moment or two to lead up to the big announcement.'

Kyra opened the door, and Karalyn looked through the entrance into a large drawing room, where four people were sitting around a low table. Edgar was reclining in his chair, his eyes dark, while Elmhirst was more agitated. He was leaning forward, as he and Konna listened to the man who was sitting next to them, a man who was speaking loudly and gesticulating with both arms.

Kyra narrowed her eyes. 'Would someone please tell me why Naxor is in my apartment?' she said. 'Who let him in?'

Naxor stopped talking, then he got to his feet and bowed low. 'Lady Kyra, how lovely to see you again.'

Kyra glared at him.

'He's Konna's uncle,' said Edgar, 'and Konna asked if he could visit. I didn't see the problem.'

'Where are the boys?'

'In bed,' said Edgar. 'It's late.'

'I assume you have had no luck in finding your mother, my lady?' said Elmhirst.

'Pour me a brandy,' said Kyra.

'We have whisky, my lady,' said Naxor, as he plucked a bottle from the low table. 'Some of the finest produce Marchbrae has to offer. Now, I was just telling Lord Edgar and Lord Elmhirst about the tremendous opportunities that lie ahead of us. Now that Konna has reconciled with her mother, I can see great scope for improving relations between Marchbrae and the Dominion.'

He filled a glass with whisky and passed it to Kyra.

'Fill another glass,' said Kyra.

Naxor raised an eyebrow. 'Thirsty, are you? You can have the whole bottle, my dear Kyra.'

'It's not for me,' said Kyra. Her gaze went to Karalyn, who had been lurking by the door.

The others glanced in Karalyn's direction.

Elmhirst frowned. 'How did a servant get past us without being seen?'

Kyra seemed to take a moment to prepare herself, then she gestured towards Karalyn.

'I would like to introduce my mother to you all,' she said. 'She has a new body.'

Karalyn limped into the drawing room. 'I would very much like a whisky,' she said. 'Kyra, could you help me to a seat?'

Kyra placed her arm round Karalyn's waist, and guided her to a chair, as the others stared in silence.

'No,' said Konna. 'Is this a trick?'

'I can see into this woman's thoughts,' said Elmhirst. 'She believes herself to be Karalyn, but I cannot fathom it. If it were truly her, then why isn't she blocking my powers?'

'Oh my word,' said Naxor. 'How the pendulum swings.'

He filled another glass with whisky, and smiled as he passed it to Karalyn.

'Thank you, Naxor,' she said.

'It was quite literally my pleasure, Karalyn,' said Naxor. 'Do you have any powers at all?'

'I have a Gift, but I don't know how to use it,' she said.

'What a day of wonders!' cried Naxor. 'The mighty Karalyn Holdfast – reduced to a feeble and defenceless old Gunstian woman. I do believe that you are at our mercy, Karalyn. Wait a moment – I know the Gunstian word for sleep.'

Naxor pointed at her, and Karalyn's eyes closed, as an overwhelming urge to fall asleep passed through her mind. She awoke moments later to the sound of her daughter shouting.

'You nasty little bastard, Naxor,' she was saying. 'If you do that again, I will rip your mind to pieces.'

Naxor was laughing so hard that tears were spilling down his cheeks. 'I couldn't resist.'

Kyra crouched by Karalyn. 'Are you all right, Mother? Look into my eyes.'

Karalyn did so, then she felt her daughter's powers permeate her thoughts.

'I have shielded you, Mother,' Kyra said. 'No one will be able to read your thoughts, apart from Cael and I – but there isn't much I can do about that. Naxor won't be able to send you to sleep again.'

'You spoil all the fun,' said Naxor.

'Be quiet, Naxor,' said Edgar. 'What you did was rude and uncalled for. But this... this changes much. What does it mean for the peace?'

'That is a very good point, my lord,' said Elmhirst. 'We should be prepared for the worst. Without Karalyn to guarantee the treaty, I fear that the Sapphire Empire might try to take advantage.'

'Are all of your memories intact, Karalyn?' said Edgar.

'Aye,' she said. 'I can remember everything. Is Esher on Zamata?'

'He is,' said Edgar.

'Esher's powers now outweigh my own,' she said. 'As an Ascendant, and as my arbiter of the peace, it will be up to him to ensure that the treaty is not breached.'

'We had best let him know,' said Kyra.

'I want to tell my sister first,' said Karalyn. 'Kyra, please take me to Colsbury.'

CHAPTER 16
NOT A PATIENT WOMAN

Marchside, Kell – 16th Day, First Third Summer 560

Lindi powered her battle-vision as the rain pelted against her face. She picked up a large timber post, and rammed it into the hole Carter had dug, driving it deep into the soil by the edge of the field. Carter moved next to her with a crossbeam. Lindi held it in place, and Carter hammered three nails into the wood, securing it to the new fence post.

'Believe it or not,' Carter said, as the rain lashed them, 'summer isnae always as bad as this.'

'Shut up and keep hammering,' said Lindi.

Carter laughed as he secured the other crossbeam, then they stood back.

'Will that keep the sheep in?' said Lindi.

'Aye, until the wind blows down another section of fence.' He gazed around. 'This rain isnae helping the barley, but. We need some sunshine to dry off the fields; otherwise, the harvest will be shite this year.'

'Does no barley mean no whisky?'

'It means that the distillery will have to buy in barley from somewhere else,' he said; 'and that costs money. Come on; we can get a cup of tea and dry off in the shepherd's hut.'

They walked along a path that lay between two fields, and entered a small, two-roomed wooden shack by the side of a road. Lindi shook her head as soon as they were indoors, and water dripped from her hair. There was a small wood stove, and Carter knelt by it. He picked up a box of matches and lit the kindling, then he set a kettle onto it. They sat, and both lit cigarettes.

'Do you think you'll still be working on this farm a hundred years from now?' said Lindi.

'Aye, maybe,' he said.

She gave him a mocking smile. 'Then it's all just talk, is it? All talk and no action?'

He eyed her.

'You are always saying that it was a great crime what happened to Cairney,' Lindi went on, 'but you don't seem prepared to do anything about it. Are you just going to let him languish in exile? Some brother you are. If Joss was taken from me, I would never rest until he was safe. Never.'

'There's fuck all I can do about it,' he said. 'Only Karalyn knows where Cairney is being held. To get to Cairney, I would have to discover something that no one else has been able to do – I'd have to find the Sextant. And then, even if I did that, I doubt I'd be able to use it. Hardly anyone can operate the Sextant, but how would I find the world where Cairney is without it? I've read a lot about this, and I know that the Sextant was designed to be used only by the Ascendants.'

'My mother can use it,' said Lindi. 'She has used it many times.'

'Aye; that's right,' said Carter, 'and, of course, Karalyn can use it, her son Cael, too. But that's it; that's the full list of people able to operate it. Not even Kyra can use it.'

'I reckon I could operate it,' Lindi said. 'How hard could it be?'

'It's not a matter of skill,' he said; 'it either talks to you or it doesn't. But, it does talk to yer mother, so maybe there's a small chance that it'd talk to you as well.'

Lindi's eyes gleamed. 'We should look for it, Carter. We should look for the Sextant and, when we find it, we should release Cairney.'

Carter snorted. 'Why do you give a shit? He's not your brother.'

'What Naxor was saying the other day,' she said, 'it struck home. The Empire should be ours – it should be ruled by the immortal Holdfasts.'

'Did you miss the part when Naxor said we should wait for a hundred years before acting?'

'I heard that bit, but I am choosing to ignore it. Why do we have to wait? Why can't we do it now? Look at me, Carter – I am going to be the Empress; do you hear me? When the Holdfast gods take over, the throne will be mine. It's my turn to wear the blue.'

Carter laughed. 'I think Cairney might have other ideas, cousin.'

'I will allow Cairney to help me,' she said. 'He can be my general, the commander of my great armies. There will be huge portraits of me in every town and city of the Empire, and anyone who refuses to worship me will be punished.'

'Ye do make me laugh, Lindi.'

'I was being serious,' she said. 'The Marchbrae Holdfasts shall be rewarded if they help me take the throne. Even you, Carter; I'll find something for you to do. You can scrub my floors.'

'Then what do you need Cairney for, eh?' he said. 'If yer so fucking wonderful, why don't ye take the throne on yer own?'

'I do need help; I realise that. But I can't get the vision that Naxor conjured out of my head. There are eight immortal gods among the Marchbrae Holdfasts, and…'

'We're demigods,' said Carter; 'and there are ten of us, if ye include Ma and Uncle Naxor.'

'All right; ten demigods; and then there's Caitlyn and Carden in Plateau City – we can't ignore them, so we'll either have to get them to join us, or they'll have to be eliminated.'

'Yer not thinking big enough,' he said. 'If we had the Sextant under our control, all we'd have to do is send Caitlyn and Carden to an isolated world. We wouldnae have to kill them. We could move entire populations around; we could create our own worlds – one for each of the Holdfasts. Let's face it – we could do whatever the fuck we liked.'

'I knew you'd thought about this,' she said.

'I've spent far too much time thinking about it, Lindi,' he said, as the kettle whistled. 'Kelsey's book on history is completely biased,' he went on, as he poured hot water into two cups; 'but she detailed a lot of the things that have been done with the Sextant. Tens of thousands were saved from Lostwell by Belinda, for example, and she'd never used the Sextant before; well, not since she had been scoured. Edmond used the Sextant to destroy Implacatus, killing millions. Yer Ma used it to send the Wystian dragons to a wee island...'

'Rigga,' said Lindi. 'She sent them to Rigga.'

'Aye, but they escaped, and then Karalyn sent them to a different world, a hidden world. If we had the Sextant, we could find the Wystians, if we wanted to. Karalyn also did something else – she sent all of Edmond's gods to a world that she then destroyed – that was fucking ruthless. She could have exiled them, but no – she massacred them instead. That's what we're up against, Lindi. Karalyn is a cold-blooded killer, and there's no way she'd allow us to get our hands on the Sextant.'

'Karalyn hates violence,' said Lindi. 'Everyone knows that.'

'I don't believe it,' he said. 'That's what we're taught, but can we trust anything written by Kelsey? She's the fucking Herald of the Empire; of course she's twisted the narrative to suit her agenda. She would be stupid not to. The other history books are the same – written by people in important positions of power.'

'Then why do you bother reading them?' she said. 'The inside of your bedroom looks like a bleeding library, Carter. Is that why you've found it hard to find a girlfriend?'

'I don't want to waste my time with mortal girls,' he said.

'Why not? Not even for some fun?'

'I've been out with plenty of the local lassies from Marchside,' he said. 'They bored me. I need someone more challenging.'

'I'll find you someone when I become Empress. Fuck it – you can have your own harem.'

Carter rolled his eyes. 'Drink yer tea, Lindi.'

Lindi slurped hot tea from her cup, and wondered what kind of god she would end up marrying. He would need to be as tall and strong as Carter or her brother Joss, but not in a way that reminded her of either of them.

'I wonder what Elmhirst is like,' she said. 'He's the last Ancient.'

'I know who he is,' said Carter.

'Of course you do, you fucking know-it-all; but have you ever met him?'

'No.'

'My mother has met him a few times, but they were usually trying to kill each other. All the same, I would have to make certain enquiries before I was willing to let him seduce me.' She grimaced. 'I mean, I couldn't bear the thought that... that...'

'That he might be yer father?'

'I want to throw up now,' she said. 'This is becoming a problem for me. How can I ever look at a god in that way, without being terrified that I might be his daughter?'

'Have ye told yer mother this?'

'I have asked her many times, but I have never framed it like that.'

'Ye should. When she realises how ye feel, she'll have to tell ye. Ye cannae live like that; not knowing.'

They finished their tea, and Lindi got up to look out of the window.

'The sun is out and the rain has stopped,' she said.

'Let's get our arses up the hill before it starts again,' said Carter.

He dropped their cups into a sink and gave them a quick wash with the warm water from the kettle; then he set them onto the drying rack. He opened the front door of the shack, and they walked outside into the sunshine.

'This is more like it,' said Carter. 'And look – the sky to the west is clear.'

'So?'

'The weather rolls in from the ocean, Lindi,' he said, 'and the ocean lies to the west. I can tell ye right now that the rain is done for the next few hours; maybe longer, if we're lucky. We can change into dry clothes in the farmhouse before we head out for this afternoon's work.'

They set off along the path that led up the hill to the house. The wind was still blowing, but for once it had a hint of warmth in it, and Lindi smiled as she gazed at the raw beauty of the Kell landscape.

'The sunlight changes everything about Kell,' she said. 'It's so beautiful, but only when the sun is out.'

'I find beauty in the greys as well,' he said. 'The dark clouds and the long nights have a poetry about them, and the farm and hills are majestic in the snow. When everything is a perfect white, and yer boots sink deep into the drifts; it sometimes makes me want to weep for the joy of it.'

'You should spend a few days on Dragon Eyre,' she said. 'A few days would be enough to appreciate what it's like all year round.'

'I don't think I'd like somewhere that doesn't change with the seasons,' he said. 'I would miss the rhythm of the year.'

They reached the top of the hill and entered the farmhouse. As they were taking off their boots and coats, Lindi heard the sound of raised voices coming from the kitchen.

'It sounds as though Uncle Naxor is excited about something,' Carter muttered.

'Either that or he is in pain,' said Lindi, 'from all the shrieking he's making.'

They walked through the house and into the kitchen. Aila was sitting by the kitchen table, as Naxor was pacing up and down the floor, his eyes wild with enthusiasm, and his hands gesturing.

He gazed at Carter and Lindi, and beamed at them.

'O happy day!' he cried. 'What wonders I have to tell you. Sit. Go on; sit down, both of you.'

'Naxor has got himself into a bit of a tizzy,' said Aila.

'And who would begrudge me that, my fine cousin?' said Naxor. 'Sit,

Carter; yes, and you, Lindi. You will need to be seated in order to hear what I have to say.'

Carter and Lindi eyed each other, then they took seats by Aila at the table.

'This sounds as though it could be exciting,' said Lindi. 'Has Thorn dropped down dead?'

'No, this has nothing to do with our dearly-beloved and gracious Empress. My news is of far greater import. Are you ready? Someone else has died. Someone we all know. Now, for most people, death brings a certain finality, but this person has died before; this was her third death, in fact.'

Carter's eyes widened. 'Karalyn?'

'Indeed, my boy,' said Naxor. 'The mightiest being in existence has had her head chopped off by a Gunstian. Who would have believed it?'

'Has she found another body?' said Carter.

'She has,' said Naxor, then he started to laugh. He wheezed and coughed, one hand on his knee, as gales of laughter left his lips.

The others watched him for a while, then Aila slapped him on the back a few times.

Naxor sat down, still laughing, though he was no longer shaking.

'Listen carefully,' he said. 'Karalyn, in her undoubted wisdom, has for some reason decided to take the body of a very elderly Gunstian mortal woman; a woman with no self-healing, no vision, and no powers of any kind. Nothing. She has reduced herself to a feeble mortal. She can barely hobble about on her legs, never mind transport herself with a mere thought. Elmhirst and I were able to get into her thoughts, and...'

'Elmhirst?' said Lindi.

'Yes, I was in Nom Karta; I have just returned. I was there when Kyra retrieved the Gunstian version of Karalyn from Great Gunst. I was with Elmhirst, Edgar and Konna, and we were having a very productive chat when Kyra appears with this doddering old lady standing next to her. We all assumed she was a servant.' He started to laugh again. 'And then

I sent Karalyn to sleep; can you imagine? It was one of the greatest moments of my life.'

'It was one of the most stupid moments, you mean,' said Carter. 'As soon as Karalyn gets herself a better body, she will make you pay for that, Uncle.'

'Don't ruin the moment, Carter,' said Naxor. 'I fear Karalyn has a lot more to worry about than a silly trick carried out by me.'

'But her mind is now open?' said Lindi.

'Not any more,' said Naxor. 'Kyra sealed it up nice and tight, after she threatened to turn my brain into mush.'

'Where is she now?' said Aila.

'Kyra took her to Colsbury at dawn this morning. Karalyn wanted to go last night, but the poor old dear realised that she was too tired, and so Kyra found her a bed. I was only in Karalyn's mind for the briefest of moments before Kyra sealed it, but I saw her fear and confusion. She knows she has made a most dreadful error; an egregious error, the consequences of which shall reverberate around the Known Worlds. Elmhirst is already making plans to repel an expected invasion by the Empire of the Sapphire Throne; and who knows what Thorn and Kelsey will make of it?' He gazed at the others. 'I smell an opportunity.'

'What are you talking about?' said Carter. 'Don't dance around it, Uncle – tell me what you are planning. Does it involve rescuing Cairney from exile? If it does, then I want to be part of it. With Cairney back, we could overthrow the government of the Empire, and take over. Are we going to hunt down the Sextant?'

'Steady yourself, Carter,' said Naxor. 'I spoke of opportunity, not a reckless revolution that could end very badly for us. Now is the time for clear thinking. Ponder your own words from a moment ago – there is no doubt that Karalyn's body will soon expire of old age; and then, if she decides to take a more powerful form, her revenge against us would be swift indeed. I was talking more of incremental manoeuvrings; stealing a bit more power here, taking some more advantage there. The Hold Fast estate, for instance – now is the perfect time for Killop to push forward in his campaign to become the next Holder. There are also opportunities in Nom Karta to increase our influence there. The point is that, by the time Karalyn has recovered from this setback, we should be in a far stronger position overall.'

'You speak very well, Naxor,' said Lindi.

'Thank you,' he said.

'But you said almost nothing of any use,' she went on. 'If this is a great opportunity, as you say it is, then all you seem to be planning is a little tinkering around the edges. I have a better idea – we strike now, while Karalyn is incapacitated. We rescue Cairney from exile, and then I seize the throne.'

Naxor sighed. 'And for how long would you be able to sit upon it, Lindi?' he said. 'Karalyn will likely come back stronger than ever.'

'What if I am able to use the Sextant?' said Lindi. 'My mother can, so why not me? I could send Karalyn to a remote world that is cut off from the others. Let us do to her what she did to Cairney.'

'She would be able to escape when her mortal Gunstian body died of natural causes,' said Naxor, 'as her immortal spirit would be able to roam free. And what if Karalyn recovers her full abilities when she takes hold of a new body? She would be able to return to this world with a mere thought. Karalyn is not going away. We could kill her a hundred times over, and she would return every time. This time, she has returned in an enfeebled state, but I have no doubt that she will learn from this.' He frowned. 'If I was Laverne, I would be getting quite worried around now.'

'Who is Laverne?' said Lindi.

'She's a goddess released by Bailey from the Palace of the Almighty,' said Carter.

'She is the most powerful goddess in the Dominion,' said Naxor; 'a granddaughter of Edmond; not quite an Ancient, but not far off it. I imagine that Karalyn might already be eyeing her up for the future.'

'What a disgusting thought,' said Aila.

'What do you think we should do, Ma?' said Carter.

'We should do absolutely nothing,' said Aila; 'as this is none of our business. A few years ago, I might have been laughing along with

Naxor, but now I am worried about the stability of the peace. Marchbrae's success depends upon a peaceful and secure Empire, and I don't want anything to jeopardise that. When, one day, the immortal Holdfasts inherit the Empire, we shall have to work with Karalyn, not against her. It would be extremely unwise to act against her at this stage; she will never forgive us if we betray her at her weakest.'

Lindi frowned, though she could see the logic of Aila's words.

'But I want to be Empress,' she said.

'If that is your true desire, Lindi,' said Aila, 'then I suggest that you offer your services to Karalyn. She will need a protector and, in years to come, she will remember that you helped her when she most needed it.'

Lindi was about to retort when the air shimmered and her mother appeared.

'I already know,' said Sable. 'I have just been on Colsbury; I have seen her.'

'Admit it, Sable,' said Naxor; 'did you laugh?'

Sable eyed him. 'Sorry to intrude like this, Aila. I wish there was a way I could tell you in advance that I was about to appear in your kitchen.'

'It's fine,' said Aila. 'You are always welcome here. I assume that you haven't come to talk about Karalyn?'

Sable sat down. 'What is there to say? I offered to put her out of her misery, but Karalyn was having none of it; so I gave her some salve, instead, to fix her aching knees. I give that body a decade.'

'Are you here to see me, Mother?' said Lindi.

'I am indeed,' said Sable. 'Your birthday is in seven days, and Lara and I have been talking about what to do.'

'There is only one thing I want for my birthday,' said Lindi: 'to be allowed to stay here for the whole summer.'

Carter smiled. 'You want to work on the farm for the entire summer?'

'I do,' she said. 'I would also like to do some other things as well, though, such as go to Threeways, and visit Severton; maybe go through the Brig Pass if the weather is all right. And I'd like to see where the battle was fought in the Kell Pass. Could I fit that in too, please, Lady Aila?'

'It's not up to me,' said Aila.

'Lara and I have a different idea,' said Sable. 'We have decided to collect you from Clackenbaird on your birthday, and take you back to Dragon Eyre. You can spend the morning of your birthday in Kell, and then, with Aila's permission, I will bring Lara and Joss here. We could maybe have a birthday lunch in the farmhouse, and then we will take you home.'

'I can agree to all that,' said Aila, 'but I would also be happy to allow Lindi to stay for the summer, if that's what you decide. I enjoy having her here. She is very high-spirited and has some rather odd opinions, but she has brightened up the house.'

'I'm afraid my mind is made up, Aila,' said Sable.

Lindi decided that a dramatic gesture was required. She got off her chair and went down onto her knees before her mother, her hands clasped together in supplication.

'Please, Mother,' she said, her eyes wide; 'I am begging you to let me stay here for the summer. Please. I am your only daughter and I love you so much, but this is what I want. I will come home at the beginning of autumn, and then I will do whatever you and Lara want of me. I will clean the heads of the *Mischief Maker* every day for a month, and I will never get into trouble again. I will be kind and considerate, and I will call Lara mother, if that's what you want. Please let me stay.'

Sable gazed down at her, and Lindi knew that her mother's will was crumbling. Lindi put on her most appealing look, her eyes welling slightly, and her lower lip quivering, and her mother had to look away.

'I am going to need you to give me the Quadrant you stole from Bedig,' Sable said.

'No, Mother,' said Lindi; 'that I shall not do.'

'Then you will have to return to Dragon Eyre on your birthday.'

'I won't be here on my birthday,' said Lindi. 'I will have fled, and you will never find me. You will have forced my hand, and I will have no choice but to hide myself in some remote corner of a world until you and Lara die. Please don't make me do this, Mother. Let me stay, and let me keep my Quadrant.'

'It is not *your* Quadrant.'

'It is now,' said Lindi. 'Did you give back any of the Quadrants you stole from the gods, Mother? I am the most powerful Holdfast god – I need a Quadrant. I deserve a Quadrant.'

'So first you beg,' said Sable, 'and now you are blackmailing me?'

'You are out of options, Mother,' said Lindi. 'Make your decision – let me stay, and I will be a dutiful daughter come the autumn; or threaten to take me home, and you will never see me again.'

Sable narrowed her eyes in anger, and got to her feet. 'Lara, Joss and I will be here on your birthday, Lindi,' she said. 'As for what happens after that, I'm going to leave it up to Lara; she can decide what to do with you. You had better be here, though. If you're not, I will hunt you down and drag you back to Dragon Eyre. Is that understood?'

'Yes, Mother.'

Sable nodded to Aila, put a hand into a pocket, and disappeared.

Lindi leapt to her feet, a huge grin on her face. 'Ha! Did you see that?'

'I certainly did,' said Naxor. 'It isn't every day that you get to see both Karalyn and Sable humbled. I rather enjoyed it.'

'It was unbecoming of you, Lindi,' said Aila. 'Your poor mother; how could you threaten to run away like that? And to tell her, a mortal, that you would hide until she was dead? That was cruel, Lindi.'

'But effective,' said Lindi. 'I didn't mean any of it; or maybe I did. All I have to do now is win over Lara, and I know exactly how to do that.'

'How, pray tell?' said Naxor.

Lindi smiled at him. 'By calling her *mother*,' she said. 'As soon as the words *Please, Mother* leave my lips, Lara's heart will melt, and she will give me whatever I want. It will be nice to see Joss, though; I am looking forward to you all meeting him. I think you'll like him.'

'If they allow you to stay,' said Aila, 'then I think I will spend the summer trying to teach you how to respect the feelings of others.'

Lindi laughed. 'Good luck with that.' She eyed Carter. 'Come on, cousin; don't we have work to do?'

'But I haven't had any lunch,' he said.

She gave him a look, and he rolled his eyes.

'Fine,' he said, getting to his feet. 'With any luck, the sun will dry off my clothes.'

He picked up an apple from a bowl, then he and Lindi walked out of the kitchen. Lindi whistled to herself as they pulled on their coats and laced up their boots, then they walked back outside into the sunshine.

Lindi breathed in the warm summer air of Kell, and gazed at the view.

'What are we doing first?' she said.

'We have a bull to move into a different field,' said Carter. 'We'll introduce him to a few lady cows.'

'And what shall we talk about on the way to this romantic destination?' she said. 'Wait – I know. Let's discuss how we are going to take advantage of Karalyn's mistake.'

She eyed her cousin. 'I have a throne waiting for me, Carter, and I am not a patient woman.'

CHAPTER 17
THE NEW THEOLOGY

Great Gunst, Gunstian Empire – 25th Abrinch 1613

Cael moved through the crowded streets close to the centre of Great Gunst.

You cannot see me.

Gunstian merchants were selling their wares at a line of stalls under a long canvas awning by the side of the road, and Cael noticed that the busiest stalls were those selling flowers. Great bunches of them were being taken away by citizens towards the central square where the Temple of the Great Mother lay. It was the direction in which Cael was already going, so he followed a large family as they carried their flowers along the busy street.

A great press of people was blocking the road ahead, and Cael recognised where he was. He skirted the back of the crowd, then he placed a hand into a pocket and activated his Quadrant. He appeared on the roof of a nearby building, and gazed down at the ruins of the Temple of the Martyrs. He had expected the site of the temple to have been cleared, but the mound of rubble he had created eight years before was still there. Bushes and shrubs had been allowed to grow on the blackened remains, and the edges of the site were covered in flowers. They were being placed there by the crowds, who were each waiting their turn to approach the ruins. They were kneeling on the roadside, praying aloud to Chadura, thanking their god for the great blessings she had bestowed upon them.

Cael heard Bailey's name being mentioned – the Gunstians referred to him as the *Great Betrayer*, then he heard the name of the *Demon Witch* being called out, as the Gunstians left their flowers by the ruined temple. Cael turned. He could see the vast open square ahead of him. To the left was the enormous Temple of the Great Mother, its balconies and loggias packed with priests and government officials. The square itself was full of people, chanting and praying around a tall, unlit pyre. Cael had come to Great Gunst to observe the long queues of those volunteering to be sent on martyrdom operations – a previous scouting expedition had identified them as assembling in the central square, and Cael had wished to follow them, to see if he could discover the location from where they were being dispatched to the Gunstian raiding camp. If he could find that, he might be able to locate the position of the camp itself, and he might even be able to retake one of the Quadrants the Empire had lost.

There were no queues of volunteers in the square that day, however – the packed crowds were there to watch the pyre being lit. But first, there were prayers and speeches to get through, and the crowds were listening to an archpriest speak from a balcony of the Temple of the Great Mother. Cael activated his Quadrant, and appeared by the edge of the largest balcony, a mere two yards from the nearest Gunstian priest.

You cannot see me.

'And let us bless the holy names of the martyrs who fell in the mighty struggle that ensued,' the archpriest was saying; 'and let us celebrate their sacrifice, for even now, they are sipping the blood-red wine of Chadura, and are honoured in her sacred presence. But it fell to one of the Gifted to subdue the beast in woman form; a sacred warrior of Chadura, whose Gift of Immolation devoured the demonic spirit from within, rendering flesh to ash; and behold! The body that now lies upon the pyre is that of the monstrous Demon Witch!'

The crowd roared and cheered.

A large, golden box was brought on to the balcony, and the priests put on white gloves, as though they did not wish their own flesh to touch whatever was being held with the reliquary. The box was opened, and an archpriest lifted up a golden skull. He raised it over his head, and the crowd began chanting.

'Death to the Empire; death to the Dominion; death to the Holdfasts!'

Over and over went the refrain, as the crowd whipped themselves into a frenzy of religious devotion. Cael ignored the sound, his gaze on the gilded skull.

He put his hand into his pocket, the air shimmered, and he appeared over twenty miles away, next to a cave where Cole and twelve Imperial Marines were waiting for him.

'Did you find the volunteers, sir?' said Cole.

Cael shook his head. 'There is no queue today,' he said. 'The square is busier than I have ever seen it – packed from one end to the other. They are celebrating the death of my mother.'

Cole emerged from the cave. 'I'm sorry, cousin. Are you certain?'

'The body of the Demon Witch has been placed onto a pyre,' said Cael, 'but the priests are keeping her skull as a prize. They have coated it in gold.'

'Bloody savages,' muttered one of the marines.

'What are your orders, sir?' said Cole.

Cael lit a cigarette. 'My sister and I already suspected what might have happened to our mother,' he said; 'and now we know. She was burned by the Gift of Immolation.'

'Should we report this to Colsbury?' said Cole.

'Not yet,' said Cael. 'We have been in Gunst for two days, searching for the location of the raiding camp, and I don't want to return home empty-handed. And after what I've just seen... I am in the mood for a little retribution.' He eyed the marines. 'Load your Battanaras and your Jackdaws. We will have time for one shot each from both weapons. Fire your Battanaras first, then pick off individual targets with your Jackdaw. Do not target the civilians in the square; restrict your actions to the priests and officials on the balconies of the temple. If they want a fucking show, we shall give them one.'

Cael smoked as the twelve marines got to work. The Mark Seven Battanaras were loaded first, then each marine primed the experimental Mark Two Jackdaws that had been distributed to them a few days before. They had yet to be used in anger by the forces of the Empire, and Rosie had asked Cael to report back to her on their reliability and accuracy. Cael picked up his own Jackdaw. The barrel was identical to the one he had seen before, but a wooden stock had been added to it as a handle. He loaded a solitary lead pellet into the Tempest-lined barrel, and then he fixed the small paper packet of Ectus powder into place by the trigger mechanism. No matches were required to fire the Jackdaw, and the marines were understandably dubious about whether they would work or not, or if they might even explode, as some of the earliest Battanaras had done.

'Are you sure about this?' Cole said to him. 'Our orders were to find the raiding camp, not strike at the heart of Great Gunst.'

'The Gunstians have hit Nom Karta twice, and Colsbury once,' said Cael. 'Perhaps they need to experience some pain in their own capital.' He turned to the marines. 'Two staggered lines,' he said. 'Jackdaws holstered; Battanaras on shoulders.'

The marines moved into position by the entrance to the cave, with Cole on one flank, and Cael on the other. Cael kept his loaded Jackdaw in his right hand, and the Quadrant in his left. He took a moment to breathe, trying to control his anger.

Cael activated the Quadrant, and they appeared on one end of the main balcony of the Temple of the Great Mother.

You cannot see us.

A senior Gunstian officer was standing three yards from where they had arrived, and Cael raised his Jackdaw, aimed, and fired. The lead pellet shot out of the barrel with a crack, and half of the officer's head was blown off from the impact.

'Battanaras!' shouted Cole, and all twelve fired at once. Amid the noise and smoke, the screams and destruction, Cael had difficulty seeing what was happening. He reloaded his Jackdaw, counting in his head to seven, and walked into the chaos. Part of the balcony had collapsed, and fires were starting to rage in the chambers just behind where the priests had been standing. The twelve Battanara projectiles had killed most of the people who had been on the balcony, but a few were staggering around, their clothes in tatters and covered in blood.

'Jackdaws!' Cael heard Cole shout through the smoke.

Cracks rippled through the air, and more Gunstians on the balcony fell. Down in the square, the crowds had descended into a crazed hysteria. They could see what was happening up on the balcony of the temple, but were powerless to intervene. Cael saw what he was looking for. He crouched down by the debris and scattered body parts, and picked up the golden skull. He shoved it into a bag tied to his belt, then he gazed at two priests who were trying to crawl away to safety, leaving smears of their own blood on the floor of the balcony. Cael raised his Jackdaw, and shot one through the head.

You can see me.

'I am Cael holdfast,' he said to the other priest, who was cowering and whimpering in terror. 'I am the son of the Demon Witch. Remember this day.'

He felt a hand on his shoulder, and saw Cole. Cael got to his feet, and they ran back to the marines. Cael activated the Quadrant. The air crackled, and they appeared on the island of Zamata, in the grounds of the monastery of Tsallon Anura, where they were due to meet Lord Elmhirst. The marines checked each other for injuries, but none of them had been harmed. Several were jubilant, and they began comparing stories of what they had done, and what they had seen.

'Rosie will be happy,' said Cole.

'Aye,' said Cael. He opened the bag by his belt, and pulled out the golden skull.

Cole's eyes widened.

'This is exactly what you think it is,' said Cael. 'My mother's head. Where is she now, cousin? She could be anywhere.'

Cole nudged him, and he turned to see Lord Elmhirst walking through the cloisters of the monastery.

'We were unsuccessful,' said Cael. 'We were trying to locate the volunteer martyrs, but the centre of Great Gunst was celebrating the death of my mother.' He held aloft the skull.

'But we did strike the Gunstian leadership,' said Cole. 'I estimate at least sixty casualties on their side – priests, officers, and government officials.'

'I am sure your marines performed very well, Secretary Cole,' said Elmhirst, 'but I have news from Nom Karta that you need to hear.' He pointed at the skull in Cael's hands. 'It concerns your mother.'

'Has Kyra found her?' said Cael.

'Found her, brought her back, and taken her to Colsbury, Adjutant Cael,' said Elmhirst. 'I can debrief your marines about the details of your raid; I will understand if you have to get yourself to Colsbury with all haste.'

'Thank you, Elmhirst,' said Cael.

'Wait a moment, sir,' said Cole. 'Is it wise to leave twelve Battanaras and twelve Jackdaws with the commander of the Dominion's armed forces?'

Elmhirst eyed him with a wry smile. 'We are not interested in the Empire's trinkets, Secretary Cole. Lord Edgar has made it absolutely clear that we are not to concern ourselves with these obscene new weapons; he sees them as an abomination. I will not be trying to steal any of your precious Battanaras or your... what were the other ones?'

Cael raised his side arm. 'The Mark Two Jackdaw,' he said.

'Ah,' said Elmhirst. 'Queen Blackrose's rider will be so proud.'

'Stay here, Cole,' said Cael. 'I will go back to Colsbury.'

'Before you go,' said Elmhirst, 'you should know that your mother's new body might not be as impressive as you were hoping for. Good luck, Adjutant.'

Cael triggered his Quadrant, and arrived on the middle balcony of the Summer Palace on Colsbury. It was raining, and the balcony was deserted. Cael glanced down into the forecourt, but it, too, was empty.

After the attack on the gardens, the Empress had ordered that all non-essential personnel leave the small island, and it felt more like how it had been during Cael's youth.

He walked off the balcony, placing the Jackdaw into its leather holster, and his Quadrant behind his leather breastplate. Several soldiers from the Imperial Guard came to attention as he passed them, then a courtier bowed and opened a door. Cael walked into one of the Empress's smaller audience chambers, where a few members of the Imperial Court were standing before the throne.

'Welcome back, Adjutant,' said the Empress, who was on her feet next to Kelsey.

Cael held up the gilded skull. 'Look what I found in Great Gunst, Your Majesty,' he said. 'Is my mother here?'

The Empress eyed him and the golden skull with a mixture of emotions. 'She is in the palace, Cael,' she said. 'Kyra brought her here this morning, after fetching her from Gunst last night. She is resting at the moment, after she was given some salve to ease her pains.'

'What pains?' he said.

'The usual mortal pains of getting old,' said Kelsey. 'She wasn't wounded or anything like that; just a bit worn out. The salve will help. Do you want to see her?'

'Aye,' said Cael.

Kelsey gestured to a doorway, then she and Cael bowed before the Empress and left the audience chamber.

'She's with Shella,' said Kelsey, as they walked along a passageway, 'and it's hard to tell which of them looks older.'

Cael frowned.

Kelsey opened a door, and led Cael into a comfortable drawing room. His sister was there, sitting opposite two elderly women. Kyra got to her feet, but Cael barely noticed, his gaze on the old woman sitting next to Shella.

'What have you done, Mother?' he said. 'Of all the bodies to have chosen, why this one?'

'There is nothing wrong with being old,' said Shella.

'Maybe for mortals like us,' said Cael; 'but my mother could have chosen any body she wanted – a god, a warrior – anyone.'

'I didn't mean to take this body, son,' said Karalyn.

'Your accent,' said Cael; 'it sounds a little strange, as though it has been mixed with Gunstian.'

'It has,' said Karalyn. 'I am in the body of the Gifted Gunstian who burned me as Albany.'

Cael lifted up the skull, and a tear rolled down his mother's face.

'I was shown that yesterday,' she said. 'I had to pretend I was the Gifted agent; I had to pretend to be overjoyed by my own death.'

Cael set the gilded skull onto the table and sat down. Kyra retook her seat next to him, and they glanced at each other.

'How bad is this?' said Cael. 'What consequences are we looking at?'

'The Empress is worried that the Dominion might use this as an opportunity to invade the Empire,' said Kyra, 'but let me tell you that nothing is further from Edgar's mind. In fact, Elmhirst believes it is far more likely that the Empire will invade the Dominion.'

'We are not going to invade the Dominion,' said Kelsey. 'The peace has been working well for us – why would we change that?'

Kyra raised an eyebrow. 'Are you sure about that, Aunty? I know the Empire covets the Tempest mine upon Inopei; are you certain that the Empress won't try to take advantage of my mother's absence?'

'I am not absent,' said Karalyn. 'I am here, in front of you.'

'I meant your absence as guarantor of the peace, Mother,' said Kyra.

'Is that true?' said Cael. 'Are you unable to guard the peace, Mother?'

'I have lost nearly all of my powers,' said Karalyn. 'I managed to use dream vision last night, which is how Kyra was able to find me, but I was sleeping. I cannot always be sleeping, son; and when I am awake, I can do nothing. I feel the loss of self-healing the most; I had started to take it for granted.'

'How old are you?' said Cael. 'How old is the body you have taken?'

'I don't know,' said Karalyn. 'I destroyed the memories of the woman who burned me.'

'I would guess she's around my age,' said Shella. 'Early eighties, maybe? A mixture of salve and whisky will keep her going for a while. That's what I live on.'

'It pains me to suggest this,' said Cael, 'but have you considered...'

'Don't say it, son,' said Karalyn. 'Kyra, Sable and the Empress have already offered to end my life, so that I can take another body. A better body, as they see it. I shall not oblige this request. This is my body now, for better or worse; and there is another important question that no one will answer. Which new body should I take? Tell me, son – whom should I murder so that I can steal their form?'

'We could go to the prison in Plateau City,' he said, 'and visit the cells of those condemned to death. If you had a Kellach or a Holdings body, then wouldn't your vision powers start to work again? Just like they did when you were in your original body?'

'I think I would require someone descended from both the Kellach and the Holdings for that to work,' she said; 'but I admit that I am uncertain.'

Cael narrowed his eyes. 'You don't sound the same; and I'm not just talking about your accent. You seem more... reflective. Less... I don't know.'

'Less haughty and aloof,' said Kelsey, who was standing by the door with her arms folded over her chest. 'My sister has been humbled, and her arrogance snatched away by her mortal weakness.'

'That is unfair, Kelsey,' said Karalyn.

'Is it?' said Kelsey. 'For years, you have spoken to us as though you existed on a higher plane than any of us mere mortals. You were the most powerful being in existence, able to scare two massive empires into agreeing to a peace. Everyone behaved themselves, because they were frightened of what you might do if you got angry. You're not so scary any more, sister.'

'But this is temporary,' said Kyra, 'and none of us should forget that. When my mother's mortal form passes into death, her spirit will rise again, free and untethered; and her powers will return at that point.'

The door opened, and Arrosa entered the room with Cowie. Cael got to his feet and embraced his wife. They kissed, then Cael gazed down at his son.

'Granny Karalyn is an old lady now,' said the boy.

'Aye,' said Cael.

Cowie pointed at the gilded skull. 'What's that?'

'It is my old head, Cowie,' said Karalyn. 'Albany's head. The Gunstian priests covered it in gold and jewels.'

Arrosa walked over to the table, and peered down at the skull. 'I count four Serpent Eye jewels,' she said. 'Could I take them to repair a couple of Quadrants?'

'You see my mother like this,' said Kyra, 'and that is your first thought, Arrosa?'

Arrosa eyed her sister-in-law. 'I was being practical,' she said. 'We are fighting a complicated war on several fronts against the Gunstians, and we are losing. The Gunstians are bound to strike while Karalyn is incapacitated.'

'Take the damn jewels, Arrosa,' said Kelsey, 'but do it carefully.'

'Thank you,' said Arrosa. She glanced at Karalyn. 'Where are you going to live?'

'I shall return to my own world in a few days, I think,' said Karalyn.

'Why?' said Arrosa. 'What will you do there?'

'I need to find out if I can still use the Sextant,' said Karalyn. 'If I cannot, then... then I don't know what I will do. Esher will guard the peace.'

Kyra snorted. 'Esher cannot guard the peace, Mother; you are being unrealistic. He was only appointed as arbiter a few days ago, and he has no experience of negotiating or diplomacy. He was a draughtsman, for Pyre's sake; he drew up plans for turrets and battlements – that's all he knows.'

'But he is a good man,' said Karalyn.

'Kyra has a point,' said Cael. 'Esher might be an Ascendant, but this task seems beyond his abilities. Does he have access to all of his god powers?'

'He does,' said Kyra, 'though I believe he has yet to use many of them. I dislike the idea of you living alone on your own world, Mother. Cael and I have been there, and...'

'You had no right to trespass upon my world, daughter,' Karalyn said.

'We have gone over this,' said Kyra. 'Cael needed to look for you through the Sextant – what choice did we have?'

'It's a beautiful world,' said Cael, 'but how would you look after yourself on your own?'

'I would need a Quadrant,' said Karalyn, 'so I could buy food; and some salve, to maintain my health.' She bowed her head. 'I realise I have made a terrible mistake, and from the way you are all looking at me, you realise it, too. I want to be on my own; I am better on my own.'

'But maybe you are too frail to live on your own, Mother,' said Cael. 'Don't be afraid to ask for help.'

'The irony of this amuses me,' said Kelsey. 'Did you know, sister, that your little cult is spreading and growing? You now have over a thousand devoted worshippers in Plateau City, with three temples where they assemble every morning to pray to the great Karalyn. They even have their own scriptures.'

'What scriptures?' said Kyra.

'They claim to have discovered ancient prophecies,' said Kelsey, 'that date back to the time of the first Prophet of the Holdings. They say that in these scriptures, the Creator foretells the coming of Karalyn. It's all horseshit, of course. I've read the old prophecies and they say no such thing; but try telling that to the folk in Plateau City who worship your mother. Give it a hundred years, and Karalyn might become the Chadura of the Empire.'

'I wonder how it happened in Gunst,' said Arrosa. 'Did Theodora appear to the people who lived there? Is that how it started?'

'Your guess is as good as mine, Arrosa,' said Kelsey, 'but we are witnessing the formation of a new religion before our eyes.'

'It is happening because the Empire is a godless place,' said Arrosa. 'Every religion that used to exist here has been swept away, but the people need to believe in something.'

'Gullible people, maybe,' said Kelsey.

'Then all humans are gullible,' said Arrosa; 'because we all have that need within us; the need to believe in a higher power that exists beyond the material world. Something that makes us feel safe and loved; that each of us matters, that we all have value. I don't believe in Chadura any more, but I can see the attraction.'

'I don't have that need,' said Cael. 'Reality is enough for me.'

'Then how do you explain your mother?' she said. 'I am not concerned that she has found herself within the body of an old Gunstian woman, because Karalyn transcends flesh. Her spirit is eternal, and she will rise again; sometimes more powerful, sometimes less so, but always there. I think she is a fine god to worship; she is worthy of her own religion.'

'I always knew you were a little crazy, Arrosa,' said Kelsey.

'Maybe she's right,' said Shella. 'The Rakanese believed in a thousand gods, demigods and spirits when I was growing up. I think Karalyn would have fitted in well. Every household in Rakana would have had their own little statue of Karalyn.'

'I don't want any of this,' said Karalyn. 'I just want to be left alone. All of you expect too much from me. When I tried to lead a private life, you berated me for not acting as your shield and protector; and then when I relented and did my best to keep the peace, I was criticised for being cold and aloof, and for neglecting my children. And now you are discussing me as though I wasn't sitting among you. In a perverse way, I am glad to be in this body. I have no powers, and no strength; I am mortal and old – and yet I feel a certain kind of peace at last. Do you know why? Because no one expects anything of me like this. You take one look at me and dismiss me out of hand, because, to you, I am just an old woman. Useless, a burden; unable to care for myself, and certainly unable to keep the peace between the Empire and the Dominion. You all want me to hurry up and die, so that I can steal a *better* body and get back to my job of stopping you from killing each other. Look to your own hearts, before you condemn me.'

Arrosa walked over to Karalyn and crouched by her, taking her hand. 'I do not dismiss you, Karalyn, for I know who you truly are. When the Gunstians arrested me, their priests asked me if I believed in the one, true god. I said *Yes*, and I told them that her name was Karalyn Holdfast. You did not ask for this, and I can see that you do not want it, but you cannot fight what fate has decreed for you. I am at your service, Karalyn, whether you are Lyla, Albany or the woman I see before me; for I love you now as I loved you as a girl on Zamata. You are a god, the only god, no matter the form you take. Let me help you; tell me how I can help you, for my love for you will never die.'

Karalyn stared at her. 'I love you, too, Arrosa; thank you.'

'What a load of bullshit,' said Kelsey.

'Arrosa is clearly deranged,' said Kyra; 'but then, she always was.'

'That's enough,' said Cael, getting to his feet. 'Kindly refrain from criticising my wife's beliefs, or I am liable to lose my temper.'

Arrosa stood. 'When we get back to Plateau City,' she said, 'I intend to investigate this new religion. If a cult of Karalyn is growing, I want to be part of it.'

'You want to be high priestess, you mean,' said Kelsey.

'If Cael becomes Emperor,' Arrosa said, 'then perhaps, as Empress, I might make this new faith the official state religion of the Empire.'

'Over my dead body,' said Kelsey.

'If necessary,' said Arrosa.

Kelsey glared at her.

'Let's go,' said Cael. 'Cowie, it's time to leave.'

The boy joined them, then Cael nodded towards his mother, and they left the room.

'Please tell me you didn't mean that,' Cael said, as they walked along the hallway.

Arrosa shrugged. 'Some of it was to annoy Kelsey and your sister, I admit.'

'Some, but not all?'

'Kelsey and Kyra think I am insane,' she said; 'do you?'

'Of course I don't,' he said, 'but that doesn't mean I agree with what you were saying to my mother.'

'But, Cael; can't you see? Your mother is living proof that death is not the end.'

'Only for her, though; the rest of us die. I love her dearly, but my mother is an aberration.'

'And what are gods but aberrations?' she said. 'How else would you define a god? They are not the same as other people. The gods of the Doomed Worlds are merely long-living mortals; they are not divine in any real sense of the word. If they are lucky, they can stretch out their existence for a few millennia, but Karalyn will live for all eternity. The correct response to this is awe and devotion. Are you going to try to stop me from looking into her cult in Plateau City?'

'I wouldn't do that. You are free to believe what you like.'

'But you don't believe it?'

'I believe what I can see with my own eyes,' said Cael, 'and what I can smell and touch and hear. This life is the only one we get, and that's what matters to me. Our family, our friends, the Empire – these are the things I want to preserve; the things I love. I cannot explain why my mother is the way she is, but I am not going to get on my knees to worship her.'

'I am going to help her,' said Arrosa. 'I think I might be able to unlock her Gift; I could sense it when I was holding her hand. That will return a little of her power to her, but I might need your assistance. Will you help me, husband?'

Cael gazed at her. 'Would I ever let you down?'

CHAPTER 18
A DANGEROUS CURIOSITY

Nom Karta, Inopei – 24th Abrinch 1613

'Where are we going?' said Konna.

'Nowhere in particular,' said Esher.

'But you said you wanted to walk; we must be going somewhere.'

'I suggested we went for *a* walk,' he said. 'I wanted to talk to you, and I felt like stretching my legs before the delegates from the Empire arrive.'

Konna raised an eyebrow.

'It's the kind of thing mortals like to do,' Esher went on. 'They like to go for walks.' He gestured at the streets and palaces of Nom Karta. 'And just look – I lived in this city for years, and yet I have never seen these palaces before. Who lived in that one, I wonder?'

Konna gazed at the palace. 'I think it was Lady Lenta Min Gahad.'

'Was she another casualty of King Naghad's ill-fated invasion of Gunst?'

'She died on Zamata in mysterious circumstances,' said Konna. 'The dragons who returned from Gunst blame her death on Karalyn Holdfast or, as they called her back then – the Demon Witch. I think that's why Lady Abda reserves such hatred towards Karalyn; she has never forgotten.'

'You saw her, didn't you?'

'Who – Karalyn?

'Yes.'

'I was with Edgar and Elmhirst when Kyra rescued her from Gunst. I saw her.'

'I have met with her a few times since she... died,' said Esher. 'She wants me to take over the responsibility of preserving the peace treaty between the Dominion and the Empire, but I don't think I can do it.'

'You volunteered for the job.'

'That was when Karalyn was all-powerful. Let's imagine that she lives on in that mortal body for another decade – does that mean I have to watch over the worlds for ten years? That might not seem like a long time to many gods, but it does to me. And will anyone listen to what I say? Will Edgar or Empress Thorn obey me? What about Queen Famula or the Holdfasts? It's hopeless.'

'You have every god power imaginable, Esher,' she said.

'That's true, but I have not yet found the will to use them. Deep in my heart, I still see myself as Draughtsman Reece.' He caught her gaze. 'That is why I have asked Sable to come to today's gathering. She helped me get through the grand convention that took place ten days ago, when Karalyn was missing.'

'Really? And how exactly did Sable help you?'

'She went into my mind and spoke encouraging words, helping me to know what to say; and she made me feel relaxed and confident.'

Konna laughed. 'Oh, Esher, she was manipulating you. She was planting ideas and feelings into your mind. She will do the same today, if she comes.'

'I don't care,' he said. 'She made me feel as though I could handle anything. She was very friendly. I like her.'

Konna eyed him. 'Have you ever met her before, say around seventeen or eighteen years ago?'

'No, that was the first time I had ever seen her.'

'She has a daughter.'

'She told me all about her,' said Esher. 'Alindi'osso, or Lindi Holdfast, depending upon which world you are on. Why do you ask?'

'No reason,' she said. 'Lindi has a wide range of powers.'

'I know; Sable told me.'

'Her father must have been a very powerful god.'

Esher came to a halt. 'Don't toy with me, Konna. Say what you want to say.'

'I don't think it's my place to say it.'

'But you were quite happy to bring up the subject of her daughter. Are we friends?'

'I... I hope so.'

'Then tell me what you suspect. I want to hear you say it.'

'Sable will not be happy if I gossip about this.'

Esher narrowed his eyes and walked away.

'Wait,' cried Konna, as she hurried after him. 'I'm sorry. It's just... well, isn't there a possibility that, maybe, you might be Lindi's father?'

'How could I be her father? Prior to ten days ago, I had never met Sable.'

'I'm going to get into fucking trouble for this, but did you know that Sable can alter people's memories? You could have met her a dozen times, and you wouldn't remember. She is notorious for this sort of behaviour. And everyone knows that she has kept the identities of her children's fathers a secret.'

'This is ridiculous,' said Esher, 'but let's imagine for a moment that you are right. Lindi is almost seventeen, so I would have had to have met Sable nearly eighteen years ago. I was a mortal back then, with no powers – how could I have fathered a child with Lindi's abilities?'

'You didn't have *no powers*, your powers were still there; they had just been blocked. They still existed; otherwise, how was my crazy brother able to unlock them? You were blocked, aye, but you would have passed those powers on to any children.'

Esher's eyes darkened. 'No. I refuse to believe it. If I were Lindi's father, then Sable would have told me. I could have been there for Lindi; I would have wanted to see her growing up. I cannot believe that

Sable would have been so cruel as to deny me the knowledge that I had a daughter.'

'Then you don't really know Sable, do you? And to be fair, she didn't know that your powers were going to be awoken by Cairney. She probably assumed that you would die as Draughtsman Reece.'

Esher fell silent, and for a moment Konna thought he might start to weep.

'I shouldn't have said anything; I'm sorry,' Konna went on. 'Just forget this conversation ever happened.'

'How am I supposed to do that?' he said. 'Can you alter memories?'

'No.'

'There are others who could be Lindi's father; you are just guessing.'

'That's true,' she said. 'It might have been Bailey, for instance. Or Elmhirst; but that's about it. Sable has told Lindi that it wasn't Edgar.'

'Who does Lindi most resemble?'

'She is the image of her mother,' said Konna. 'She doesn't particularly remind me of you, or any of the gods I've mentioned. Are you going to tell Sable what I've said?'

'I am going to be direct, Konna. When Sable gets here, I shall ask her to her face if I am Lindi's father, but I won't mention you.'

'You won't need to; she'll read it out of your mind if you bring it up.'

'But I need to know. If Lindi is my daughter, then that changes everything. I will need to meet her, and attempt to get to know her. What is she like?'

Konna tried to word a response without making it seem as though Lindi was a power-crazed god who wished to seize the throne of the Empire.

'She is headstrong,' said Konna. 'A little rebellious, perhaps. Cocky, like her mother, only more so, if such a thing is possible.'

'I heard several stories about Sable when I lived in Jezra,' he said. 'She isn't as well known in the City as she is on other worlds, but even there we knew that she was a great god-killer. At the time, of course, I didn't know any gods, and I obviously didn't know that I was a god, and the term *god-killer* seemed quite noble.'

'We should probably go back to the Palace of King Gahad,' she said. 'You should be there to greet the delegates.'

Esher nodded. They began to walk back the way they had come, but Esher remained silent for the entire time, and Konna cursed her loose tongue. She wondered which would be worse – that he was Lindi's father, or he wasn't. Either way, Sable would likely be furious.

Several dragons, gods and mortal humans from the Dominion government were outside the Palace of King Gahad waiting for the imperial delegates to arrive, and Konna's eyes tightened when she noticed Naxor whispering into Lord Edgar's ear.

'Why the fuck is Naxor here again?' she muttered under her breath.

'He has been seeing a lot of Edgar recently,' said Esher.

'Has he? Why?'

'I don't know. Presumably he wishes to sell more whisky to the Dominion.'

'If only it were that simple,' she said. 'He will be plotting something.'

'Edgar will be able to read his mind,' said Esher; 'I wouldn't worry about it.'

Sable stepped out from the crowd, and smiled at Esher. 'I made it on time,' she said. 'I thought I was going to be late, as I was helping Joss select a present for Lindi's birthday tomorrow, and he was taking forever to decide.' Her smile faded when she saw the sombre expression on Esher's face. 'Is everything all right?'

'Sable,' said Esher, 'is Lindi my daughter?'

Sable's face fell and, for the briefest of moments, she seemed almost too shocked to speak.

'Who told you that?' she said.

'Does it matter?' said Esher. 'I need to know the truth.'

'You are not Lindi's father,' she said. 'Don't take it personally – I am sure you would make a very good father, but Lindi is not your daughter.'

Esher nodded. 'I'm not sure how I feel about that. Relieved, I supposed, but also disappointed. When I say relieved, Sable, I mean that I am relieved that I didn't miss her childhood years; that would have been hard to take.'

Sable's smile returned. 'It's all right; I knew what you meant. Shall we go inside?'

They turned and started to walk into the palace, then Sable glanced back at Konna, and gave her a brief look of pure anger. She was smiling again a moment later, and Konna watched them enter the palace.

'I saw that look,' said Elmhirst, as he walked towards Konna. 'Have you upset the mighty Sable Holdfast?'

'I certainly hope not,' said Konna.

'Why are so many gods still terrified of her?' said Elmhirst. 'It is true that she was a great warrior, but that was a while ago. She is now just another aging mortal.'

'Her battle-vision is probably still better than ours, Elmhirst,' she said. 'The day I'm not a little scared of Sable will be the day she's dead and buried.'

'Your father could have beaten her.'

'Aye, but there was no one like my father. He could have beaten anyone.'

'Ward defeated him.'

'Ward had four gods and twenty dragons with him,' said Konna, 'and my father killed them all.'

'Then I am glad I never had to face him.'

Konna eyed him with a smile. 'He would have kicked your arse.'

'Indeed. I saw the latest imperial weaponry while I was on Zamata. I daresay a Battanara or a Jackdaw could have defeated your father. What use is battle-vision, when set against such ferocious weapons? What use self-healing, if a projectile can remove one's head?'

'I agree, but what can we do about it?'

'Nothing, for the moment. The time for change will come when the immortal Holdfasts inherit the Sapphire Throne.'

Konna rolled her eyes. 'You have been speaking to my Uncle Naxor, haven't you?'

Elmhirst laughed. 'Maybe.'

'What else has he been telling you?'

'His main focus has been on the future relationship between the Dominion and the Empire, once the Holdfast gods take over. He was saying that this will herald a new era of cooperation, that the gods on both sides should be allies rather than adversaries. Most of it made sense.'

'And what is he whispering to Lord Edgar?'

'I cannot say for certain, as I have not been privy to those conversations. I fear that Lord Edgar may have spoken to him about the issue he discussed with us some time ago. Do you recall? The issue concerning Kyra's mortality, and Edgar's plan to remedy it.'

'Why would he mention that to Naxor?'

'Your uncle is very good at getting people to open up to him,' said Elmhirst, 'and Edgar is desperate to talk about that particular subject. I believe Naxor was present when Karalyn ascended into godhood?'

Konna nodded. 'He was there.'

'This is starting to concern me, Konna. Has Edgar mentioned it to you again?'

'Not once.'

'Please tell me if he does.'

The air shimmered as Konna was considering how to respond, and several people appeared in the middle of the street outside the palace.

Edgar and Elmhirst walked towards the new arrivals and Konna and Naxor followed them.

'Welcome back to Nom Karta,' said Edgar.

'Thank you,' said Cardova. 'Herald Kelsey sends her apologies, but she is currently with her sister.'

'I assume that Kyra is also with Karalyn?' said Edgar. 'I was hoping she would return today.'

'Karalyn is finding it difficult to adjust to her new life,' said Cardova, 'but her son Cael has come along today. Secretary Cole and Postmaster Arrosa are also here, and Chamberlain Brogan has come in place of Kelsey.'

'Welcome, Brogan,' said Edgar. 'Shall we go into the great hall?'

Banner soldiers stood to attention as Edgar led the imperial delegates up the broad steps and into the palace. Cael and Cole fell in with Konna and Naxor, and Cael shot Konna's uncle a fierce glance.

'I see you have found your way to Nom Karta, Naxor,' Cael said. 'I shall have to warn the Dominion leadership about you.'

'Feel free to do so,' said Naxor. 'I have nothing to hide; my mind is open to you, Cael – what could I possibly be concealing from the Empire?'

'I would need about four days to find out,' said Cael; 'or a couple of hours and a restrainer mask.'

Naxor laughed. 'The Empire is truly in safe hands with you as Thorn's anointed successor, Cael. Of course, you would still have to be chosen by the Succession Council; do you think you will win enough votes?'

'It makes no difference to me,' said Cael.

'How about we do a little deal?' said Naxor. 'The Marchbrae Holdfasts possess one vote on the Succession Council, a vote which is currently held by Aila. If you were to support Killop's bid to become the next Holder Fast, then I guarantee that Aila's vote would be yours when the time comes to choose a new Emperor.'

Cael eyed him. 'Why is Killop bidding to become Holder Fast?'

'Why not? He manages the Hold Fast estate, he lives in the Holdings, and he is forging strong connections with the other Holders, as well as the members of the Holdings parliament. Holders Terras, Clement, Wain and Elance have already indicated that they would prefer Killop to be chosen. They know him, and they trust him. Can you think of a better choice?'

'It doesn't matter what the other Holders think,' said Cael. 'It's Kelsey's decision.'

'Yes, but all I ask is that you mention to her that you would prefer Killop's bid. I understand that you have no power over the decision.'

'I will think about it.'

'Excellent,' said Naxor.

They walked into the cavernous hall. It had been set up in the same manner as the previous convention, and the delegates from both sides approached the horseshoe-shaped table, as Queen Famula, Lady Abda and Lord Konran stood close by, the three dragons gazing down at the humans.

'Your Majesty,' said Cardova, bowing; 'it is a pleasure to see you again.'

'Thank you, Lord Constable,' said the dragon. 'Lord Esher, are we ready to begin?'

Esher inclined his head. 'We are, Your Majesty.'

Konna narrowed her eyes as everyone took their seats. Sable remained standing by Esher's side, but she was avoiding Konna's gaze. Konna had no doubt that she would have read Esher's mind – she was probably in it at that moment – and she would know for certain who had mentioned the possibility that Esher was Lindi's father. Konna wondered if Sable had been telling the truth. She had seemed honest in her denials, but Konna recalled the look of horror and shock that had appeared on her face for the split-second before she had answered. And everyone knew that Sable was a very good liar.

'Renowned dragons, ladies and gentlemen,' Esher said, 'welcome to this, the second official convention between the Dominion and the Empire of the Sapphire Throne. I have been informed that Constable Lucius Cardova of the Empire wishes to speak first.'

'Thank you, Lord Esher,' said Cardova. 'My first point is to mention that Her Imperial Majesty Empress Thorn has approved the draft agreement we produced at the last convention. Her Majesty would also like to propose a formal truce between the Empire and the Dominion, to last for as long as it takes for Karalyn Holdfast to be able to resume her duties as guarantor of the peace. This truce would forbid any hostile action between the two sides, and it also proposes a greater degree of cooperation against our mutual enemy, the Gunstian Empire. Her Majesty feels that a united front against the Gunstians is of paramount importance.'

'We are already cooperating with the Sapphire Empire, Constable,' said Queen Famula. 'What more does your Empress want?'

'The establishment of embassies and the appointment of ambassadors, Your Majesty,' said Cardova. 'The Dominion would have a permanent diplomatic presence in the heart of the Empire, and we would have the same in Nom Karta. This would reduce the possibility of misunderstandings and help foster an atmosphere of friendship.'

'We are not your *friends*, insect,' said Abda. 'This truce is a temporary state of affairs, and will expire once we have dealt with the perfidious Gunstians. We have no need for your friendship.'

'If I may, my lady?' said Elmhirst. 'Let us not be distracted by any notions of sentiment. It might be wise to have embassies in both capitals – that does not mean we would suddenly become friends with the Sapphire Empire.'

'I agree,' said Edgar. 'I like the idea of ambassadors. It will save us having to arrange meetings through Zamata.'

Abda's eyes burned with rage, but she fell silent at a glance from Queen Famula.

'We shall consider this request, Lord Constable,' said the dragon queen. 'Now tell me – are we any closer to defeating Gunst?'

'So far, Your Majesty,' said Cardova, 'the Empire and the Dominion have raided Gunstian military installations a total of eleven times. Between us, we have destroyed ships, naval facilities, army depots and bases, fortifications and other military targets. Adjutant Cael also led an attack on Great Gunst that eliminated around eighty priests, army officers and government officials.'

'We agreed that we would not strike their capital city,' said Abda; 'to avoid civilian casualties – those were your words, Constable. You are a liar.'

'The attack was my responsibility, my lady,' said Cael. 'I went against orders when I commanded my team to assault the Temple of the Great Mother, and I apologise for my actions. Seeing the skull of my murdered mother filled me with a rage that could only be satisfied by vengeance.'

Abda stared at him. 'I see. In that case, I withdraw my earlier words;

for you acted as a dragon would, Adjutant Cael.' She tilted her head. 'I apologise.'

'Thank you, my lady,' said Cardova.

'I want to see an increase in the number of raids being carried out,' said Queen Famula.

'The Dominion could conduct more raids, Your Majesty,' said Elmhirst, 'had we more Quadrants at our disposal.'

'Perhaps there are the makings of another deal here,' said Edgar. 'Lord Constable, would the Empire be interested in receiving more Tempest ore in exchange for Quadrants?'

'Unfortunately,' said Cardova, 'we have no remaining stock of Serpent Eye jewels. The Empire is not currently creating any new Quadrants, and the four we gave you at the last convention represent all we could spare.'

'The Dominion holds a certain quantity of Serpent Eye jewels,' said Edgar. 'We could deliver them to you, and you use them to build Quadrants.'

Cardova sat in silence for a moment, then he gazed at Edgar. 'There are some in the Empire,' he said, 'who struggle to understand why the Dominion has not been able to construct their own Quadrants. Bailey knew much about the inner workings of these devices, and we are sure that he passed on his knowledge to the Dominion. You also have ample supplies of Tempest and Serpent Eye jewels, you have Lady Kyra, who learned about Quadrants at Plateau City University, and, finally, you have a collection of very fine research institutes and colleges in Aucteran. Teros City and Naeth, in particular, have facilities that seem to be the perfect environments in which to design and build Quadrants.'

'How do you know so much about Aucteran?' said Abda. 'Does the greedy Empire wish to annex our richest province?'

'Not at all, my lady,' said Cardova. 'We were merely curious.'

'This is irrelevant,' said Edgar. 'I am sure, Lord Constable, that you already know the answer to the question you have posed. In order to have the facilities on Aucteran develop a Quadrant, the gods and dragons of Nom Karta would have to share a great deal of hidden knowledge with the mortals who live there. We shall not be doing that.'

'I see,' said Cardova. 'Might it be the case that you are hindering your own efforts? Why not unleash the great minds of the academies of Teros City? Millions of mortals live in the cities and towns of Aucteran; are they not a great potential resource?'

'Why is it always the same with mortals?' said Elmhirst. 'Their thirst for knowledge can never be assuaged – this is a known fact for those who have lived for centuries and millennia. If we gifted everything we knew to the mortals of Aucteran, their curiosity would lead them to look into areas that could only harm us.'

'Areas like the advanced weaponry of the Empire?' said Cael.

'Indeed,' said Elmhirst. 'Where would it end? We gods know the answer to that – it would end as it always does, in a great war between mortals and immortals. As soon as mortals are able to create weapons that can kill gods with ease, the result never varies. Take the imperial Battanara as an example. Here you have a weapon that can be used by a mere child – one simply points and looses, and a god can be obliterated. We may talk of truces and pacts between our two sides as we band together to face our mutual foe; but let no one be in any doubt – the weaponry of the Sapphire Empire is an existential threat to the Dominion.'

The cavernous hall fell quiet, and Konna watched as the mortals sitting opposite the delegates from the Dominion eyed each other.

'Let us return to the matter at hand,' said Edgar. 'I propose that the Dominion delivers a batch of twenty Serpent Eye jewels to the Empire; in return, the Empire shall then deliver four Quadrants to the Dominion. This deal will supply the Empire with sufficient extra jewels to construct a Quadrant for themselves. Do you agree to this?'

'We shall take this request to the Empress, my lord,' said Brogan, 'but I think it would be acceptable.'

'Thank you, Chamberlain,' said Edgar. He glanced at Esher.

Sable nudged the Ascendant, and Esher looked up.

'We shall adjourn for a short break,' said Esher. 'Let us reconvene in twenty minutes.'

The delegates started to get to their feet.

'This is where I leave you all,' said Naxor, who had been standing behind the delegates from the Dominion, close to where Lady Abda had been positioned. He spoke in a low voice to Abda, then he tilted his head in Edgar's direction. Konna narrowed her eyes as Naxor walked from the hall, then, on an impulse, she followed him. Naxor went into the large hallway that led to the street outside, and Konna watched him take out his Quadrant. She glanced over her shoulder to make sure no one was close by.

You see me as Lord Edgar.

'One moment, Naxor,' she called out.

Naxor turned, then he smiled and bowed his head. 'My gracious lord,' he said.

'What did you think of that discussion?' Konna said.

'I found it dreadfully ominous, my lord,' said Naxor. 'The cycle is about to restart, it seems. Back in the City of Salve, we gods also had our problems with mortals attempting to learn things that should always be kept from them. A certain Prince Aurelian had to be subdued by force, and his works destroyed. But, as fortune would have it, there is a way out of this situation – when the immortal Marchbrae Holdfasts inherit the throne of the Sapphire Empire, we shall put an immediate end to this learning. The universities shall be instructed to teach only poetry and literature; the science faculties shall be closed, and all dangerous knowledge shall be suppressed. This process will be disruptive, but it is far better than the alternative.'

'Will Karalyn allow this to happen?' said Konna.

'That remains to be seen, my lord,' said Naxor, 'but I have faith that she will come around to the notion that it is better for everyone if we keep the mortals ignorant to a certain extent. She will not wish to preside over wars that consume entire worlds. Now, as for the other matter we discussed, be assured that I will speak to the person I mentioned; but it must be stated that we are dealing with a very strong-willed individual. I shall have to use all of my wiles to persuade her.'

'Thank you,' said Konna.

Naxor bowed again. 'It is an honour and a privilege to be of service to the gods who rule the Dominion.'

He swiped his fingers over the Quadrant and vanished.

Konna dropped her disguise, her eyes tight. She had no idea to whom Naxor had been referring, or what he was going to ask of her; but Konna didn't like it.

Naxor and Edgar were up to something, and Konna was determined to find out what.

CHAPTER 19
OLDER AND WISER

Colsbury Castle, Republic of the Holdings – 22nd Day, First Third Summer 560

'I love sitting in the harbour,' said Shella, 'but I've been doing it on my own since Olo'osso died. It's nice to have you here, Karalyn; it's good to have the company.'

Karalyn gazed out over the calm waters of the lake. The mountains to the west of Colsbury were reflecting perfectly on the surface, and the sky was a deep blue.

'I'm sorry I missed Olo'osso's death,' she said.

'You missed a lot of things,' said Shella. 'For the last fifteen years, you have been unapproachable. Were you happy living alone? You were on that world by yourself, yeah?'

'I was the only human on the entire world.'

'I don't know how you managed. Who did you speak to? Yourself?'

'I spoke only to the Sextant,' Karalyn said. 'Time began to lose its meaning, and months would pass without me noticing.'

'Your mother would have been able to snap you out of it.'

'I'm not sure about that,' said Karalyn. 'I can be quite stubborn.'

'Yeah, we've noticed,' said Shella. She eyed Karalyn from her deck chair. 'You seem more normal again, in your new body; well, now that you've had salve and a few healings. You were pretty grumpy while you were still in pain.'

'Is that how you've made it to your age, Shella? Salve and healings?'

'Of course, and I fully intend to outlive your Gunstian body. I've had years of regular healings; I strongly recommend them. I've noticed Sable doing the same thing. She always has a little vial of salve on her, and her daughter has been giving her doses of healing ever since her powers emerged – I'm sure of it. Have you meet Lindi?'

'Maybe; I can't remember.'

Shella shook her head.

'I understand,' Karalyn went on. 'I have neglected my family; you don't need to tell me this.'

'And now?'

'Now I realise how selfish I've been,' she said. 'The Sextant took over my every thought; there is nothing like creating your own world, Shella. I could lose myself for years at a time, and then, whenever I pulled away from the Sextant, I would feel regret about everyone I had ignored; but then I was too embarrassed to make amends. And on it went.'

'At least it worked out for Lucius Cardova,' Shella said. 'He and Kelsey seem very happy. How does that make you feel?'

'It makes me feel stupid, Shella. Looking back, I can now see all of the occasions when Lucius tried to speak to me about our marriage, but I never had any time for him. He wasn't a bad husband, but I lost interest in everyone around that period. My husband, my children, my family, and my friends. But I am glad he is happy. I am glad my sister is happy. Lucius and Kelsey are better suited to each other than I was with Lucius, or Kelsey was with Van.'

'Then why did you marry him?'

'I loved him, Shella. I read his mind when I took Cairney into custody; that was when I saw his feelings towards Kelsey. But I saw other things, too. He thinks I never got over Lennox; he thinks I always saw him as coming second, that Lennox was the only man I ever loved – but it's not true. I loved Lucius. The feelings I still have for Lennox are more complicated, because I feel guilty for the way I treated him.'

'You thought he'd burned down a hospital.'

'I believed that right up until the moment he died,' said Karalyn. 'That's what I regret. At some point, I am going to have to go back to my unnamed world, if only to check on the Sextant. The Empress wants me to ensure that it is safe. Would you come with me when I go?'

Shella raised an eyebrow. 'Are you inviting me to your secret world, Karalyn? I thought you made it for yourself.'

'I don't want to go there on my own,' she said.

'I will come with you, but only for a visit,' said Shella. 'My home is here.'

Karalyn eased herself off the deck chair and stood. 'I am going to ask Arrosa for a Quadrant.'

'Do I need to pack?' said Shella.

'I have plenty of spare clothes and food on my world.'

'Do you have dreamweed?'

Karalyn raised an eyebrow. 'No, Shella, I don't have any weed.'

'Then I'd better pack. Help me up.'

Karalyn reached out, and helped Shella stand. They walked off the pier and into the wide forecourt of Colsbury Castle.

'I miss the days when I could just think of where I wanted to go, and I would appear there,' said Karalyn.

'That power might come back when you take your next body,' said Shella. 'Choose more wisely next time.'

'People keep saying that to me, but I don't think you realise how this works. Am I supposed to murder a random woman because she has powers? For the last two times, I happen to have been killed by a woman, and it made sense to take their bodies; but what if this body expires of old age?'

'You could use the Sextant to create a world stocked with spare bodies,' said Shella.

Karalyn rolled her eyes. 'That doesn't sound very humane.'

They entered the Summer Palace, and Shella turned left to walk to her rooms, while Karalyn started climbing the stairs to the quarters used by Cael and Arrosa. She was out of breath, and her knees were aching by the time she reached the apartment. She knocked, and Arrosa opened the door.

'Ah, there you are, Karalyn,' said Arrosa. 'I was hoping to see you today. Come in.'

Karalyn walked into Arrosa's sitting room, and sat on a couch. Kelvin and Carrie were playing a game by a table, and they looked over at Karalyn.

'Can I get you something to drink?' said Arrosa.

'No, thanks,' said Karalyn. 'If it is all right, I would like to ask if I could please borrow a Quadrant.'

Arrosa smiled. 'I have one set aside for you,' she said. 'The Dominion were asking us for more Quadrants, even after we gave them four from our own stock; then there was a slight row when Lucius asked them why they couldn't make their own.'

Karalyn frowned. 'Why don't they make their own?'

'Because they want to keep all advanced technology a secret from the mortals,' said Arrosa. 'They were quite open about it; they don't want the mortals under their control to become too knowledgeable. They think it will lead to the mortals getting rid of the gods. Anyway, wait here a moment, and I will fetch you your Quadrant.'

Arrosa left the room just as Cael and Cowie entered.

'Mother,' said Cael. 'I am glad you're here. Arrosa and I have had an idea about how to access your Gift.'

'Were you in Nom Karta recently?'

'We were there this morning,' said Cael. 'Lord Esher hosted a second convention.' He sat down, as Cowie walked over to his brother and sister. 'We managed to agree to a few things; it looks as though we will be sending ambassadors to each other.'

Arrosa walked back into the room, and presented a Quadrant to Karalyn. Karalyn reached out to take it, then she hesitated.

'This is the moment I have been dreading,' she said. 'What if it doesn't speak to me?'

'There is only one way to find out,' said Cael.

Karalyn took the Quadrant, her fingers touching the engraved surface.

Nothing. No voice, just silence.

Karalyn bowed her head. 'I cannot hear the Tempest.'

'Do you remember how to use it correctly?' said Arrosa.

'Aye, but I was hoping... You both know what I hoped for. There is something quite different about Gunstian physiology. I don't know exactly what Theodora did when she created the Gifts, but it altered the Gunstians to some degree.'

'It couldn't have altered us that much,' said Arrosa. 'We are all humans.'

'The Holdings are the only true human species native to the Star Continent,' said Karalyn. 'The Kellach Brigdomin are close, but Nathaniel changed them, just as Theodora changed the Gunstians.'

'That idea I mentioned,' said Cael. 'Shall we try it?'

'What does it involve?' said Karalyn.

Cael picked up a wooden bookend and placed it onto the low table in front of Arrosa.

'I will enter Arrosa's mind,' he said, 'while she turns that piece of wood into glass.'

The children got up and walked over.

'Is mummy going to turn that into glass?' said Carrie.

'Aye, sweetie,' said Cael. 'Do you want to watch?'

'Aye,' said Kelvin.

'Once that has been done,' Cael went on, 'I should be able to detect the part of Arrosa's mind that controls the Gift of Vitrification. It might not be the same place that controls the Gift of Immolation, but we think it's worth a try.'

'All right,' said Karalyn.

Arrosa placed her fingers onto the bookend. 'Are you in my mind, Cael?'

'Aye,' he said. 'Any time you're ready.'

Arrosa gazed at the carved block of wood. There was a crack, and it transformed into dark green glass.

Carrie laughed. 'Do it again, mummy.'

'Maybe later, darling,' said Arrosa. 'Did you see anything, Cael?'

'Aye. I felt it, though it was coming from a part of your mind completely unrelated to where mage and god powers emanate. Shall I go into your mind, Mother?'

'Kyra erected a barrier.'

'I know; I've seen it,' said Cael. 'I will be able to get through it.'

'Kyra suspected you might. Where is she?'

'My sister is with Kelsey, I think,' said Cael, as he gazed into Karalyn's eyes. She felt nothing, but knew that he was in her mind.

Arrosa opened an old book, and flicked through a few pages. 'The Gift of Immolation,' she said, 'works only on living organisms – animals, fish, birds; not plants, and certainly not inanimate objects. You should select something before trying to activate your Gift; if you find it.'

'Perhaps we should move the children into a different room,' said Cael, 'in case it's triggered accidentally.'

Arrosa got to her feet. 'That's a good idea,' she said. 'Come on; let's leave daddy and granny alone for a minute.'

She shepherded the children out of the room and closed the door.

'I might have found it,' said Cael.

'I have a concern, son,' said Karalyn.

'Aye?'

'The Gifts of Theodora and Nathaniel's dream mage powers were never supposed to mix.'

'And?'

'Well, you and Arrosa... the children...'

Cael narrowed his eyes. 'I wondered if folk said the same thing to your mother,' he said. '*Holdings and Kellach Brigdomin shouldn't mix*. The church told your mother that you were an abomination.'

'I am not calling your children *abominations*, son. I would never do that, but you must be careful. And the comparison is wrong, because the Holdings and the Kellach Brigdomin used to be the same people, long ago. My mother and father were bringing together two peoples who had been separated. The natives of Athumia were never meant to come into contact with others. Your children's abilities could be very unpredictable.'

'I am glad you waited until Arrosa had left the room before saying this,' said Cael. 'Her opinion of you as an ever-living god might have been damaged.' He broke off his gaze. 'I've found it; I've found your Gift.'

'Show me.'

'Not until we have something you can immolate. I am the only organic material in this room, and I don't particularly want to be burned from the inside out. What if I were to catch you a rat?'

Karalyn frowned.

'It's the nature of your Gift, I'm afraid,' said Cael. 'You will kill whatever you practise on; and you might not be able to control it for a while. The Lesser Keep has a few rats; we could catch a dozen, and you could test your Gift on them.'

'Maybe later,' she said. 'I don't see why a poor rat should have to suffer to satisfy my curiosity.'

'That's the mother I remember well,' he said. 'If you ever need your Gift and can't find it, it will be because you felt sorry for a rat.'

There was a knock on the front door of the apartment and Cael got to his feet. He opened the door, and Karalyn heard the hushed voices of Kelsey and Kyra.

'Mother,' said Cael. 'You have visitors. Kyra and Aunty Kelsey have brought someone to see you.'

Karalyn got up from the couch. Standing behind Kelsey and Kyra at the doorway were Caitlyn and Carden. Both were staring at Karalyn, their eyes wide.

'Mother?' said Carden.

Karalyn said nothing, too shocked for words to form in her mind.

'Come in,' said Cael.

Karalyn remained where she was as her immortal children entered the room. She felt a sense of panic ripple through her, and she would have vanished if she had been able. Her eyes went to the Quadrant given to her by Arrosa – it was lying on the table, just out of reach.

'Don't even think about it, Mother,' said Cael. 'Take a seat.'

Karalyn sat on a chair. Cael and Arrosa remained standing, while Kelsey, Kyra, Caitlyn and Carden sat on a couch.

'Sorry about surprising you like this,' said Kelsey.

'You should have told me,' said Karalyn.

'I went to Plateau City to talk to Caelius,' said Kelsey, 'and I was ambushed by your children. They had heard the rumours, sister; the rumours that you were back, but that you had changed. What was I supposed to do – lie to them? And when they learned the truth, they demanded that they be allowed to come here.'

Karalyn glanced at her immortal children, but they were still staring at her, and she had to look away. Shame and guilt bit deep into her heart.

'Maybe we should leave the three of them alone,' said Arrosa.

'I agree,' said Kyra.

'Do you know something?' said Carden. 'This is the first time in many years that Mother has been in the same room as all four of her children. And who knows? – it might be the last time.'

'Let's hope not,' said Cael, as he stood. 'We will take Cowie, Carrie and Kelvin for a walk down to the village. Carden, send me a message when you are finished.'

'There is no need to walk,' said Kyra. 'Gather round.'

Everyone apart from Karalyn and her two younger children walked up to Kyra, and they vanished.

Karalyn stared at the floor.

'Do you hate us, Mother?' said Caitlyn.

Karalyn felt her eyes well. 'No.'

'Then why did you abandon us?' said Caitlyn. 'I have been rehearsing this moment over and over again, for years. I have gone over it so many times that I could give you a dozen different little speeches. Some were angry, some sad, some both. Help us understand, Mother.'

Carden shook his head. 'She can't even bring herself to look at us. She has been on Colsbury as an old mortal woman for eleven days, sister. She had no intention of letting us know what had happened to her. She doesn't care.'

'I do care,' said Karalyn. 'I was lost.'

'And yet you were able to sit with Cael and Kyra,' said Carden. 'You have been with them for days. What is it about me and Caitlyn that you don't like? Did we offend you in some way?'

'Of course not. I knew I had been neglecting you, and I was too ashamed to make amends. I kept thinking that we would be able to spend centuries together; that there was no rush. I was obsessed with the Sextant, and with trying to keep the peace between the Dominion and the Empire. I lost sight of what was important.'

'Father told us that you disapproved of our choices,' said Caitlyn. 'He told us that you were angry that I wanted to join the cavalry, and that Carden was going to enlist in the marines.'

'Father didn't force us to make those choices,' said Carden. 'We talked about the future with him, and we made up our own minds.'

'I am glad Lucius was there for you.'

'So are we, Mother,' said Carden.

'Aunty Kelsey has been more like a mother to us for years,' said Caitlyn; 'even before she and Father decided to be together. We all lived in the Holdfast townhouse, with Cael and Arrosa. Uncle Caelius and Cousin Caelius were there, and Calpurnia, too. We were like one big family; only you were missing. I grew up thinking that I must have done something wrong.'

'But Father told us that it wasn't our fault,' said Carden. 'He kept defending you, Mother. He kept saying that you wanted to be with us, but couldn't. But you abandoned him, too. Is it any wonder he left you?'

'Don't say that,' said Caitlyn. 'We cannot know what our mother has been thinking all this time. I wish Mother and Father were together again, just like it was when we were younger, before Mother left us.'

'Lucius and I will not be getting back together,' said Karalyn. 'I still love him, but he and Kelsey are happy now, and I would do nothing to upset that.'

'You still love him?' said Caitlyn.

'Not enough to be his wife,' she said.

'Do you love us?' said Caitlyn.

'Of course I do.'

'I don't believe you,' said Carden. 'You are only saying that because you have been forced into this situation. You didn't know we were coming, and you had no plans to visit us.'

'I did have a plan to visit you,' she said. 'Just before I was killed by the Gunstians, I was about to go to Plateau City with Lucius.'

Carden laughed. 'Do you expect us to believe that? Admit it, Mother – you wish you had never had us.'

'That's not true. You are my children, and I will always love you; but I have been drifting from one body to the next.'

'But we only knew you as Albany,' said Carden. 'You had that body for our entire lives, up until a few days ago.'

'I know I was selfish.'

'You still are,' he said.

'Stop it, brother,' said Caitlyn. 'I want to be reconciled with Mother, but the things you are saying are only making it worse.'

'I don't think I care any more,' said Carden. 'When I walk through the streets of Plateau City, I sometimes see the religious fanatics who have decided to worship you, Mother; and I think – they cannot possibly understand what you are like. They have heard of the things you have done, but none of them know you. I feel like shaking them by their collars, and telling them that the god they follow abandoned her children when they were little. I have seen you three or four times since I was five, Mother, and it used to make me so angry; but now I feel nothing.' He got to his feet. 'Are you coming, sister? I have seen and heard all that I can take.'

Caitlyn glanced up at her brother, and shook her head.

Carden nodded, then he walked out of the room, closing the door behind him.

'He is very angry,' said Caitlyn.

'He is right to be,' said Karalyn. 'I let him down; I let you down.'

'But what now? Where do we go from here, Mother? Are you going to hide yourself away on your secret world for another fifteen years?'

'I don't know what I am going to do,' she said. 'I have clearly disappointed the Empress, who cannot understand why I don't simply choose a *better body*. By that, she means the body of a powerful god, so that I can go back to watching over the peace. But I don't have the will to murder someone for their body.'

'I am glad about that,' said Caitlyn, 'but the body you are in won't last forever. How does it feel to be mortal again?'

'Terrible,' she said. 'It would have been better if I had never been in Albany's body, for then I wouldn't know what I was missing – the feeling of safety and strength, knowing that nothing could hurt me. And now I feel so weak and helpless. I do have to go back to my own world, but only to check that the Sextant is safe.'

'Will you come back?'

'Aye.'

Caitlyn narrowed her eyes. 'I will stay here if you promise to come back, Mother.'

'Shella is waiting for me,' she said.

Caitlyn said nothing.

Karalyn got to her feet, then she picked up the Quadrant.

'Don't do this to me, Mother,' said Caitlyn.

'I am sorry,' said Karalyn.

She swiped her fingers over the surface of the Quadrant, and appeared outside Shella's quarters on the ground floor of the palace. The old Rakanese woman was standing with a bag over her shoulder, but her smile vanished when she saw the expression on Karalyn's face.

Karalyn activated the Quadrant again. The air crackled, and they appeared on the long balcony upon Karalyn's unnamed world.

'Wow,' said Shella. 'Nice view.'

Karalyn started to weep. 'My children hate me.'

'What?' said Shella. 'Sit down.'

Shella pushed Karalyn onto a chair, and sat beside her. 'What happened?'

'Caitlyn and Carden arrived,' she said, as tears fell down her face. 'Carden... he wants nothing to do with me, and I hurt Caitlyn so badly.'

'Then what the fuck are we doing here?' said Shella. 'Take us back to Colsbury before they leave.'

'I can't face them, Shella,' she said. 'They are better off without me.'

'If I was Daphne Holdfast,' said Shella, 'I would slap you across the face right now. Your children came to Colsbury, and you walked out on them, again?'

'I listened to their complaints, but it was all too much for me.'

'Are you actually a Holdfast, Karalyn?' said Shella. 'Are you giving up?'

'What else can I do?'

'We can go back to Colsbury, and you will try again. But first, where is the damn Sextant? We came here to check that it was safe; so let's do that.'

Karalyn wiped her eyes, and they both stood. Shella gazed at the cliffside house.

'Who built this place for you?' she said.

'I hired a hundred Aucterians to do it,' said Karalyn, 'and then I removed their memories.'

'That figures.'

They went into the house, and entered the Sextant chamber. The large device was humming quietly, and Karalyn almost broke down again at the sight of it.

'You should probably see if you can operate it,' said Shella.

Karalyn placed her hand onto the Sextant's flat surface, but nothing happened. She shook her head.

'Well, that's what we were expecting, I suppose,' said Shella. 'Should the Sextant go to Cael? He is able to operate it.'

'Cael would be devoured by the Sextant if it were his,' said Karalyn. 'I cannot do that to him. I love him too much.'

'Right,' said Shella. 'The Sextant is safe. Let's go back.'

'Maybe we could stay here for a few days,' said Karalyn. 'I don't think I'm ready to go back.'

'You mean wait here until Carden and Caitlyn have gone back to Plateau City?'

Karalyn said nothing.

'You are better than that, Karalyn,' said Shella. 'Your children have grown up, and you missed the last fifteen years of their lives. There is nothing you can do to change that – the past is done. But you can change your future. I know it will be hard. You will probably still be apologising twenty years from now; but Carden and Caitlyn are immortal, and so are you. You are going to run into them throughout the coming decades and centuries. This is your chance, right now, to ensure that you have some sort of amicable relationship with them. If you allow this opportunity to slip away, you will never forgive yourself. Be their mother, Karalyn; that's all they want from you.'

'I have been so stupid.'

'This new body is affecting you in all kinds of ways,' said Shella. 'You are old and mortal, like me; but you have also lost your confidence. Remember who you are, and who you were. Remember all you have done. The Ascendants would be running the Star Continent if you hadn't kicked their asses.'

Karalyn took out her Quadrant and gazed at it.

'That's it,' said Shella. 'Just a few finger movements, and we'll be back on Colsbury. Please, Karalyn; do the right thing.'

'I am scared.'

'Yeah, I know. Guess what? – tough shit. Take it on the fucking chin, Karalyn.'

Karalyn touched the Quadrant, the air crackled, and they both appeared inside Arrosa and Cael's apartment on Colsbury. The room was empty.

'She's gone,' said Karalyn.

'Try the middle balcony,' said Shella.

Karalyn triggered the Quadrant again, and they arrived on the middle balcony of the Summer Palace. Carden was standing by the railings alone, smoking a cigarette, his face dark with anger. Caitlyn was a few yards away on a chair, crying, while Calpurnia was sitting next to her with an arm over her shoulder.

Calpurnia turned, and saw Karalyn and Shella.

'Caitlyn,' she said. 'Your mother is back.'

Caitlyn looked up, as Carden turned.

'I thought you had left us again,' said Caitlyn.

'I love you both so much,' said Karalyn. 'Please forgive me.'

Carden turned away again, but Caitlyn got to her feet. She walked over to Karalyn, and embraced her mother. Shella and Calpurnia moved to the side of the balcony as Karalyn and Caitlyn wept in each other's arms. Carden tossed his cigarette over the balcony railings. He eyed his sister and his mother for a few moments, then he walked off the balcony.

'I'm sorry,' said Karalyn.

'Yes, Mother,' said Caitlyn. 'I know.'

CHAPTER 20
SEVENTEEN

Marchside, Kell – 23rd Day, First Third Summer 560

Carter climbed up onto the cart. He gripped the reins, and the ponies started pulling the cart along the track. In the rear, Lindi was lying on her back with her eyes closed as she allowed the sunlight to warm her skin.

'The barley's drying out nicely,' Carter said. He frowned, and peered over his shoulder. 'Are ye sleeping, Lindi?'

'I am sunbathing,' she said.

'Why? Yer skin's already dark.'

'I'm not trying to get a tan, you cretinous oaf; I am enjoying the miracle of the sun being out. There isn't a single cloud in the sky. I wish it was always like this in Kell.'

'Then it wouldnae be so green. The rain makes it beautiful.'

Lindi lit a stick of dreamweed, and reclined against a pile of empty sacks.

'Are ye sure that's a good idea?' said Carter. 'We'll be back at the farmhouse in five minutes.'

'It's my birthday,' she said. 'I can do whatever I like.'

'Are ye ready to face yer parents?'

'Lara is not my parent,' she said.

'Come on, Lindi; the woman raised ye. I would ask, as a favour to me, that ye treat Lara with respect when she arrives.'

Lindi started to laugh.

'I was being serious,' said Carter.

'I know,' she said. 'That's what makes it so funny. You haven't ever met Lara; she might be a complete bitch for all you know.'

'I bet she's not, but. Sable wouldnae have married a bitch.'

Lindi sat up. The cart was climbing the hill to the farmhouse. 'I am going to ask my mother for a special present today,' she said. 'I'll get her to promise to agree to it before I tell her what it is.'

'Aye?'

'And then I will ask her to tell me who my father is.'

'As a present?'

'Yes. It might work. Have you got me a present?'

'Maybe.'

'If you haven't, I will beat you up.'

'I'd like to see ye try.'

'Have you ever killed anyone, Carter?'

He laughed. 'Of course I haven't.'

'I would like to crush a mortal's skull with my bare hands.'

'I think ye might be smoking too much weed, Lindi.'

Lindi frowned, then she used her self-healing to expel the dreamweed from her system. She gazed around the cart, and climbed up onto the driver's bench.

'Do I stink of weed?' she said.

'A bit.'

'Bollocks. I should be trying to make a good impression on your mother. Tell her it was you who was smoking.'

He eyed her as he pulled on the reins, bringing the cart to a halt in the courtyard outside the farmhouse. They climbed down, and Lindi walked into the house, as Carter dealt with the ponies. She pulled off her boots, and left them in an untidy pile by the door, then she walked into the dining room. Aila and Clova were there, setting up the table for lunch.

'All the morning farm chores have been done,' said Lindi.

'You didn't have to do that on your birthday,' said Aila.

'I wanted to,' she said. 'I don't mind hard work; I want to pay my way.'

'Is Carter with ye?' said Clova.

'He's putting the ponies away,' said Lindi. 'Is there anything I can help you with?'

'Not on your birthday,' said Aila. 'Go into the kitchen, and I'll gather the others.'

Lindi gave Aila her sweetest smile, then she walked out of the dining room. She noticed Carter at the end of the hallway neatening Lindi's boots, and she laughed to herself. She walked into the kitchen. The side of the coffee pot was still warm, so she poured herself a cup and sat down. A few moments later, the rest of the family crowded in and joined Lindi by the table.

'Happy birthday,' said Carla, holding out a wrapped bundle. 'This is from me and Ceres.'

'Thank you so much,' said Lindi. She unwrapped it. 'Clothes – exactly what I needed.'

'This is from me,' said Aila, placing a bottle of whisky onto the table, 'but it's only a small part of my present. The real gift is the offer of a job, if you want it. We have a vacancy in the distillery for an apprentice, and I will keep it open for you.'

Lindi smiled to hide her disappointment. Did Aila honestly believe that she wanted to work in a distillery, where she would be surrounded by mortals? She was an immensely powerful god, and she should be ruling empires, not working like a peasant.

'Thank you,' she said; 'that is so thoughtful.'

'I made this for you,' said Carter. He set down a sword in a scabbard of dark green leather.

'That's not true,' said Carla. 'You were making that sword for yerself, Carter.'

'Aye, all right,' said Carter, 'but I thought I'd give it to Lindi. I can make myself another one.'

Lindi gripped the handle. The sword was heavy, so she powered her battle-vision as she drew it. The blade was long and dark, almost black.

'It's not Tempest, is it?' she said.

'It's got Tempest in the alloy,' said Carter.

Lindi narrowed her eyes. 'And you made it yourself?'

Carter laughed. 'Aye. I've been forging for a few years; I know how to make a sword.'

'Does it have a name?' said Lindi. 'A good sword should have a name.'

'Should it?' said Carter. 'In that case, ye'll have to think up a name on yer own.'

'Then I shall call it *God's Will*,' said Lindi. 'Thank you very much.'

'Do you know how to use a sword?' said Aila.

'My mother gave me a few lessons,' said Lindi. 'I'm a natural.'

'Me next,' said Clova. She lifted a large basket onto the table. 'I made this up for you,' she said. 'It's got chocolate, that cider you like, cheese and honey; all sorts of stuff.'

Lindi suppressed her initial response, which was to wonder aloud why her Kell cousins were all so damn rustic. Cheese? On what world was *cheese* an appropriate gift for a seventeen-year-old goddess?

'That is so wonderful, Clova,' she said. 'Thank you. I might open the cider now. Whose birthday is next?'

'Mine,' said Ceres. 'I'll be sixteen in the Last Third of Summer.'

'I hope I am still here for that,' said Lindi.

'Let's crack open the ale and the cider,' said Carter. 'Is the dining room ready?'

'Aye,' said Clova. 'Me and Ma set it up.'

Lindi got up as the others made their way out of the kitchen. She held the sword to her belt, but she would need some way to attach it properly. It was easily the best present she had received from the Marchbrae Holdfasts, though the whisky would go down well. She drew the sword again, and held it with both hands. It was longer than she was used to, and she could well imagine that Carter had made it for himself, but her battle-vision could cope with the weight. She swung *God's Will* over her head, and smiled.

Aila eyed her from the doorway. 'It might be too big for you, that sword.'

'I can handle it,' said Lindi.

'But how are you going to draw it?' said Aila. 'It's too long to go by your waist. You might have to carry it about on your back.'

'Then I will carry it on my back.'

Lindi slid the blade back into its scabbard, and left the kitchen with Aila.

'Sable and the others will be here soon,' Aila said. 'You will have to accept whatever they have decided.'

'I am prepared to beg again.'

'Let's hope it doesn't come to that.'

They entered the dining room, and they all took their places. Cider was served to the younger children, and Lindi took a mug. Cider had been her favourite discovery in Kell. She had already known about whisky, but Kell cider had been unfamiliar to her, and she had taken to it so much that she would always choose it over ale.

Aila, Carter and Clova each took a dram of whisky, and Aila raised her glass.

'To Lindi Holdfast on her seventeenth birthday,' she said.

The others drank, and Clova slapped Lindi on the back. The door opened, and Naxor walked into the farmhouse with Konna. Aila got to her feet and hugged her daughter.

'I'm only back for the day, Ma,' said Konna. 'I still haven't decided if I want to stay in Nom Karta.'

'Take all the time you need,' said Aila.

'Is Sable here yet?'

'Not yet.'

Konna nodded, then she eyed Lindi. 'Could I have a quick word with you?'

Lindi got to her feet. 'What is it?'

'It's private,' said Konna.

Lindi frowned, then she followed Konna out of the room. They walked to the other end of the farmhouse, then Konna came to a halt.

'I might have fucked up, Lindi,' she said. 'I'm sorry.'

'What did you do?' said Lindi.

'I should have kept my big mouth shut, as I know it's none of my business.'

Lindi placed a hand on her hip. 'Well?'

'I was speaking to Lord Esher,' said Konna, 'and I mentioned the possibility that he might be your father.'

Lindi's temper started to build.

'And so Esher decided to ask your mother if it was true,' Konna went on.

'What did she say?'

'She denied it.'

'So Esher is not my father?'

'Not according to your mother. Sable knows it was me who brought it up with him, and she's not exactly happy about it. I thought you should know.'

'If it's not Esher, who does that leave?'

'I can only think of two others – Elmhirst and Bailey. But, I don't know if your mother was telling Esher the truth. There was a look on her face before she denied it, just the briefest of looks – but it was enough to put some doubt into my mind. Anyway, I'm sorry.'

'My parentage is of no concern to you.'

'Aye, I know that, but Esher is my friend. I was asking because of him, not because of you, but I should have taken your feelings into account.'

Clova appeared at the other end of the hall. 'Lindi, yer Ma's here.'

Lindi walked back to the dining room, her mood sour. She put on a smile as she entered the large chamber, then her smile became genuine as she caught sight of her brother.

'Joss!' she cried.

She ran to him, and he flung his big arms round her.

'All right, my little tiddler?' he said.

She beamed up at him.

'This is our son Anaj'osso,' said Sable; 'or just Joss.'

'Good afternoon, Marchbrae cousins,' said Joss. 'I hope my little sister hasn't been a right pain in the arse; but that would be a first, eh, Lindi?'

'Shut up,' she said.

'And this is Alara'osso,' Sable went on.

Lara smiled. 'It's nice to see you all again; it's been a while. But I don't think I've met you before. You must be Carla, right?'

'Aye, that's me,' said the girl.

'And it's bleeding well sunny,' said Lara. 'I was led to believe that it always rained down here.'

Lindi steeled herself. She took a slow breath, and clasped her hands together. She gazed at Lara.

'Please, Mother,' she said, 'I...'

Lara laughed. 'That's enough, girl; that's all I wanted to hear.'

'But...'

'Sable and I have already decided that you can stay,' said Lara. 'If Lady Aila says it's all right.'

'I am more than happy to let her stay,' said Aila. 'Sit down, everyone.'

Lindi noticed Sable eye Konna for a brief moment as they all sat by the dining table.

'We do have a plan for the beginning of autumn,' Lara said.

'What plan?' said Lindi.

'Queen Blackrose wants to try out the *Mischief Maker* on a proper voyage,' Lara went on; 'and so we'll be sailing Her Big Scaly Majesty all the way to Alef and Olkis – and you, Lindi, will be coming along as the ship's second lieutenant. Tilly will be first lieutenant, and Joss will be master. I, of course, will be the bleeding captain; and Sable, as per bloody usual, will be a passenger.' She eyed Lindi. 'That is our condition; do you accept?'

'Yes, Captain,' said Lindi.

Joss rubbed his hands together. 'I can hardly wait; it'll be a grand test for the *Maker*. I'll be taking us through the Luckenbay to Langbeg; right through the damn Skerries.'

'I have no idea what yer all talking about,' said Carter.

'Ship stuff,' said Lindi.

'Do you sail, Carter?' said Joss.

Lara eyed him. 'What did I tell you, Joss? They ain't got no boats that sail on the ocean here. All they have is a piddling little sea in the middle of the continent.'

Joss smiled, but he looked puzzled. 'No ships on the ocean, eh?'

'Carter made me a Tempest sword,' said Lindi.

'Did he now?' said Joss.

'I've called it *God's Will*.'

Joss laughed. 'Of course you did. So, what are we drinking?'

'Try this,' said Lindi, as she shoved a mug of cider in front of her brother.

'I'll get some whisky ready for ye, Joss,' said Carter. 'Ye'll need it after trying that stuff.'

Joss picked up the mug and drained it. He raised an eyebrow. 'Funny sort of ale, this is, eh?'

Aila smiled. 'It's cider,' she said. 'Apparently, it's what all the locals used to drink in Kell.'

'It's made from apples,' said Carla.

Joss nodded to Carter. 'I'll be needing that whisky now.'

'What's that smell coming from the hall?' said Ceres.

'I smell it, too,' said Carla. 'It reeks.'

'That was me,' said Joss. 'I brought fish.'

'You brought fish?' said Aila.

'From this morning's catch in Udall harbour, ma'am,' he said. 'It's all fresh.'

'I haven't eaten fish in years,' said Aila. 'Children, we shall be having fish for dinner today. Thank you, Joss.'

'It was my pleasure,' he said. He picked up the whisky Carter had poured for him and took a sip. 'That hits the bleeding spot and no mistake.'

'Is the fish my birthday present?' said Lindi.

Joss laughed. 'It was a gift for the house,' he said. He took out a small box and handed it to her. 'This is for you.'

Lindi opened the box. Inside, resting on a soft velvet cushion was a silver necklace with a pearl mounted on a golden pendant.

'Happy birthday, little tiddler,' said Joss. 'Do you like it?'

Lindi picked it up and fastened it round her neck. 'I love it.'

Sable, Lara and Joss stayed in the farmhouse for two hours, eating and drinking with the Marchbrae Holdfasts. Lindi cried when it was time for them to leave, but she wasn't sure if it was because she was sad they were going, or because she had drunk too much cider. Or perhaps it was because she had lacked the courage to ask her mother about the identity of her father.

'I'll see you in the autumn, Lindi,' Joss said.

'Behave yourself, girl,' said Lara. 'I hope you have a good summer.'

Lindi wiped her eyes, then Sable activated her Quadrant, and the three of them disappeared. Clova handed Lindi a handkerchief, as the younger children started clearing away the table. Aila had retreated to the kitchen in order to prepare the fish, and Naxor sat down next to Lindi, a glass of whisky in his hand.

'Such a charming family you have,' he said.

Lindi nodded.

'I was wondering,' Naxor went, 'if you might be interested in a little experiment.'

She eyed him.

'I understand that you do not hear a voice when you touch a Quadrant,' he said.

'That's right,' she said. 'I know that some people hear a voice, but I don't.'

'But your mother is able to operate the Sextant,' said Naxor, 'and she doesn't hear the voice of the Quadrant. Therefore, it can be deduced that hearing the voice of the Quadrant is not essential in order for one to be sensitive to Tempest; sensitive in a way that allows one to operate the Sextant.'

Lindi narrowed her eyes. 'Spit it out, Naxor,' she said. 'What do you want from me?'

He leaned in closer. 'There is another device; did you know that? It was constructed by the renowned Professor Elbannon, and its purpose is to locate sources of Tempest. It is called the Compass. Have you heard of it?'

'Nope.'

'Would you like to see if you can use it?'

'Why would I want to do that?'

'As a favour.'

'As a favour for who?'

'Lord Edgar of Nom Karta.'

'Hasn't he got Kyra for that kind of stuff?'

'Kyra is not in Nom Karta at present,' said Naxor. 'It wouldn't take long.'

'What's in it for me?'

'Lord Edgar would owe you a favour in return.'

Lindi gazed around the room. Konna was talking to Carter by the bay windows as they tidied away plates and glasses.

'Is Konna coming along?' said Lindi. 'She lives in Nom Karta.'

'Konna's presence is not required,' said Naxor. 'You and I would be visiting Nom Karta alone.'

'I noticed you waited until Lady Aila had left the dining room before asking me this,' she said. 'Is it a secret?'

'It is not exactly a secret,' said Naxor, 'but perhaps a little discretion would not go amiss. Shall we leave now?'

'All right,' she said.

Naxor rose to his feet, and Lindi did the same. Naxor glanced over at Carter and Konna.

'Lindi and I won't be long,' he said, then he triggered his Quadrant.

The air crackled, and Lindi appeared with Naxor on the roof of a gargantuan building. Dragons were soaring and circling through the sky above them, and there was a series of other, equally-massive buildings set out along the streets.

'This is Nom Karta,' said Naxor, 'the capital city of the Dominion. What you are looking at are dragon palaces. Hold on a moment – I will let Lord Edgar know that we have arrived.'

Lindi lit a cigarette as Naxor's eyes glazed over. She powered her self-healing a little to sober herself up, and watched the dragons fly over the city. The air shimmered, and two men appeared. At once, Lindi could sense that both were extremely old gods.

'Which one is Edgar?' she said.

'I am he,' said the man on the left. 'My colleague is Lord Elmhirst.'

'Greetings, Lindi Holdfast,' said Elmhirst. 'Welcome to Nom Karta.'

Lindi regarded him, wondering if she might be looking at her father.

'Have you explained to Lindi what it is that we require of her, Lord Naxor?' said Edgar.

'I have briefly summed it up, my lord,' said Naxor. 'I have made her aware of the existence of the Compass, but I have not given her your reasons for wanting her to test if she can use it.'

Edgar dipped a hand into a pocket and retrieved a small object.

'This is the Compass, Lindi,' he said. 'I would like you to hold it in one hand, and place your thumb onto the circle near the top.'

'No thanks,' said Lindi. 'I'm not touching that; it could have been anywhere.'

'It is perfectly clean,' said Edgar, a confused look on his face.

'What if I want something in return?' said Lindi. 'What have you got to offer me? And before you answer, you should know that it's my birthday, and my expectations are high.'

'What is it you desire?' said Edgar. 'Gold? Land? A royal title?'

'Yeah, I like the sound of those,' said Lindi.

'I am open to negotiation,' said Edgar, 'but first, let us see if the Compass responds to your touch.'

He held it out, and Lindi took it.

'How will I know if it works?' said Lindi.

'A circle has been engraved on the outside of the device,' said Edgar. 'You place your thumb onto it and close your eyes. If you are sensitive to the Compass, then you should be able to feel the presence of Tempest. Right now, there is more than one Quadrant on this roof, and all Quadrants contain a small but potent amount of Tempest. You should be able to sense it.'

'And then what?'

'Test it first, and then we shall talk.'

'I get it. If it doesn't work, then you aren't going to tell me what you want me to do next – is that it? But, if I can use it, then you will want me to find some Tempest for you? Am I close?'

'Please, Lindi,' said Naxor. 'Try it; that is all we are asking for now.'

She eyed the demigod. 'And what are you getting out of this?'

'I am merely assisting Lord Edgar,' said Naxor.

'You are doing him a favour?'

'You could say that.'

Lindi narrowed her eyes as the three men stared at her. If she touched the circle that had been engraved onto the device and felt nothing, then she had no doubt that she would be whisked back to Kell without any further explanation, and then she would never find out what they really wanted.

She closed her eyes and pressed her thumb onto the device. At first, she could see nothing, then her vision went grey, as though she had stumbled into a thick sea of fog. Four dim lights appeared, lights that roughly corresponded to where the four gods were standing on the roof. She aimed her vision down, and saw that one of the sources of the faint light was coming from the pocket in which she kept her stolen Quadrant.

She resisted the urge to smile, for smiling would alert the others to her success. Let them wait a little longer, she told herself.

She opened her eyes.

'Well?' said Naxor.

'Well what?' said Lindi.

'Did it work? Could you detect the presence of Tempest?'

'Is Lord Esher in Nom Karta today?' she said.

Edgar's eyes flashed with impatience.

'She clearly cannot operate the Compass,' said Elmhirst. 'It was worth trying, my lord, but it seems that your plan can go no further.'

'Oh yeah?' said Lindi. 'Then how do I know that you have a Quadrant in your back pocket, Mister Elmhirst? Or that Edgar's Quadrant is inside the front of his robes? How do you answer that, smartarse?'

Edgar laughed in joy, then he clenched his fists and closed his eyes. Next to him, Elmhirst looked unhappy, as though he had been hoping that the experiment would fail. Lindi narrowed her eyes. She didn't know what Edgar wanted from her, but whatever it was, Lord Elmhirst did not approve.

'Well done, Lindi,' said Naxor. 'I had complete faith in you.'

Edgar opened his eyes, and he gazed at Lindi. 'This pleases me. Now I must ask you, Lindi Holdfast – are you prepared to help me again?'

'To do what?' she said.

'I will not say, not at the moment,' he said, 'as I need to prepare for what must be done. If you are willing to help me, I will call on you soon.'

'Then you'd better start working on that list you offered me,' she said. 'What was it? – gold, land and fancy titles? I'll have a bit of each, thanks. And I want to see Lord Esher.'

'Why?' said Naxor.

'That's none of your business, Naxor,' she said.

'I will grant you everything you desire,' said Edgar. 'Will you help me?'

'I will,' she said, 'unless it hurts my family in some way. It doesn't, does it?'

'No one will be hurt,' said Edgar. 'My purpose is to extend life, not to harm it. I must extract one last thing from you, Lindi, before you go.'

'Let me guess,' she said; 'I am not to mention this to anyone?'

Edgar smiled. 'You have it exactly right. Naxor, please take Lindi to Lord Esher's rooms on Zamata.'

Naxor bowed low. 'Yes, my gracious lord.'

'And thank you, Lindi,' Edgar went on. 'You have brightened the darkness of my soul.'

He held out his hand, and Lindi placed the Compass onto his palm. Naxor took out his Quadrant. He eyed Lindi, who nodded, then he activated the device. The air shimmered, and they appeared amid a wide lawn that sat next to a palace of shining white marble.

'Do you see that balcony above us?' said Naxor. 'Lord Esher dwells in there. I can see him with my vision; he is at his desk, writing a letter to the dragon that governs Aucteran. Might I ask why you wish to speak to this man?'

'You may not,' she said. 'Wait here, and if I sense you spying on me, I will use *God's Will* to cut off both of your hands.' She looked into his eyes. 'Do you believe me?'

Naxor frowned. 'Surprisingly, I do. It is the kind of thing your mother would threaten to do.'

'I will know if you use your vision, Naxor,' she said. 'Be a good little demigod, and keep your nose out of my business.'

She took out her own Quadrant, triggered it, and appeared on the balcony that Naxor had pointed out. She opened the balcony door, and saw a man sitting by a desk.

He glanced up, his eyes widening. 'What are you doing in my apartment?' he said. 'Who are you?'

Lindi peered at him. He didn't seem to resemble her in any way, but neither had Lord Elmhirst, or Lord Edgar, for that matter.

'My name is Lindi Holdfast,' she said. 'Does that mean anything to you?'

Esher got to his feet. 'You are Sable's daughter.'

'I spoke to Konna,' she said.

'Ah.'

'I know what my mother told you.'

'I see. Do you doubt it?'

'I don't know. Do you?'

'Your mother was adamant. I am not your father, Lindi. I... I wish I were.'

'Why?'

'I have no family of my own,' he said. 'I am an Ascendant whose mind was stripped bare by Karalyn Holdfast, and I cannot remember anything of my old life. All I remember is being a mortal in Jezra. I was alone then, and I am alone now. Having a daughter would... I think it might have anchored me, and given me some purpose. At the same time, I would have been angry with your mother for keeping your existence hidden from me; but, on balance, I would rather have a family.'

'Don't you have any friends?'

'Konna is my friend,' he said, 'but she lives in Nom Karta. I wish you luck in finding your father, Lindi. You seem like a lovely young woman. You look just like your mother.'

Lindi said nothing. She chewed her lip for a moment, then she activated the Quadrant in her pocket, and appeared next to Naxor on the lawn.

'Thank you for not intruding, Naxor,' she said.

'I quite like having hands, Lindi,' he said. 'Did you get what you came for?'

'No,' she said. 'Take me back to Kell.'

CHAPTER 21
THE FAITHLESS ONE

Colsbury Castle, Republic of the Holdings – 23rd Day, First Third Summer 560

'I like Colsbury when it's so quiet,' said Kelvin, as he and Cael walked through the gardens behind the Lesser Keep.

'I do, too,' said Cael, 'but we must remember why it is so quiet.'

Kelvin lowered his gaze. 'I remember,' he said. 'The Gunstians attacked us. I just meant that I don't hear so many lies when there aren't people around.'

'Are lies starting to cause you pain?'

'A little bit. It's not as bad as the pain mum feels, but I don't like it.'

They stopped by the gravestones in the middle of the apple orchard. Fresh flowers had been put down next to the grave of Cael's father – the surest sign that his mother was living on Colsbury again.

'Why does Granny have a new body?' said Kelvin. 'Will I get a new body when I die?'

'There is no one like Granny Karalyn,' said Cael.

'Then what happens when we die?'

'I don't think anything happens. Do you remember where you were before you were born?'

'No.'

'Then I think it might be like that after we die. Your mother believes something else, though.'

'She thinks Granny is a god.'

'She does. But you're too young to be thinking about death, Kelvin.'

'I saw people die when the Gunstians attacked.'

'I know you did. I wish I could have shielded you from that. I saw horrible things when I was young. You never really forget them, but you don't have to think about it all the time.'

'Cowie told me that the Gunstians want to kill you, Dad.'

'Many of the Gunstians are bad people. They don't like us because we don't believe in their god.'

'When are you going to fight them again?'

'Tonight,' said Cael. 'I will be back in the morning, though.'

'Why do *you* have to fight them? Why can't someone else do it?'

'It's my job, Kelvin. When you make a promise to do your duty, then you have to keep your word, or people will never trust you again. But it's more than that – I want to protect my family and my friends, and all of the people who live in the Empire. That's the only good reason to fight, Kelvin – to defend what you love from bad people.'

'How can you tell who the bad people are?'

Cael gazed down at the boy. He was well used to Arrosa's Gift of Truth, but sometimes it was hard to know what to say to Kelvin that wouldn't trigger his own Gift. He was too young for brutal honesty, but any lie Cael told would be instantly detected.

'You look for people who do bad things,' he said.

'Have you ever done anything bad?'

Cael's thoughts went to the massacre at the Temple of the Martyrs, and he looked away, knowing that he had been caught by his own logic.

'Have you, Dad?'

'Aye, son. I have.'

'Does that mean you are a bad person?'

'I am bad to my enemies,' Cael said. 'I think it's time for your morning classes to begin.'

Kelvin narrowed his eyes, as though he guessed that his father wished to change the subject. They carried on walking through the empty gardens, then they entered the castle forecourt, where the little harbour lay.

'Off you go to class, Kelvin,' said Cael. 'I will see you at lunchtime.'

Kelvin ran off in the direction of the Summer Palace, and Cael turned for the harbour. He was hoping that his mother would be there, but Shella was sitting alone on her deckchair by the small pier. She glanced up and saw him.

'Karalyn is with Caitlyn,' she said. 'She stayed in the Summer Palace last night; Karalyn is lucky that her daughter is so forgiving.'

'Did Carden go back to Plateau City?' said Cael.

'Yeah. He wasn't having any of it. Kelsey took him back last night.'

'At least one of them is prepared to reconcile,' said Cael. 'That's better than I had expected.'

'I said Caitlyn was forgiving,' said Shella, 'but she's still mightily pissed off with her mother. It's going to take time. Could you do me a favour? There's a little stall by the front of the Great Keep that sells hot food. Could you get me something?'

'What would you like?'

'A pie? Sausages on a roll? Something with meat in it.'

'All right; I'll be back in a minute.'

Cael walked through the forecourt towards a small row of stalls – the only stalls that remained after most of the civilians and merchants had been evacuated from the island. He bought two portions of bread with sausages, and walked back to the harbour. He gave one portion to Shella, then he sat down on the pier by her feet, his legs dangling over the water.

'You're a good lad,' said Shella, as she took a bite.

'Am I?' said Cael. 'It's my fault that the Gunstians are attacking us. I fucked up, Shella. I killed three hundred Gunstians and blew up an ancient temple to show them how dangerous it is to attack the Holdfasts, but it had the exact opposite effect.'

'These things happen,' said Shella.

'Do they?'

'You were angry, and you miscalculated. On the other hand, you have joined the ranks of those of us who have killed far too many people for the wrong reasons. I have certainly killed more than my share; and so have the Empress, and your Aunty Sable, and Keir, and Daphne. Who have I missed out? What I'm saying is that you are one of the few Holdfasts I know who actually seems to regret some of the violence they have carried out. You get that from your mother.'

'Or maybe my father.'

'Yeah – good point. Lennox walked around feeling permanently crushed by the weight of what he had done; or what he thought he had done. The greatest act of forgiveness I have ever witnessed was when your mother absolved Sable for what she did to Lennox. But you need to focus on what is happening right now. The Gunstians are kicking our asses, Cael. They need to be stopped.'

'How? By exterminating all of them? How else can we stop them? They have an unlimited number of volunteers who are prepared to die in order to hurt us – how do you fight that? No matter how many times we raid them, no matter how many ships and bases and depots we hit, they keep coming back. Every soldier of theirs we kill becomes a martyr, inspiring twenty others to volunteer in their place. I hate them, Shella.'

Shella said nothing.

'I am one of the few people with the power to kill everyone in Gunst,' Cael went on. 'The thought haunts me. I know where my mother is hiding the Sextant; I have been there. Five minutes with the Sextant, and Gunst would no longer be a problem. No – ten seconds would be enough. *Remove everyone from Gunst and place them at the bottom of the fucking ocean*. And that would be that.'

'Are you tempted?'

'Aye. Does that make me a monster? I am scared that the Gunstians will hurt or kill someone I love, and then I would have to live with the knowledge that I could have prevented it. But if I did it, I would be one of the worst mass murderers of all time. Millions of people live in Gunst – women, children, babies. How could I ever look my own children in the eye again?'

'Shut up and eat your breakfast before it gets cold,' said Shella. 'It's too early to be thinking about these things.'

Cael took a large bite out of the sandwich, but he barely tasted it.

'Hey, Cael,' said Shella. 'Who are those men? They are looking in our direction, but I don't recognise them.'

Cael glanced up. His gaze went through the archway by the end of the pier, and he saw two men standing by the entrance to the gardens. Without a moment's thought, he sent out his vision, and entered the mind of the man on the left. At first, he could not understand what the man was thinking, then he realised that his native language was Gunstian.

'Don't do anything dramatic, Shella,' Cael said, 'but they are Gunstian. Let me see why they are here, and then I will take care of them both.'

He started to root around in the man's thoughts and memories; then it became clear – it was Cael Holdfast they had come for. It was Cael they desired to kill; and it was Cael they were hoping would drop down dead at any moment, for the other Gunstian man had the Gift of Poison, and Cael's food had been contaminated.

Cael gazed at the bread and meat in his hands. 'Shit.'

He felt a tightening in his throat, then his guts seemed to explode in pain, He dropped the food, and fell off the edge of the pier and into the water of the harbour, his head going under the water. He struggled as the pain got worse. He couldn't breathe, but as he was already underwater, that seemed almost irrelevant compared to the searing pain in his stomach. His hand found the side of the pier, and he pulled his head out of the water to see Shella staring down at him.

He gasped and choked, then he sent out his vision.

Sister, he called out. *Two Gunstians... the Gift of Poison. Help me.*

He foundered, and slipped back under the water, sinking into the murky depths. There was a splash next to him, and a hand reached out and gripped his arm. Cael felt himself being pulled upwards, and his head broke through the water again.

'Help me lift him out of the water,' cried Cole.

Two soldiers on the pier leaned over, and Cael was hauled out. He was set down onto the boards of the wooden pier, then he vomited into the waters of the harbour. Dazed and in agony, he saw Cole climb out of the water next to him.

'Talk to me, cousin,' said Cole, as he crouched over him.

'The Gift of Poison,' Cael gasped.

'I know. Kyra is dealing with the two Gunstian agents.' Cole frowned. 'You should be dead.'

'He's three-quarters Kellach Brigdomin,' said Shella, who was still sitting on her deck chair. 'You can't kill a Kellach with poison.'

'Water,' gasped Cael.

Cole nodded to a soldier, who handed over a canister. Cole pulled off the lid, and held it to Cael's mouth. Cael drank, then he threw up again. He turned so that he was on his knees, gripped his stomach with both hands, and vomited for a third time.

'That's it,' said Shella; 'get it all out. That's the Kellach way. Those dozy Gunstians.'

Kelsey walked up the pier. 'Is he all right? Cael – are you all right?'

Cael nodded.

'Thank Pyre for that,' said Kelsey. 'We caught the Gifted agent, but his colleague abandoned him; he took out his Quadrant and vanished before Kyra could send him to sleep. She needs to learn damn Gunstian.' She eyed Shella. 'No symptoms?'

'I am clearly not worth killing,' said Shella.

'Many would disagree, Shella,' said Kelsey. 'Good job, Cole. I saw you dive into the water.'

'Thanks, cousin,' said Cael. 'I assume Kyra told you?'

'Arrosa alerted us first,' said Kelsey. 'She sensed the Gift of Poison being used, then Kyra got your message a few seconds later. You were the target, Cael. After Bailey and your mother, you are now the number one name on their list. They even have a title for you – Bailey was the Great Betrayer, Karalyn was the Demon Witch, and you are apparently the Faithless One. It seems you have made quite an impact on them.'

'We need a fucking vision dome,' said Cael; 'like we had over Clackenbaird.'

'Aye, but your mother isn't capable of that sort of thing, not in her new body. Kyra can kind of do it, but it doesn't work as well and anyway, she is due to return to Nom Karta soon. It would be handy if you could suddenly discover that you can do it. You helped build up Karalyn's vision dome over Kell; could you give it another try?'

Cael sat down on the crowded pier and wiped the sweat from his forehead.

Shella peered at him. 'I think he's still in a daze, Kelsey. I have some keenweed he can have.'

'Of course you do,' said Kelsey. 'Aye, what's the harm?'

Shella rummaged around in a pocket and produced a weedstick. She lit it, took a draw, and handed it to Cael. He took it, and smoked in silence for a moment, as his thoughts cleared.

'If the other agent escaped,' he said, 'then the Gunstians will know that their attempt to kill me has failed.'

'Maybe not,' said Cole. 'They saw you fall into the water, but I don't know if they saw you being pulled out again.'

'Then, at best, they are unsure,' said Cael. 'If I were the Gunstians, I would have prepared a back-up plan. I recommend we evacuate everyone from Colsbury within the next few minutes.'

'I preferred him before he smoked the keenweed,' said Kelsey. 'Up you get, Cael. I think your wife might like to see that you are still alive.'

Cael got to his feet. He took out a packet of cigarettes, but they were sodden. He tapped a pocket, and felt the reassuring presence of his Quadrant.

'How are you feeling?' said Cole.

'Like shit,' he said. 'My guts are on fire, and now my head is buzzing.'

'There's salve in the palace,' said Kelsey. 'Let's go.'

The soldiers led the way off the pier, while Cael and Cole walked at the rear.

'I am very glad you can swim, cousin,' Cael said. 'Thanks again.'

They walked through the forecourt, and came to a large group of people who had assembled in front of the Summer Palace. Arrosa was there with their children, and she hurried forward, her arms out to embrace her husband. Cael hugged her, then she leaned forward and kissed him.

'No one should have survived what that agent did to you, brother,' said Kyra. 'You are fortunate to have a Kellach constitution.'

'Where is the agent?' said Cael.

'We have placed him into the cells in the gatehouse,' said Cardova. 'This could be a breakthrough. If he knows where the Gunstian raiding camp is located, then we will get it out of him.'

'I have been asked to interrogate him,' said Arrosa, 'but I'll need your help.'

'Sure,' said Cael. 'Just give me ten minutes to change out of these wet clothes.'

His mother and Caitlyn appeared through the crowd.

'I'm fine, mother,' he said. 'Just a bit wet.'

'I heard what happened,' said Karalyn. 'I wanted to help, but... what could I do? I would only get in the way.'

'I understand,' said Cael. 'I think we should evacuate Colsbury. The Gunstians know we are here, and they won't stop attacking us. We'd be safer in the Blue Palace.'

'The Gunstians didn't use a Quadrant to arrive directly onto the island,' said Kyra. 'I would have sensed it if they had. They might have first appeared on the mainland.'

'It doesn't matter where they arrived,' said Cael. 'They know how to get here.'

'Let's think this through,' said Kelsey. 'We would need to get the Empress's approval, and you know how much she loves coming here each summer. Could you not try to build a vision shield first?'

'I have already tried,' said Cael.

'Try again,' said Karalyn. 'Kyra will help you.'

A scream arose from the direction of the bridge that led to the village on the mainland. Cael turned. A portal had been opened in front of the gatehouse, and hundreds of Gunstians soldiers were charging through, while Gifted agents in robes were subduing the imperial soldiers with the Gift of Pain. Before Cael could react, the portal closed; then it re-opened a hundred yards to their left, next to the base of the tall Spire. More Gunstians ran through, then that portal closed. By the gatehouse, the imperial soldiers were starting to recover from the Gift of Pain, but the Gunstians were tearing through them, cutting down those who were still on the ground. The portal opened again, in a different location, between the Great and Lesser Keeps. Three Gifted agents filled the forecourt with waves of Pain and Despair, as hundreds more Gunstian soldiers crossed over onto Colsbury. The agents retreated, and the third portal closed.

'Get all civilians into the palace,' shouted Cardova. 'Kelsey, start the evacuation. Get the Empress and the civilians to safety. Cole, call out every soldier and marine on the island.'

Cael ushered his children into the palace, then he turned to go back outside.

'Wait,' said Arrosa. 'We should stay together.'

'I have to fight, Arrosa,' he said. 'It's me they're here for.'

He kissed her and ran outside. With all three portals having gone, the forecourt was teeming with hundreds of Gunstian soldiers, but marines and imperial guards were piling out of the gatehouse and the barracks in the Great Keep. With no Gifted agents around, the Gunstians were being pushed back, and a thick line of soldiers was preventing them from getting close to the front of the Summer Palace. Behind the line, more soldiers were buckling on their armour, while a quartermaster was handing out packets of crossbow bolts and swords to anyone who needed them. He handed a leather breastplate to Cael, who pulled it on over his wet clothes.

Cole appeared by Cael's side with a company of marines, several of whom were carrying crates.

'Distribute the Jackdaws, sergeant,' said Cole; 'give them to anyone who has had training.'

'Aye, sir,' said the marine sergeant.

Cael glanced into the forecourt at the fighting. The Gunstians were still outnumbering those from the imperial army who had been on duty and ready to fight, but reinforcements were arriving, and their lines were holding steady.

A marine passed Cael a loaded Mark Two Jackdaw.

'Shall we?' said Cole.

'Have you organised firing teams before?' said Cael.

'I have, sir,' said Cole.

'Then take command. I'll watch, to see what I can learn.'

Cole spoke to several other officers, as the company of marines loaded their Jackdaws. Squads were carrying forward crates filled with ammunition, and others were handing out the small packets containing Ectus powder.

'Form up; three lines,' shouted Cole. He gestured to a captain out in the forecourt. 'Prepare to withdraw crossbows.'

The company of marines got into position just behind the crossbow teams, leaving gaps in their lines where their comrades could slip past them to the rear.

'Crossbow teams – pull out!' Cole cried.

Each soldier armed with a crossbow turned and filed back through the ranks of the marines, who closed up as soon as the last of them had passed.

'First rank, fire!' shouted Cole.

Seventy Jackdaws cracked, and smoke rose up into the forecourt as the front rows of the charging Gunstians were cut to pieces.

'Second rank, fire!'

The marines in the row behind fired as one, while those in front of them knelt as they reloaded.

'Third rank, fire!'

The carnage in the forecourt increased, as the Gunstians ran into the hail of lead. The other imperial soldiers drew back to the flanks and watched, as the marines in the centre unleashed volley after volley into the enemy. The last remaining Gunstians in the forecourt rallied together as a group, and threw themselves at the marines, and the Jackdaws cut them down to the last soldier.

'Cease fire!' shouted Cole.

The groans and cries of the wounded Gunstians echoed up into the sky, where wisps of smoke from the Ectus powder lingered. Cael peered into the forecourt, and saw the bodies heaped in piles over the bloodstained cobbles.

'When we get back to Plateau City,' said Cael, 'remind me to send Rosie a bottle of the finest Marchbrae whisky,'

'All ranks, reload!' shouted Cole. 'Keep your eyes open for another portal.'

Cardova walked out of the palace.

'The civilians have been evacuated,' he said to Cael, 'but the Empress is refusing to leave.' His gaze went to the slaughter in the forecourt, and his eyes tightened. 'I heard the roar of the Jackdaws being fired,' he went on, 'but I wasn't expecting this.'

'Eighteen volleys was enough, sir,' said Cole.

'That's well over a thousand rounds,' said Cardova.

'In less than two minutes, sir,' said Cole.

Cardova walked with Cael, Cole and the commander of the marine company into the forecourt. They gazed at the bodies of the fallen, as the wounded were picked up and carried to the side of the palace, where doctors were waiting to treat them. Cael's eyes went to the small holes pocking the side of the Great Keep.

'We need as many of these Jackdaws as possible for the army and the marines,' said Cardova. 'I will get the factories moving; they will be increasing their production. I knew these weapons were going to be useful, but this has exceeded every expectation.'

'I believe Rosie is working on the Mark Three, sir,' said Cole.

'I can't see how these weapons could get any better,' said Cardova.

'Rosie has a few ideas about that, sir,' said Cole, 'and Nestorian is working on a version with a longer barrel. He claims it will have a much greater range.'

Cardova shook his head. 'Imagine if the Ascendants had possessed these weapons on Dragon Eyre; imagine any army equipped with them. They would be unstoppable.'

'Until the other side gets their own versions, sir,' said Cole.

'But that's the point – the Dominion is refusing to allow the mortals under their control to develop anything that might threaten the rule of the gods. Their armies will continue with swords and crossbows and lances; while we have Battanaras, mortars and Jackdaws. They throw rocks; we throw Forty-Eighters.'

Cael glanced up at the middle balcony. 'We have an audience, sir.'

The others turned. The Empress was standing on the balcony, her gaze directed at the carnage that had taken place a few yards before the front doors of the Summer Palace.

'Can you take us up there, Cael?' said Cardova.

'Aye, sir.'

Cael touched his Quadrant, and the three men appeared by the side of the Empress.

'All Gunstians have been accounted for, Your Majesty,' said Cardova.

'I watched them fall,' said the Empress. She eyed Cael. 'I am very glad to see you on your feet, Adjutant, although I noticed that you did not fire your Jackdaw.'

'I was happy to learn what to do from Cole, Your Majesty,' said Cael.

'I think I now understand what Lord Edgar meant,' she said. 'Had our foe been Ancients with battle-vision, as I once witnessed here in Colsbury Castle, our marines would have destroyed them. The gods are right to fear these new weapons, for they are terrible indeed.'

Cardova opened his mouth, then closed it again.

'Do not worry, Constable,' said Thorn; 'I have no intention of trying to stop these technological advances. On the contrary, I want our entire army re-equipped with the latest weaponry as quickly as possible. I want more money funnelled to Rosie and Nestorian's research teams;

give them whatever they desire. Double their funding; treble it. I want to see where their creativity takes them next. No areas of research shall be forbidden under my rule; I want the Empire to become the most advanced civilisation in history, for that is the way to be secure.'

'I agree, Your Majesty,' said Cael, 'but these weapons did not stop the Gunstians from attacking Colsbury in the first place. I recommend a complete withdrawal of the government back to Plateau City. The upper floors of the Blue Palace cannot be penetrated by Quadrants; you will be safe there.'

'No, Cael,' she said. 'I will not hide behind the walls of the Blue Palace when the rest of the Empire has no such protection. If my people are at risk, then I will not flinch from sharing their danger. The people would despise me for it, and rightly so.'

'But we cannot guarantee the safety of Colsbury, Your Majesty,' said Cael. 'The Gunstians have breached our security twice on this island and, if we stay, they will return.'

'What about Shella?' said Thorn. 'Should we evict her from her home?'

'Your Majesty?'

'If we all leave, then Shella will be alone here, apart from a few gardeners and caretakers. If the Gunstians attack, she will be on her own. If Shella is brave enough to stay here, then I shall not desert her.'

'But...'

'No, Cael,' she said. 'I know why you are concerned; you feel responsible for the fact that the Gunstians are attacking the Empire. You blame yourself, and you think that any casualties we suffer are a direct result of what you did in Great Gunst eight years ago. I supported your actions then, and I support them now, so if anyone is to blame, it is me. Instead of dwelling on the past, think of how to better defend Colsbury, for I shall not be leaving.'

Cael bowed his head. 'Aye, Your Majesty.'

'I will call in another thousand marines, Your Majesty,' said Cardova. 'We currently have enough Jackdaws for all of them, and we will position them in fire teams all over the island, with depots of ammunition and Ectus powder stored in multiple locations. We will grant them operational freedom to fire upon any portal the moment it appears.'

'That sounds acceptable, Constable,' said the Empress. 'For now, though, send someone to Plateau City, and have the Imperial Court recalled to the island. I have an Empire to run.'

CHAPTER 22
THEFT

Nom Karta, Inopei – 27th Abrinch 1613

'With eight hundred soldiers coming through the portals,' said Kyra, 'this was the largest Gunstian raid so far. One Gifted agent was captured, along with over a hundred Gunstian soldiers.'

'Is Empress Thorn safe and well?' said Queen Famula.

'She is, Your Majesty,' said Kyra. 'She is also refusing to evacuate the imperial government from Colsbury.'

'And how is your mother?' said Lord Konran Mon Gahad. 'Does the Demon Witch thrive?'

'My mother remains without her powers, my lord,' said Kyra. 'She was unable to assist the Empress during the attack, and had to be evacuated along with the other civilians.'

'I am pleased to hear of the humbling of the Demon Witch,' said Abda.

'It is only a matter of time before Karalyn Holdfast will have to assume a new form, my lady,' said Edgar. 'Depending upon your viewpoint, this is either a temporary respite from her tyranny over us, or a dangerous time when the treaty has no protector. But one thing seems certain – we shall not be getting any help to defeat the Gunstians from Karalyn.'

Queen Famula kept her gaze on Kyra. 'When shall you be returning to Nom Karta for good?'

'In a few days, Your Majesty,' said Kyra. 'There is little more I can do to help my mother, and her other daughter is now staying with her on Colsbury. I will wrap up my affairs on the Star Continent and return soon. I have my own children to think of.'

'Very well, Kyra,' said Famula. 'Please inform the Empress that we send our condolences for the losses sustained in the attack on Colsbury.'

Kyra bowed her head, then she turned and whispered to Edgar for a few moments. Edgar kissed her, then Kyra vanished.

'All gods, with me,' said Edgar. He inclined his head towards the three dragons. 'We shall prepare the next assault upon Gunst, Your Majesty.'

Edgar walked from the cavernous hall, and the four other gods who had been attending the audience followed him, with Konna tagging along at the rear. She hadn't been invited to the audience, but had decided to try to impose herself on the company of the gods who ruled the Dominion. She was a Holdfast, after all, and her mortal cousin was married to the oldest god in existence.

Edgar led them into the human-sized parts of the palace, and they came to a chamber that overlooked the city of Nom Karta. Edgar sat without a word, taking his place by the head of a table. Konna sat down next to Naxor, while Laverne and Elmhirst took seats opposite them.

'Do you require my assistance in the planning of a raid, my lord?' said Laverne. 'I have business to attend to at the Tempest mine.'

'We are not here to plan a raid,' said Edgar. 'We are running out of time. My wife shall be back in a few days from now, and what we need to accomplish must be completed before she returns.'

Laverne raised an eyebrow, while Elmhirst looked distinctly unhappy.

'But, my lord,' said Elmhirst; 'is it wise to proceed without Kyra's knowledge and approval? This plan of yours is for her benefit, is it not? What if she refuses to comply with your wishes?'

'I will impress upon her the necessity of acting in this way,' said Edgar. 'The Sextant is the only chance she has to achieve immortality. She can ascend, as her mother did, and take her rightful place among the gods.'

'The Sextant, my lord?' said Laverne.

Edgar ignored her. 'Take Naxor with you, Elmhirst,' he said. 'Bring the girl here.'

Elmhirst bowed his head as he stood, but his eyes were betraying his inner feelings about Edgar's plan. Naxor also got to his feet. Elmhirst took out his Quadrant, and both men vanished.

'Why am I here, my lord?' said Laverne. 'Why did you summon me from the Tempest mine?'

'I need your assistance, Laverne,' he said. 'I want you to prepare rooms in the fortress that lie next to the mine – quarters for myself, and somewhere secure to store a large device.'

Laverne looked incredulous. 'Are you referring to the Sextant, my lord? Are you planning to steal it from Karalyn?'

'Karalyn is no longer able to safeguard the most valuable object upon any of the Known Worlds,' said Edgar. 'We are doing the responsible thing, by taking it into our custody.'

'And then you intend to use it to grant Kyra immortality?' she said. 'I don't quite understand, my lord. How exactly is this to be done? How can the Sextant do such a thing?'

'If it was done to Karalyn, it can be done to Kyra,' said Edgar. 'Return to the Tempest mine, Laverne, and do as I have commanded. Tell no one what I am intending to do. The chamber where the Sextant will be held needs to be in the most secure part of the fortress, but it should also be close to the stock of raw Tempest that has been excavated from the mine.'

Laverne stood, her eyes narrow. 'As you will it, my lord,' she said, as she took out her Quadrant. Her fingers brushed its surface, and she disappeared.

Edgar sat back in his chair, then his gaze fell upon Konna.

'Why are you here?' he said. 'I did not summon you to attend Queen Famula this morning, Konna.'

'Neither did you send me away when you saw me there, my lord,' she said.

'That is true. I wondered if you might be of service to me, and I knew that you were aware of my plans regarding the Sextant. Was I correct, Konna? Do you wish to help me in this endeavour?'

'I am tired of being dismissed as too young to be of any use, my lord,' she said.

'I see. You wish to prove yourself? You are impatient – an affliction that plagues many young gods; but I am also in need of trusted lieutenants. Can you be trusted? Will you obey every order I give you?'

'I will not obey any order that will lead to my family being hurt.'

'And I would never issue such an order. I am trying to do something good, something noble – an act that will transform a mortal woman into an immortal god.'

'But you will need someone who can operate the Sextant,' she said. 'Even then, I have my doubts about whether this plan can succeed, but without someone who knows how to use the Sextant, we will get nowhere.'

'That is true,' he said.

Konna frowned. 'Have you found someone, my lord? The *girl* you mentioned; the one Elmhirst and Naxor are fetching? Oh. I think I now see.'

'Do you?' said Edgar. He reached into his robes, and took out a small box. He opened it, revealing several sets of thin, clear eye-guards. 'I recommend you wear these,' he said. 'Lord Elmhirst and I are already protected.'

Konna leaned forward. She plucked a set of eye-guards from the box, angled her head back, and placed them over her eyes. She blinked a few times as she got used to them. It was the first time she had ever worn eye-guards, but she didn't want Edgar to know that.

The air shimmered, and Elmhirst appeared with Lindi Holdfast.

'I left Lord Naxor in Kell, my lord,' said Elmhirst. 'There is something about his manner that inspires mistrust, and I felt it better that he plays no part in the next step.'

Edgar said nothing, his gaze on Lindi, who was gazing back at him with an amused expression on her face.

'Have you arranged my gold, land and titles, Edgar?' said Lindi.

'Let us wait to see if you are successful,' said Edgar.

'Are you going to tell me what I will be looking for?' said Lindi. 'I can guess, of course; I'm not stupid. When the Empress finds out, she will not be happy. How are you going to hide it, assuming I can actually find the damn thing?'

'That has been arranged,' said Edgar. He reached into a pocket, and took out the Compass. He set it down on the table. 'Pick it up, Lindi.'

Lindi eyed the small device, then she glanced at Konna. 'I wasn't expecting to see you here, cousin,' she said. 'Does Edgar know that you are thinking about moving back to Kell?'

'Konna has agreed to help me,' said Edgar; 'just as you did, Lindi. Pick up the Compass.'

Lindi placed a hand on her hip. 'I want to know what you are planning to do with the... thing you are going to ask me to look for.'

'That is none of your concern,' said Edgar.

Lindi peered at him, then she frowned. She turned to Elmhirst, then Konna, and her eyes tightened in anger.

'You horrible little cheats,' she said. 'You know I'm stronger than any of you, so you have put those stupid things in your eyes to shield your thoughts from me.'

'Wisely, it seems,' said Edgar. 'As you have already guessed what it is I seek, I will be plain with you. I want you to use the Compass to locate the Sextant, and then I want you to reveal the location to me. That is it, Lindi; that is all I require from you.'

'No, it isn't,' said Lindi. 'You are lying to me, Edgar. I refuse to believe that you want the Sextant without having any means by which to use it. I mean, none of the gods of the Dominion can use it, can they? You need me for that. What do you want me to do with the Sextant? Do you want me to use it to slaughter your enemies? Or perhaps you want me to build a nice little world for you? Tell me, Edgar, or the deal is off.'

'I have a large estate in the centre of Aucteran that I can give you,' he said. 'It has thousands of acres of vineyards, and some of the finest horses on Athumia. A title comes with it – you shall be Lady Lindi of Belguard; and you will be rich. That is what you told me you wanted when you agreed to help me; and yet now you are adding new conditions. No, Lindi. Accept the offer as it was agreed, or Elmhirst will take you back to Kell.'

Lindi eyed Konna. 'Do you know what he wants, cousin? What is he going to do with the Sextant?'

'If Edgar wishes you to know, he will tell you,' said Konna.

'You sneaky little bitch,' said Lindi. 'You are my cousin. We are both Holdfasts. Fucking traitor; I won't forget this.'

'Shall I take her back to Clackenbaird, my lord?' said Elmhirst.

Lindi raised a finger. 'Wait.' She gazed down at the Compass on the table, then she picked it up.

'Find me the Sextant, Lindi,' said Edgar.

'One last question,' she said. 'I asked Naxor about the Compass. I wanted to know why it was made in the first place. He wouldn't say, but that didn't stop me from reading it out of his mind. Kyra used it to find a world created by her brother Cael. In other words, Kyra, your wife, knows how to use it. She could find the Sextant for you, Edgar; so why do you need me?'

Edgar said nothing.

'Why are you keeping this from your wife?' Lindi said, a sly smile on her lips. 'I don't know Kyra very well, but I heard she's a pacifist. Are you going to use the Sextant to do something terrible? Something so awful, that you know Kyra would stop you?' She laughed. 'You should see the look on your face, Edgar. Lady Lindi of Belguard, eh? Vineyards? All right, I will do it for a few acres of vines, but I'm telling you, Edgar – their wine had better be good.'

Lindi placed her thumb onto the Compass, and her eyes glazed over.

'What an infuriating girl,' muttered Elmhirst.

'We need her,' said Edgar, 'and she knows it.'

'I can still hear you,' said Lindi; 'I haven't gone deaf.' She took her thumb off the Compass and sat down at the table. 'This might take a while,' she said. 'There are worlds out there that I never knew existed, and I may have to examine each one in turn. Konna – get me a drink. No – a selection of drinks. Water, coffee, wine – white, not red, and some cold cider.'

'I am not your servant,' said Konna.

'Oh,' said Lindi. 'Did you hear that, Edgar? Konna is refusing to help me. Perhaps I should return to Kell.'

Edgar glared at Lindi.

'I will order her some drinks,' said Konna, as she got to her feet. She walked to the door of the room and opened it a few inches. 'Bring water, coffee and white wine,' she said to a courtier, who bowed. Konna closed the door and retook her seat.

'What about the cider?' said Lindi.

'We don't have any cider in Nom Karta,' said Konna.

'That's a pity,' said Lindi. 'I guess I won't be able to find the Sextant after all.'

'Cease these games!' cried Edgar. 'You gave me your word that you would help me, Lindi.'

Lindi laughed. 'You look funny when you're angry, Edgar. All right; I will search for a while, but I will need a break when the drinks arrive.'

She pressed her thumb to the Compass and her eyes glazed over again.

'I wonder if Sable was like this when she was younger,' said Elmhirst.

'My mother was very religious as a child,' said Lindi. 'She worshipped Nathaniel. She was like the Gunstians – she did terrible things, then told everyone that her faith made her do it. The Tempest mine is very bright, isn't it? The light I can see coming from that location drowns out everything else. Right; let's try a different world – the

Sextant won't be on Athumia. I can see tiny pinpricks of light coming from a few worlds. They must be Quadrants, I guess.'

A knock came from the door as Lindi was speaking, and Konna got up. She opened the door to see a servant standing in the hallway with a trolley containing a wide selection of cups, glasses and drinks. Konna wheeled it into the room, and unloaded its contents onto the table. Lindi fell silent for a long while, her eyes still glazed over, as Konna served coffee and wine to the others.

The minutes dragged past, and Elmhirst shifted uncomfortably on his chair as he kept half an eye on Lindi. Edgar sipped from a glass of red wine, his gaze staring into the middle distance, as Konna drummed her fingers off her knee.

Lindi put down the compass, took out her cigarettes, and lit one.

'Well?' said Elmhirst.

'Have some patience,' said Lindi, as she picked up her cup of coffee. 'What happens after I find the Sextant?'

'As soon as you locate it,' said Edgar, 'you will tell me how to get there.'

'Do you think it's as simple as that, do you?' she said. 'Are you stupid, Edgar? How would I know how to get there, just because I can sense the location of the Sextant? How does that knowledge translate to the required movements on a Quadrant? You haven't thought this through.'

'But Kyra can always travel to the places she sees with the Compass,' said Edgar.

'Kyra can travel without a fucking Quadrant, you pillock. She just thinks of a location and she's there. I will need to work it out manually. This is going to be a lot harder than you thought.'

'Go back to searching for now,' said Edgar. 'We can look into that problem later.'

Lindi smiled. 'There's no need. I've found it.'

'You have? Where?'

'How could I possibly describe its location to you?' said Lindi. 'It is on a world I have never seen before.' She took out her Quadrant, and examined the engravings etched onto its surface. 'My mother taught me how to use a Quadrant,' she said; 'but she didn't just show me how to get to specific places; she taught me the principles behind each finger movement.'

Edgar leaned forward on his chair, his eyes wide with excitement as he watched Lindi's fingers trace out lines on the Quadrant.

'The different worlds are not close to each other,' Lindi went on; 'I could see that through the Compass. Each world seems to exist in isolation. In other words, when you look up at the night sky from Athumia, you cannot see Dragon Eyre. They exist... separately; but the principles of movement remain consistent.' She frowned. 'I think I might now know how to travel to all of the Known Worlds, not because I have been to them, but because I can judge where they must lie; the Compass has made that clear to me.'

'What you say seems impossible,' said Elmhirst. 'The Ascendants searched in vain for the world of salve, and for the world of the Holdfasts. They could not intuit their locations merely by studying the lines on a Quadrant.'

'They didn't have the Compass,' said Lindi. 'It's the Compass that has revealed this truth to me; the truth of how the worlds are connected to each other. This device not only senses Tempest, but it shows the user its precise location relative to the other worlds.' She smiled at Elmhirst. 'It's such a shame that you lack the skill to use it.'

'Show me your best guess, Lindi,' said Edgar. 'Show me where to place my fingers on a Quadrant.'

'Nope,' said Lindi. 'I won't be doing that. By placing those stupid things in your eyes, you have proved that you don't trust me. Why should I trust you? I will take us there; I will take the four of us to the location of the Sextant.'

'Very well,' said Edgar. 'Let us leave immediately.'

'Wait,' said Lindi. 'You are going to get the Sextant out of this deal, and I am starting to feel as though you have bought my services too cheaply. What is the Sextant worth to you, Edgar?'

'I am providing you with exactly what you asked for, Lindi,' said Edgar. 'This has already been agreed.'

'Then I'm tearing up the agreement,' she said. 'What are you going to do about it? I have something you need, and the only way you will get it is by giving me what I want.'

Edgar's fists clenched, and his eyes flashed with rage.

'Why don't you name your price?' said Elmhirst. 'Tell us what you desire, Lindi.'

'That's easy,' she said. 'I want to become the Empress of the Sapphire Throne. When the Holdfast gods take control of the Empire, it shall be me upon the throne wearing the crown – not Karalyn's immortal children, and not the Marchbrae Holdfasts.'

'This is ridiculous,' said Edgar. 'I cannot promise that which is not in my power to give, Lindi. I have no say over the succession to the Sapphire Empire.'

'But you *can* promise to do everything in your power to help me,' said Lindi. 'Are you prepared to do that?'

'You are out of yer fucking mind, Lindi,' said Konna. 'There are at least two of my brothers who should be ahead of you when it comes to inheriting the Empire. Pyre's arse – I'd probably do a better job. What the fuck do ye know about ruling an Empire?'

Lindi smiled at her. 'I will have plenty of time to figure it out. All of the other immortal Holdfasts can have places in my Imperial Court, if you behave yourselves. Well, Edgar? Will you promise to support my bid for the throne? Do you swear to come to my assistance when the time comes?'

'What you are demanding may well result in war,' said Elmhirst. 'The mortals will not give up power without a fight, and with every year that passes, their weapons get more terrible.'

'That is why we should act quickly,' said Lindi. 'We can take care of the Gunstians and the mortal Holdfasts, then we can destroy all of the new weapons, and I will take the throne. The war will be short, and we shall emerge victorious.'

Elmhirst turned to Edgar. 'My lord,' he said, 'we cannot agree to this condition. We have a treaty with the Sapphire Empire, and we have pledged to never interfere in their internal affairs. Lindi may well become Empress one day, but we cannot get involved.'

'But what if this is the only way?' said Edgar.

'She is trying to blackmail us, my lord,' said Konna. 'I agree with Elmhirst; we cannot allow this.'

Edgar bowed his head. 'It is inevitable that, one day, the immortal Holdfasts will inherit the Empire from their mortal cousins – this cannot be altered. If that is the case, then does it matter to the Dominion which Holdfast becomes Emperor or Empress? And if it is inevitable, then would it not be better to overthrow the mortals now, in order to prevent the Empire from developing even more powerful weapons? I can recall a time when mortals built explosives that could destroy entire cities. Everyone living within that city, whether mortal or immortal, was killed, their bodies rendered to ash and dust. If we do not stop the mortals of the Empire, they will reach this stage in due course, and then it will be the end for all gods. You said it yourself, Elmhirst – the weapons of the Sapphire Empire are an existential threat to the Dominion; a threat that we will one day have to face. We cannot escape this fate; for have we not seen it happen before? But the last time these events occurred, there were thousands upon thousands of gods in existence; thousands of Ancients willing to fight, and even then, the wars were terrible. If we wait this time; if we do nothing, it will be too late. The mortals will annihilate what remains of our numbers, and the era of the gods will be over.'

'And we don't want that,' said Lindi.

Edgar raised his gaze. 'You win, Lindi; I will help you become Empress; I will help you destroy the weapons made by the mortals. Take us to the Sextant.'

Lindi got to her feet, her Quadrant in her left hand. Elmhirst and Konna eyed each other, and also stood. Edgar was the last to get to his feet. He nodded at Lindi.

'Here we go,' she said. 'Let's see if the intuition I gained from the Compass is any good. If it isn't, then we might all end up in a volcano, or at the bottom of an ocean, or perhaps we shall be stranded in the void for eternity.'

'Stop wasting time,' said Edgar. 'Activate the device.'

Lindi picked up the Compass and placed it into a pocket, then she smiled again, and triggered the Quadrant.

The air crackled and spat, and Konna found herself floating in complete darkness. The silence was absolute, and she could feel nothing, as though she had no physical form attached to her consciousness. She tried to speak, but it was as though she had no mouth. She started to panic, then a blue sky appeared above her, and she plummeted down from it. She saw clouds, then mountains to her left and right. She looked down, and saw a forest hurtling towards her. She smacked into the branches of a tall tree, and was flung forward. She hit the side of a cliff, then another tree, and then the hard ground, breaking several of her bones when her legs struck a jagged boulder.

Konna lay on the ground in agony as her self-healing got to work. She tried to remain still as the bones in her legs knitted themselves back together, then she noticed the sound of birds singing and calling to each other from the trees, and the noise of a stream as it flowed down the hill to her left.

Elmhirst crashed through the forest a few yards from her. He gazed down at her.

'Why are you not wounded?' said Konna.

'I received multiple injuries,' he said, 'but my self-healing is more powerful than yours. Can you stand?'

He reached out with a hand, and she took it. He pulled her up, and she winced in pain. Elmhirst eyed the patches of blood on the jagged boulder.

'You're lucky your head didn't hit that,' he said. 'It might have been the end of you.'

'Have you seen Edgar or Lindi?' she said.

'No, but I saw a large house as we were falling through the air.'

'And before that – the darkness?'

'The void,' said Elmhirst. 'It was my first time in it, but I have heard of its existence. It was described to me as being the nothingness between worlds, and I guess we travelled through it.'

Konna tried to walk, and her healed legs responded.

'I'm ready,' she said. 'Shall we try to find the house you saw?'

They set off through the forest, climbing the slope that ran by the side of the stream. Insects were buzzing by their heads, and butterflies and bees were darting from flower to flower.

'It's like a sunnier version of Kell,' said Konna. 'Green, but warm.'

'Presumably, Karalyn designed it that way,' said Elmhirst.

'Did you know Simon?'

'Yes. Why do you ask?'

'He created Dragon Eyre, and everyone says it has the perfect climate. That must have been Simon's doing.'

'I suppose it was. Out of the thousands of insane things Simon did during his life, he was bound to get something right occasionally.'

Konna laughed. 'Didn't you like him?'

'I certainly did not. You might not agree, but Edmond was a paragon of virtue and moderation compared to Simon. I danced for joy when I heard that he had been killed on the salve world; it was the only time I have been grateful to Kelsey Holdfast. She and her dragon did us all a tremendous favour.' He glanced up, and pointed. 'There it is.'

Konna looked up the slope, and saw that a large dwelling place had been carved out of the side of a cliff. There were windows and openings, and a long, wide balcony that stretched across the entire front of the house. Elmhirst took out his own Quadrant. He activated it, and he and Konna appeared on the balcony.

Konna walked up to the railings and gazed out at the view. 'This is breathtaking.'

'I wonder how many times Karalyn has stood here,' said Elmhirst, 'and I wonder how she had this place constructed. Albany possessed no power over stone.'

The air shimmered next to them, and Edgar appeared next to Lindi.

'I sensed you use your Quadrant, Elmhirst,' said Lindi. 'Thanks for that; it told me exactly where you were.' She turned, and gestured towards a large open entrance leading into the cliffside house. 'The Sextant is this way.'

They walked through the arched opening and entered a chamber. In its centre was a large device that seemed to be hovering just above the level of the floor.

A tear fell down Edgar's cheek. 'The Sextant; at last.'

Elmhirst walked forward. He crouched by the device, examining its sides. 'I can see the Weathervane,' he said, 'but no Quadrants have been inserted.'

'Get out of the way,' said Lindi. 'I want to see if it responds to me.'

The others moved back as Lindi approached the Sextant. She raised a hand, then she positioned it over the flat surface of the device. She held it there for a long moment, then she exhaled, and pressed her palm down, making contact.

Lindi started to laugh. 'What is my desire?' she said. 'I can hear it; I can hear the voice.'

Edgar took out his Quadrant and activated it. The air crackled, and they appeared in a volcanic landscape. Dark smoke was blotting out the heavens, and burning streams of lava were rolling down the broken slopes. The Sextant was sitting on a ridge of rock, as ash rained down from the leaden sky. Konna gazed around – she knew they must be close to the Tempest mine, but she couldn't see it.

'Where are we?' said Lindi.

'Take Lindi back to Kell, Elmhirst,' said Edgar, 'then come back for Konna. Do it now.'

Elmhirst swiped his Quadrant as Lindi opened her mouth to protest, then both of them disappeared.

'It is important that Lindi does not learn where I intend to hide the Sextant,' said Edgar. 'Do not allow her to read your mind, Konna. You may have to wear eye-guards for a while, until I have mastered the secrets of immortality this device can offer.'

'But how will you use it without Lindi?' said Konna.

'There must be a way,' he said. 'If I can get Kyra to commune with it, then...'

'But Kyra can't use it, either,' said Konna. 'Only Cael, Sable and Lindi can.'

Edgar glared at her. 'I will think of something.'

The air shimmered, and Elmhirst appeared again, alone.

'Take her back to Nom Karta, Elmhirst,' said Edgar; 'I have much to do.'

Konna narrowed her eyes. Elmhirst triggered his Quadrant, and they vanished.

CHAPTER 23
ESTRANGED

Colsbury Castle, Republic of the Holdings – 26th Day, First Third Summer 560

Karalyn gazed down from the bay window at the masses of marines in the forecourt of Colsbury Castle. Hundreds had been arriving over the three days since the latest Gunstian attack, and every marine had been armed with one of the new Jackdaw weapons, as well as their usual swords and war axes. Marines had been training with their Jackdaws, shooting them out over the waters of the lake, and drilling in lines as they practised loading and aiming. One in every dozen marines also had a Battanara, and the noise they made when fired had broken the peace and calm of the little island.

Karalyn loathed the new weapons being built by the Empire, but as she had been unable to help defend Colsbury during the attack, what right did she have to complain? The Empress was merely using the tools she had to hand; where once she might have deployed death powers to slaughter any invaders, now she had ranks of marines with Jackdaws and Battanaras. The evacuation had been humiliating. Caitlyn had wanted to stay and fight, but her powers would have been useless while Kelsey remained on Colsbury, and Karalyn had begged her daughter to come with them. It had been Kelsey who had whisked them off to the Blue Palace in Plateau City with the other helpless civilians, and Karalyn had felt nothing but shame.

Wasn't it her job to protect her family and friends? Hadn't she once defeated Agatha and her gods on her own? Hadn't she crushed Edmond's army of gods and Ancients? These days, she could barely walk up a flight of stairs without getting tired, and only Shella seemed to understand how she felt.

Like the Empress, Shella had refused to be evacuated, and the story went that she had fallen asleep on her deck chair by the harbour after smoking dreamweed and drinking whisky; and that she had slept for the entire duration of the Gunstian raid, while the carnage had unfolded just a few dozen yards to her right. Shella had teased Karalyn about it after Kelsey and Lucius Cardova had ferried everyone back to Colsbury; she had asked Karalyn why she had run away, when she was the only one able to survive death. Karalyn had been wary to admit the truth – that she had been scared. Scared of the Gift of Pain, scared of being hurt, scared of falling over in the panic and being abandoned – her fears had overwhelmed her. Kelsey had seen it in her eyes, and so had Cael, and her humiliation was complete.

Squads of marines were also on the roofs of the two keeps, keeping watch over the gardens, harbour and forecourt, and Karalyn remembered fighting Agatha's army of Rahain from one of those roofs, back when she was still in her original body.

The door opened behind her, and she turned. Caitlyn eyed her as she came into the small dining room, then Lucius Cardova entered after her.

'Thank you for the invitation to share lunch with you both,' said Lucius.

'I thought the three of us should talk about Caitlyn's future,' said Karalyn.

Caitlyn rolled her eyes at Karalyn's words, then the three of them sat. The table had been laid with cutlery and glasses, and Karalyn picked up a bottle of white wine.

'How have you been feeling?' said Lucius.

'I have been better,' said Karalyn. 'Wine?'

'Yes, thank you,' he said.

Karalyn half-filled three glasses. She passed one to Lucius, and the other to Caitlyn.

'You didn't ask if I wanted any,' said Caitlyn, 'and I think it's a little ironic that you want to talk about my future, when you have never shown the slightest interest in it before now.'

'I can only start from where I am,' said Karalyn, 'no matter how much I wish I could change the past. Tell me why you want to join the cavalry.'

'I have been riding my three horses for years, Mother, and...'

'You have three horses?' said Karalyn.

'Two are kept in the cavalry compound in Plateau City,' said Caitlyn, 'and the other is stabled on Colsbury.'

'I thought it was important that she kept some of her Holdfast roots,' said Lucius. 'They have always been known for horses.'

'Does Carden also have horses?' said Karalyn.

'He didn't take to them,' said Caitlyn. 'Might I continue?'

'Of course,' said Karalyn; 'sorry for interrupting.'

'I enjoy being out on my horses,' Caitlyn said, 'so when Father asked me what I wanted to do after school, the cavalry seemed the obvious choice. I will be able to use my battle-vision, and I will learn how to lead companies of troopers.'

'Those sound like your father's words,' said Karalyn. 'Did Lucius coax you towards the military?'

Caitlyn eyed Lucius, who gave her a gentle shrug.

'Father suggested the military,' said Caitlyn, 'but I am not being forced to join. I think it could be a useful skill to learn.'

'What – killing people?'

'Come on, Mother; do you think we should disband the armed forces? Should we, the Holdfasts, ask others to serve, but not serve ourselves? That would be hypocritical. The peace of the Empire is defended by the army, navy, marines and the cavalry, and I want to make a contribution.'

'You could make a fine contribution by attending university for a few years,' said Karalyn. 'What areas might you like to study?'

'Warfare,' she said.

'Now you are just mocking me,' said Karalyn.

'Did you get upset when Cael joined the marines?' said Caitlyn.

'That was different – he was forced to join as a punishment; whereas, you are choosing a life I do not like.'

'Both of your husbands were in the armed forces, Mother. You can't hate the life that much.'

'Lennox had left the army when I met him,' said Karalyn, 'and he knew I didn't approve of some of the things he did as a soldier.'

'And me?' said Lucius. 'You knew I was in the Banner of the Lostwell Exiles.'

'Look at how many times we argued over your career, Lucius,' said Karalyn. 'It was our main source of disagreement during our marriage. I did not approve of bringing hundreds of thousands of Banner soldiers over from Dragon Eyre, but you insisted on doing it anyway. And you failed to keep Cael out of danger during the battles on Na Sun Ka.'

'Cael was an officer in the marines,' said Lucius; 'I couldn't intervene. The Holdfasts would have been publicly shamed had I shown Cael any special treatment; and Cael would have been furious.'

'You preferred the army over me.'

Lucius shook his head. 'That's exactly what my first wife used to say.'

'Then perhaps there is some truth in it,' said Karalyn.

'Can we go back to my future?' said Caitlyn. 'I am going to join the cavalry, Mother, so you had better get used to the idea. I will earn my commission as a junior lieutenant, and I will not let the family down. I will serve for at least three years, and then I will look again at what I want to do. I might decide to go to university then, or I may stay with the cavalry. Three years isn't that long, Mother.'

'It will feel like an eternity if another war breaks out. What if you are posted to Gunst? It may come to that. Thorn has no idea how to defeat the Gunstians, but she knows that continual raids aren't going to bring her victory.'

'There are no plans to invade Gunst,' said Lucius; 'and I would know.'

'Aye, but things can change very quickly, Lucius,' said Karalyn. 'Can you promise our daughter that imperial forces will never be sent to Gunst?'

'Imperial forces are already operating in Gunst,' said Lucius. 'Small, elite teams, under the leadership of Adjutant Cael.'

'Aye. I know,' said Karalyn, 'and it sickens me.'

'What would you do, Mother,' said Caitlyn, 'if you were still able to assert your authority?'

'I don't know. The Gunstian raids aren't affecting the peace between the Empire and the Dominion. I might have intervened to stop a full-scale invasion, but a few raids are insignificant in the larger context.'

Cardova's eyes widened. 'You call what the Gunstians did on Colsbury *insignificant*?'

'Aye, Lucius,' she said. 'A few hundred soldiers here and there is not the same as armies in their tens or hundreds of thousands invading and occupying someone else's land. I did not watch over the worlds in order to stamp out every example of criminal behaviour, for not only would that be impossible, it would also encourage the populations of the Empire and the Dominion to become complacent. Why prevent crime, if I am there to catch the criminals?'

Cardova said nothing for a while, then the door opened, and servants entered bearing large trays. They set down large bowls of food, bowed, and left the room.

'Shall we help ourselves?' said Cardova, as he picked up a serving spoon.

'I know you think I don't care about the people of the Empire,' said Karalyn.

'I didn't say that,' said Cardova.

'A parent shouldn't do everything for a child,' Karalyn went on, 'because the child will learn nothing.'

'Is that how you saw the situation?' said Cardova. 'With us as the children, and you as the parent?'

'It's how I had to act when Thorn tried to wipe out the entire leadership of the Dominion,' said Karalyn; 'and again when I had to stop Cael from driving nails into Cairney's head.'

'Perhaps this is the problem,' said Caitlyn. 'You treated everyone like children and, in the process, you forgot who your own children were.'

Karalyn said nothing. Cardova piled some food onto his plate and passed the serving spoon to Caitlyn.

'I have been meaning to ask about Cairney,' he said. 'Can we assume that he will be safely contained until...'

'Until I possess a body able to use the Sextant?' said Karalyn.

'Yes.'

'Cairney will be fine,' she said. 'He has access to food and water, and shelter. He might wonder why I haven't visited to bring him any books, but he will be safe.'

'You brought him books?' said Caitlyn.

'Aye. A wide selection. He needed something to stimulate his mind.'

Caitlyn served herself some food, and passed the spoon to her mother.

'Your next body might be one that can use the Sextant,' she said.

'That is what everyone seems to expect of me,' said Karalyn.

Caitlyn nodded.

'What else did you want to say?' said Karalyn.

'This is what I fear, Mother,' said Caitlyn; 'that this new attitude of yours is only temporary. You have been greatly weakened, and you are vulnerable, and so you reached out to me and Carden. But, as soon as you are back in a powerful body, like Albany's was, you will go back to the Sextant and forget about us. I am scared you will abandon us again.'

Karalyn said nothing.

'I visited Carden yesterday,' said Cardova.

'How is he?' said Caitlyn.

'His emotions... are in turmoil,' said Cardova. 'He is angry, and not in the mood for any kind of reconciliation with your mother; not yet, at any rate. I am glad Caelius is there to keep an eye on him.'

'What did he say?' said Karalyn.

'He said a lot of things.'

'Can you summarise?'

Cardova sat back. 'Well, it's a little like what Caitlyn was just saying. Carden feels that you ignored them when you were powerful, but now that you are weak and in need of assistance, you have remembered that you have children who can help you. You have returned to your family on Colsbury, not because you love them, but because you need them.'

'I see.'

'I tried to tell him that this wasn't true,' Cardova went on, 'but he wasn't receptive to my words. He said that I shouldn't even be talking to you.'

'Should I go down to Plateau City to speak to him?'

'I don't think that would do any good,' he said; 'not yet. He needs time for his more turbulent emotions to settle. If you went now, I fear any meeting would quickly descend into acrimonious shouting and recriminations. It would only make things worse.'

'But if I don't see him, he will think I am ignoring him again.'

'He knows that you want to reconcile; he understands that. It's your motivation he questions. He compared you to someone who has become addicted to salve or narcotics, who has just had their supply cut off. You have awoken from a stupor, and you feel weak and disorientated, but, deep down, you still crave that which you cannot have. And, as soon as you can have it again, you will return to your old ways.' He glanced at her. 'I am sorry to have to pass on these words, Karalyn; it is not my intention to hurt you. I think you are trying your best, but Carden needs more time.'

For a few moments, they ate in silence, but Karalyn's appetite had gone. She chewed the food without tasting it, and concentrated on not crying. She had hardly ever cried while she had been in Albany's body; such extreme displays of emotion had seemed crass to her, but the shock of becoming mortal again, even if only temporarily, had robbed her of self-control.

She was trying to think of something to say to restart the conversation when the door opened again, and Cael and Kyra walked into the small dining room.

'We came to tell you that we will both be leaving Colsbury this morning,' said Cael, 'although I'll only be gone for an hour or so.'

'I will be gone for a little longer,' said Kyra. 'It is time to return to Nom Karta, Mother.'

'Thank you for spending so much time with me, Kyra,' said Karalyn.

'You are welcome, Mother. I will come back soon, but only for brief visits, to see how you are doing.'

'I understand. You have already given me time that you could have spent with your two sons. Why don't you bring them with you when you next come? I would like to see my grandchildren.'

'Are they both gods?' said Caitlyn.

'Aye,' said Kyra; 'my immortal boys.'

'I would like to see them, too,' said Caitlyn.

'You are welcome to visit Nom Karta,' said Kyra. 'The only good thing to come out of the Gunstian attacks is that relations between the Dominion and the Empire have improved a little. You would be able to appear in Nom Karta without triggering a crisis.' Kyra leaned forward and kissed her mother on the cheek. 'Take care.' She glanced at Cael. 'I will be seeing you soon, no doubt, brother.'

'No doubt,' said Cael.

'Farewell, Lucius; farewell, Caitlyn,' said Kyra, then she vanished.

'It was very kind of Kyra to spend so much time here,' said Karalyn.

'And it was very good for Empire-Dominion relations,' said Cardova. 'Much of the tension between the two sides has eased.'

'My sister still thinks little of the Empress,' said Cael, 'but I got her to admit that the Empire is now more democratic than the Dominion. I have an appointment this morning with Lord Holdsmith in Plateau City, to formally congratulate him on becoming the first elected Lord

Marshal of the Plateau. I had to squeeze the meeting in between two raids on Gunst.'

'Will Holder Smith be a good leader?' said Karalyn.

'He seems moderate and cautious,' said Cael. 'More than half of the people living in Plateau Province are Holdings, and Lord Holdsmith got his votes from them, and from the former Banner veterans settled along the shores of the Inner Sea. The Kellach voted for a Kellach candidate, and the Rahain barely voted at all. He'll be forming a government soon, but I wouldn't expect anything too radical.'

'You can be very proud of what you achieved, Cael,' said Cardova.

'Now all I have to worry about are the Gunstians.'

'Your raids upon Gunst are worse than useless, son,' said Karalyn. 'They achieve nothing but more pain.'

'Attacks on imperial territory cannot go unpunished,' said Cardova.

'My mother has a point,' said Cael. 'Each raid creates more martyrs, and martyrs encourage more Gunstians to volunteer. I cannot see how this will end without a major escalation of violence. If we could locate and destroy their raiding camp, then we might be able to knock them off course for a while, but none of the prisoners we captured a few days ago knew where they were being held before the raid on Colsbury began. I have seen the same image in their minds of fields and mountains – just as you described, Mother; and we know that their camp is based in Aucteran; but Aucteran is a large continent, with vast mountain ranges that run down the length of its spine. We are looking, but it is like trying to find a solitary ship amid the ocean.'

'We shall discuss this more when you get back,' said Cardova.

Cael nodded, then he took out his Quadrant.

'I will see you all later,' he said, then he activated the device and disappeared.

'He sounded as though he agreed with you, Mother,' said Caitlyn.

'I found that strange,' she said.

'Cael is not as ruthless as many imagine him to be,' said Cardova. 'Or, more accurately, he regrets having to be ruthless at times.'

'I very clearly remember him trying to hammer nails into Cairney's eyes.'

'Yes, but Cairney had just tried to assassinate Kelsey and the Empress. Cairney was fortunate that Cael didn't remove his head. Cael sometimes acts out of anger and, when he does, the results can be devastating, such as when he destroyed the Temple of the Martyrs.'

'Why doesn't the Empress rein him in?' said Karalyn.

Cardova smiled. 'The Empress and Cael usually agree on these matters. Her Majesty sees Cael as her iron fist, smashing her enemies. There is a reason that he is her favoured successor.'

'In other words, Thorn approves of his methods? That does not surprise me.' She glanced out of the window. 'It would be nice to get out of Colsbury for a little while. Caitlyn, would you like to come with me?'

'Where would we go?' said Caitlyn.

'Would you like to see the world I built for myself?' said Karalyn. 'It doesn't have a name, but you will be able to see where I lived for so many years.'

'Are you sure you want me to see it?'

'Aye, I'm sure.'

Cardova wiped his hands on a napkin and got to his feet. 'I shall return to work. Rosie and Ravi should be arriving soon to discuss how we are going to increase the production of the new Jackdaws.'

'And you wonder why we argued, Lucius,' said Karalyn.

He smiled. 'We should do this again.'

Karalyn kept her gaze on him as he walked out of the room, then she turned back to her daughter.

'You managed to get through that without too many cross words being spoken,' said Caitlyn.

'Shall we go?'

They both got to their feet, and Karalyn took out her Quadrant. She gazed at the surface, then moved her fingers over the engraved symbols. The air crackled, and they appeared on her wide balcony. Karalyn smiled. Her unnamed world still felt like home, and she was looking forward to showing Caitlyn around.

'This is very beautiful,' said Caitlyn, as she gazed at the view of the mountains and valleys.

'I stood out here every day,' she said.

Caitlyn turned, and looked up at the cliff face. 'And you lived in there?'

'It had everything I needed. There is a little stream at the top of the ridge, and I got the builders to pipe the water throughout the house. It has taps, and even a bath. I used to cook my own food in the kitchen, and I have a little library where I could read. The balcony was my favourite place, though.'

'What did you eat? Did you have to go out hunting and foraging?'

'I was far too lazy for that,' she said. 'I used to go to a market in Naeth to buy my provisions.'

'Naeth? Why did you go all the way to Aucteran when there are markets in Plateau City?'

'No one knows my face in Naeth.'

'Oh. You were worried you might bump into me or Carden.'

'I didn't want to be recognised by anyone. It would have... distracted me from the worlds I was building.'

Caitlyn said nothing.

'I am so sorry for how I acted,' said Karalyn.

'I know you are, Mother, but can you honestly say that you won't allow the Sextant to consume you if you become powerful again? Will you be able to resist the temptation?'

'I don't know. Perhaps it is time for someone else to look after the Sextant, or maybe the Tempest sword that activates the device could be put in a different location. If Cael kept hold of the sword, then I wouldn't be able to use it.'

'How about you give me a tour of your house?' said Caitlyn.

'I would love to. The first room we'll come to contains the Sextant, but don't worry – I am unable to use it. There will be no temptation to face.'

They walked through the arched opening and into the large, empty chamber. Karalyn's eyes widened, and she staggered back a step.

The Sextant had gone.

'Are you all right, Mother?' said Caitlyn.

'The Sextant should be here,' she said. 'This is the room where I keep it. It's gone.'

Karalyn walked forward, as though to prove to herself that she wasn't hallucinating. She stood on the exact spot where the Sextant had been, too stunned to react.

'Where could it have gone, Mother?' said Caitlyn. 'This is bad, isn't it? Has it been stolen?'

'I... I...'

'Deep breaths, Mother. Try to think – who could have taken it? Who else knew it was here?'

'Everyone knew that I kept it here.'

'You're not listening, Mother – who would have known how to find this world?'

Karalyn turned to face her daughter. 'We had better go back to Colsbury; I need to tell Kelsey about this.'

She took out her Quadrant, triggered it, and they appeared back in the small dining room where they had eaten lunch with Cardova. Karalyn went to the door, and took a right along the hallway, as Caitlyn followed her. They came to the middle balcony of the Summer Palace, where over two dozen people were sitting out in the sunshine, and Karalyn went over to a table where Kelsey was eating lunch with her daughter Calpurnia.

'Kelsey,' said Karalyn.

Kelsey glanced up. 'Aye?'

'The Sextant has gone, Kelsey,' said Karalyn. 'It's not in my home; it's gone.'

Kelsey's expression darkened. She stood. 'Kyra?'

'Why would my daughter steal the Sextant?'

'I don't know, Karalyn, but she's the only person I know who would have been able to track it down. Kyra must know how to find it;

she took Cael there when they were looking for you. Have you asked her?'

'Caitlyn and I came straight back here. It can't have been Kyra, Kelsey – she was here less than an hour ago.'

Kelsey eyed her daughter. 'Sorry, Calpurnia, but we'll have to continue our conversation later. Tell Lucius what you just heard, and I'll be back as soon as I can. Take us to Nom Karta, Karalyn.'

'Now?' said Karalyn.

'Aye, now; and you're taking me with you.'

Karalyn activated her Quadrant. The air shimmered, and she appeared next to Caitlyn and Kelsey on a street outside the huge dragon palaces. Kelsey turned for the palace of Naghad, and they hurried along the street. Soldiers from the Banner of the Doomed Worlds stopped them on the steps in front of the open entrance to the palace, then Kyra appeared by their side.

'I sensed you arrive,' said Kyra. 'What's wrong?'

'Can we speak in private?' said Kelsey.

Kyra inclined her head, then the four women appeared in Kyra's private rooms, where she had been unpacking her clothes.

'The Sextant has gone,' said Karalyn.

Kyra frowned. 'What?'

'It's not in my house on the unnamed world,' Karalyn went on. 'Someone has taken it.'

'But how could anyone have found your world?'

'That's why we're here,' said Kelsey.

'Do you think I had something to do with it?' said Kyra. 'I've been on Colsbury for much of the last month; you've seen me every day.'

'The Compass, daughter,' said Karalyn; 'do you have it?'

'Aye; it's in the bottom of a drawer. I'll show you.'

Kyra walked over to a large chest of drawers. She slid one open, and rummaged around under a pile of clothes. She frowned after a moment, and removed the clothes entirely.

'It's not here,' she said.

'Oh, bollocks,' said Kelsey. 'Who knew that you kept the Compass in there?'

'Edgar, but he can't use it, Kelsey. He has tried.'

'I'm going to need to speak to Edgar.'

'You can't; he isn't in Nom Karta at the moment. He has gone on a raid with Elmhirst. He left a note for me in case I came back while he was still away.'

Kelsey paced up and down the room. 'I need the names of every single person we either know or suspect that could use the Compass. Cael?'

'No,' said Kyra. 'He also tried.'

'Sable?'

'Probably,' said Kyra. 'I don't know. As far as I am aware, she might be able to use it.'

'She can use the Sextant.'

'Aye, but so can Cael. It's not an exact science. I can use the Compass, but not the Sextant; it's the other way around for Cael. The only person I know that could definitely use both is Mother.'

'But Sable is a suspect?'

'I guess so,' said Kyra; 'and if we include her, we might as well include her children. These things are probably passed on.'

'What about your sons?' said Kelsey.

Kyra raised an eyebrow. 'Neither is sensitive to Tempest.'

'The Marchbrae Holdfasts?'

'I don't know,' said Kyra. 'Konna lives in Nom Karta, but her dream powers are very limited. It's possible that one of her siblings might have the correct abilities.'

'I will send Cael down to Kell once he gets back from meeting Lord Holdsmith,' said Kelsey, 'and he can question the Marchbrae Holdfasts. Sable's daughter Lindi also happens to be staying there, so he can talk to her as well. I'll go to Ulna to ask Sable directly. Kyra, you can speak to Konna. Let me know if she has heard anything, and let me know when Edgar gets back.'

'All right,' said Kyra. 'I don't know if this is connected in any way, but Naxor has been spending a lot of time in Nom Karta recently.'

'Has he? I heard he was present at the second convention between the Dominion and the Empire, and I did wonder why he was there.'

'He has been trying to ingratiate himself with the dragons, especially Lady Abda,' said Kyra.

'Did you read his thoughts?' said Karalyn.

'I did, Mother, but you know how good he is at hiding his true feelings. I would need a few days to sort my way through all of his secrets.'

Kelsey shook her head. 'And now I will have to tell the Empress that we have lost the most valuable object in existence. It's only lunchtime, and I'm already in line for an arse-kicking.'

'We will find it, Aunty,' said Kyra.

'We must be in trouble if you're calling me that,' said Kelsey. 'Take us back to Colsbury, Karalyn.'

Karalyn triggered the device, and the three women vanished.

CHAPTER 24
GOING ALL-IN

Marchside, Kell – 26th Day, First Third Summer 560

Lindi reclined on the grassy slope, and basked in the warm sunshine. In her left hand was the Compass, and her gaze remained fixed on it. She wondered why Edgar hadn't come to Kell to ask her to give it back to him, but he had seemed to lose interest in it the moment Lindi had found the Sextant. And what was he planning to do with the huge device?

Overnight, Lindi had used the Compass to search for the Sextant, but she had been unable to find it, and that had worried her. Had Edgar destroyed it? Perhaps he had removed the sword that was needed to make it operational, but if that were the case, then why had he bothered to steal it in the first place?

Lindi gazed down the hillside. She could see both the farmhouse and Corthie's cairn from where she lay on the soft grass, and beyond them, the buildings of the distillery spread out along the valley. Carter would be down there, working in a field while wondering why Lindi hadn't joined him that day. She hadn't told him where she had been the day before; she hadn't told anyone about her trip to Nom Karta and then on to Karalyn's own world. Naxor knew some of what had occurred, and he had questioned her about it when Elmhirst had delivered her back to the farm on the previous evening; but Lindi had said nothing to the demigod.

It had dawned on her that morning that things were starting to get serious. One of the leaders of the Dominion had stolen something precious from the Empire, and Lindi had helped him do it. A lot of people, including many Holdfasts, were going to be extremely pissed off when they found out. How long would it take them to realise that Edgar was responsible? And then the clues would lead directly to Lindi. If they caught her, she would be punished. Would her mother intervene to save her? The worst part had been the business about her wanting to become Empress – what had that been about?

At first, Lindi had told Naxor and the others about her desire to sit upon the throne as a sort of joke; she had been teasing them in her usual way. She would say provocative things to watch the response of others, and she had laughed at the way people like Aila had rolled their eyes at her. But everything had changed when Edgar had promised to support her claim to the throne.

What the fuck had she been thinking? Edgar's unwise promise had somehow made her exaggerated boasts seem real, and the knot of tension in her stomach had worsened as the hours had passed. At the time, she had felt invincible. She had known how desperate Edgar was to get his hands on the Sextant, and she had wanted to see how far she could push him. The last thing she had expected was for him to commit to supporting her bid to become Empress. Maybe he had been lying to her; she hoped so. Lindi had talked of eliminating her mortal cousins, and she now realised how that had made her sound – greedy, cruel and arrogant.

A tear escaped her eye. As far as she could see, she had two options open to her, and neither was appealing. She could either run back to Ulna and confess everything to her mother; or she could commit to what she had done, and follow that path to its conclusion. She could go *all-in*, as the sailors used to say when they were playing cards on the *Mischief Maker*.

But how could she go all-in if she couldn't find the Sextant?

She was about to press her thumb back onto the Compass when she sensed a Quadrant being activated close to the farmhouse. She peered down the slope, expecting to see Naxor arrive, and saw a much taller man walking towards the front door of the farmhouse.

It was Cael.

Lindi swore under her breath as she watched her older cousin enter the house. Had he come for her? Had they discovered what she had done so soon? She shoved the Compass into a pocket, and took out her Quadrant. All of her clothes were in the farmhouse, along with the presents she had received on her birthday, but if she stayed to collect them, Cael would see her, and if he saw her, then things could get messy very quickly.

She needed to hide, but where?

She took the Compass back out of her pocket, and pressed her thumb against the engraved circle. Her vision went grey. She saw two small pinpricks of light coming from the farmhouse, which presumably represented the Tempest within Cael and Naxor's Quadrants, then she switched to looking for other worlds. She considered looking for a world without a Quadrant, one that was not in contact with any other world, but that was too risky. If she went there and her Quadrant was damaged or lost, she would be stranded there forever. An outpost of the Doomed Worlds might be ideal; one that contained just a single pinprick of light for the entire world. She found one, worked out its location relative to the Star Continent, then she placed the Compass back into her pocket, stood, and activated her Quadrant.

The void swallowed her up, just as it had done when she had travelled to Karalyn's world. She had panicked that time, but she was now expecting it, and it passed quickly. She fell a few feet, and landed in the midst of a great forest, falling into a large pile of brown pine needles. She glanced up. Something seemed wrong. The trees were taller and wider than any she had ever seen in her life, and the air was stiflingly hot and humid, making it difficult to breathe. Fallen tree trunks lay everywhere, all heaped up one on top of the other, while the living trees were each competing for a glimpse of the clear blue sky that shone overhead.

Lindi struggled to her feet, her clothes already soaked through with sweat. Thick ferns were blocking the view of her surroundings, and she fought her way through them, looking for higher ground. Within minutes, she had to call upon her self-healing. It was so humid that every movement was tiring, and she felt as though she was being slowly suffocated.

She sat down, her head spinning, and sent out her vision. It soared upwards, racing past the towering tree trunks until it broke through the branches and emerged into the dazzling sunlight. All around her was the great sweep of forest, then she noticed a range of tall mountains to her right. She estimated the distance and altitude, cut her vision, and triggered the Quadrant. The air shimmered, and she appeared on a stone ridge high above the treeline. She gasped in relief. It was still warm, but the humidity had dropped, and she felt as though she could breathe again.

Where was she? She stood, and gazed at everything she could see before her. The vast forest covered much of what was in her line of sight, but it frayed at one side, so she sent out her vision to investigate. It soared over the trees for dozens of miles, then she saw what lay beyond the forest – an even larger desert of dry, baked earth where nothing grew. She skirted the liminal area between the forest and the desert, and noticed a few abandoned settlements. It occurred to her that the desert was spreading inexorably, swallowing up the forest foot by foot, and the settlements had been overtaken by the arid wasteland. After another hour of searching, she at last found a settlement that was still thriving. It had a small marketplace, and a large but half-deserted military compound. In fact, the settlement was far too large for the small number of people Lindi could see. Was it being slowly evacuated by the gods of the Dominion? Lindi didn't know much about the Doomed Worlds, but she was aware that most if not all of them were dying. They had once supplied Implacatus with everything it required, and when Lindi saw a large logging operation by the edge of the settlement, she realised the function of the world she was on – to supply timber to Serene. Implacatus had possessed no reserves of trees, but Athumia was different. The Dominion no longer had any need for a world that supplied wood – was that why it was almost deserted?

She saw a small detachment of Banner soldiers standing next to where logs were being loaded onto long wagons, and entered the head of an officer. She quickly gleaned the basics – the world's name was Viridia, and it was indeed in the midst of being evacuated. Barely five hundred people remained, and the Dominion was hoping to complete the evacuation after a few final loads of cut timber had been exported to Inopei. Lindi noted the quantity of supplies in the settlement, and their locations, then she turned her attention back to the mountains. She searched the high peaks, looking for something she had seen in the officer's mind, and she found it fifty miles south of where she was standing on the ridge. An old, abandoned complex of stone buildings with its own well. It had once been an observatory, designed to predict certain eclipses that played havoc with the weather on Viridia, but it had been closed for decades.

Lindi triggered her Quadrant, and appeared on a stone veranda next to the observatory. She congratulated herself. She had found shelter, a place where she could get food and supplies, and she had evaded capture.

All she had left to do was find the Sextant.

Two hours later, Lindi was sitting in the shade of a wall of the observatory, a bag of stolen food by her side, and a lit cigarette in her fingers. She had wiped the memories of those she had robbed in the settlement; and she had also stolen clothes that were more appropriate for the intense heat, as well as a few blankets in case it got cold at night.

She ignored the nagging feeling of dread in the pit of her stomach. There was no time for regrets or doubts; she had chosen her course. She had gone all-in.

She activated the Compass with her thumb, and resumed her

search for the Sextant. She had found it quite quickly on the previous day when she had been sitting with Edgar, Elmhirst and Konna, and she had already spent a far longer amount of time looking for it again. She went from world to world. She looked at the Star Continent and Dragon Eyre, and then the City of Salve, in case Edgar had been so bold as to hide the Sextant within the lands of the Empire, then she took another look at Athumia. She saw several pinpricks of light as she gazed down at Nom Karta, then she gazed to the east, where the great glow of the Tempest mine dominated the horizon. The presence of so much Tempest in one place overpowered everything else in its vicinity, and then it finally struck her. She laughed aloud. Of course. Hadn't the damn volcanoes been a big enough clue? The perfect place to hide the Sextant was right on top of the Tempest mine; no wonder Lindi couldn't see it.

Without waiting, Lindi got to her feet, replacing the Compass in her hand with her Quadrant. She triggered the device, and she appeared under the dark, smoke-filled skies in the western half of Inopei. The desolate landscape was being illuminated by the red glow from the multiple lava flows, and ash was drifting through the air. She sat down on the rocky ground, and got to work.

Fifteen minutes later, her vision was soaring through the buildings by the minehead. The town and fortress by the Tempest mine were connected by walls, where soldiers stood, keeping watch over the workers as the Tempest was excavated from beneath the ground. Lindi went from room to room, but saw no sign of the Sextant, and she was about to give up when she went into a room where a god was sitting with a few officials. Lindi smiled, and entered the god's mind.

Laverne – the governor of the mine. Despite her appearance of outward calm, Laverne was keeping a dark secret, one that had been causing her a considerable amount of concern. Lindi delved into her recent memories until she saw an image of Edgar.

'But how long will I have to keep it here, my lord?' Laverne was saying.

'For as long as it needs to be here,' said Edgar.

'But the forces of the Empire will be mobilised to find it,' said Laverne. 'They may even deem this theft as an act of war.'

'No one will find it,' said Edgar. 'If my plan works, I will gladly hand it back to the Empire with my sincere apologies.'

'But...'

'Calm yourself, Laverne,' said Edgar. 'I know what I am doing. I am going to leave it here for now, but I will return soon.'

'Where are you going?'

'I have to be seen in and around Nom Karta, so people don't begin to connect my absence to the Sextant. And I have to speak to Kyra.'

'It will never work, Edgar,' cried Laverne. 'This dream of yours – it's impossible. Kyra is not Karalyn.'

'And yet I must try,' said Edgar. 'My sons need a mother, and I need my wife.'

Lindi focussed on the location where the events of the memory had taken place, and found it. She activated her Quadrant again, and appeared in a deep basement under the keep of the fortress – the same place where Edgar and Laverne had been talking. It was in darkness, so Lindi lit her cigarette lighter. She peered around, saw a lamp, and touched the flame to its wick. She increased the flow of oil, and a soft glow permeated the dank chamber. She turned, and smiled.

Sitting in front of her was the Sextant.

'Oh Edgar, you silly boy,' she said. 'Did you think you could outwit me?'

She took a step forward and placed her hand onto the flat surface of the device.

What is your desire, Lindi?

Lindi cackled with laughter. 'I want to move myself and the Sextant to a different place; can I do that?'

Specify the location.

'The large hall in the observatory on Viridia; can you see it?'

Everywhere you can see can be seen.

'That was a little cryptic, but all right. Take us there. Now, if you please.'

The air crackled, and Lindi appeared within the walls of the abandoned observatory, her hand still on the Sextant. She whooped and laughed.

'Could I destroy an entire world if I wanted to?' she said.

Specify the location.

'Oh shit,' Lindi muttered. 'Not just now, Sextant. Can I create a new world?'

Order the creation, and we shall begin.

'I want to, but maybe later. Can you show me Udall?'

Her vision went blurry, then it focussed on the town where she had grown up. She saw the ships in the harbour, and the bridge palace. Dragons were flying overhead in the dimming light of evening, and the sight made Lindi a little homesick.

'Show me Joss.'

Joss cannot be located.

'Why not?'

Joss cannot be located.

'Is that because you can't find individual people?'

Silence.

'So, you don't like tricky questions, eh? Show me Clackenbaird Farm.'

Her vision went blurry again, then it centred on the farmhouse.

'Show me Carter.'

Carter cannot be located.

'For fuck's sake; you can be annoying, Sextant. I need a list of what does and doesn't work. Look into the farmhouse; go room by room until I say stop.'

Her vision appeared in the front hall of the farmhouse, then it switched into the kitchen, then Aila's bedroom, then the dining room, each image flashing into her mind after the other.

'Stop,' she said. 'That makes my head hurt. Can I use my own vision through you? That would be simpler.'

Silence.

Lindi frowned, then she eased her vision out, and she found herself looking down on the farmhouse again.

'I am a fucking genius,' she said.

She scanned around the farm with her dream vision, then she noticed a cart climbing the hill from the direction of the barley fields. Carter was up on the driver's bench, and the cart was loaded with farming equipment.

'All right, Sextant; let's see if you can do this. Bring Carter here. Now.'

Lindi took her hand off the Sextant in time to see the air shimmer a few feet away. Carter appeared, still in a sitting position, then he fell three feet and landed on the solid stone floor.

'Fancy meeting you here,' said Lindi.

'What the fuck?' cried Carter.

'Look what I've got,' she said.

Carter scrambled to his feet, his eyes wide. 'Where am I? Where are we, Lindi? Did you know that Cael Holdfast wants to speak to you?'

'I know,' she said.

She pointed at the Sextant, but Carter seemed too taken aback to notice anything. He stared out through a hole in the half-ruined wall, his mouth half-open.

'Fuck, it's hot here,' he said.

'You should try it down in the forest,' she said.

'Cael questioned everyone in the farmhouse,' Carter went on; 'but the arrogant bastard wouldnae even tell us what he was looking for. He was in my fucking mind, raking around. Ma wasnae pleased, I can tell ye. The only person he didnae get to speak to was you, Lindi. Have ye been here all day? Where are we? Is this Sanang?'

'It's not Sanang.'

Carter turned around, and he finally glanced in the direction of the Sextant.

'Ta dah,' said Lindi. 'It turns out that I am an expert thief, although I only stole something that had already been stolen by someone else first.'

'What is it?'

'It's the Sextant, you dozy pillock. Edgar stole it from the Empire, and I've just stolen it from Edgar. Do you have any idea what this means?'

'Cael did mention Edgar,' said Carter. 'He was asking Naxor why he had been spending so much time on Nom Karta. Naxor was trying to be cocky about it, but I could see that he was shitting his pants. What have ye done, Lindi? The whole Empire will be after ye.'

'Yeah, probably,' she said. 'I could destroy the Empire. It would take me a few seconds, and every world ruled by Empress Thorn would be reduced to dust.'

'Why the fuck would ye do that?'

'I'm not going to do it. I'm just saying that, with the Sextant, I could, if I wanted to. I used it to bring you here; it was easy.'

Carter walked up to the Sextant. 'How does it work?'

'You place your palm onto the top, and if you hear a voice, it will work for you.'

'Can I give it a go?'

'Of course.'

Lindi watched with a little trepidation as Carter placed his large hand onto the flat surface of the device.

'How long do I have to wait for the voice to appear?' he said.

'You should have heard it by now.'

'Oh well. I guess it doesnae work for me.'

Lindi smiled in relief. 'What a shame. Don't take it personally though; it doesn't work for the vast majority of people. It was designed only to be used by the Ascendants, but a few Holdfasts have the ability. There's Karalyn, of course, though she can't use it any more. And there's my mother, and Cael, and now me.'

'Then why would Edgar steal it?'

'That's what puzzles me. I assume that Cael didn't provide you with an answer to that question?'

'He told us nothing. Can Kyra use it?'

'I don't think so.'

'Then it makes no sense, unless Edgar is trying to provoke a war with the Empire. What about Esher?'

'What about him?'

Carter gave her a look. 'He's an Ascendant, ya numpty. You said it was designed for them. Maybe Edgar was hoping that Esher would use it for him.'

'I never thought of that. I did read a strange conversation out of Laverne's head.'

'Who?'

'Never mind – a god who lives on Athumia. She was speaking to Edgar just after he stole it; and he said that he would hand the Sextant back to the Empire if his plan worked. And then Laverne said that his plan was stupid – that *Kyra wasn't Karalyn*. What do you think that meant?'

'It could mean anything,' said Carter. 'It sounds as though Edgar wants Kyra to become more powerful, like her mother, but I have no idea if the Sextant could help with that.'

'Yeah, I agree. I suppose it doesn't matter what Edgar wanted it for, because it belongs to us now. Just wait until you hear my plan, Carter. If it's successful, which it will be, we will get everything we want. We will...' She paused. 'Actually, before I tell you my plan, we should probably go back to Kell to collect our things before it is too late.'

'What?' said Carter. 'Is this plan so dangerous that it won't be safe for us to return to Kell for a while? Will people be looking for us?'

'They won't find us here, not on this world.'

'But will it be safe to go back to Kell?'

'Probably not,' she said, 'which is why we should go back right now, while we still can.'

Carter frowned. 'If we're gonnae be living in this dump,' he said, 'we'll need clothes, weapons, food, tools – a whole shitload of stuff. We can split up – I will gather food, tools, blankets, weapons and fuel; and you can get clothes, soap, towels, and maybe even a mirror. In other words, I'll deal with the downstairs of the farmhouse, and you can deal with the upstairs. Ceres and Carla are still at school just now, but they will be home in around half an hour, while Clova will be in the distillery. My mother and Naxor might be there, though, which is why I will gather stuff from the ground floor – it's best if they don't know that yer in the house. Have you got all that?'

'My word,' said Lindi, 'you are an organised chap.'

'One of us has to be.'

Lindi took out her Quadrant. 'I'll drop you off in the courtyard, then I'll go straight to your bedroom and start packing.'

'I have a large luggage case under the bed – use that.'

She triggered the device, and they appeared next to one of the large barns by the front of the farmhouse.

'I will meet you back here in five minutes,' said Lindi, then she activated the Quadrant again.

The air shimmered, and she found herself in Carter's room. She pulled the heavy case out from under the bed, and started throwing Carter's clothes into it, along with a pair of boots, and a knife she found by his pillow. She dragged the case into the room where she had been sleeping, and packed away her own clothes, as well as the ones she had purloined from Caitlyn. She threw in a hairbrush and a small oval mirror, then a box containing money, make-up and some jewellery, including the necklace Joss had given her on her birthday.

She crept to the door, and peered out of the bedroom. No one was on the landing, so she padded to the large bathroom. She laid a towel onto the tiled floor, and set down a variety of soaps, their toothbrushes, and anything else she could find that might be of use. She picked up the towel by its corners, and hurried back into her bedroom, where Naxor was standing by the luggage case, a quizzical look on his face.

'Ah, Lindi,' he said. 'Off on your travels, are you?'

'Something like that,' she said.

'While you were out this afternoon,' he went on, 'I had a most unpleasant encounter. Would you like to hear about it?'

'Not really.'

'I was interviewed by Cael Holdfast,' he said. 'Naturally, I told him nothing about Lord Elmhirst taking you to Nom Karta yesterday, nor did I mention anything about the time Edgar asked you to see if you could operate the Compass. Needless to say, none of what I said mattered, for Cael then took it upon himself to raid my mind. I hide my thoughts and memories well, but the simple truth is that I have no idea what, if anything, Cael took from my mind. He might know nothing, or he might know everything.'

'I don't have time for this Naxor,' she said.

'You will find the time, Lindi. What did Edgar want with you yesterday? What did he ask you to do? One must assume it was related to the Compass, and that thought leads me directly to the Sextant. Answer me, Lindi. What did you do for Edgar?'

Lindi frowned. 'That's none of your fucking business, demigod. Who do you think you are, to question me like that? I have moved far beyond your pathetic little plans and schemes. Now get out of my way, before I kick your sorry arse.'

Naxor stared at her, and she punched him in the face, using her battle-vision to break his nose. He cried out, as blood gushed from his face, and Lindi placed the toiletries into the case and closed it.

'See you around, Naxor,' said Lindi.

'Wait!' he cried.

She activated the Quadrant, and appeared by the barn. Carter had filled an entire handcart with items, and he nodded to her. She triggered the Quadrant again, and they both arrived back in the half-ruined observatory on Viridia.

'That was easy,' said Carter. 'My mother must be out – there was no one downstairs.'

'I ran into Naxor,' she said.

'Aye? What happened?'

'He started acting as though he was my father or something, asking me all these questions; so I broke his nose.'

Carter laughed. 'Right; do I finally get to hear the plan? It had better be good.'

'It is magnificent,' she said.

'Give me the gist.'

Lindi smiled. 'All right. It's quite simple really. The first thing we shall do is use the Sextant to locate something.'

'What?'

Lindi smiled. 'Your brother,' she said. 'We're going to rescue Cairney.'

CHAPTER 25
INDESTRUCTIBLE

Eastern Coast of Gunst – 2nd Lexinch 1613

The military harbour was in flames. Warehouses, boat sheds and dockyards lay in smoking ruins, devastated by a mass barrage of Battanaras, and smoke was drifting up into the blue sky. Five Gunstian warships had been sunk in the harbour basin, and only the masts of the two largest vessels were poking above the surface of the water.

Cael stared out to sea as a line of captured Gunstian sailors and dockworkers was being corralled behind him on the quayside.

'Zamata is only a couple of hundred miles due east of here,' said Cole.

'Is that right?' said Cael. 'We have raided so many Gunstian installations that I have lost track.'

'This harbour was the one the Gunstians used if they needed to ship agents or supplies to the island,' Cole said. 'It was also a forward base to launch an invasion of Irlan and Elso. Without it, the Gunstians will have to postpone any notions they had of re-conquering the western half of Athumia.'

'I hope the Irlanians are grateful.'

'You can ask them yourself, if you like,' said Cole. 'We have released over sixty Irlanian sailors who were being held here.'

'A captured crew?'

'Most likely pirates, sir. They are happy to be free, but they are a little upset that we destroyed every ship in the harbour.'

'Tell them that we'll take them directly back to Irlan, or to Zamata; wherever they want. We won't leave them stranded in Gunst.'

'Yes, sir.' He glanced to his left. 'Lord Elmhirst is approaching.'

'Go and talk to the Irlanians, Cole,' said Cael. 'I want to speak to Elmhirst alone for a moment.'

Cole saluted. 'Yes, sir.'

Cael lit a cigarette as Elmhirst walked up to him. The Ancient was in full battle armour, and had a long war axe slung over his back. Cael tried to access Elmhirst's mind but, as he had suspected, the Ancient had protected himself with eye-guards.

'Congratulations to you and your forces,' said Cael.

'And to yours, Adjutant,' said Elmhirst. 'Dare I say that our combined forces worked quite well together? This was a powerful military establishment and yet, between us, we destroyed it completely.'

'Any casualties?'

'A dozen Aucterian infantry. No gods. You?'

'Six slain; eleven injured. Where is Lord Edgar, Elmhirst?'

Elmhirst smiled but said nothing.

'Does he have the Sextant?' Cael went on.

'I cannot comment on that,' said Elmhirst.

'Then you are not denying it?'

'I am neither denying nor confirming anything, Adjutant. My loyalty is to the Dominion.'

'The Empress is extremely displeased,' said Cael. 'If it so happens that Lord Edgar is responsible for the theft of the Sextant, the consequences could be grave.'

'That is understood.'

'I fail to comprehend the motivation behind his actions, if, indeed, Edgar is the thief. Can you enlighten me?'

'Again, I have no comment to make.'

'Lord Naxor knows something,' Cael went on, 'but I couldn't stay in Kell long enough to dig my way through his memories.'

Elmhirst said nothing.

'But I shall be returning to Kell today,' said Cael, 'for I still need to talk to Lindi Holdfast. When I am there, I will press deeper into Naxor's mind. I will find what he is hiding.'

'Indeed.'

'Does Lindi have anything to do with the theft?'

'No comment.'

'Was Naxor acting as an intermediary between Edgar and Lindi?'

'I could not possibly comment on that, either. I have my own opinions regarding the wisdom or otherwise of certain actions taken by the gods of Nom Karta; but you must understand, Cael, that my loyalty to the Dominion outweighs my personal views. Is it not the same with you? If your Empress makes what you consider to be a grievous error, would you not remain loyal?'

Cael smiled. 'I don't know what you're talking about,' he said. 'The Empress never makes mistakes.'

Elmhirst laughed. 'Of course. Regardless, I hope my inability to comment on any of this does not come between us. We have been working well together against the Gunstians, and I hope our cooperation can continue.'

'As do I, Elmhirst.'

A few imperial marines approached, leading a small group of bedraggled-looking sailors.

'Sir,' said a marine sergeant, 'these men wished to speak to the leaders of the raid.'

'We want to show our gratitude,' shouted one of the sailors.

Cael turned to them. 'Irlanians?'

'Aye,' said the sailor. 'We just wanted to say thank you. Those bastard Gunstians have been holding us in their cells for nigh on three months, and it's good to breathe the sea air again. And thank you for offering to take us all home. So which are you – Dominion or Sapphire Throne?'

'Both,' said Cael. 'I am the Adjutant of the Sapphire Empire, and the gentleman standing next to me is Lord Elmhirst of the Dominion.'

'Well, you lads have done us a tremendous favour. I hear you've cleared the entire coast of Gunstian warships; business is going to be good.'

'Where have you asked to be taken?' said Cael.

'One of your officers is going to take us all the way to Linnagatz,' said the sailor. 'He says we'll be home in a few minutes.'

'Make sure you spread word of what is happening to those you meet in Irlan,' said Elmhirst. 'Let them know that the Dominion protects its allies.'

'Righto, sir.'

The marines led the sailors away, and Elmhirst frowned.

'It appears, Cael, that we have made the seas safe for pirates,' he said. 'An unintended consequence.'

He extended his hand, and Cael shook it.

'Until next time, Adjutant,' said Elmhirst, then he turned and walked back to the soldiers and gods he had brought from the Dominion.

'Gather everyone,' Cael said to Cole. 'We're leaving.'

'Yes, sir; and the prisoners?'

Cael gazed at the corralled crowd of Gunstians. 'We will leave them here. I'm not going to order the execution of unarmed sailors and labourers, and it would be a waste of good money to house them all in imperial prisons.'

'Do you think it's working?' said Cole. 'Do you think the Gunstians will back down because we are disabling their military installations?'

'No, Cole, I do not. But what else can we do?'

Two hours later, Cael stepped out of the shower in his quarters in the Summer Palace on Colsbury. He dried himself, and dressed in a clean uniform. He had taken to wearing military garb since the Gunstians had begun raiding the Star Continent, and he buckled his holstered Jackdaw to his belt.

Arrosa and Cowie were in the sitting room when Cael walked in.

'We heard you in the shower,' said Arrosa. 'How was the raid?'

'Another tactical success; another strategic waste of time,' he said. 'Zamata will be safe from Gunst for a while, though; we hit the harbour closest to the island, left it in smoking ruins.'

'Did you kill anyone?' said Cowie.

'Not personally; not today,' he said. 'I let around three hundred prisoners go.'

Arrosa frowned. 'You are supposed to bring captured Gunstians back to the Star Continent for internment.'

'I know, but I fail to see the point. Our jails are already full of poor, uneducated Gunstian peasants. Imprisoning them doesn't make them change their minds about us – they still want to kill us all.'

'I questioned the agent with the Gift of Poison again,' she said. 'He is telling the truth – he is ignorant of the location of their raiding camp. He is aware that it is in Aucteran, but that is as far as his knowledge reaches. I also learned that you were the sole target that day. The agents, the portals, the eight hundred Gunstians – they were all for you. They are offering a massive reward to anyone who can capture you alive.'

'It's nice to know I am appreciated. I spoke to Elmhirst about Edgar.'

'Let me guess – he wouldn't say anything?'

'His refusal to comment was a comment in itself. He hinted that Edgar may have done something that he personally disagrees with, but his loyalty comes first. I have to admit, I am growing to like Elmhirst, for all that he fought against us when the Ascendants invaded. He's cynical and a bit jaded, but he isn't evil.'

'He wants to keep mortals in a permanent state of ignorance.'

'Aye, that's true; but it makes sense, from his point of view. I think the fear of death grows the longer you are alive, so gods like Elmhirst must be terrified of mortals creating weapons that can obliterate them with the press of a small lever.'

'Then what's the answer?'

'Perhaps there isn't one. I am firmly on the side of the mortals in this; I refuse to accept that any god should be able to hold back progress. It's not just weapons they want to stifle – it's everything else, like printing presses, steam engines, factories, better agricultural techniques, better navigation at sea. They want us all to live like peasants, uneducated and servile.'

'To keep us in our place.'

'Exactly,' he said. 'I won't stand for it. Three mortals with radically different backgrounds and upbringings – Ravi, Rosie and Nestorian are, between them, responsible for developing the most devastating weapons ever made on the Star Continent. They could do that because the Empire allowed them free access to money and research, with no fields of study forbidden to explore. Imagine what else we mortals could create, if left to our own devices. I will not allow the gods to hinder us.'

There was a knock at their front door, and Cael walked to the entrance and opened it.

'Good afternoon,' said Cole.

'I wasn't expecting to see you again today,' said Cael. 'I'm about to travel down to Kell to see if Lindi is there.'

'I know. Aunty Kelsey has asked me to accompany you.'

'Why?'

'Lord Naxor has made a formal complaint regarding your *attitude and behaviour*. He claims that you were very rude to Aila and her children when you were last there.'

'I wasn't rude,' said Cael. 'I remained curt, but polite. I was told not to mention why I was there, and small talk seemed out of the question; so I did what I had to do with the minimum amount of disruption.'

'I believe you, cousin,' said Cole, 'but Kelsey wants me to take the lead this time. For some reason, Aila is more comfortable with me. I will do the talking, giving you time to root around Naxor's memories.'

'Why are we pandering to Naxor?'

'Kelsey doesn't want to risk any potential reconciliation between us and the Marchbrae Holdfasts. She wants us to be on our best behaviour, and that means you are not allowed to use your persuasion skills on anyone.'

Cael was about to swear, then he remembered that Cowie was watching him from the couch.

'All right,' he said. 'I shall be courteous and well-mannered in front of our delightful cousins and their charming mother.' He turned to Arrosa and Cowie. 'I will be back for the meeting of the Imperial Court.'

He and Cole left the apartment, then Cole took out his Quadrant.

'Five minutes with that prick Naxor,' Cael muttered, 'and I could get everything we need out of him.'

'I think torturing him might upset Lady Aila, cousin.'

Cole triggered his Quadrant, and they appeared in front of the farmhouse of Clackenbaird.

Cael glanced up at the clear blue sky. 'It was like this the last time I was here. Contrary to rumours, Kell does have a summer.'

Cole knocked on the door, and they waited. After a moment, it was opened by Carla, who narrowed her eyes at Cael.

'Hello, Carla,' said Cole. 'We were wondering if Lindi is here today?'

'She's not,' said the girl.

'Do you know when she will be back?'

'No.'

'Could we speak to your mother for a moment?'

Carla frowned, then she turned to glance over her shoulder. 'Ma,' she shouted. 'The Colsbury Holdfasts are here again.'

Aila appeared by the door a few moments later.

'Ma'am,' said Cole, inclining his head. 'We would like to speak to Lindi for a few moments, please. She is the only Holdfast we haven't talked to.'

Aila chewed her lip. 'What has she done?'

'We are not at liberty to discuss the precise allegations, ma'am,' said Cole.

'Then you can leave.'

Cole eyed Cael.

'I think we should be honest with them,' said Cael. 'The last time I was here, ma'am, I was under strict instructions not to reveal anything to you, and I apologise if my manner appeared rude or abrupt. Frankly, though, I no longer see any good coming from this secrecy. Lady Aila, the Sextant has been stolen, and we suspect that Lord Edgar might possibly be involved. We hope that Lindi has nothing to do with it, but until we are able to speak to her, we cannot be sure. Is she here?'

Aila glanced at Carla. 'Go back inside,' she said.

The girl scowled at Cael, but did as her mother had told her. Aila stepped outside into the farmhouse courtyard, and eased the door shut behind her.

'Lindi vanished two days ago,' she said. 'She went out for a walk on the morning when you arrived to question us, then Naxor saw her briefly in the house after you had gone. We haven't seen her since.'

'But...' said Cael.

'Let me finish,' said Aila. 'There is more. Carter has also gone. He did not return from work that day, though Naxor saw Lindi packing away some of his clothes. Naturally, I have asked my cousin if he knows any more about this, and it seems that, through an innocent mistake on Naxor's part, he introduced Lindi to Lord Edgar in Nom Karta a few days ago.'

'Is Lord Naxor available for us to question, ma'am?' said Cole.

'Naxor is not in Clackenbaird at the moment,' said Aila. 'I am not sure when he will return.'

Cael narrowed his eyes. 'Do you know what Edgar wanted with Lindi?'

'I didn't, but after what you have told me, I imagine that he wanted Lindi's help to track down the Sextant. Sable can use the Sextant, so it is likely that Lindi also has that ability. Believe me, I am greatly annoyed at Naxor for this – he had no right to take Lindi to Nom Karta without first seeking Sable's permission, but I genuinely believe that he was ignorant of Edgar's plans for the Sextant, if indeed Edgar has taken it. When he questioned Lindi about it just before she vanished, her reply was to punch him in the face and break his nose.'

'Do you think Carter is Lindi's willing accomplice in this?' said Cole.

'Carter knew nothing of Edgar's plans,' said Aila.

'I can confirm that,' said Cael. 'I read his mind when I was last here. There was no sign of Edgar or the Sextant in his thoughts.'

'Then why would Carter vanish with Lindi?' said Cole.

Aila frowned. 'Isn't it obvious? Carter longs for one thing above all, and he needs the Sextant to accomplish this. He and Lindi have been working closely together this summer, and I can well believe that he told her his thoughts on this matter.'

'And what matter is that?' said Cael.

'If Lindi and Carter can access the Sextant,' she said, 'they might try to release Cairney from exile. That is Carter's dream. For years, Naxor and I have told the children to be patient, that there is no need to confront the mortal Holdfasts, not when the Empire will fall to us in time – all we have to do is wait. And I am tired of the divisions between us. I hate to admit this, but Karalyn was right to exile Cairney for what he did.'

'Let us imagine that this is the case,' said Cole. 'And let us imagine that Lindi and Carter are successful, and Cairney is free again. How would the others react? Specifically, I mean Killop, Konna and Carron. Would they support Cairney?'

'I have no idea what Cairney would do,' said Aila; 'but if he were to promote the idea of a violent overthrow of the Empire, then I would oppose him. I cannot speak for my children, however.'

'And what would Naxor do?' said Cael.

'The idea of Cairney returning would terrify my cousin,' said Aila. 'You all think Naxor is waiting to betray you, but that is only partly correct. He has no desire to provoke a violent confrontation, as it would destroy his slow and gradual accumulation of power. Naxor's plan is one that spans centuries; it is a plan that will affect none of the mortal Holdfasts currently alive, nor their mortal children. The plan uses our one advantage over you – that we will still be here long after you are all dead. So yes, we do mean to betray you, but not now, not while any of you live. The Empire shall be ruled by immortal Holdfasts – it might take centuries to come to pass, but it is inevitable.'

'If I understand you correctly,' said Cael, 'then you might be willing to help us find Lindi and Carter?'

'I am willing, but I cannot see how I could be of any use. I have told you everything I know. I only ask that you show Carter some measure of mercy and sympathy. He has never hurt anyone in his life, and I can well believe that Lindi has him twisted around her little finger, playing to the fact that Carter longs to see his brother again. As for Lindi, I do not believe that she is evil. She has a lot of her mother in her, and she seems a little too desperate to prove herself. It may be that she is an innocent victim of Edgar's folly.'

'Thank you for all your help, ma'am,' said Cole. 'I think we are done.'

'We will let you know if we discover anything,' said Cael.

Aila eyed them both, then she slipped back into the house and closed the door.

'Should we go back to Colsbury?' said Cole.

'Not yet,' said Cael, as he lit a cigarette. 'We might as well visit the whisky shop while we are here.'

They turned away from the farmhouse and started walking down the hill.

'Only three of Aila's children are now living with her,' Cael said, as they walked. 'Two are on the Hold Fast estate, one is in Nom Karta, one is in exile, and the other is with Lindi.'

'What do we know about Lindi?' said Cole.

'Too little, it seems. Let's say that Edgar tricked her into helping him. She could have decided to confess what she has done but, instead, she ran away with Carter.'

'Is Edgar allowing them to use the Sextant?'

'Edgar won't want to see Cairney being released,' said Cael. 'He attacked Nom Karta before he tried to kill the Empress and Aunty Kelsey.'

'I don't get it,' said Cole. 'Why would Edgar do something so foolish? Does he want another war? It's obvious that he has taken advantage of your mother's fall from power, but that implies that he has been secretly awaiting an opportunity to stick a knife in our back.'

'Elmhirst doesn't approve, and I think that's important,' said Cael. 'Whatever Edgar has done, he lacks the support of other gods.'

They reached the bottom of the slope, and walked along a track in the sunshine towards the first buildings of the huge distillery complex.

'Aila has installed three steam engines here,' said Cole.

'I can see the smoke they are giving off,' said Cael.

'Yes, but did you miss my point?' said Cole. 'Aila is a god, but she is taking advantage of the same mortal technology so despised by the rulers of the Dominion.'

'But will her children do the same when they eventually take over the Empire?' said Cael. 'Would Killop or Cairney close down the universities? Would they order the burning of books to stifle our knowledge? How do we stop that from happening, cousin?'

'I don't know if we can,' said Cole. 'Aila is right – they will outlive us all. Naxor's plan is fucking genius, if you think about it. Do nothing for centuries, and wait for the Empire to fall under their control. And once one of them becomes Emperor or Empress, they could sit on the throne for thousands of years. Imagine the entire Imperial Court populated by immortal Holdfasts.'

'Or,' said Cael, 'we increase the development of new weapons as quickly as we are able, arming the mortals with devices capable of destroying any god who opposes them. The immortal Holdfasts will never be able to take over if they wait too long, for our mortal descendants will be armed to the teeth by then.'

'And thus begins the war that Elmhirst so fears,' said Cole.

'But this time, the mortals will win.'

They walked into the whisky shop, and the old woman who worked there smiled at them.

'Good afternoon, ma'am,' said Cole.

'Yer far too polite to be from around here, son,' said the woman. 'Wait – are ye Holdfasts?'

'Aye,' said Cael. 'The Colsbury variety.'

The woman raised her palms. 'Then sorry, lads – no discount for you. Naxor's orders.'

Cael laughed. 'We suspected as much.' He took a bottle of Twenty-Year-Old Pitburn from a shelf.

'That's the most expensive whisky in the shop, son,' said the woman.

'Aye, I know,' said Cael, as he set it down on the counter.

'I see,' said the woman. 'Yer showing off in front of yer pal, eh?'

'You sound like you don't want me to buy it,' said Cael. 'All I'm doing is working my way through Marchbrae's entire catalogue, and I haven't had this one before as you rarely see it on sale in the Plateau. Are you saying that it's not worth the money?'

'Naw, it's a fine whisky,' she said.

Cael handed over the coins to pay for it, then he glanced at Cole. 'Are you getting anything?'

'Not today,' said Cole. 'I have four unopened bottles in my quarters; I don't need another one.'

'What are you doing after today's meeting of the Imperial Court?'

'I don't have any plans.'

Cael smiled. 'Shall we tan the Twenty-Year-Old?'

Cole raised an eyebrow.

'It's a Kell word,' said Cael. 'It means we drink the whole fucking bottle in one night.'

'It's meant to be sipped,' said the old woman. 'I'm not responsible for the raging hangovers ye'll have in the morning.'

Cael took out his Quadrant. 'I would never dream of blaming you,' he said to the woman. 'Are you up for it, Cole? I could do with a night off, and it'll be like the old days; just the two of us.'

'I'll need to check with Alva first,' he said, 'but all right.'

Cael smiled, then he swept his fingers over the Quadrant.

. . .

Four hours later, Cael and Cole were sitting on Cole's tiny balcony overlooking the forecourt in front of the Summer Palace on Colsbury. The meeting of the Imperial Court had been a tense and fractious affair, with no one having any concrete ideas about how to locate Edgar, Lindi or the Sextant. With the Compass also missing, and Karalyn's inability to sense the Sextant, they had argued back and forth about what to do. The Empress's rage had permeated the meeting, along with Her Majesty's disbelief that the most valuable and dangerous object on the Known Worlds had been so easily stolen.

Cael tore off the wax seal that topped the bottle of Twenty-Year-Old, then he pulled out the cork and filled two glasses. Cole took his and they both sipped.

'Aye, it's not bad,' said Cael.

'You can get stuff almost as good for a quarter of the price,' said Cole.

Cael lit a cigarette. 'But I can strike it off the list. There is one good thing about the theft of the Sextant – do you want to hear it?'

Cole nodded.

'I no longer have the temptation to annihilate the Gunstians,' said Cael. 'When the Sextant was still sitting on my mother's world, I always knew that I could use it to end the raids for good.'

'By massacring the entire population?'

'Aye. I wasn't going to do it, but the fact that I could was always in the back of my mind.'

'Maybe that's what Edgar wants to do,' said Cole. 'The Gunstians murdered his best friend. Killing them all would seem like a god-like response to that.'

'But Edgar would have to ask someone else to do it for him,' said Cael. 'He cannot use the Sextant himself.'

'So it would be either Lindi or Esher who would use it for him?'

'I don't know about Lindi, but we can discount Esher. I've been in his mind. He would refuse to help Edgar. If he knew anything, he would tell us.'

'He's quite useless, for an Ascendant.'

'And thank Pyre for that,' said Cael; 'though I dread to see how he would act if someone properly pissed him off. He has all that power within him, and yet he has never used even a fraction of it. He's a bit like you.'

'I used my fire powers today.'

'Aye, but only to ward the flames away from the marines by the quayside. You never use your fire powers aggressively.'

'Once was enough,' said Cole. 'That village on World Three still haunts me.'

Cael nodded, then he turned to gaze out at the night sky. As his head was moving, he caught a brief glimpse of Cole's eyes, and his vision blurred over. When it refocused, he was looking at the tall battlements of a city at night. The city was in flames, and great pillars of smoke were rising above the buildings and towers. Kelsey was close by, and her gaze was on the figure of an enormous purple dragon, whom Cael recognised at once. The dragon descended to the parapets of the city walls, where a young Kellach woman was standing. Her face was obscured by the smoke, but her voice rang clear.

'You know what to do,' the woman said. 'Kill them all.'

Cael blinked, and his vision returned to the small balcony and Cole.

'What just happened?' said Cole.

'Something that hasn't happened for a long time,' said Cael. 'I think I just had a glimpse of the future through your eyes. And no, you didn't die in it. Aunty Kelsey was also there, and she didn't die, either. Neither of you will die until after you have seen Lady Sigra Min Sigmund descend over a burning city. I guess that's nice to know.'

'Which city?'

'I'm not sure; I could only see a section of the city walls, but there were smoke and flames behind you. There was also a woman up on the battlements, but I couldn't see her face. She was telling Lady Sigra to kill everyone.'

'Fucksake, Cael; why did you tell me this?'

'You now know that you are pretty much indestructible until this happens,' said Cael. 'It means that you can be as reckless as you like. I thought you would want to know. You can jump off a fucking building and you would survive.'

'You definitely saw it through my eyes?'

'Aye. I'll be sending you out on the most dangerous operations from now on.' He laughed. 'Folk will marvel at how you manage to survive the shit I'll be putting you through.'

Alva opened the balcony door. 'Sorry for interrupting your night together, boys, but could I borrow my husband for a moment?'

Cole got to his feet. He narrowed his eyes at Cael for a moment, then he followed Alva into their apartment.

Cael stared out at the mountains in the distance. The night was dark, but all seven stars were out, and he could just make out the border where the sky and mountains met. He thought about Cole for a moment. He had been joking about sending him on perilous operations, but he was also very glad that he wouldn't have to worry about his cousin dying for a while. Cole was more than just a cousin, though; he was Cael's best friend. Cael would always put his wife and children first, but Cole came a close second; and who else but Cole could ever be Herald of the Empire, if Cael ever ascended to the throne? Cael's mood soured. Did he even want to be Emperor? The role held ever less attraction for him as time went on. He knew what he had said to Kelsey – that he wanted to lead the Holdfasts and the Empire, but he was finding it ever more difficult to obey every order he was given. He had broken two that day – he had released the captured Gunstians, and he had admitted to Aila the real reason they wanted to talk to Lindi. Neither breach had been brought up in the meeting of the Imperial Court. Did that mean the Empress was unaware of his petty transgressions, or did she know but not care?

Cole emerged from the house and sat down. He wiped the tears from his eyes.

'Is everything all right?' said Cael.

Cole nodded. 'Yes.'

'Am I going to have to beat it out of you, cousin?'

'Alva's pregnant,' he said. 'After years of trying, I'm going to be a father.'

Cael's arms reached out, and he embraced his cousin.

'I'm so happy for you, Cole,' he said. 'I know how much you and Alva wanted this. Can I tell Arrosa?'

'Arrosa already knows,' he said. 'The girls all knew before me, because Alva had to ask Kelsey to leave Colsbury for five minutes so Shella and Caitlyn could check if it was true. Alva was worried that she might be imagining it; she needed confirmation.'

Cael gazed at his best friend. 'I want you and Alva to move back to the Blue Palace in Plateau City. You can't stay on Colsbury, not if the Gunstians might raid it again at any moment. Let's not take the risk.'

'But your children are here,' said Cole. 'Alva and I will not leave if your family stays.'

'I agree,' said Cael. 'We should all evacuate.'

'We can't go if the Empress insists upon remaining here. If she stays, we all have to stay.'

Cael frowned. 'Now I wish we still had the Sextant. To protect our families, Cole, I would not hesitate to annihilate the Gunstians, and I don't care if that makes me a bad person.'

Cole raised his glass. 'To the future.'

'Aye,' said Cael, 'and to avoiding Lady Sigra for as long as possible.'

CHAPTER 26
ADMISSION OF GUILT

Nom Karta, Inopei – 3rd Lexinch 1613

'This was a good idea, Esher,' said Kyra. 'I can't remember the last time I went for a walk.'

Esher smiled as he led Kyra and Konna up the steps to the parapet on the wall that encircled Nom Karta.

'Back when the Bullan garrisoned this city,' he said, 'no one was allowed up here. Just look at that – what a view.'

Konna gazed out at the ocean and the river estuary. The small island at the mouth of the river was topped by a small castle, and gulls were circling over it as vessels of all sizes sailed in and out of the estuary. Further up the river, short piers jutted out from the banks by the city of Sat Orma, and the harbour was bustling with activity.

'When I first moved here,' said Kyra, 'Sat Orma was in ruins. The civil war between Tegru and Famula had devastated whole districts, and the harbour had been utterly destroyed. And the fort on the little island had been razed to the ground. What a difference now.'

'I credit the work ethic of the humans evacuated from the Doomed Worlds,' said Esher. 'I think they were so grateful to be living on Athumia, that they were prepared to work long hours for very little reward. They rebuilt Sat Orma with their own toil and sweat.'

'I am very glad they did,' said Kyra. 'I hated seeing Sat Orma when it was falling to pieces.'

Konna remained a little apart from Kyra and Esher as they talked. There was only one emotion on her mind – guilt. Kyra was far too trusting, and she had taken Konna's denials at face value. She must have, since she clearly knew nothing about Konna's involvement in the theft of the Sextant. The thought that Kyra trusted her so much that she hadn't used her powers to read her mind made Konna feel terrible. She wanted to grab Kyra by the arm and tell her to stop being so naïve, but, of course, that was the last thing she was going to do.

As a god, Konna never got ill, but she felt sick with worry. She had seen no sign of Edgar for four days, and whenever Elmhirst had made an appearance in Nom Karta, he had always been wearing his eye-guards. Konna had taken hers out after a few hours; they were so irritating that she could hardly think straight with them in – and maybe part of her had wanted to get caught. She had assumed that Kyra would read her mind, but she had been wrong. The Empire knew that the Sextant was gone, and they also knew that the Compass and Edgar had not been seen for the same length of time – and yet Kyra seemed to be clinging to the hope that Edgar had not been involved; that the father of her children would not have acted so irresponsibly. Esher had sensed Kyra's mood when he had arrived from Zamata that morning, and he had suggested going for a walk as a way to take her mind off Edgar for a while.

Several dragons soared over them, some just a few feet above the heads of the three humans standing on the city walls, and Konna felt the rush of air that passed in their wake. One of the dragons banked to the left, flying over the fringes of the ocean before circling back. She approached the walls from the south, then hovered over Konna, Kyra and Esher.

'Kyra-insect,' said the dragon, 'not once have I ever seen you out on these walls; not once in fifteen years.'

'Do you object?' said Kyra.

'Not at all,' said the dragon. 'You insects spend far too much time locked up inside the palaces of this city. Do you remember why I came to Nom Karta?'

'I do.'

'I fear I will never be able to fulfil my grandfather's command. No one in the Dominion wishes to aid me; no one cares about my purpose here.'

'Then perhaps you should return to your grandfather,' said Kyra.

'Are you mocking me, Kyra-insect? I cannot return in failure; I would rather die. Do not insult me again. I know you are a powerful witch, but I am also powerful.'

'No insult was intended,' said Kyra.

The dragon peered down at Kyra, then she swept out her wings and soared away.

'Who was that?' said Esher. 'I have occasionally seen her in the great audience halls, but she is usually near the back, and she never speaks.'

'Her name is Sigra,' said Kyra. 'Have you met Lahnos?'

'No, never.'

'Lahnos is the rider of a dragon named Sigum, and Sigra is Sigum's niece. Her grandfather commanded her to kill his son Sigum, but Sigra has no way of finding him, and no one will take her off Athumia to allow her to look for him. Lahnos is being protected by the Empire, and his location is a well-kept imperial secret. The Dominion knows this, and they refuse to help Sigra carry out her grandfather's wishes. Hence, she lingers in Nom Karta like a bad smell, unable to move forward, and unwilling to go home.'

'And she has been here for fifteen years, the same as you?' said Esher.

'We arrived together,' said Kyra.

'She is a most beautiful dragon,' said Esher. 'I have never seen scales of that purple hue on another. It seems a shame that her life is now devoted to seeking the death of her uncle. Why does Sigum's father wish to kill him?'

'It's over something petty,' said Kyra. 'Sigum disgraced the family name by refusing to honour his betrothal to Queen Famula's daughter.'

'I don't think dragons would deem that petty,' said Esher. He glanced at Konna. 'You are being very quiet today.'

Konna's face flushed. 'Am I?'

'Yes, you are,' said Esher. 'Is everything all right with you?'

'I... it's uh...' She lowered her gaze. 'I am so sorry, Kyra.'

Kyra frowned at her. 'Sorry for what? Is this about Edgar? Do you know something?'

The air shimmered next to them and Elmhirst appeared on the parapet.

'What in the name of the Ascendants are you three doing all the way out here?' Elmhirst said. 'It took me an age to find you.'

Esher smiled. 'We were going for a walk.'

Elmhirst raised an eyebrow. 'I will be taking you back to the palace immediately. Lord Edgar has returned.'

Elmhirst swiped his Quadrant before any of the others could respond, and they appeared in Edgar's private study within the palace of Naghad. Edgar was seated on a chair, his face downcast, and his eyes red.

'I have found Lady Kyra, my lord,' said Elmhirst.

Edgar raised his gaze and stared at Kyra. 'I have made a grievous mistake, my love, but I did it for you.'

Kyra stared back at him. 'Why are you wearing eye-guards?'

'This is something I need to tell you of my own volition,' he said. 'I do not wish you to witness the depths of my despair.'

'Should we be alone for this?'

'The others can stay,' said Edgar. 'Both Elmhirst and Konna know already what it is I did, though I ordered them both to remain silent.'

Kyra cast an angry glance at Konna and Elmhirst, but Konna could not meet her gaze.

'Yes,' said Edgar; 'it was I who stole the Sextant from its home upon Karalyn's hidden world. It was me, I freely confess to my crime.'

'But why?' said Kyra. 'We have to give it back right away. We can make this right if we hand it back to the Empire.'

'That we cannot do.'

'But, Edgar, we must.'

'We cannot, for it has in turn been stolen from me. I went to where I had placed it a few hours ago. It has gone.'

Kyra collapsed into a chair, her head in her hands.

'It has gone, my lord?' said Elmhirst.

'It has,' said Edgar. 'A second thief has stolen from the first.'

'And what did the Sextant's protector have to say about this?' said Elmhirst.

'She knows nothing. She saw nothing. She did not know it was missing until I told her.'

'I cannot believe Laverne could have been so careless,' said Elmhirst.

'She wasn't careless,' said Edgar. 'She did exactly as I commanded.'

'Laverne had the Sextant?' said Kyra.

'I placed it into her hands for safekeeping,' said Edgar. 'I knew the Tempest from the mine would smother any signal coming from the Sextant. It wasn't enough.'

'Give me the Compass, Edgar,' said Kyra. 'I presume you took it? Give it to me, and I will find the Sextant, and we can return it to the Empire.'

'I do not have the Compass,' said Edgar. 'I gave it to someone, and they did not give it back. I was so taken by the Sextant that it slipped my mind to ask for it.'

Kyra leaned forward. 'Who did you give it to?'

'It was Lindi,' Konna blurted out. 'Lindi has the Compass, and she must have stolen the Sextant.'

Edgar shook his head. 'Did you not hear what I said? The Compass would have been useless, since the Sextant was placed amid the great deposits of Tempest by the mine. Lindi could not have found it that way.'

'I feel betrayed,' said Kyra. 'You told everyone about this but me, Edgar.'

'I didn't know anything about this,' said Esher.

'At least I have one honest friend,' said Kyra.

Elmhirst bowed his head. 'I apologise deeply for the deception, my lady.'

'Elmhirst tried to talk me out of stealing the Sextant,' said Edgar. 'He begged me to consult with you first, Kyra, but I refused; and then I ordered him to say nothing.'

Kyra's glare turned to Konna. 'What about you? Did you also try to dissuade my husband from this folly?'

'Not hard enough,' said Konna. 'I wanted to prove to Lord Edgar that I could be useful; that I wasn't too young and inexperienced to be of any assistance. I'm sorry.'

'But I still don't understand why,' said Kyra. 'Edgar – tell me. What were you going to do with a Sextant that you are unable to use?'

'If you look deep enough into your heart, my beloved, you will see the reason. We have spoken of it before.'

Kyra's eyes narrowed. She lowered her gaze for a moment.

'No,' she said.

'Yes,' said Edgar. 'I want you to remain by my side for millennia, not decades. What use are mere decades to me? I was going to find a way to make the Sextant change you, as it changed your mother. The secret of transforming a mortal into an immortal lies within the workings of the Sextant. I was going to ask Esher to look into these secrets for me. As the last of the Ascendants, he would have power over it; he would have been able to fathom its secrets.'

'You were going to ask me?' said Esher. 'Had you done so, I would have informed the Empress of the Sapphire Empire. I am not beholden to the Dominion, Edgar; I am the arbiter. What you have done is a grave betrayal of the treaty, and I am forced to find you in breach of your obligations and oaths.' He took out his Quadrant. 'I shall inform Queen Famula of what has occurred,' he said, 'and then I am going to Colsbury. I hope you will all accompany me there, so that you can tell the

Imperial Court the truth of what has transpired, but I will go alone if necessary.'

'Wait,' said Kyra. 'We will go with you, Esher, but first, I want to hear from Edgar why he wants me to become immortal.'

'You know why!' Edgar cried. 'I judge time in centuries, and yet the time we are allotted together spans a mere handful of years. If I am forced to watch you grow old and die, I shall mourn for a millennium.'

'But, Edgar,' she said, 'did you not stop to think about what I might want? The thought of being immortal fills me with a sense of dread that I can barely begin to explain. I look at you and the other gods who live in Inopei, and I pity you. I see the changes that happen to those who linger on for centuries. Esher and Konna are yet to experience these changes, and our own sons are far too young to understand what it feels like to watch generations of mortals come and go. I wish you were mortal, Edgar; I wish we could grow old together, and I wish I could spare you and our boys the pain of seeing me wither and die – but I don't want to live forever. By its nature, life is transient, and that's the way it should be. We live, and then we die; or that's what should happen. It is the gods who have flouted the natural order. You all seem to think that we mortals long to be like you, and maybe some do, but I am glad I am mortal; it gives my life a meaning that the gods seem to have lost.'

'You cannot mean that,' said Edgar.

She reached out and touched his face. 'If you truly know me, my husband, you will understand that I meant every word. My mother is cursed. What happened to her was a punishment, not a blessing.'

Edgar bowed his head. He crouched by the chair where Kyra was sitting, took her hand, and kissed it, as the others watched in silence.

'Let us give them a moment,' said Esher. 'I will speak to Queen Famula, and then I shall return here to take us all to Colsbury.'

'I shall not be going,' said Elmhirst. 'I am guilty only of obeying my lord's commands, and there is nothing for which I feel a need to apologise.'

'Very well,' said Esher, as he opened the door to the study. He led

Elmhirst and Konna out into the hallway, and closed the door. 'Will you be coming with me, Konna?'

'I don't want to,' she said, 'but I shall.'

Esher's eyes narrowed as he gazed at her. 'I am so disappointed in you,' he said. 'You, too, are in breach of the treaty, Konna. Why did you do it?'

'I was tired of being treated as a child,' said Konna. 'I wanted to prove to Edgar that I was just as capable as any of the other gods.'

'When I was Draughtsman Reece,' he said, 'I heard much about your father. In the City of Salve, one could hardly escape hearing the stories of how he fought the greenhides, and how he returned with Karalyn to defeat the Ascendants.'

'Don't do this,' said Konna. 'Don't drag my father into the conversation. I am perfectly aware that he would not have approved of me helping Edgar.'

'And what would he have thought of your rift with the other Holdfasts?' said Esher. 'From everything I have heard and read, your father was loving and forgiving – do you think he would have enjoyed seeing his children filled with such hatred for their mortal cousins? For ten years, your mother's anger poisoned your hearts, and so, I suspect, did the whispered words of Lord Naxor. This, I believe, would have hurt your father far more than any mistake you made in helping Edgar.'

Konna said nothing as Esher turned and walked away.

'Pay him no attention, Konna,' said Elmhirst. 'The last Ascendant is angry, but his little tantrum reminds me that he still thinks like a mortal. He will gain perspective as the years roll by.'

Elmhirst inclined his head at Konna, then he walked off in the opposite direction to Esher. Konna gazed at the marble floor of the hallway, the words of the Ascendant going round her mind. Her mother's grief and rage had passed, but the damage had been done. To a centuries-old demigod like Aila, her decade-long bitterness towards the other Holdfasts might seem like a small period of time, but it had occurred during the formative years of her eight children, and the effects ran deep. Konna had loathed Cael, Kelsey and Thorn since the moment she had seen her father's body in Colsbury Castle, and that hatred had been maintained by her mother's anger, and by Naxor's determination to drive a wedge between the mortal and immortal Holdfasts. Konna had a few memories of Cael from before the time her father had died on Dragon Eyre. When Cael had been sixteen and seventeen, he had worked in Marchside during the cold and dark winter thirds, helping her father on the farm. Konna had often seen the two of them together – her father and her cousin – and it had been obvious that her father had held a great affection for Cael. And then, after her father's death, Cael had seemed different – more remote, more arrogant, more ruthless; and it struck Konna for the first time that her cousin had also suffered from the death of the great Corthie Holdfast. Cael had been there, and he had failed to save his uncle. He had held Corthie's hand in his last moments, and had wept over his body – what had that done to him? A deep sense of shame and regret flowed over Konna. She had blamed Cael, when he had been going through his own personal anguish. Had the hatred of the Marchbrae Holdfasts contributed to the hardening of Cael's heart?

She heard footsteps, and looked up to see Esher walking towards her.

'I am sorry for mentioning your father,' he said. 'It's none of my business, and I should have kept my big mouth shut.'

'It's fine,' said Konna. 'How did the Queen take the news?'

'Her greatest concern is that the Sapphire Empire will want to punish the Dominion for Edgar's crime,' he said. 'We did something bad to them, so they will need to do something bad to us, to balance things out.'

'That's dragon logic,' she said.

'I am to offer the Empress a sizable amount of Tempest free of charge,' Esher went on, 'as a suitable recompense.'

'Is she angry with Edgar?'

'I think she understood his motivation. He wants his mate to live forever, and took action to try to accomplish this. It's the consequences that worry her, not the crime.'

He knocked on the door of Edgar's study, then eased it open. Inside, Edgar and Kyra were sitting together, and they got to their feet.

'Kyra will be staying here,' said Edgar. 'She has no desire to see the Empress.'

'It's not the Empress I wish to avoid,' said Kyra; 'it is the sight of my husband having to apologise to her.'

'Then I shall take only Edgar and Konna,' said Esher, his Quadrant in his hand.

Edgar and Kyra kissed, then the god moved closer to the Ascendant. Esher activated the Quadrant, and Konna found herself on Colsbury, in the wide courtyard between the Summer Palace and the two keeps. Several heavily-armed marines emerged from the entrance of the palace, and a loaded Battanara was pointed at them.

'Hold,' said a marine lieutenant. 'Greetings, Lords Edgar and Esher, and Lady Konna.'

Konna stared at the marine with the Battanara. The weapon was balanced on his right shoulder, and he was aiming its barrel at Edgar, as he gazed down the sights. More marines appeared from the direction of the Great Keep, and they surrounded the small party of arrivals.

'We are here to see the Empress,' said Esher.

'While the current crisis endures,' said the lieutenant, 'I would ask that you arrive in the village on the mainland, and send a message that you wish to enter Colsbury. The island has been attacked twice by Gunstians, and we are under orders to eliminate any raiding party that appears unannounced.'

The air shimmered a few yards away, and Cole appeared.

'I will take it from here, Lieutenant,' he said to the marine officer.

The lieutenant saluted. 'Aye, sir.'

Cole and the others waited as the marines moved back into their positions.

'Sorry about that,' said Cole, 'but we aren't taking any chances with the Gunstians. What can I do for you?'

'We need to speak to the Empress,' said Esher. 'It concerns the Sextant.'

Cole's gaze went to Konna, then he triggered his own Quadrant. The air shimmered, and they appeared in an anteroom inside the Summer Palace, where more marines were on duty. Cole whispered something to a courtier, who bowed and went through a large set of doors. Konna folded her arms across her chest as they waited, then the tall doors opened, and the courtier rejoined them.

'Her Imperial Majesty is ready to see you,' said the courtier.

Cole led Edgar, Esher and Konna into a large audience chamber, where several members of the Imperial Court had gathered. Cael was there with his wife Arrosa, along with Kelsey and Lucius Cardova, while the Empress was seated upon a throne. Konna felt her spirits sink. She hadn't been in the company of the leadership of the Empire since Cairney's arrest on Dragon Eyre eight years before. That time, she had been reprieved thanks to the fact that her brother had been manipulating her; this time, she had no such excuse.

'Good afternoon,' said Kelsey, from where she was standing by the base of the throne. 'We hear that you have news regarding the Sextant? Good news, I hope.'

'Bad news, Madam Herald,' said Esher. 'It is my unfortunate duty to announce to you, Your Majesty, that the thieves who stole the Sextant from Karalyn Holdfast are standing before you. Lord Edgar has admitted the crime, and Lady Konna has confessed to being his accomplice.'

The Empress remained silent, her features unmoved, but Konna could see the rage start to build in Kelsey's eyes.

'You two stole the Sextant?' Kelsey cried. 'What the fuck were you thinking?' She jabbed her finger in Edgar's direction. 'How long were you planning this? You waited until Karalyn lost her powers before striking, you backstabbing little thief.'

'Maybe we should listen to what they have to say before we lose our tempers, Aunty,' said Cael. 'I am more concerned by the fact that they haven't brought the Sextant back with them. If you stole it, Edgar, then where is it?'

Edgar moved forward a few paces, then he got down onto his knees before Thorn. 'I humbly apologise for my grievous error of judgement, Your Majesty,' he said. 'I not only stole the Sextant, but it has now been stolen from me.'

Thorn glanced at Arrosa, who nodded.

'Pyre's tits,' said Kelsey. 'Who stole it from you?'

'I do not know for certain, Madam Herald,' said Edgar.

'But you can't even operate the damn thing,' said Kelsey.

'I was going to ask Esher to operate it on my behalf.'

'I would have refused,' said Esher. 'I had no knowledge of Edgar's actions until a short while ago, when he admitted to me what he had done. Queen Famula was also unaware and, as compensation, she wishes to offer the Empire five tons of unrefined Tempest ore.'

'We appreciate the gesture,' said the Empress, 'but I would rather have the Sextant back. Lord Edgar, did you and Lady Konna act alone?'

'We received assistance from three others, Your Majesty,' said Edgar. 'Lord Elmhirst and Lady Laverne carried out my orders, though both were unwilling, and both counselled me against the course of action I had chosen. They are blameless; their only fault is loyalty.'

'Who was the third?' said Kelsey. 'Who else helped you?'

'Lindi Holdfast, Madam Herald,' said Edgar. 'She used the Compass to locate the Sextant.'

'She still has the Compass,' said Konna. 'She must have stolen the Sextant from Edgar.'

Thorn turned her gaze to Konna. 'What was your role in this?'

Konna felt some of her old anger and hatred return to her as she stared back at the Empress.

'I wished to be of service to Lord Edgar,' she said.

'I see,' said the Empress.

'The treaty has been breached,' said Esher. 'Both sides agreed that the Sextant should remain with Karalyn alone, and Lord Edgar has violated that clause.'

'We get that,' said Kelsey. 'Why did you do it, Edgar?'

'I wished to find a way for my wife to ascend into immortality,' he said. 'Karalyn did it; I wanted the same for Kyra.'

Cael's eyes tightened. 'You wanted my sister to become a god?'

'Yes.'

'Did she know what you were planning?'

'She did not. She was greatly angered when she found out. She does not wish to be immortal, and so my heart is doomed to a lifetime of grief. All I wanted was to have Kyra with me through the long centuries to come, for she is the one true love of my life, and so I allowed my passions to overwhelm me. I intended to return the Sextant to the Empire once I had exhausted every possibility to achieve my aims; but I now know that my efforts would have been in vain, for Kyra would have refused to cooperate.'

'If you cannot bear the thought of being without my sister,' said Cael, 'perhaps you should have asked her to block your self-healing powers.'

Edgar paid no attention to Cael's remark, then he raised his hands in supplication towards Thorn.

I throw myself upon your mercy, Empress of the Sapphire Throne,' he said. 'I shall accept whatever punishment you deem fit.'

Thorn moved her gaze back to Konna. 'Daughter of Corthie,' she said, 'what punishment do you believe would be appropriate for you and Lord Edgar?'

'I'm not playing this game,' said Konna. 'If you want to place us in restrainer masks, then do it. I am not afraid of you.'

'I do not require you to be afraid,' said Thorn; 'all I wish from you, Konna, is an apology. Lord Esher, please inform Queen Famula that I accept her generous offer of compensation. The Empire shall not hold the Dominion responsible for the actions of a few misguided gods. Lord Edgar, you have placed us all into a most delicate position. We already suspected that Lindi and Carter were in possession of the Sextant, and this news seems to confirm it. I accept your apology, but it is not enough. I require you to lend all assistance to the task of finding Lindi and Carter. Are you in agreement?'

'I am, Your Majesty,' said Edgar, 'and I thank you for your clemency.'

Konna frowned. 'How do you know that Carter is with Lindi?'

'Cole and I were in Kell yesterday,' said Cael. 'We spoke to your mother. Carter and Lindi have both vanished. We are working on the assumption that they intend to free Cairney.'

'No,' said Konna. 'Is that even possible?'

'You tell me, cousin,' said Cael. 'Can Lindi operate the Sextant?'

'Aye,' said Konna. 'We saw her do it.'

'There's your answer,' said Cael. 'It might take her a while to locate Cairney, but if she looks long and hard enough, she'll get there in the end.'

'But why would Lindi want to release Cairney from captivity?' said Esher, his eyes wide.

'Knowing Lindi,' said Konna, 'she would do it for a laugh. But Carter... he has dreamed of being reunited with our brother. If Cairney returns, we are all in grave danger.'

'And yet you helped Edgar place the Sextant into their hands, cousin,' said Cael. 'Do you really hate us that much?'

Konna stared at Cael, but said nothing.

Kelsey eyed her. 'It might be time for that apology, niece.'

'I'm sorry,' said Konna. 'I didn't help Edgar to spite any of you; though I doubt you will believe it. I did it because I was tired of being treated like a child by the other gods in Nom Karta. I wasn't trying to hurt the Colsbury Holdfasts.'

'She is telling the truth,' said Arrosa.

'Thank you, Postmaster,' said the Empress. 'Herald, inform Sable immediately of this news; she deserves to know, and she may have some inkling of where to find her daughter.'

'Aye, Your Majesty,' said Kelsey. 'One thing bothers me though – why would Lindi help Edgar steal the Sextant in the first place? Was she planning to take it into her own possession?'

'I think it was opportunistic, Madam Herald,' said Edgar. 'As for your first question, I swore to support Lindi's bid to become Empress; an oath that was insincere. I would have promised anything for her assistance.'

The hall fell into silence.

'Would you mind repeating that, Edgar?' said Kelsey. 'Was this Lindi's idea?'

Edgar bowed his head. 'She said it was her condition, along with gifts of gold, land and titles. Lindi wishes to overthrow the rule of the Empress and install herself upon the throne.'

'And you agreed to help her?' said Cael.

'I did. It is inevitable that the immortal Holdfasts will inherit the Sapphire Empire; should I care which of them wears the crown?'

'This is the first I have heard of this,' said Esher.

'Take Edgar and Konna back to Nom Karta, if you would, Lord Esher,' said the Empress. 'I have heard enough.'

Edgar rose to his feet.

'We must be ready for anything,' the Empress went on, 'as we not only have to contend with the Gunstians; we must also be prepared for the return of Cairney.'

CHAPTER 27
APPROACHABLE

Hold Fast, Republic of the Holdings – 2nd Day, Second Third Summer 560

'You look as old as I feel, Karalyn,' said Celine, as the two women reclined on the front porch of the Holdfast mansion.

'I'm getting used to it, I think,' said Karalyn. 'I have learned to move a little slower, and to be more careful. All the same, I had forgotten how warm the Holdings gets in summer. I don't know how you cope with it, Celine.'

'I have lived here all my life,' she said. 'Iced tea helps.'

Karalyn smiled as she gazed out over the vast expanse of the Holdings plain. A heat haze was rising from the parched earth and, even under the shade of the large awning, it was uncomfortably hot. Carron appeared from the direction of the square, where the fountain would be filling the air with cooling spray. The tall son of Corthie and Aila climbed the steps onto the porch and sat down by the two women.

'I thought you were with Killop and the others,' said Celine.

'Killop is showing Caitlyn and Arrosa around the stables,' said Carron, as he filled a glass with iced tea. He glanced at Karalyn. 'Are you really *her*? Are ye really the great Karalyn Holdfast?'

'Aye,' she said.

Carron smiled and shook his head. He leaned back on a reclining chair, and put his feet up.

'And ye've lost all yer powers?' he said.

'Temporarily,' she said. 'How is life on the estate?'

'Fucking hot,' he said. 'I have never experienced anything like it; I feel like I'm melting. Killop's used to it, but. He's been here for eight years.'

'It took him a couple of summers to acclimatise,' said Celine.

'I cannae wait for winter,' said Carron; 'words I never thought I'd say.'

'Winter in the Holdings is similar to the summer in Kell,' said Karalyn.

'Aye? That'd be braw. I still cannae ride a horse, but I've got plenty of time to work it out.' He gestured out towards the stables. 'Here they come.'

Karalyn turned to look, and saw Killop leading Caitlyn and Arrosa through the heat haze. They climbed the steps to the porch, and Killop served the two younger women iced tea. Caitlyn was beaming with joy despite the oppressive heat, and her happiness made Karalyn happy.

'Killop has gifted me two horses, Mother,' Caitlyn said. 'A grey mare and a dappled gelding. They are going to stay here, of course, but Killop says that they are mine, and I will be able to come and visit them whenever I like.'

'That was very generous, Killop,' said Karalyn.

The eldest son of Corthie smiled at her. 'I admit to having an ulterior motive, ma'am,' he said. 'Over my time here, it has occurred to me that the Hold Fast estate is a bit neglected these days. The other Holdfasts congregate in Plateau City or Colsbury, or down in Kell, and very few bother to visit the estate.'

'Tell me about it,' said Celine.

Killop laughed. 'If I can interest Caitlyn in coming up here more often, I will count it as a success. I want the estate to play a bigger role in the life of the family.'

'I recall Kelsey trying that with Cael,' said Karalyn. 'For a few years, she had him moving between all those places you mentioned, and he spent a few summers here.'

'Much to his annoyance,' said Arrosa. 'I was also here for a couple of summers; this heat reminds me of that time.'

Killop took a seat, and Karalyn gazed at him. In his looks, stature and voice, he brought back memories of her own father.

'You are well-named,' she said.

'How so?' said Killop.

'You are just like my father, except you look younger than I remember him.'

'I am twenty-eight,' he said, 'but, you know – the immortality keeps me looking twenty-one. Do you remember how it feels?'

'Aye, I do,' said Karalyn.

'Do ye miss it?' said Carron.

'I miss not being worried about hurting myself,' said Karalyn. 'Self-healing makes you feel invincible, and no little injuries trouble you. Now, if I cut my finger, it does not heal. It is disconcerting, to say the least.'

'It's how we mortals live,' said Celine. She eyed Killop. 'Are you going to ask her?'

'I'm not sure any more,' said Killop. 'I was certain I was going to, but now I feel a little embarrassed. It will sound as though I have a large opinion of myself.'

Celine rolled her eyes, while Karalyn noticed Arrosa frown, a clear sign that Killop had not been completely truthful.

'Don't be embarrassed,' said Karalyn. 'Ask me your question.'

'All right,' he said. 'I was wondering if you might support my claim to become the next Holder Fast, ma'am. I understand that Aunt Kelsey has yet to choose her successor, and I was hoping that you might speak to her about this. Would you be prepared to recommend me for the position?'

Karalyn narrowed her eyes.

'I personally think it would be an ideal solution,' said Celine. 'The other Holders are always complaining that the current Holder Fast does not reside in the Holdings. Indeed, Kelsey barely sets foot in this part of the world – she hasn't taken up her seat in the Holdings parliament for many years. It would be good for the family to have a Holder Fast who lives on the estate.'

'I have been looking for a suitable house to buy in Holdings City,' said Killop. 'It seems very odd to me that the Holdfasts have allowed themselves to have no property in the capital of the Holdings. If I were Holder Fast, I would play a full role in the parliament, and attend to the other duties the role requires. I have the backing of several other Holds, including Terras, Clement, Wain, Stringer and Elance; while Holder Smith has intimated that he would have no objection to me assuming the role. Of course, he is now busy with ruling the Plateau Province as Lord Marshal, so he has had to resign his seat in the Holdings parliament.'

Karalyn said nothing, and a flicker of concern passed over Killop's features.

'I understand,' he went on, 'that the title should by rights be yours, ma'am. Why did you give it up? Why did you allow it to pass to your sister?'

'It wasn't as simple as that,' said Karalyn. 'I died on the same day as my mother and Keir, so, by law, the title went to Kelsey as the next in line. When I returned from Athumia, I wanted a quiet life with my family on Colsbury, and Kelsey was already established as Holder Fast. I saw no reason to change that. Do you realise that the role of Holder Fast comes with an awful lot of property? You would not only control the estate, but Colsbury itself would legally belong to you, along with the townhouse in Plateau City. There are also a great number of business concerns – mines in Northern Kell, shipping companies in the Inner Sea, land in the Plateau, and so on. Kelsey pays little attention to these; she has them managed by others on the family's behalf. In other words, the next Holder Fast will have many responsibilities, most of which are not on the estate. You would be head of the family – why is this something you want?'

Killop pursed his lips. 'How do I phrase this without sounding callous? I am committed to the Holdfasts, ma'am, but I have an advantage over many of the others – I will outlive them. I am also not part of the imperial government. There is a conflict of interest here – Aunt Kelsey is the Herald of the Empire as well as Holder Fast, so her loyalties are divided. The same goes for Cael and Cole, while Kyra lives in the Dominion.'

'Let me ask you a question,' said Karalyn. 'If you succeeded in your claim, for how long would you intend to remain as Holder Fast?'

Killop raised an eyebrow.

'Would you continue in that role for a century?' Karalyn went on. 'A millennium? Would you never give it up? It might not be healthy for the family to be governed by someone who cannot die, and who feels no obligation to relinquish the post.'

'But this is the direction in which the family is travelling,' said Killop. 'You could say the exact same thing about Caitlyn – what if she were to become a member of the imperial government? Imagine that she starts at the bottom, say as Imperial Secretary. She could be in that post for centuries. Eventually, the entire Imperial Court could be full of immortal Holdfasts. That being the case, why shouldn't the role of Holder Fast also be held by a demigod?'

Karalyn turned her gaze back to the endless plains. 'And if Cairney returns? I assume you have heard the rumours regarding your brother?'

'If Cairney returns, I shall attempt to restrain him,' said Killop. He eyed Arrosa. 'Was that a lie?'

'It wasn't,' said Arrosa. 'The only lie you have spoken was about being too embarrassed to ask for support.'

Killop laughed. 'Then you must forgive me that little slip; I was trying to sound humble.'

Arrosa glanced at Carron. 'Would you also oppose Cairney?'

'I'm not fucking answering that,' said Carron.

'Language, brother,' said Killop.

Carron rolled his eyes. 'Does it matter if Cairney comes back now, or in a hundred years from now? The result will be the same. Cairney will kick the arses of every Colsbury Holdfast; well, maybe not all of them. You lot sitting here will be all right. I cannae see Cairney killing ye now, Karalyn, not while yer an auld woman.'

'Why will I be all right?' said Caitlyn. 'I would never agree to help Cairney.'

'That'll be your choice, hen,' said Carron. 'I reckon Cairney will want to find out if you and yer brother Carden would be willing to join him. As for you, Arrosa, yer fate will depend on how far yer prepared to go to help yer husband. Aunty Celine will be fine, but. Who'd ever want to hurt Aunty Celine?'

'I suppose I should feel flattered,' said Celine, 'but if Cairney does return, and if he decides to kill members of my family, you can be assured that I will resist him.'

Karalyn smiled. 'I think it might be time to go,' she said. 'It has been wonderful to see you all. Killop, I will consider your words carefully.'

They got to their feet, and Karalyn noticed Killop glare at his younger brother. Arrosa took out her Quadrant, as Karalyn kissed Celine on the cheek.

'Thank you for visiting,' Celine said.

Karalyn smiled, then Arrosa swiped her fingers over the Quadrant. The air shimmered, and they appeared in the gardens on Colsbury.

'That little bastard,' snapped Arrosa. 'Carron cannot be trusted; I hope Celine realises that.'

'You brought us back while I was still saying my farewells,' said Karalyn.

'I'm sorry about that,' said Arrosa, 'but I could barely control my temper. This is what Killop has been planning for years; you must see that. And from where did he get the idea about being Holder Fast? Naxor, that's where. Naxor has poisoned their minds against us. Tell me honestly, Karalyn – how would the Empress react if I had Naxor killed? I could make it look like an accident, or we could blame it on the Gunstians.'

Caitlyn eyed her. 'You aren't being serious, are you?'

'Of course I'm being serious,' said Arrosa. 'Naxor has been openly defying us for years. Cairney is his creation, moulded by a long campaign of lies and innuendo. Carter is clearly lost to us, and it looks as though Carron feels the same. As for Killop, I don't trust him. All of this is Naxor's fault.'

'Nothing Naxor has done is treasonous,' said Karalyn. 'You may find that hard to believe, but I have read his thoughts on multiple occasions. He believes that mortals and immortals should remain aloof from each other, and he is planning to have Corthie and Aila's children inherit the Empire, with him remaining in the shadows behind the throne.'

'That is reason enough to kill him,' said Arrosa. 'I could make a nice glass statue of him, and we could put it in the Teal Garden to remind ourselves not to be so damn gullible.' She took a breath. 'Apologies. I have a hundred things to worry about at the moment.'

'I will say one last thing about Naxor,' said Karalyn. 'From reading his mind, I am certain that he will not be happy if Cairney returns. Naxor may have moulded him, but Cairney's aims are not the same as Naxor's. Naxor does not advocate violence; he wants to take control of the Empire peacefully, over centuries, and Killop is in tune with those feelings. Cairney lacks such patience and foresight. I have also read his mind. It is full of blood and revenge. If Naxor stands in his way, you won't need to kill Naxor, Arrosa; Cairney will do it for you.'

They fell into silence as they walked through the garden. They came to the shores of the lake, and Karalyn gazed out at the mountains.

'I don't think Aunty Kelsey is on Colsbury,' said Caitlyn. 'I can still feel my powers.'

'I brought us to the far edge of the island,' said Arrosa. 'We are out of Kelsey's blocking range. I feel so damn helpless. Lindi and Carter could be anywhere. With each day that passes, Lindi will be getting closer to finding Cairney, and there isn't a thing we can do about it.'

There was a noise to their right, and Cael emerged from the trees with Cowie by his side. Behind them, a squad of armed marines lingered by the edge of the woods, their hands gripping their weapons. Cael smiled at the sight of his wife, then he narrowed his eyes when he saw the expression on her face.

'Did your trip to the estate go well?' he said.

Arrosa tried to smile. 'Caitlyn now owns two horses,' she said. 'Killop wants your mother to support his bid to become Holder Fast.'

'I thought he might,' said Cael. 'Naxor was asking me to support Killop's claim, in exchange for a vote in the Succession Council.'

'That vote belongs to Aila,' said Karalyn.

'And Naxor felt confident enough to vouch for it,' said Cael. He glanced down at Cowie, and his frown deepened. 'Stop that, son. Now. Get out of Caitlyn's head.'

Cowie looked up, his cheeks reddening.

'What have we told you?' Cael went on.

'Sorry,' said Cowie.

'Don't apologise to me,' said Cael; 'apologise to Caitlyn.'

'Sorry, Caitlyn.'

'Thank you,' said Cael.

'You were far worse as a child, son,' said Karalyn. 'You and Kyra were always reading people's minds without permission.'

'I didn't feel a thing,' said Caitlyn. 'You were very quiet, Cowie.'

'I have been practising on the marines,' said the eleven-year-old boy. 'It was harder to get into your mind, Caitlyn.'

'Are you a full dream mage?' said Caitlyn.

The boy frowned.

'I am the only full dream mage,' said Karalyn, 'though I have lost most of my abilities while in this body. Cael and Kyra are both strong, but neither have the complete suite of powers. You can vision with your eyes closed, can't you, Cowie?'

'I can do it with my eyes open or closed,' he said.

'Why is it getting weaker with every generation?' said Arrosa.

'I have a theory,' said Karalyn. 'My mother was a Holdings mage, and my father a Kellach mage; they produced me and my siblings. Lennox was a Kellach mage, and my first two children are also dream mages. But you, Arrosa, are Gifted, and the powers don't seem to mix. With Kelsey, the father of her children was a man from Implacatus, and none of them are mages, so her children also lost powers. Caelius can block powers, but Calpurnia seems to have no extra abilities. Corthie married a demigod with a long lineage of powers, hence their children are powerful indeed.'

'How do you explain Sable?' said Caitlyn.

'My grandfather Godfrey is responsible, I think,' said Karalyn. 'My mother got her powers from him, and so did Sable, so I would guess that Godfrey possessed trace elements of dream powers, just as Daemon did.'

Cael smiled. 'So you're saying that I should have married a Holdings mage?'

Arrosa punched him on the arm.

'Lindi is also very powerful,' said Caitlyn. 'Do you know who her father is?'

'Only Sable knows for certain,' said Karalyn. 'I have always had my suspicions, but they have never been confirmed.'

'Were you never tempted to pry?' said Arrosa.

'Never. I would like to think it was because I was being considerate, but the truth is that I didn't care.'

'I like you in this body, Mother,' said Cael. 'You seem so much more... approachable. Engaged. Will it continue when you eventually move on?'

'I want to say aye, son,' she said, 'but I am starting to believe that my personality is shaped at least a little by the body I inhabit.'

'You were nice when you were Lyla,' said Arrosa. 'A bit naïve at times, but friendly and open. I think that...' She paused, her eyes widening. 'Gifts. Pain and Immolation. There are Gifted on the island.'

The marines ran forward as soon as the words had left Arrosa's lips. They were forming up around the five Holdfasts when four figures burst through the trees to their left. Two were Gunstian soldiers, and one of them was clutching a Quadrant in his hand, while the other two were robed, and were raising their hands.

The Gift of Pain swept over the edge of the garden, and the marines started to fall, followed by the Holdfasts.

'Galina?' cried one of the Gifted agents.

'Forget her,' shouted the other. 'Kill the Faithless One.'

The second agent lifted his hand and pointed at Cael, who was down on one knee as he tried to shield Cowie from the Gift of Pain. Cael glanced up, then one of the marines threw himself in front of him. The marine screamed as he burst into flames, the cold blue fire covering his body. Another marine fired his Jackdaw at the Gunstians, but he was contorted with Pain, and the lead pellet went astray. Karalyn tried to move, but the Gift of Pain was keeping her down. The agony was all-consuming, and she could feel herself starting to slip into unconsciousness as she lay on the grass by the edge of the lake. The burning marine cried out for a last time, then fell silent, his clothes, skin and hair smouldering. The Gifted agent lifted his hand again, then all four Gunstians screamed as the flesh melted from their faces. They fell to the ground, their skulls exposed through the mess of blood and tissue. Karalyn felt the Gift of Pain recede, and she gasped for air as she looked around. Crouching behind Cael was Caitlyn, her eyes wide with shock as she gazed at what she had done to the Gunstians.

'I killed them,' Caitlyn whispered.

Karalyn checked Cowie. The boy was pale with fear, but his father had managed to keep most of the Gift of Pain from reaching him. Arrosa got to her feet, and helped Karalyn stand, as the marines started to recover. They stared down at the body of the fallen marine, which was still smouldering and smoking, then they turned to the bodies of the dead Gunstians.

Cael walked closer to them, then he leaned down and pulled the Quadrant from the fingers of the dead Gunstian soldier. He glanced at Caitlyn, who had remained where she was.

'You saved us, sister,' Cael said.

'You saved me,' she said. 'I was sheltering behind you like a coward.'

Arrosa looked down at the bodies. 'You are not a coward, Caitlyn. You acted, even though you were scared.'

Caitlyn burst into tears, and Karalyn crouched down next to her, an arm over her shoulder.

'I killed four men, Mother,' Caitlyn said.

'They were trying to kill us,' said Karalyn. 'You defended your family; I am very proud of you.'

'We are all proud of you, sister,' said Cael. He held up the Quadrant. 'And we got this.' He turned to the marines. 'One of your comrades sacrificed himself to save me; I'll not forget it. What was his name?'

'Corporal Lanach, sir,' said a sergeant. 'He was a good lad.'

Cael stared at the body of Corporal Lanach, then at his own son, who was holding on to his mother's hand. Caitlyn was weeping openly, her shock at having killed the four Gunstians overwhelming her. Karalyn kept her arms round her daughter as she wept, holding her close.

More marines arrived on the scene, some armed with loaded Battanaras. A marine captain ran over to Cael, and ordered the marines to form a square around the Holdfasts.

'The attack is over,' said Arrosa. 'I sense no more Gifts.'

'It was me they were after,' said Cael.

'We got two Gifted agents and retrieved a Quadrant,' said Arrosa. 'Caitlyn Holdfast deserves the credit; as does Corporal Lanach, who gave his life to save the Adjutant. Will you please escort us back to the Summer Palace?'

The marine captain saluted. 'Yes, ma'am.'

'You are not to blame,' said Thorn. 'Despite the sad death of a marine, we must count today's raid as a small victory – two Gifted agents and a Quadrant.'

Cael said nothing, his gaze on the view from the Empress's private balcony. Thorn glanced over at Karalyn.

'Speak to us, son,' said Karalyn. 'I know you hold yourself responsible.'

'I am responsible,' he said.

'Then so am I,' said Thorn. 'I supported your actions in Great Gunst eight years ago, and I made the decision to remain on Colsbury. Do you blame me?'

He eyed her. 'Of course not, Your Majesty.'

'Don't call me that when we're speaking in private,' she said. 'It's only me, you and your mother, Cael. You were once my adopted child, and I love you like a son. I will never have children of my own – you are the closest I will ever get to that.'

Karalyn said nothing. She hated when Thorn spoke to Cael in that way, and she had her own ideas about who to blame for the Gunstian raids. Perhaps if she had been in Albany's body, then she might have had no hesitation in telling Thorn exactly what she thought; but, instead, she remained silent.

'Corporal Lanach's death was my fault,' said Cael. 'Cowie could have been killed, and that is also my fault. Arrosa, Caitlyn and my mother's lives were threatened, because I massacred three hundred Gunstians and obliterated their oldest temple. I am unfit to be your heir.'

'Kelsey mentioned that you had brought this up with her,' said Thorn. 'You remind me of your father, Cael. Lennox also had a fierce conscience, and was troubled by some of the things he had done.'

Karalyn bit her lip to stop herself from rebuking the Empress. How dare she talk about Lennox like that? She had barely known him.

'He was also very brave,' Thorn went on. 'He rescued me and Keir from Amatskouri when Agatha and her gods were burning it to the ground; and, as you know, he gave his life protecting you and your sister. You say you are like Daphne, but I also see a lot of Lennox in you. Do you agree, Karalyn?'

'Partly,' said Karalyn. 'The event Lennox felt most guilty about wasn't his fault. I wish he had known the truth about Rainsby, but he died believing he was a wicked monster.'

'I have no such excuse, Mother,' said Cael. 'No one went into my mind and forced me to destroy the Temple of the Martyrs. I did that on my own, and now we are reaping the consequences.'

'But what else can we do but keep moving forward?' said Thorn. 'I have complete confidence in you, Cael.'

Cael kept his gaze on Karalyn. 'How is Caitlyn?'

'She is sleeping,' said Karalyn. 'She cried herself to sleep. Killing those Gunstians... well, we three know what it feels like to take the life of another. Caitlyn has never killed before, and I think she will be deeply affected by what happened.'

'You blame me, don't you, Mother?'

Karalyn gazed at him. 'A little,' she said. 'Some of what you believe is true. Would the Gunstians be attacking us if you hadn't slaughtered so many of them?'

Thorn glared at Karalyn, her eyes flashing with anger.

'But the Empress is correct,' Karalyn went on. 'We have to move forward. Learn from what happened, son. None of us are blameless; we all make mistakes. All you can do now is reflect on your decisions, and try to do better.'

There was a light knock on the balcony door, then it opened, and Sable walked out of the palace.

'Am I interrupting?' she said.

Thorn smiled. 'It's fine, Sable,' she said. 'Did you hear about the latest attack?'

'I heard you got one of the missing Quadrants back,' said Sable, 'and I heard about what Caitlyn did. That took guts. I'm glad she's on our side.' She glanced down at Cael. 'I spoke to your wife. She told me that you are blaming yourself for the Gunstian attacks.'

Cael said nothing.

'You are right to do so,' said Sable. 'This is your fault, Cael. But so fucking what? Imagine if I had given up after every stupid mistake I made. I can't even remember every stupid mistake I've made; there have been so many. One little massacre shouldn't bring you down. And, if I'm honest, I can't help but admire what you did to the Gunstians that day eight years ago. You were acting like a Holdfast. Anyway, that's not why I came to Colsbury.' She turned to Thorn. 'I cannot find my daughter, Your Majesty. I have been searching for days, flitting from world to world. Lindi is too clever for her own good at times, and I think she has found a decent place to hide. Should we construct another Compass?'

'You would have to ask Karalyn about that,' said Thorn. 'She was present at the making of the first. With Elbannon gone, she is likely the only person who might know how he did it.'

'It was something to do with silver and Tempest,' said Karalyn. 'I will ask Kyra about it, as she was also there.'

'Is it true that Edgar wanted Kyra to ascend to godhood?' said Sable.

'That is apparently why he stole the Sextant,' said Thorn.

'It wouldn't have worked,' said Karalyn. 'Kyra cannot operate the Sextant; it doesn't speak to her.'

'It speaks to me,' said Cael. 'Does that mean I could become immortal?'

'Perhaps.'

Sable smiled. 'Are you tempted?'

'Not in the slightest,' said Cael. 'I cannot imagine anything worse than having to watch my family die while I remain alive, moving from body to body.' He glanced at Karalyn. 'I'm sorry to put it like that, Mother.'

'No, I understand,' said Karalyn. 'Do you think I want to be like this? I should have died twenty-six years ago, in the farmhouse in Clackenbaird. I am glad I was able to see my children become adults, but I am terrified by the thought of the millennia to come. How many bodies will I use up? I think that was why I wanted children with Lucius, so that I would have someone to talk to when everyone else I know is dead and buried.'

'There is only one Karalyn,' said Thorn. 'What has happened to you is a blessing, and a curse.'

'You will also have Lindi for company,' said Sable. 'She will be around for a very long time to come, if she can keep her head on her shoulders.'

'Will she release Cairney from captivity?' said Cael.

'I don't know,' said Sable, 'but why else would she have taken Carter along with her? How strong is Cairney? I wasn't on Ulna when he was last on the loose.'

'It took the combined strength of me and Cole to put him down,' said Cael, 'and he was only sixteen back then. He'll be twenty-four now, and if his powers have matured, he might be too much for any of us to handle.'

'There is a solution,' said Sable. 'I kill Karalyn, and she finds a stronger body. Perhaps Laverne? She is the granddaughter of the Second Ascendant, and she is every bit as powerful as Albany was. Just say the word, Karalyn; I'll make it quick.'

Karalyn gazed at the others. From the look on Thorn's face, she suspected that the Empress agreed with Sable's suggestion, but Cael's features were unreadable.

'I will not murder Laverne,' Karalyn said, 'or anyone else, for that matter.'

'I thought you'd say that,' said Sable. 'I guess it will be up to me and you, Cael, to deal with Cairney if he returns.'

'It won't just be us,' said Cael. 'We'll have Cole and Caitlyn, and Kyra, too.'

'And Killop,' said Karalyn. 'He has pledged to oppose his brother.'

'It will be like fighting the Ascendants,' said Sable, 'only this time, the damn Holdfasts will be battling each other.'

CHAPTER 28
ASSERTING DOMINANCE

Observatory, Viridia – 23rd Abrinch 5281

'Of course I've asked it,' said Lindi, as she watched Carter work.

'What does it say?' he said.

'If you ask it a question it doesn't like,' said Lindi, 'it doesn't say anything. If I say, *Where is Cairney Holdfast?* it doesn't respond with, *I don't know*; it stays silent.'

Carter leaned on the long-handled axe, as sweat rolled down his face. 'I always thought the Sextant could find people,' he said. 'Did it not find Karalyn after she was killed?'

'I think Karalyn must be different from other people,' said Lindi. 'I've tried that question, and it says, *The connection to Karalyn is broken*, or something like that.' She lit a cigarette, and leaned back against the half-ruined wall of the Observatory. 'Karalyn has become entwined in some way with the Sextant; that's my guess. It must be related to how she became immortal.'

Carter swung the axe, and its blade drove through another log. A large array of tools had been gathered by Carter inside the Observatory, and he had spent hours each day working to improve their living quarters. He had built a wooden roof over one of the more intact rooms, which kept out the night rains; he had unblocked the deep well that took water from a mountain stream; he had constructed the chairs upon which they sat, and the low pallets upon which they slept; and he had begun work on a large stone oven, fuelled by chopped wood taken from the forest below the treeline. In seven days, he had almost succeeded in transforming their rudimentary accommodation into something approaching comfortable. He had cooked their meals, washed their clothes, fetched drinking water, and had sawn through untold numbers of wooden beams. He had also been giving her lists of items to steal – knives, nails, pots, pans, mattresses... the lists went on and on. To allay suspicion, Lindi had not been robbing the items from the sweltering settlement at the foot of the mountains. The Banner officer who governed the community had a Quadrant, and would have noticed if everything on Carter's lists had been taken from his territory; so, instead, Lindi had been travelling to Dragon Eyre and Athumia, targeting random villages and towns, and stealing from there.

It was the most fun she had ever had.

As far as she could tell, everyone in the Empire and the Dominion was hunting her, but they hadn't come close to catching her. Her mother was prowling the Known Worlds, and Kyra was searching for her. Cael was also searching, when he wasn't off killing Gunstian sailors and soldiers. Lindi knew this because she could see them all through the Sextant. She could watch and listen to conversations held within the Empress's most private rooms within the Summer Palace on Colsbury; then she could turn to the dragon palaces of Nom Karta to check what Edgar and his gods were doing. She was getting better at using the Sextant – quicker and more efficient, and yet she had been unable to locate the one person she and Carter most longed to find.

'Have ye tried the worlds Karalyn created?' said Carter.

Lindi rolled her eyes. 'Obviously. I found the most awful swamp world; just an entire continent ringed with marshes and flies. What's the point of that?'

Carter frowned. 'Is it for the Rakanese?' he said. 'I remember Naxor saying something along those lines – that the Rakanese breed so quickly, that Karalyn was going to make a new world for them.'

'She's going to deport them all to a vast swamp?' said Lindi. 'Seems a little extreme. I'll tell you what I did find – the damn Wystians. Thousands of dragons from Wyst, all congregated on these large islands. There are no humans there, just thousands of Wystians. They have no idea what has happened to them – one minute they were on Dragon Eyre, getting ready to invade Na Sun Ka, and then – whoosh – they are stranded on a different world.'

Carter laughed. 'They might be used to it by now; did your mother not send them to an island?'

'To Rigga,' said Lindi, 'but they managed to escape. They won't be escaping from the new world where Karalyn put them; well, not unless I help them escape. That could be funny. Where would thousands of dragons cause the most disruption?'

'Send them to Gunst,' said Carter. 'Coffee?'

She nodded. Carter leaned the axe against a wall, then he lit the fire under his new stove. A kettle was already sitting atop the stone oven, and Lindi watched as the flames began to intensify.

'I can't help but feeling,' she said, 'that you are enjoying this a little too much, Carter.'

'I'm just keeping busy,' he said. 'I feel a bit guilty about abandoning my job on the farm, but what else am I supposed to do all day while you're communing with the Sextant?'

'We could be here for months.'

'Aye. I know. Food is the biggest problem. The forests are teeming with animals we can eat, but it's a long trek down there and back; and I don't want to eat nothing but meat every day. A wee farm would be nice, but ye cannae grow anything this high up the mountains, but it's too hot to move any lower.'

'If you want me to teach you how to use the Quadrant,' she said, 'all you have to do is ask.'

'That might be handy,' he said, as he prepared the coffee pot and mugs. 'Then I could find the stuff on my lists without bothering ye.'

She eyed him. 'We are in a shitload of trouble, Carter.'

He shrugged.

'Doesn't that concern you?'

'Nah,' he said. 'As long as they cannae find us, we'll be all right.'

'I reckon the last of the Banner soldiers and workers will be evacuating this world within a month or so,' she said; 'then we can pillage whatever they leave behind.'

'Only one thing matters,' he said: 'finding my brother.'

'And then what?' she said. 'What if Cairney is in a bloodthirsty mood? What will we do if he starts slaughtering people?'

'Cairney won't do that. He'll have a plan; he'll have worked out the best thing to do.'

'How do you know that? According to Maddie Jackdaw, the last plan he had was utter horseshit. He tried to provoke a war between the Dominion and the Empire, but nobody fell for it. And didn't your sister sell him out?'

'She only did that to save Cairney from being executed,' said Carter; 'but ye've got a point – his last plan was bollocks. He was only sixteen, but.'

'And you're hoping his wisdom has improved since then?'

'I'm keeping my expectations low,' he said, as he poured hot water into the coffee pot. 'Cairney might need time to recover, which is another reason I've been getting this place more liveable. I also have a few ideas of my own.'

'What ideas?'

'Ideas about how to take over the Empire.'

Lindi laughed.

Carter smiled at her. 'You may mock, Lindi, but I've thought of little else for years. The fragmented nature of the Empire allows for a little flexibility; but the power structures are ordered to be controlled from the centre; therefore...'

'Fucking shut up,' she said. 'I couldn't give a toss about your political philosophy bullshit. I want to sit on a comfy throne with servants seeing to my every whim.'

'Ye won't be Empress if Cairney's back; do ye realise that?'

'We'll see,' she said.

'There's something I need to tell ye about him,' Carter went on. 'It's his voice that ye need to be aware of – Cairney can command folk with his words; just as you can go into minds and implant suggestions.'

'But he hasn't got vision powers.'

'He cannae read minds, but he doesnae need to. He can just say, *Tell me the truth about so-and-so*, and before ye know it, yer blabbing all yer secrets.'

'It won't work on me,' she said. 'Karalyn shielded my mind when I was a baby, just as she shielded yours.'

'Cairney was able to twist Esher round his little finger, and that bastard's an Ascendant.'

'Yeah, but Esher doesn't have any dream abilities – that's what makes us special, Carter. We're not just gods – we're dream gods.'

'He can change his appearance; make ye believe that he's someone else.'

'An illusion,' she said. 'That won't fool me.'

Carter laughed, then he filled two mugs with coffee, and passed one to Lindi.

'Thank you, servant,' she said.

'Are ye actually gonnae do any work today, Lindi, or are ye just gonnae sit on yer arse?'

'I might just sit on my arse,' she said. 'How can I work when you have handed me coffee? Pass me a stick of keenweed.'

Carter delved into a pouch, and gave her a weedstick. She lit it, and relaxed in the shade of the wall, her coffee in one hand, and the keenweed in the other. Her senses sharpened as she smoked, and she gazed out at the view of the vast, humid forest that stretched out below them. She hated going down there. Within a minute or two, her clothes would be sodden with sweat, she would be covered in insect bites, and she would be gasping for breath. The Banner soldiers and workers in the settlement had a large infirmary, which was always full; the mortals down in the forest were always getting sick and, at any given moment, around half of them were unfit to work. It was no wonder Viridia was being evacuated; it was a sickly world – sticky, hot and pestilent.

She thought about what she was doing. It was stupid and rash; she knew it, and yet she had committed to her decision. Go all-in. No turning back. See it through. Carter was convinced that they were doing the right thing. They were correcting an injustice; righting a wrong. Cairney had been the victim of the nefarious Colsbury Holdfasts, and his return would see power shift irreversibly to the immortal Marchbrae Holdfasts. Lindi was neither. Was she an Ulna Holdfast?

'What does Cairney think of my mother?' she said.

'No one's gonnae harm Sable,' said Carter. 'My mother taught us to respect Sable. If that bitch Kyra hadnae blocked Sable's powers during the battle for Na Sun Ka, she would have stopped my Da from being killed.'

'And what if my mother decides to oppose Cairney?'

Carter eyed her. 'Is that likely? Why would she do that?'

'Well, let's see – she might get upset if Cairney kills Aunty Kelsey or Cael or someone like that.'

'Yer mother will have to stay out of it; but I refuse to believe that Cairney will start killing members of the family.'

'He has already tried to kill them.'

'Aye, when he was sixteen. Look – we've got the damn Sextant; we don't need to kill anyone. We can exile them, just as Cairney was exiled.'

Lindi finished her coffee, then she stubbed out the weedstick and got to her feet. 'I will be laying down a few rules for Cairney when we finally get him,' she said. 'He will have to understand that certain people are not to be touched.'

'I get it,' said Carter.

Lindi eyed him, then she walked into the part of the Observatory that Carter had roofed. She passed their wooden beds, and came to the Sextant. She smiled as she gazed at it. Despite the frustrations of not being able to locate Cairney, Lindi had loved the experience of being connected to the huge device. Her vision felt liberated, and her senses satiated. When she looked upon a world, it felt as though she were there, flying above it, her spirit untethered from her body. She wondered if Edgar's mad plan would have worked. No, she thought – how could it have worked for Kyra, if Kyra heard no voice?

She placed her palm onto the flat surface of the device.

What is your desire, Lindi?

'You know my desire,' she said. 'I want to find Cairney Holdfast.'

Silence.

'Show me Colsbury,' she said.

Her vision blurred over, then she found herself looking down onto the little island. She gazed at the Summer Palace and the two keeps, then at the gardens and harbour. Heavily-armed marines were everywhere, holding their odd-looking weapons. The Gunstians were a useful distraction, Lindi decided. With those crazy Chadura-worshipping fanatics liable to attack at any moment, the Empire was unable to concentrate all of its strength on searching for the Sextant.

Lindi had been trying to vary her questions to the device, and she had thought of a few more during the night.

'How many people live on Colsbury?' she said.

Silence.

'How many immortals are on Colsbury?'

Two.

Lindi smiled. 'How many mortals are on Colsbury?'

Seven hundred and sixty-one.

'That's more like it, Sextant,' she said. 'Show me Empress Thorn.'

Silence.

'Show me Cael Holdfast.'

Cael Holdfast is not connected.

Lindi frowned. Why did the device recognise Cael's name, but not that of the Empress? Was it because Cael had used the Sextant in the past?

'Show me Karalyn Holdfast.'

The connection to Karalyn Holdfast has been broken.

'Show me the swamp world.'

The vision altered, and moved to a different world, the world she had been examining on the previous day.

'How many mortals are on this world?'

None.

Lindi smiled again. 'How many immortals are on this world?'

None.

Lindi clapped her hands in joy. If her suspicions were correct, then she had discovered a shortcut that would save her untold amounts of time. The Sextant could see hundreds of worlds, and she had been laboriously searching through them one at a time. If she could discount an entire world with a single question, then her job had become far easier.

'Show me another world made by Karalyn.'

Specify.

'Show me the oldest world made by Karalyn.'

Her vision blurred again, then she looked down on a desolate wasteland of bleak deserts and barren plains.

'How many immortals are on this world?'

None.

'Show me the next oldest world made by Karalyn.'

Her vision changed again, and she looked down on a vast continent of mountains and fertile land. Rivers flowed down through forested hillsides, and birds were circling over the wide golden beaches.

'This is nice,' she said. 'How many immortals are on this world?'

One.

Lindi froze. 'Uh, Carter,' she said. 'Carter! Get in here.'

Carter appeared by the entrance. 'What is it? I have work to do.'

'I think I might have found something,' she said. 'A solitary immortal is on one of Karalyn's worlds. I discovered the right combination of words to ask.'

'A solitary immortal?'

'That's what I said, donkey-brains. It's got to be him, unless Karalyn has been using her creations to stash away other gods. Stick your hand on the Sextant, and you will be able to see what I see.'

Carter walked up to the device, and laid his large hand onto it.

'Show me the immortal,' said Lindi.

Silence.

'Fuck,' she muttered.

Carter eyed her with a wry smile, then he walked back out of the chamber. Lindi glared at his back, then she focussed her vision powers, and sent them into the world she had found. Her vision soared down, sweeping over the valleys and hills. She passed lakes fed by rivers coming down from the mountains, and saw animals drinking along the muddy banks.

'How many mortals are on this world?' she said.

None.

It had to be Cairney, she told herself. Who else could it be?

She spent two hours roaming over the continent, before giving up and soaring over the ocean to a neighbouring island that was so large it could have been another continent. She scanned the ground, searching for any signs of human habitation or influence. Another two hours passed, but Lindi felt no sense of exhaustion; being with the Sextant was exhilarating.

She saw a waterfall spilling down from a high ridge of cliffs, and paused to take a closer look at something that might be a track. She gazed down at it – had it been made by animals, or by Cairney? She followed the track for several miles, until it disappeared amid the rocky scree by the foot of another cliffside. Sitting by the entrance to a cave was a tall, broad-shouldered man dressed in the skins of wild animals, though some tattered remnants of his old clothes remained.

Lindi smiled to herself, then she tried to push her powers into his mind.

The man immediately looked up, aware that someone was attempting to access his thoughts. Lindi tried again, but was rebuffed, then the man narrowed his eyes.

'Whoever you are,' he said, 'try again.'

Lindi did so, and her powers slipped into the mind of the man with ease.

At once, Lindi found herself walking in a grassy meadow. The sun was shining, and butterflies were flitting among the tall wild flowers.

'This is a good trick,' she said, as she gazed around. 'I assume you have created this illusion somewhere deep within your subconscious? Where are you?'

'Behind you,' came a voice.

Lindi turned. The man standing in front of her looked like a cleaner, more smartly-dressed version of the man she had seen by the cave entrance, while his dark eyes shone with a pitiless intelligence.

'Who are you?' he said.

'Don't you know your own cousin, Cairney?' she said.

The man narrowed his eyes.

'I felt you trying to get into my head,' he said. 'You are strong, but you're not that strong.'

'And yet I am in your mind,' she said.

'I allowed you in,' he said. He gestured around the meadow. 'This is the only part of my mind you are going to see. Are you Alindi'osso?'

'Lindi Holdfast, if you don't mind,' she said.

'How did you find me, Lindi?'

'Oh, I might have stolen the Sextant,' she said, a hand on her hip. 'It was easy. Karalyn is... well, she's not the woman you might remember. The Gunstians killed her, and she took the body of a feeble old mortal woman. She's lost her powers.'

The man said nothing.

'You don't talk much, do you?' she said. 'I was expecting a little gratitude.'

'Why should I be grateful?'

'Because I am here to set you free, you dozy pillock. But, I have conditions.'

Cairney eyed her.

'First,' she went on, 'you must not try to steal my Quadrant. Second, you will not try to manipulate me with your words of persuasion. They wouldn't work on me anyway, but you are not to try. Third, I am in charge, not you. When we overthrow the mortals, I get to be Empress. You can be my Herald, or something like that. Fourth, my mother and brother are completely off-limits. You hurt them, I will kill you. Do you agree to my conditions?'

A hint of a smile crossed Cairney's features, but he remained silent.

'Is anyone home?' said Lindi. 'Answer my fucking question, or I'll leave you here to rot. I could be creating worlds with the Sextant instead of wasting my time with you. Carter will be disappointed, but there ain't much I can do about that.'

'Carter?' he said.

'That is what I said. Carter is with me. He can't use the Sextant, though.'

'I agree to your terms,' said Cairney.

Lindi smiled. 'Get ready to be free, Cairney; today is your lucky day.'

She withdrew from his mind, and pulled her vision back from the world. She shook her head and laughed, then she glanced at the entrance, but there was no sign of Carter. She would surprise him; that would be funny. She reconnected with the Sextant, then hesitated. Her mother had transported the Wystians to Rigga, so Lindi knew that what she was about to attempt was possible.

'All right, Sextant,' she said, 'transport the immortal from this world to here; place him into this chamber, a few yards to my right.'

Silence.

'Eh, do it now.'

The air next to her crackled and spat, then Cairney appeared, dressed once again in the skins of wild animals. His hair was much longer than it had been in his imaginary meadow, reaching halfway down his back. He gazed at her, then he noticed the Sextant.

'You're welcome,' she said.

Cairney walked up to the Sextant, and placed his hand onto to it as Lindi watched. A slight frown crinkled his features, and Lindi laughed.

'No voice, eh?' she said. 'What a shame.' She turned to the entrance. 'Carter!'

'For fuck's sake, Lindi,' came his voice. 'What is it this time? I'm busy.'

Cairney removed his hand from the Sextant, and eyed the entrance, just as Carter walked into the chamber. The brothers stared at each other. They looked the same age despite their difference in years, and Lindi felt a little on the short side as she peered up at them.

Carter broke first. He hurried towards his brother, his arms out, and embraced him. Carter choked back a sob, as Cairney eyed him warily.

'We did it,' said Carter. 'Cairney, yer back. How are ye feeling? Do ye need anything? Are ye hungry?'

Cairney remained silent.

'After eight years on his own,' Carter went on, 'he might have forgotten how to speak. Are ye all right, brother?'

'Aye,' said Cairney. 'Where are we?'

'We're on a world called Viridia,' said Carter. 'It's one of the Doomed Worlds. Come and take a look.'

They walked outside into the heat of the afternoon sun, and Cairney gazed down from the mountain top at the spread of forest below them.

'We've been here for seven days,' Carter went on. 'Ye don't want to go into the forest, though; it's too hot down there. That's why we're high up in the mountains, where it's cooler. Did Lindi tell ye how she stole the Sextant? Did she tell ye about Karalyn?'

'She told me,' said Cairney.

'The Empire and the Dominion are hunting us,' Carter went on. 'They'll know by now that Lindi took the Sextant from Edgar; and they'll guess that I'm with her.'

'Can we trust her?' said Cairney.

Carter eyed him. 'Who? Lindi?'

'I'm standing right here,' said Lindi.

'She's been a great help,' said Carter. 'As soon as she stole the Sextant, she came to look for me, so that we could find you, brother.'

Cairney turned from the view and stared down at Lindi. 'Why?' he said, his dark eyes piercing her. 'Why would you help me?'

Lindi frowned, and folded her arms across her chest. 'I don't care for the way you're looking at me,' she said. 'Is this the thanks I get? I risk everything to rescue my cousin, and you're wondering if I can be trusted.'

'You want to rule, and you want my help,' he said.

'Maybe,' she said.

'I renounce your four conditions,' he said, turning back to gaze at the view. 'I am not beholden to you, or to anyone, Lindi.'

'What?' said Lindi. 'You can't do that. You promised.'

'What conditions?' said Carter.

'I made him agree to a few things before I brought him here,' said Lindi. 'He's to keep his hands off my Quadrant, leave my mother and brother alone, not use his persuasion powers on me – not that they'd work, anyway; and... well, he had to accept that I was in charge.'

Cairney laughed, then he abruptly turned and walked back into the Observatory.

'No offence, Carter,' said Lindi, 'but your brother is weird.'

'He's been on his own for so long that...'

'Yes? He's gone insane; is that what you were going to say?'

'No, but it might take him some time to adjust.'

Lindi frowned as she peered through the entrance of the building into the darkness beyond. 'What is he doing in there?'

Cairney emerged from the building, a long, black-bladed sword in his right hand.

'Hey!' Lindi cried. 'You can't take that; the Sextant doesn't work without it.'

He walked up to Lindi, then he raised his arm, holding out the Weathervane so that its tip was an inch from Lindi's throat. Her eyes widened.

'You did not save me,' he said, 'because you know me or care about me, or because you share the same cause of righteous vengeance against my enemies. You saved me because you want power for yourself. Do not try to deny it, daughter of Sable. You saved me because you wanted me to feel obligated towards you. Until I trust you, I will not be permitting you to operate the Sextant. You will have to earn that trust.'

Lindi bared her teeth. 'Go fuck yourself.'

'You may keep your Quadrant, for now,' Cairney went on, 'but your first job for me will be to find me my own Quadrant. You will deliver it to me and, in return, you may keep your head. You work for me now, Lindi Holdfast of Dragon Eyre. Every time you do as I say, you shall be rewarded, but if you oppose me in any way, I will show you how the long years of isolation have stripped me of any notions of mercy or pity.'

'You arrogant bastard,' she cried. 'I should rip your fucking head off.'

'Try,' he said.

Lindi clenched her fists.

'What the fuck is going on?' said Carter. 'Lindi is our cousin, brother; without her, you'd still be stranded on that world.'

'She needs to learn which of us is the superior god, brother,' Cairney said. 'She has much of Sable's rebellious spirit within her, and if she cannot be tamed, she will be of little use to me.'

Lindi's hand inched towards the pocket where her Quadrant was kept.

Cairney smiled, but there was no joy in it. '*Get on your knees, Lindi*,' he said.

Lindi felt a great weight of compulsion bear down upon her. Her knees weakened, and she staggered. Cairney's eyes tightened, and Lindi realised that he was surprised at how strong she was; that she was able to resist, even a little. If she continued to fight him, what would he do? He was immune to her powers, and she could sense the great strength of his battle-vision. Would he lash out with the Weathervane, which remained just inches from her throat? Her head would be gone before her hand would be able to reach her Quadrant.

She decided to pretend.

She fell to her knees, as though defeated by his words of persuasion, and Cairney smiled.

'Who do you work for?' he said.

'You, Cairney,' she said.

'What is your first task?'

'To find you a Quadrant.'

'Good girl,' he said. 'There are two paths ahead of you, Lindi. If you do as I say, you shall rise to become one of the greatest gods in the Known Worlds – I shall give you realms to rule over, and great power and riches. You shall be a queen, worshipped and feared by the mortal masses; and I will be your greatest ally. If anyone wrongs you, I will destroy them. But, Lindi, if you disobey me; if you choose the other path, then my revenge upon you will be worse than anything you can imagine. I will not kill you, for that would be a mercy, and I have none left to give. Which path do you choose?'

'I will serve you,' she said.

Cairney lowered the Weathervane. '*Stand.*'

Again, Lindi felt the power of compulsion attempt to grip her, but she got to her feet of her own accord. Cairney embraced her, his strong arms almost smothering her.

'Cousin,' he said, 'we shall do great things together.'

CHAPTER 29
TARNISHED

Colsbury Castle, Republic of the Holdings – 5th Day, Second Third Summer 560

Cael crouched to tie his daughter's shoelaces.

'Keep still, Carrie,' he said.

'We need to be leaving,' said Arrosa. 'We're going to be late.'

'I know,' said Cael. 'Just give me a minute.'

He finished with the girl's shoes, and they both stood.

'What are you thinking of getting Cole for his birthday?' Arrosa said.

'I haven't had a moment to think about it,' said Cael, as he ushered Carrie towards their other children.

'I will take them to their tutor,' said Arrosa. 'You're the Adjutant; it will look worse if you're late for the Imperial Court.'

'Thanks,' he said. 'My mother and Sable are going to be there.'

'I know,' she said, 'and so will Lord Marshal Holdsmith. I think the Empress wants the widest possible group to advise her on the Gunstians and the Sextant.'

Cael opened the front door of their apartment within the Summer Palace on Colsbury, then he led the three children out into the hallway, where four armed marines were waiting to escort them.

'Arrosa is going to the classrooms on the ground floor to drop off the children before she attends the meeting,' said Cael.

'Right you are, sir,' said a marine sergeant. He gestured to two others. 'You pair, guard Lady Arrosa and her children; the rest of us will stick with the Adjutant.'

The group split into two, with Arrosa leading the children along the hallway with two marines, and Cael heading in the other direction, with his own two marine escorts following a pace behind.

'If I might, sir?' said the sergeant, as they walked. 'The lads and lassies of the Thirteenth Company of Imperial Marines would like to thank you for your words at the funeral of Corporal Lanach this morning. They were very moving, sir.'

Cael nodded to the sergeant but said nothing. In truth, he wondered why the marines didn't seem to hold him responsible for the corporal's death at the hands of a Gifted Gunstian agent. Every death caused by the Gunstians could be traced back to Cael's destruction of the Temple of the Martyrs, and Cael knew he was to blame. Sable had said as much, and so had his mother. He had been finding it hard to sleep, his thoughts going round and round, circling the decisions that had led him to conclude that the appropriate punishment for Arrosa's arrest was the slaughter of three hundred Gunstians. He had killed many other people since that day in Great Gunst; he was a finely-honed weapon in the hands of the Empress – but none had affected him as much as those he had massacred in Great Gunst. But none of the other deaths had led to a campaign of vengeance against the Empire, and Cael suspected that his guilt was measured by consequences, and not by any sentiment or morals.

He had inherited his violent streak from the Holdfasts – his grandmother, his uncles, Sable, Keira, his grandfather Killop – all had killed untold numbers of people, some guilty, some innocent. Daphne had often said that she had never lost any sleep over those whose lives she had ended, while Sable's morals were more selective. She regretted some of her actions, but by no means all of them. For all her pacifism, his mother had also killed multitudes, from the entire Rahain army serving under Agatha, to the thousands of gods attacking the Kell Pass. Keir and Corthie had also played their roles in the mass killing of the enemies of the Holdfasts; but Keira remained at the top of the list – her toll ran into the hundreds of thousands, and her last act had been to cut off the head of an Ascendant as he had snapped her neck. The family was drenched in blood, and now Caitlyn had joined them. Were there any left in the family who hadn't taken someone's life? Corthie's younger children had surely retained some of their innocence, but the only adult Holdfast Cael could think of who had never shed blood was Kelsey. She had given orders that had resulted in people dying, but she had never actually done the deed herself.

Cael turned a corner, and ran into three soldiers from the Imperial Guard, who were escorting two Rakanese.

'Adjutant,' said an army officer, 'might I have a moment?'

'I am due to appear at the meeting of the Imperial Court, Captain,' said Cael.

The officer gestured at the Rakanese. Cael gazed at them. Both seemed distraught about something, and Cael felt his impatience rise.

'This lady and the gentleman have just arrived from Amatskouri, sir,' said the army captain. 'They have news from Adorati.'

'What news?' said Cael.

'Something that you have to see for yourself, Lord Adjutant,' said the Rakanese woman. 'My words will not do it justice.'

Cael took a breath. 'Where?'

'Along the beachfront of Amatskouri, sir,' said the Rakanese man. 'We implore you to come with us; a few moments will suffice. The prime minister herself has sent us here, to beg the help of the Empress. If you could just take a moment to witness.'

Cael almost brushed them aside, then he calmed his irritation. Was he not a servant of the Empire? It was the Adjutant's job to travel around the provinces, solving their problems, and dealing with their enemies.

'It involves the Gunstians, Lord Adjutant,' said the Rakanese woman.

'All right,' said Cael. 'He glanced at his marine escort. 'You two, stay here. Captain, please let the Herald know that I will be late for the meeting.'

The captain inclined his head as Cael took out his Quadrant.

'The beachfront of Amatskouri?' Cael said to the two Rakanese.

'Yes, sir,' said the man.

Cael swept his fingers over the device. The air shimmered, and the three of them arrived under the summer skies of Amatskouri. The first thing Cael noticed were the cries of lamentation, then he gazed along the beach. Hundreds of butchered Rakanese bodies were lying on the blood-streaked sand, their severed limbs being lapped by the edge of the Inner Sea. Women, children, men – all civilians; while crowds of mourners were being held back by the Adorati militia.

'This happened less than an hour ago,' said the Rakanese woman. 'It was just another normal day, and the beach was full of people out for a morning walk. There were food stalls, and musicians, and...' She broke down, and started weeping.

'And then Gunstians arrived,' said the man. 'Hundreds of them, through a portal on the esplanade. Gifted men and women subdued the crowds, so no one was able to run away to safety, and then the Gunstian soldiers moved in, slaughtering everyone. We have heard that the Gunstians abandon their soldiers to die on these raids, but that did not happen in this case. The portal remained opened until every Gunstian soldier was able to escape.'

'Has there been a count?' said Cael.

'Not a thorough one,' said the man. 'I estimate perhaps five hundred casualties. The Gunstians left very few people injured. Those who were unable to run away were killed.'

'Tell him about the others,' said the woman.

'What others?' said Cael.

'We believe,' said the man, 'though we are yet to gather any firm evidence, that the Gunstians may have taken civilians back through the portal with them. Women, children. Some witnesses watched what happened from the upper floors of the residential housing blocks on the other side of the esplanade – they have told us that they saw civilians being dragged or carried through the portal.'

Cael said nothing. Men and women from the Amatskourian militia were moving through the carnage on the beach, crouching by bodies and checking for survivors, while the crowd on the main road was growing.

'Why would the Gunstians do this?' said the man. 'The people of Adorati have never hurt them.'

'They attacked Colsbury three days ago,' said Cael; 'their third attack on the island. It was a failure, and we recovered one of their Quadrants. Perhaps they have decided to change tactics.'

'We want our people back,' said the woman. 'I cannot bear the thought of helpless civilians in the hands of those monsters.'

'What will the Empress do?' said the man.

'We will soon find out,' said Cael. 'Inform your government that I will speak of this to the full Imperial Court today. Her Majesty will likely want to talk to the prime minister of Adorati.' He lowered his gaze. 'I… I am sorry for your loss. I will report this to the Empress.'

He triggered his Quadrant, and arrived in the gardens behind the Lesser Keep on Colsbury. Four marines emerged from the trees, but they relaxed when they saw who had arrived, and returned to their positions. Cael sat down on a bench and lit a cigarette, as the images of what he had seen on the beach pulsed through his mind. He had managed to hold back his emotions while he had been standing on the bloody sand, and the effort had made him feel empty. He smoked until his hands had stopped shaking from anger, then he stood and transported himself to the anteroom next to the audience chamber.

Eight marines were on duty in the room, and they stood to attention when Cael appeared among them. A courtier opened a door, and Cael entered the audience hall. The Empress was on her throne, behind which lay the large, curving window that overlooked the island; while the rest of the Imperial Court were arrayed by two rows of semi-circular tables. Chamberlain Brogan was on her feet, talking about the need for more prison spaces for the Gunstians soldiers who had been captured on their previous raids, but she fell into silence as Cael approached the throne. Cael saw Arrosa seated in the second row, but he could barely meet her eyes as he bowed before Thorn.

'Your face tells me a story, Adjutant,' said the Empress. 'What has happened?'

'The Gunstians have attacked Amatskouri, Your Majesty,' said Cael. 'Perhaps five hundred civilians have been killed; and some might have been taken back through the portal into captivity.'

The hall hushed.

'It was on the beach,' Cael went on. 'The Gunstians didn't leave their soldiers there this time; they kept the portal open long enough to make sure everyone got out. The prime minister's representatives want to know what we are going to do about it.'

Cael heard a muffled sob, then out of the corner of his eye he saw Chancellor Fenu, who was from Amatskouri, raise her hands to her face.

'Five hundred civilians?' said the Empress, her voice quiet.

'Aye, Your Majesty. As well as an unknown number who might have been taken back with the Gunstians. The massacre was indiscriminate. The children... the children on the beach were not spared.'

'Take your seat, Adjutant,' said the Empress.

Cael kept his head bowed as he walked to the front row of chairs. He sat down next to Lucius Cardova, who eyed him in silence.

No one said anything for a long moment, then Kelsey stood.

'I propose that we take a break, Your Majesty,' Kelsey said, 'to gather more information and to send word to Zamata. We have contacts on that island whom the Gunstians might accept as intermediaries. If Rakanese civilians are being held by Gunst, we should begin negotiations to secure their release.'

The Empress raised her head. 'No,' she said. 'We shall not pause for breath. The gathering of more information is not required, for no new knowledge will overturn what we have learned. I confess to a feeling of intense anger and bitterness, and I fear I am about to make a rash decision. Secretary Cole, please chair.'

Cole rose to his feet as Kelsey sat. 'Your Majesty?' he said.

'Canvas opinion,' said the Empress. 'I need to hear what my court believes we should do next.'

'Yes, Your Majesty,' said Cole. 'We shall go down in order of rank. Herald Kelsey, what is your opinion?'

'I have already stated it,' said Kelsey. 'A delegation needs to go to Zamata immediately, to set up a group of Zamatans willing to reach out to the authorities in Great Gunst. If civilians are in their hands, we need to know what it will take to bring them back alive. Until that process is underway, I counsel no other action.'

Cole inclined his head. 'Lord Constable?'

Lucius gazed at the members of the Imperial Court. 'I agree with the Herald in every respect bar one. We should reach out to the Zamatans, but we should also plan an immediate retaliatory strike upon a suitable Gunstian target. If we do not respond, the Gunstians will perceive that as weakness on our part, and they will be encouraged by our inertia to raid again.'

Cole nodded. 'Chamberlain?'

'We could offer to swap the Gunstian prisoners in our custody for the Rakanese civilians who were taken,' said Brogan. 'Over eight hundred Gunstian volunteers are currently languishing in our prisons. I do not believe that we should stoop to the level of the Gunstians; I am opposed to any retaliation against the civilians of Gunst.'

'Chancellor?' said Cole.

'I agree with Herald Kelsey and Chamberlain Brogan,' said Fenu. 'My heart is breaking for Amatskouri. I used to walk on that beach every morning, listening to the singers as the sun rose over the Inner Sea. I would like to travel there as soon as possible, to convey my sympathies to the prime minister, and to visit the families of those whose loved ones have been killed.'

'Adjutant?' said Cole.

Cael stared at the surface of the table in front of him. 'Between the Empire and the Dominion,' he said, 'we have raided Gunstian installations nearly twenty times. We have destroyed barracks, naval facilities, ships, fortresses and training grounds, and none of it has made the slightest difference. We are not fighting against a traditional army; the Gunstians are not doing this for political gain – they are doing it because they hate us. Striking them again will not change that. Nor do I believe that they will negotiate over any captives they have taken from Amatskouri. They think we are demons – why would they talk to godless demons? There is nothing we can do, short of annihilating them.'

Cael felt the gaze of his mother upon him, but he did not lift his head.

'Chief of Staff?' said Cole.

'I do not agree with the nihilism of the Adjutant's comments,' said Claudian. 'I call for immediate, and brutal, retaliation. We should make a powerful demonstration of our resolve, and lay down to the Gunstians the consequences of what they have done. I suggest we destroy a major landmark in the city of Great Gunst, and take our own captives. We should not target civilians directly, but the Gunstians need to understand that none of them are safe while they continue to attack us.'

Cole nodded. 'Treasurer?'

'I have no opinion,' said Slaeon.

'But...'

'My opinion,' said Slaeon, 'is that I have no opinion, dear Secretary.'

'Very well,' said Cole. 'Chief Jurist?'

Toripadeni raised his eyes. Like Fenu, Tori was from Amatskouri, and his face was twisted with anger.

'The only thing we need to discuss is the target for our response,' he said. 'I agree that it needs to send a strong message to the Gunstians, but we should try our best to avoid any civilian casualties. We are not animals; we do not slaughter civilians. We should consider sending an expeditionary force to seize the port city of Toraq, to cut Great Gunst off from the ocean. We sent Sanang into Rahain; why can't we send them into Gunst?'

'Lord Marshall?' said Cole.

Holder Smith drummed his fingers on the table. 'The people of the

Plateau Province will support any retaliatory action,' he said. 'We are tired of the Gunstian raids, and there is a swell of feeling among the populace that they need to be taught a lesson. We have the most advanced weapons on any of the Known Worlds. It is time to use them.'

Cole nodded. 'Quartermaster?'

Commander Quill cleared her throat. 'My opinion is that we should do two things at once, as the Constable suggested – reach out in the hope that we may be able to get the civilians back through negotiation, while also hitting the Gunstians where it hurts. As the Adjutant said, however, I do not believe that the Gunstians will negotiate, but we should be seen to be trying that approach. I also believe that, as harsh as it sounds, we should treat all those taken by the Gunstians as already dead. As for Tori's suggestion about occupying Toraq City, the empire is ready for such an action to be taken. We could have a full division of infantry in place within a few days.'

'Postmaster?' said Cole.

'The Dominion tried that strategy,' said Arrosa. 'If we invade Gunst, we must be prepared for a long, drawn-out campaign of attrition. What would we regard as success? The return of every captive? If that is the case, we may never be able to leave Toraq, for I do not believe that the Gunstians will willingly hand our people back to us alive. The cost in gold and blood would be stupendous. The simple truth is that we have no answer to the Gifts – our best mages and most powerful gods have no defence against them, and our casualties would be high. How long will the people of the Empire tolerate a war in Gunst? They are angry now, but that anger will be turned upon us if we embark on an occupation of Toraq, and our forces get whittled away day by day. If we have to retaliate, I propose several lightning strikes along the lines of those suggested by the Chief of Staff – let us make a demonstration in Great Gunst, and then let us withdraw quickly.'

'Thank you,' said Cole. 'I will now give my opinion, if I may. I am opposed to any invasion of Gunst, for the reasons outlined by the Postmaster, and I am at a loss to see any advantage from making a violent demonstration in their capital city. We would only succeed in filling the ranks of volunteers if we destroyed a major landmark. Thousands more Gunstians would long to martyr themselves if we obliterate another temple. We should continue with our previous strategy, and ignore this obvious provocation. Why did the Gunstians strike civilians, if not in the perverse hope that we will do the same to them? Let us not give them what they want; instead, let us remain calm and considered. The key remains the Quadrants – the attack on Amatskouri has not changed that. If we can capture their Quadrants, this conflict will be over.' He bowed to the Empress. 'Should I also canvas the opinions of our guests – Karalyn and Sable Holdfast?'

'There is no need,' said Thorn, 'for I already know what they will counsel.' Her eyes simmered with fury. 'My decision is this – we shall send a regiment of Imperial Marines directly to the centre of Great Gunst, where they shall use all means necessary to destroy the Temple of the Great Mother. We shall not specifically target civilians, but nor shall we risk the lives of our marines to protect them. The Temple of the Great Mother functions as the headquarters of the Gunstian religion as well as being the heart of their government. Raze it to the ground, and make a pyre of all those inside. I care not that this will encourage more Gunstians to volunteer, for they have already proved their willingness to sacrifice their own soldiers in order to harm us. The Gunstians must be forced to understand the consequences of their government's decisions. Adjutant, you shall lead this force. I want it carried out within the next few days, and I want all of our marines brought home safely. You may expend as much of our reserves of explosives as you deem fit, but do not leave the temple standing.'

Cael remained where he was, his gaze lowered.

'The Empress requires an acknowledgment of her orders, Adjutant,' said Kelsey.

Cael raised his glance. 'I cannot obey these orders,' he said. 'I have already destroyed one temple in Great Gunst; I shall not do so again. I will not have the blood of civilians on my hands.'

'What about your oath?' said Lucius. 'We have all sworn to obey the commands of the Empress.'

'Then I resign my post,' said Cael. 'If you wish to arrest me, Lord Constable, I shall not resist.'

'Why, Cael?' said the Empress. 'Do you believe the Gunstians should escape punishment for this atrocity?'

'No, Your Majesty,' said Cael. 'I loathe the Gunstians more than any words can express, but this is revenge for the sake of revenge. It will achieve nothing but death, horror and bloodshed. The Gunstians cannot be reasoned with; they want to drag us down to their level. They want their people to see that we are evil and worthy of destruction, and the obliteration of the Temple of the Great Mother will do precisely that. Cole is right – all we can do is try to capture their Quadrants, and then we cut the Gunstians off from all contact; we shun them completely. Ideally, we retrieve the Sextant. If and when we do, I will transport every Gunstian to another world, where they can follow their religion without becoming a menace to their neighbours. Either that, or I will send them to the bottom of the fucking ocean.'

Kelsey got to her feet. 'I propose a break, to allow tempers to cool,' she said. 'I implore Her Majesty not to take the Adjutant's refusal to obey this command as his final word on the matter.'

The Empress stared at Cael, then she inclined her head. 'Let us reconvene one hour from now,' she said, 'when we shall again hear from the Adjutant.'

Thorn rose from her throne, and the members of the Imperial Court got to their feet. Several walked over to Cael, until he was surrounded.

'You cannot resign over this,' said Claudian.

'I will not slaughter civilians,' said Cael.

'The Temple of the Great Mother is full of priests and government officials, Cael,' said Lucius Cardova. 'There is no need to regard them as civilians – they are the very people who ordered the attack on Amatskouri.'

'Let me talk to my husband alone,' said Arrosa. 'No – Cole, you stay as well. The three of us need to discuss this in private.'

The others walked away, leaving Cael, Cole and Arrosa by the foot of the throne. On the other side of the hall, Cael could see the Empress arguing with Kelsey and Brogan.

'If you go, I go,' said Cole.

Cael eyed him. 'What?'

'You heard me, cousin,' said Cole. 'If you refuse to lead the expedition to Great Gunst, then I will be ordered to do it. I won't; I shall also resign.'

'Let's think about this rationally,' said Arrosa. 'If attacking Great Gunst will make no difference, as both of you have said, then why not do it? Lucius is right – the Temple of the Great Mother is not an ordinary place of worship – it is the centre of the Gunstian government.'

'Hundreds of civilians work there,' said Cael, 'and I will not soil my heart with their needless deaths. I will fight our enemies, but I will not debase myself any further. The Gunstians want us to retaliate; they long to die for Chadura.'

'Then let them die,' said Arrosa.

'No.'

Arrosa shook her head. 'Very well. We three should remain as one, and if that is what you both believe, then I shall also resign. The Empress will not wish to lose us, but neither will she be able to back down in front of the entire Imperial Court. We should prepare to be arrested. Our careers will be over, and we shall be lucky to escape prison. This is the end of the dream; do you understand?'

Cael took her hand. 'I'm not sure it was ever my dream.'

Arrosa smiled sadly at him. 'You would have made a fine emperor, husband.'

The doors to the audience chamber were swung open, and a squad of armed marines entered, with Lord Elmhirst in their midst.

'Your Majesty,' said a marine officer. 'A delegation from the Dominion has arrived.'

'Might I address the chamber, Your Majesty?' said Elmhirst.

'Everyone to their places,' said Kelsey. 'Let us hear what the Dominion has to say.'

The members of the Imperial Court walked back to their seats, but they remained standing until the Empress retook her throne.

'Greetings, Lord Elmhirst,' said Thorn; 'I pray the news you bear is good.'

Lord Elmhirst smiled, his eyes revealing his pent-up excitement.

'The news I bear is indeed good, Your Majesty,' he said. 'This morning, I conducted a raid on a peripheral naval facility on the southern coast of Gunst; you can ask Cael about those types of raids – they usually amount to little other than the destruction of a few ships and warehouses. This time was different. Volunteers were being trained at this facility in seaborne operations, and several high-ranking officials from the Gunstian army and navy were present. It is my belief that the Gunstians were intending to carry out some sort of naval assault upon either the Dominion or the Empire. I have taken care of that threat; the entire facility has been destroyed, and the volunteers dealt with.'

'You have our thanks,' said the Empress.

'There is more, Your Majesty,' said Elmhirst. 'I personally read the mind of a senior Gunstian officer from their army.' He turned, and directed his gaze at Cael. 'I have it, my friend. I have the location of the Gunstian encampment, from where they have been coordinating their attacks. It is in Aucteran, as we suspected. Shall we destroy it together, Adjutant Cael?'

A wave of relief passed over the chamber, and Cael saw Arrosa put a hand to her face. Cael glanced at the Empress, who inclined her head.

'I would be more than happy to assist,' said Cael.

Elmhirst beamed. 'We must move quickly, my friend, before the Gunstians discover what we have learned. We must give them no opportunity to relocate their encampment; we must strike hard and fast.'

'I can have a regiment of marines armed and ready to go within two hours,' said Quill.

'Thank you, Quartermaster,' said the Empress. 'Go, Adjutant, and take Quartermaster Quill with you. We shall talk about other matters when you return.'

'Please be careful, Adjutant,' said Fenu. 'The Gunstians may have taken the civilians from Amatskouri to their encampment.'

'Civilians?' said Elmhirst.

'I will tell you all about it as we prepare,' said Cael. He bowed before Thorn. 'Your Majesty.'

'Rescue as many Rakanese civilians as you can,' said the Empress, 'and recover our missing Quadrants. As for the Gunstians in this encampment, I trust you understand what to do with them?'

'I understand, Your Majesty.'

'Show them no quarter, Adjutant.'

'Aye, Your Majesty,' he said; 'I will show them none.'

CHAPTER 30
TO THE MOUNTAIN

Nom Karta, Inopei – 9th Lexinch 1613

'I'm sorry, ma'am,' said the Banner sergeant, 'but Queen Famula has informed us that you are no longer welcome to attend royal audiences.'

'On what grounds?' said Konna.

The sergeant shrugged. 'I didn't ask, ma'am.'

Konna stared over the soldier's shoulder at the closed doors to the Queen's main hall. She had been partly expecting that some form of action would be taken against her following Edgar's confession, and she had been keeping her head down for several days, hoping that the dragons of Nom Karta would prove forgiving.

She heard a sound behind her, and moved to the side as Lady Abda walked down the wide hallway, her teal-coloured scales gleaming in the lamplight. The Banner soldiers swung open the tall doors as Abda approached, but the dragon came to a halt next to Konna, then she lowered her head.

'Filthy insect-thief,' said Abda, 'you have brought shame to the Dominion. Not only did you steal from the Empire, you then lost what you had stolen. Is there anything more pathetic than an incompetent criminal?'

Konna bowed her head. 'I was merely trying to serve Lord Edgar, ma'am.'

'That fool has imperilled us all,' said Abda. 'The Queen is being too soft on him; for all we know, that insect Cairney will be back here with his tricks and illusions. The Demon Witch should have killed your brother when she had the chance; it was a strange time for her to learn the art of mercy, when she showed Lady Lenta none.'

Konna said nothing, and the huge dragon went into the audience hall. The Banner soldiers closed the door behind her, as Konna stood in silence. She turned, and began walking away from the hall. There had been news she had wished to hear – two rumours she had wanted confirmed. She walked to a flight of stairs, and ascended a few levels of the gargantuan palace to a rooftop loggia, where a few chairs had been placed. Konna sat and gazed out at the palaces of Nom Karta.

She had never felt so alone. She had tried to prove her worth to Edgar, and had ended up being humiliated in front of Empress Thorn. The insufferable bitch had looked down at Konna from her throne as though she were nothing; and Edgar's grovelling behaviour had been intolerable. Elmhirst had been avoiding her, Kyra had been staying in her quarters with her boys, and Esher had been absent from Nom Karta for days. She thought about returning to Kell, but she knew that her mother would be angry about the part she had played in the theft of the Sextant. It was a little ironic that her mother had been upset by Konna's involvement in the capture of Cairney; and now she would be upset about the prospect of Cairney escaping with Carter's help. Naxor had not been seen in Nom Karta since the incident; he had been played for a fool by Edgar, who had exploited his desire to ingratiate himself with the gods of the Dominion. That gave Konna some consolation – at least she wasn't the only person feeling humiliated.

'I thought I might find you here,' said Esher, as he walked into the loggia.

'Are you here to tell me how disappointed you are in me?' said Konna.

'I apologised for that,' he said, as he took a seat next to her. 'I want us to remain friends, Konna. Is that possible?'

'You hauled me in front of the Empress to be berated.'

'You went willingly,' he said. 'You took responsibility for your actions, and I admire that. While Elmhirst slinked away, you stood your ground.'

'I have been barred from the audience hall.'

'Yes, I know. I have just come from there – it was the soldiers on the doors who told me that you had tried to enter. Lady Abda also mentioned seeing you. She is of the opinion that Lord Edgar should also have been forbidden from attending the audience with the Queen.'

Konna narrowed her eyes. 'Edgar was allowed in?'

'He was,' said Esher. 'He was contrite, but it wasn't enough for many of the dragons, and the entire meeting turned into an argument about whether or not Edgar should even be there. But, he is the Queen's leading human counsellor, and the Dominion owes him much. Her Majesty said exactly that, and told Abda to keep her opinions to herself. The Queen is very pleased that the Empress accepted the offer of Tempest ore. To her mind, that means the affair is settled.'

'Lindi and Carter have the Sextant,' she said. 'It's hardly settled.'

'Queen Famula doesn't seem too concerned about that,' said Esher. 'She views this as an imperial problem that has little to do with the Dominion. After all, it is the Empress that Cairney wishes to overthrow. Abda is worried that he will attack Nom Karta, but the Queen reminded her sister that Cairney's purpose in assaulting Nom Karta last time was to try to provoke a war.'

'I heard a couple of rumours.'

'Oh yes? Which ones?'

'The first was about a Gunstian attack on Elidus, where another Quadrant was stolen. I heard it happened yesterday, but the Dominion wants to keep it quiet.'

'The attack did take place,' said Esher, 'and a Quadrant was indeed stolen, but, personally, I doubt it was the Gunstians.'

'Why?'

'Because no one was injured or killed, and I don't believe the Gunstians know how to travel to Elidus. I wouldn't even describe it as an *attack*, more of a *burglary*. Someone sneaked into the rooms of the Governor of Elidus and made off with gold, maps and, of course, a Quadrant. If I had to guess, it sounds more like something Lindi might have done. If she was capable of stealing the Sextant from under Laverne's nose, doing the same for a Quadrant would have been easy for her.'

'Why would Lindi need another Quadrant?' said Konna.

'Your guess is as good as mine. What was the other rumour?'

'That Lord Elmhirst went to visit Cael in Colsbury with important news.'

'That is also true. Elmhirst says he has found the hidden Gunstian encampment on Aucteran. He is assembling a team of gods and Banner soldiers, who will join forces with Cael and the Imperial Marines. They are due to attack either tonight or at dawn tomorrow.'

'I wish I could go with them. Anything would be better than sitting here. Part of me wishes I had never come to Inopei in the first place.'

'Perhaps you need to get away for a while,' said Esher. 'Would you like to return to Zamata with me?'

'When are you leaving?'

'Now. I took a small detour to talk to you.'

Konna smiled. 'All right. Thank you, Esher.'

'We young gods need to stick together,' he said, as he got to his feet and took out his Quadrant.

Konna also stood. 'Do I need to pack? Are you inviting me to stay for a few days?'

'Certainly. Shall I collect you from your quarters one hour from now?'

'That sounds perfect,' she said.

After packing some clothes and letting Kyra know that she would be leaving Nom Karta for a few days, Konna met Esher outside the front door of her apartment at the allotted time.

Esher activated his Quadrant, and they appeared on a balcony overlooking the smooth lawn in front of the Dragon Palace in Igatz.

'Put your bag into the spare room,' said Esher.

Konna had visited Esher's quarters in the palace before, so she walked through his large sitting room and into an unused bedroom. The bed and much of the floor were covered in piles of books, and Konna dropped her packed bag onto the blanket.

'Please excuse the mess,' said Esher, from the doorway. 'I am collecting books for when Zamata Gataza is rebuilt. Would you like to visit the site? All of the bodies have been cleared away and buried, and builders and architects have begun work.'

'Shall we go by Quadrant?'

Esher raised an eyebrow. 'Certainly not. It is a beautiful summer's day. We shall walk; and, of course, take a couple of ferries – I'm not expecting you to swim across the Cyasarta.'

Konna pulled a face. 'How long will that take?'

'Around four hours? The first half will be through Igatz and Kaugatz, and then we shall have the long walk up Mount Hodzulat when we reach the opposite bank of the Hansarta.' He laughed. 'Come on, Konna – we are gods. We have self-healing. A few miles of walking won't hurt us.'

They left the Dragon Palace via a side door, and walked along the streets of Igatz. The town looked prosperous and well-maintained, with clean roads and neat houses with flowerboxes by their windows.

'Igatz is almost entirely inhabited by Aucterians,' Esher said. 'Doesn't this remind you of parts of Plateau City?'

'The wealthier parts,' said Konna.

'Yes, the aristocratic district where the Holdfast townhouse lies, or the area near the university. I wish the two peoples would realise how much they have in common.'

'I didn't know you'd been to Plateau City.'

'I have been several times, when I have been meeting members of the Imperial Court. I am never there in summer, though.'

'What do you think of the Blue Palace?' she said.

Esher puffed out his cheeks. 'It is quite the architectural statement.'

'It's a fucking abomination,' said Konna. 'It screams, *Look at me; aren't I pretty and important?* It's got Thorn's fingerprints all over it.'

'It certainly dominates the city.'

Konna laughed. 'Aye.'

It took them forty minutes to traverse Igatz, then they took a ferry to Kaugatz and crossed the Cyasarta. One hour after that, they took another ferry over the Hansarta, and left the town of Kaugatz behind. The ferry deposited them onto a jetty by a coastal road, and the mountain of Hodzulat loomed up ahead of them. Konna grimaced at the sight, but Esher was persistent, and they started the long climb up the slope. They passed terraced fields and farms, and took a track that wound its way up the side of the mountain, climbing ever higher, until the whole of the island could be seen behind them.

'This was once a famous pilgrimage route,' said Esher. 'Irlanians would sail to Zamata, land at Igatz, and make their way around the monasteries, visiting each one in turn, or perhaps staying in the same one while they read and prayed. There were Serpent Pillars along every road that led to a monastery, to guide their steps, and some of the monasteries functioned more as large hostelries, where hundreds of pilgrims could stay. The kings and queens of Irlan used to come here, and they showered money on the island, just as the Empire has done in recent years.'

'When was this?' said Konna.

'Around a thousand years ago,' said Esher, 'before the Dominion had learned how to cross the ocean, and while Gunst was in the midst of a long period of civil strife.'

'Ancient times.'

'To the Zamatans who live here now – yes. To us – yes. But to people like Edgar and Elmhirst? This is the point I am trying to make, Konna. I know that I have existed for over thirty millennia, but I feel as young as you do. When a thousand years has elapsed, will we look upon these present times as *ancient*? Or will we still remember the details, the emotions? Will we think – *President Bauchlie? Oh yes, I remember him*; or will we have forgotten the names and faces of the countless mortals that we will have seen come and go? A thousand years may seem like an impossibly long period of time to us right now, but it is nothing compared to the yawning abyss of eternity. These are the thoughts that grip my mind while I try to sleep each night. Right now, I feel human, alive. I am curious about the peoples who inhabit the Known Worlds, and I am eager to learn all that I can. Will I still be able to say the same a millennium from now?'

'I don't know,' said Konna. 'I try not to think about it.'

Esher smiled. 'Sometimes, it is all that pervades my mind.'

'Would you rather be mortal?'

'Maybe. Life seemed simpler, and yet more precious, before I learned who I was. When your time is short, every moment counts, and one little decision could change the entire course of your life. One small injury could lead to a life-threatening infection, or a debilitating illness might overcome you at any moment. We never have to worry about these things, but I can remember what it felt like to be mortal. Here is what I think – mortals *experience* life, while we merely *observe* it.'

'I feel as though I am experiencing life.'

'Yes, but you are still young, Konna. Will that sentiment remain true as the centuries begin to pass? There must come a moment in the life of every god, when they think to themselves – *I have seen all this happen before*. That is when it begins, I think; the slow degeneration into cynicism and apathy.'

'You are starting to depress me.'

He laughed. 'Sorry. Anyway, here we are.'

They came to a halt in front of what to Konna looked like a village of large tents. Between the tents were neatly-arranged piles of masonry and timber, and carts filled with tools and equipment. A large dusty area by the foot of tall cliffs had been cleared, and Konna imagined that it had been the place where the old monastery had sat. She could see large foundation blocks that were still in place, and several stairwells that descended into the darkness. A few workers were out, measuring distances over the cleared space and taking notes.

'The Gunstians did not destroy Zamata Gataza by chance,' said Esher. 'They chose to attack this site not only because it was the home of Lord Bailey, but in response to the destruction of their own oldest temple – the Temple of the Martyrs, which was also a thousand years old.'

'The temple that Cael obliterated?'

'Precisely, though I doubt that many people in the Empire have made that connection. The Gunstians may imagine that the destruction of Zamata Gataza has struck a grievous blow to Empress Thorn but, in reality, she probably hasn't given it a single thought.'

'That's because she's an arrogant, self-centred bitch.'

'She is not,' said Esher. 'She is trying her best.'

Konna laughed. 'Wait – are you being serious?'

'Your impression of the Empress does not match mine, Konna,' he said. 'I don't wish to cause offence, but do you think that perhaps the words of your mother and Lord Naxor may have influenced your opinion of Thorn?'

'I am prepared to concede that I might have been wrong about Cael and Kelsey,' she said, 'but I will never forgive the Empress. Her greed started the war that killed my father.'

Esher gazed into her eyes. 'Why not blame Bailey, who opened the Palace of the Almighty, thereby releasing the god who slew your father? Why not Queen Blackrose, who enticed the Empire into intervening upon Na Sun Ka in order to secure her southern frontier? Why not Sable, who imprisoned the Wystians on Rigga, where they festered for years and thirsted for revenge? And, dare I say it? – why not your own parents? Corthie Holdfast was not a mindless cipher – he understood the risks. And did your mother not ask him to kill those who had attacked Clackenbaird?'

Konna said nothing.

'I am not trying to claim that Thorn is a perfect Empress,' Esher went on; 'far from it – she has certainly made mistakes. But I stand by my assertion that she is trying her best. She longs to be remembered as a good Empress, a wise and compassionate leader – this is her heart's desire, or so I believe. She is a mortal who longs to create a legacy that lasts the ages. In other words, she is trying to be like us; she wants the memory of her deeds to live forever.'

'I still don't like her,' said Konna.

'You are free to hold that opinion,' said Esher. 'Give me a moment or two; I wish to talk to the architects about their designs for the new building.'

Konna waited by the edge of the tents as Esher walked to the cleared area. He clambered over a few foundation blocks, and began speaking to a group of Zamatan workers. Konna turned, and peered through the open entrance of a large tent. Two monks were inside, sorting through heaps of items that had been retrieved from the ruins of the monastery – tattered old books, paintings, reliquaries and candlesticks sat piled on tables, and the monks were noting down their details. Konna wandered among the other tents, and saw several large fragments of statues; some of serpents and dragons, and others of venerable old monks and prelates from the past. Around a dozen carved marble pillars had also been saved from the wreckage, and they lay in neat rows between two long tents.

Konna knelt to examine one of the pillars, and a shadow moved over her, blocking out the sunlight.

'Ah,' said a voice, 'the great betrayer. How is your conscience, sister? Does it keep you awake at night?'

Konna froze, as a base terror swept over her. She turned her head, and saw Cairney standing a few feet away. He was dressed for battle, with a steel breastplate, and a longsword buckled to his belt. He looked older, and his face held a threat of violence.

'Should I forgive you?' he said.

'Brother,' she said.

'You have lost the right to call me that,' he said. 'To regain it, you will have to prove your loyalty to me. Call Esher over.'

Konna's mouth went dry.

'No?' said Cairney. 'Then you are no sister of mine. Should I compel you?'

Konna rose to her feet. 'What do you want from me?'

'Isn't it obvious?' said Cairney. 'I desire your undivided and complete loyalty and obedience. If it is not forthcoming, then I will be forced to subdue you. But first, tell me why you did it. Tell me why you sided with the Colsbury Holdfasts over your own blood and kin.'

'If you had killed the Empress that day,' she said; 'if you had killed Kelsey or Cael, then Karalyn would have executed you.'

'I see,' he said. 'You are claiming that you betrayed me for my own good.'

'Your plan was stupid, Cairney. You were a sixteen-year-old numpty; you were defeated not by me, but by your blind over-confidence.'

'If my plan had been sound, you would have supported me?'

'I... I don't know. Mother has changed; did you know that? She no longer blames the Colsbury Holdfasts for Da's death.'

'Lies,' he said.

'Where is Carter?'

'Safe.'

'Ask him about Mother's change of heart. He will tell you the same. I assume it was Lindi who found you?'

'Lindi now works for me,' he said. 'Will you do the same? Let us forget the past for a moment; let us think only of the future. I have a new plan to assume control of the Empire; will you help me, Konna?'

'I have grown to believe that Uncle Naxor's plan might be the most sensible course of action,' she said. 'Why can't we be patient? We don't have to do anything but wait.'

'I had one great fear while I was in exile,' he said. 'Do you want to know what it was? I will tell you. My greatest fear was that I would not be released until everyone responsible for the death of our father was themselves dead. That Kelsey, Thorn and Cael would be but memories by the time I set foot in the Empire. I will not be patient; I shall not wait. I will spill the blood of the Empress and spit on her remains. I long to make her suffer, and her death will be drawn out and lingering. For Kelsey, I will be more merciful; I will merely snap her neck. Cael's death will also be quicker than he deserves. A nail through each eye should suffice. All of this is essential. Give me these deaths, and I will spare the others. Do we have a deal?'

Konna lowered her gaze. 'Cael is innocent.'

Cairney slapped her across the cheek with the back of his hand, his eyes flashing with rage. Konna stumbled, then her self-healing asserted itself, and she glared back at her brother.

'You bastard,' she cried.

'It was less than you deserved,' said Cairney. '*Get on your knees.*'

Cairney's words of compulsion struck Konna like a wave, and she fell to her knees before she had realised what she was doing.

Cairney smiled. 'I have grown in power since we last met; did you feel it? My will is the strongest, my battle-vision is unparalleled, my powers supreme. I will be Emperor for a thousand millennia, and all will kneel before me, just as you are now doing. *Call for Esher.*'

'Esher,' Konna cried. 'Please come here. Esher.'

'That's right,' said Cairney. 'You cannot resist. I had hoped that you would be my willing servant, Konna; how I had hoped that you would repent of your earlier transgressions against me – but so be it. You will help me, Konna, whether willing or not.' He stared into her eyes. '*You will never be able to hurt me.*'

Konna felt changes sweep across her mind. Cairney was right – his powers had grown during his exile. She began to sob.

Cairney glanced up as Esher walked into the gap between the tents where the recovered pillars lay.

'Did you call for me, Konna?' he said, then his eyes widened with fear.

'*Do not move, Ascendant,*' said Cairney.

Esher came to an abrupt halt, as Cairney stared into his eyes.

'*Your powers are blocked,*' Cairney said. '*Go to sleep.*'

Esher toppled over, and fell to the ground. The side of his face brushed off one of the stone pillars, and the cut began to bleed.

'Leave him alone,' said Konna. 'Esher is a good man.'

'He is weak,' said Cairney. 'For eight years, he has known of his great powers, and yet he has done nothing with them. He is unworthy of the name of Ascendant.'

'What about Karalyn?' she said.

'What of her? I know what happened; Carter and Lindi told me about the frail mortal body she now inhabits.'

'But that won't last,' Konna cried. 'When she dies again, she could return just as powerful as she was in Albany's body. Think, brother. You might believe that you have a free hand to do anything you want, but Karalyn won't forget.'

'The problem of how to deal with Karalyn has dominated my thoughts for years,' he said.

'It is a problem that cannot be solved.'

'I believe otherwise,' he said, as he took out a Quadrant. 'Lindi, my faithful servant, procured this for me yesterday from the ice world of Elidus. I gave her a command, and she obeyed.'

'Did you compel her?'

'I didn't need to. I revealed to her a small portion of my power, and she fell into line. I am now going to take you and Esher to the mountain where we have been staying.'

He moved his fingers over the surface of the device. The air crackled, then Konna found herself kneeling on a solid stone floor within a half-ruined building, with Esher lying a few yards to her left.

'Konna,' cried a voice.

Konna looked up, and saw Carter hurrying towards her, a large smile on his face. He glanced at the body of Esher, frowned, then he turned to his sister.

'Why are ye on yer knees?' he said.

'Konna has refused to assist us,' said Cairney.

'Aye?' said Carter. 'Why would ye do that, Konna?'

'Cairney will bathe the Known Worlds in blood,' said Konna.

Carter laughed. 'Come on; do ye really believe that? Three people –

that's all who are on Cairney's list. Three people, and then we can take over the Empire.'

'He wants to kill our cousin, our aunt, and the Empress.'

'Nah,' said Carter. 'He isnae gonnae kill them; we have the Sextant. We can exile them.'

Cairney smiled.

'I don't know what he's told you, Carter,' said Konna, 'but he's been lying to you.'

Carter rolled his eyes, then he looked down at Esher again. 'Why did ye bring him back?'

'Insurance,' said Cairney.

'Eh?' said Carter. 'Yer gonnae have to explain that.'

'Where is Lindi?' said Cairney.

'She's outside; I'll get her.'

Carter walked away towards a large opening, where sunshine was entering the building.

'How will Carter react when he discovers that you've been lying to him?' said Konna. 'Carter might accept the death of the Empress, but not Cael or Aunty Kelsey.'

'Carter will accept my decisions,' said Cairney. 'His mind is sharp, and he has been thinking about the politics of the Empire throughout my exile. His plans are sound, and I intend to use them. Do you see, Konna? – I am quite prepared to take advice, if it is good, and if it is offered willingly.'

Carter walked back into the chamber, as Lindi trailed along behind him. The daughter of Sable had a cocky expression on her face, and Konna wondered if it was for show, or whether she was under Cairney's spell.

'Cairney brought Esher and Konna back with him,' said Carter.

'I'm not blind, Carter,' said Lindi. She peered down at the unconscious body of the Ascendant. 'Why can't I detect his self-healing powers?'

'I blocked them,' said Cairney.

Lindi narrowed her eyes.

'I sense doubt in your mind, Lindi,' said Cairney, 'so perhaps it is time for a small demonstration. Watch carefully, and you might realise how fortunate you were that you pledged your loyalty to me without having to be forced.' He glanced at Konna. '*Remain exactly where you are. Do not move unless I command it.*'

Konna felt her body still, as she knelt on the hard stone floor.

Cairney walked over to Esher and crouched by him.

'*Listen to my words, Ascendant,*' he said. '*You are under my authority. You shall awaken and stand to attention.*'

Esher opened his eyes and rose to his feet.

'*Throttle Konna,*' said Cairney.

'Wait,' said Carter. 'I don't think...'

Cairney raised a finger. 'Silence. Konna will not suffer any lasting harm; this is for Lindi's benefit.'

Esher walked up to Konna, then he reached out with both hands and gripped her throat. He had no battle-vision, but he was naturally strong, and Konna began to choke, as her self-healing battled his tightening grip.

'*Ascendant, stop,*' said Cairney.

The grip around Konna's throat loosened, and she gasped for breath.

'This is the part you really need to see, Lindi,' Cairney went on; 'to confound any thoughts you might have that you are indispensible to me. *Ascendant, walk over to the Sextant. Konna, rise and follow us.*'

Esher walked away, and Konna got to her feet. Lindi eyed her for a moment, then she, Carter and Cairney went after Esher, and Konna followed them. They entered a chamber that had been recently roofed, and Konna saw the huge Sextant sitting on the stone floor. Cairney drew his sword. It was the Weathervane, and he slid it into the flank of the Sextant. The device began to hum, and it lifted a little off the floor.

'Gather round,' said Cairney. 'Let us witness the reason I have brought Esher here. Lindi believes that I need her, as she is the only one of us who can use the Sextant. She is wrong. *Ascendant, place your hand onto the Sextant and tell us what it says to you.*'

Esher raised his right hand, and placed it onto the flat surface of the device. 'It said, *What is your desire, Esher?*'

Cairney smiled. '*Take your hand off the device.*'

Esher removed his hand from the Sextant, and Cairney pulled the Weathervane from its flank. The humming ceased, and the Sextant settled back onto the stone floor.

Cairney walked up to Lindi, and gazed down at her. 'Anything to say, daughter of Sable?'

Lindi frowned. 'You didn't need to do that,' she said. 'I have already sworn to be loyal to you.'

Cairney laughed, then his features changed, and he peered more intently at Lindi. 'There is something else going on here,' he said. 'I was watching your eyes when you first saw Esher.' He frowned. 'Are you fond of the last Ascendant, Lindi Holdfast?'

'Of course not,' she said. 'Don't be stupid.'

Cairney turned to Esher. '*Ascendant, have you ever spoken to Lindi before?*'

'I have,' said Esher.

'*Tell me about the conversation.*'

'Lindi wanted to know if I were her father,' said Esher, 'but Sable told me that I am not.'

'Konna put the idea into my head,' Lindi cried.

Cairney laughed, his eyes lit with delight. 'Of course,' he cried. 'Who else would Sable choose to father a god with her but the last Ascendant? Sable always reaches high.'

'But it's not true,' said Lindi, her gaze lowered.

'And what if I ordered you to kill Esher?' said Cairney. 'Would you obey?'

Lindi stared at the floor, then nodded. 'I would.'

'This isnae necessary,' said Carter. 'We should be talking about the plan.'

Cairney tore his gaze away from Lindi and smiled. 'You are correct, brother. My little demonstration is complete. Let us sit, and we shall discuss the downfall of Karalyn Holdfast.'

CHAPTER 31
ADVICE NOT TAKEN

Colsbury Castle, Republic of the Holdings – 5th Day, Second Third Summer 560

Karalyn kept her gaze on Cael as he, Elmhirst and Quill walked out of the large audience chamber.

Sable shook her head from the seat next to her. 'Elmhirst will probably never know just how welcome his news was,' she whispered to Karalyn. 'I really thought Cael was about to resign.'

'I am not sure I have ever been more proud of him,' said Karalyn. 'He was prepared to go to jail to avoid having to slaughter civilians.'

Kelsey rose to her feet from her place in the first semi-circular row of tables. 'Shall we continue with the meeting, Your Majesty?'

Thorn was still gazing at the doorway that Cael had used to leave the room. She turned her head, keeping her gaze lowered.

'Was I too rash?' she said.

'We can hold a more private discussion when Cael returns from Aucteran, Your Majesty,' said Kelsey. 'Should we move on to discuss the missing Sextant?'

Thorn said nothing for a moment, then she shook her head. 'Not today,' she said. 'I need time to think about the Gunstian attack on the Rakanese.' She glanced at Chancellor Fenu. 'You mentioned that you wished to travel to Amatskouri to meet the prime minister and the families of the fallen. I shall accompany you.'

'Might I journey with you, Your Majesty?' said Tori. 'Amatskouri is also my home.'

'Secretary Cole,' said Thorn, 'you shall escort me, the Chancellor and the Chief Jurist to Amatskouri.'

The Empress stood, and the other members of the Imperial Court also got to their feet.

Cole walked forward and bowed before the Empress, then Fenu and Tori joined them.

'We shall pick up a squad of marines on the way, Your Majesty,' said Cole.

'Very well,' said Thorn. She glanced at Kelsey. 'We shall be back by sunset.'

Thorn nodded to Cole, who activated his Quadrant. The air shimmered, and all four of them vanished.

Sable rolled her eyes. 'I came all this way to discuss my daughter, and she wasn't even mentioned.'

Kelsey eyed her. 'Is that your reaction to the news that five hundred Rakanese civilians have been massacred by the Gunstians?'

'If my daughter fetches Cairney back from exile,' said Sable, 'then we might have a lot more to worry about than the Gunstians. It was worth at least five minutes of the Empress's time.'

'All right,' said Kelsey; 'I'll sum up our progress on how well we are doing in tracking down your errant daughter – we have found fuck all. She could be anywhere.'

Sable narrowed her eyes. 'And what, my dear niece, do you intend to do to my daughter if you find her before I do?'

'She's a god,' said Kelsey, 'so maybe five hundred years in jail? More if she's freed Cairney. Let's face it, my dear aunt; your daughter is out of control. And if you find her first, don't try to sneak her to safety; she's endangering every Known World, and she deserves to be punished. A seventeen-year-old crazy girl in charge of the Sextant; it's like our worst nightmare come true.'

Sable put a hand on her hip. 'I will find her, Kelsey, have no fear of that.'

Kelsey snorted, then she and Lucius Cardova left the audience chamber.

'Your sister is a pain in the arse,' Sable said to Karalyn.

'Then don't rile her up,' said Karalyn. 'Where are you going to look next?'

Sable shook her head. 'I don't know. You must have seen every world created by the Sextant, yeah?'

'Every one that still exists.'

'Where would you hide the Sextant?'

'I hid it upon a world of my own creation – but it isn't there now. Kyra has gone back to check; Lindi hasn't returned to my world.'

'How many worlds did you make?'

'Altogether?' said Karalyn. 'Forty-three, but I destroyed over half of those not long after creating them. There are eighteen of my creations left.'

'All right,' said Sable. 'We have the Known Worlds, which include the Doomed Worlds; we have your eighteen creations, and we have the worlds that were created ages ago that have slipped out of contact with the others. Is that right?'

'There are hundreds of worlds in that last category,' said Karalyn. 'Many are desolate, but some are thriving.'

Sable frowned. 'Are there gods on any of these worlds?'

'Gods, dragons, mortals,' said Karalyn; 'some have all three. There is a world entirely populated with green-skinned people, like the Fordians; and there are several worlds where gods rule millions of mortals. I tended not to interfere in any of those.'

'Finding you on Athumia was simple compared to this,' said Sable. 'All I knew was the world you were on, and that you had killed a dragon king. It wasn't much to go on, but it was enough. This is... no, it's not impossible, and I am not going to give up.'

Caitlyn walked into the audience hall, passing those who were leaving.

'That was over quickly, Mother,' she said.

'The Empress called an early halt to proceedings,' said Karalyn. 'There was no time to discuss the missing Sextant.'

'The news about what happened in Amatskouri is all over the palace,' said Caitlyn. 'I saw Cael leave with Lord Elmhirst – are they organising a reprisal attack?'

'No,' said Karalyn; 'they are going to attempt to rescue those taken by the Gunstians.'

'That's a relief,' she said. 'For a moment, I thought we were going to strike back at Gunstian civilians.'

Sable raised an eyebrow. 'Would our beloved Empress order such a thing? Anyway, I had best be off. So many worlds, so little time. I will see you both later.'

Sable dipped a hand into a pocket and disappeared.

'Poor Sable,' said Caitlyn. 'Imagine having a daughter as wild as Lindi. I hope my cousin is all right.'

'Would you like to go for a walk?'

'Where?' said Caitlyn.

'The gardens?'

'I thought you might say that, Mother. All right; let's go.'

They walked out of the audience chamber and descended a flight of stairs to the main entrance of the Summer Palace. The sun was shining, and the air was clear and fresh.

'How are you feeling?' Karalyn said, as they made for the tunnel that went under the two keeps.

'About killing those men?' said Caitlyn. 'I feel terrible, Mother. I know they were going to kill us; I know they weren't innocent, but it felt so... so final. All it took was a wave of my hand, and I could feel the death powers leaving my fingertips. I struck them too hard. I didn't mean for... for the flesh to melt off their heads. I wish I had given them heart attacks, not for their benefit, but for ours. I subjected little Cowie to seeing that. It was horrible. But I panicked, and so I lashed out without a thought for the intensity of powers I was unleashing on them. Did you see what Cael did?'

'Aye.'

'He shielded Cowie from the Gift of Pain,' said Caitlyn.

'He did the same for me when the Gunstians attacked Nom Karta,' said Karalyn. 'Cael has many attributes, but cowardice has never been one of them.'

They emerged from the tunnel and entered the gardens of Colsbury. They made their way through the apple orchards until they reached the small graveyard, where they stopped. Karalyn lowered herself down to one knee by the grave of Lennox, and tidied up the flowers, removing any that had withered in the summer heat.

'I knew you wanted to come here,' said Caitlyn.

'Do you object?' said Karalyn.

'No, but I don't really understand what draws you here again and again. You visit the grave every day.'

'I have done the same whenever I have lived on Colsbury.'

'It has been thirty-three years since he died, Mother.'

'I made a terrible mistake with Lennox,' she said. 'I blamed him for something for which he was innocent. It always came between us, and I think I come here partly to remind myself of that. It used to be my biggest regret.' She glanced up at Caitlyn. 'Neglecting you and your brother has displaced it. Caitlyn, I have decided to visit Carden today. It has been thirteen days since he went back to Plateau City, and I don't want him to think that I am ignoring him.'

Caitlyn bit her lip. 'I'm not sure if that's a good idea.'

'Why not?'

'I saw how angry he was, Mother. Perhaps you should send him a letter. Write down your feelings, and someone with a Quadrant can deliver it. He might just rip it to pieces, but he will know that you are thinking of him.'

'What if he is in pain? I need to see him face to face; do you want to come with me?'

'I want to persuade you to think again,' said Caitlyn. 'Give it a few more days.'

'But you seem fine with me,' she said. 'Perhaps Carden will also be fine.'

'Oh Mother,' she said. 'Do not underestimate how angry I remain with you. I love you – yes; but I am still angry. All those wasted years – we can never get them back. I do want this to work though; I want us to be close, and I know how hard you are trying. Please take my advice on this – leave Carden be for a while longer. He is not ready to form any kind of relationship with you; not yet.'

Karalyn got to her feet and brushed the soil from her knee. 'If Carden doesn't wish to talk to me, I will return here immediately; but I have to try. I will keep trying for as long as it takes.'

Caitlyn said nothing, but a sour expression remained on her face. They walked through the rest of the gardens in silence, then emerged through the gate that led to the harbour. A large shadow passed overhead, and Karalyn looked up to see Frostback circling over the island. The silver dragon began her descent, and landed in the great forecourt between the keeps and the Summer Palace. Karalyn and Caitlyn walked over to the dragon, just as Calpurnia climbed down to the ground.

Caitlyn smiled. 'Cousin. I didn't know you were flying up from Plateau City today.'

'I thought I might see you here,' said Calpurnia. She eyed Karalyn. 'It is strange to see you in a different body, Aunty.'

'Not as strange as being in it,' said Karalyn.

Frostback swung her head round, and she gazed down at Karalyn.

'Halfclaw and I heard what had happened to you, witch,' said the dragon. 'Is it true that you are powerless in this form?'

'I have a Gift,' said Karalyn, 'but I haven't been able to use it. Apart from that I am as you see me – a mortal woman with no powers.'

'For the security of the Empire,' said Frostback, 'you should remedy this situation at once. It is selfish of you to linger in this reduced state. What of your duties, your responsibilities?'

'Are you suggesting I take my own life?' she said.

'Another can do it for you, if you have not the courage to do it for yourself. I would be content to oblige you.'

'And then?'

'Then you would be free to take on a more powerful vessel.'

'In other words, I would have to murder someone?'

The dragon's red eyes glowed. 'If the peace collapses because of your reluctance to do what is necessary, Karalyn-witch, the fault will lie upon your shoulders. Halfclaw and I also heard that the Sextant is missing – it could only have been stolen due to your current weakness. What other calamities will befall us while you remain diminished? For the good of all, you must rectify this at once.'

'I will not take the life of an innocent.'

Frostback lowered her head so that she was level with Karalyn. 'Not all beings are innocent, Karalyn-witch. Find someone guilty; it does not have to be a god – you were powerful enough in your original body. Select a Kellach Brigdomin from the jails of the Empire, and your dream vision will rise again.'

Karalyn lowered her gaze. 'I cannot.'

'This folly may lead to the ruin of all,' said the silver dragon. 'I am tempted to snuff out your life right now, but I fear your vengeance when you return. Come, Calpurnia; let us visit your mother. I have missed my former rider.'

Karalyn said nothing as Frostback walked away. Calpurnia gave a gentle shrug towards Karalyn and Caitlyn, then she ran after her dragon.

'Frostback might be right,' said Caitlyn. 'There are bound to be a few Kellach women in prison, and some of those will be serving sentences for murder.'

'I cannot bear the thought of it, Caitlyn,' she said. 'What right do I have to take the life of another? I know that I have killed before; but each time has been in order to defend those I love. To kill merely to become more powerful cannot be right. I think I will go to Plateau City now. It is nearly noon, and Carden is likely to be in the townhouse. Do you wish to accompany me?'

'Are you going to brush away all of the advice I give you, Mother?' she said. 'I beg you not to visit Carden, and you ignore me. I ask you to consider what Frostback said, and you change the subject. Is it because I am only seventeen? Do you think of me as a child?'

'You killed four Gunstians,' said Karalyn; 'you are not a child.'

'And yet you treat me like one. I think I will remain here today. I would like to be on my own for a while.'

Karalyn nodded. 'All right. I am not sure when I will return; perhaps this evening? It depends on...'

'I know what it depends on, Mother. Be prepared for disappointment with Carden; that's all I'm saying.'

Karalyn took out her Quadrant, then she activated it. The air shimmered, and Karalyn appeared in the quiet, elegant streets of the aristocratic district in Plateau City. She glanced over her shoulder, and saw the spires of the university rise into the cloudy sky. She turned to gaze towards the centre of the city, and the monstrous size of the Blue Palace caught her by surprise. She had viewed it many times before, but never from down in the streets of the city. It so dominated the horizon that it seemed to have been made to the wrong scale. It was beautiful – its exterior glistening in a dozen shades of blue; but it was also overwhelming. It was noon in the height of summer, so the shadow it was casting over the city was at its smallest, and Karalyn wondered what it would feel like in the evening or in winter, when the palace would be blocking the view of the sun for many of the city's inhabitants. Had Thorn considered the effect of her palace on the people who had to live next to it? When Karalyn had first moved to the city, Empress Bridget had lived within a modest villa that had been converted into her palace. From the outside, it had been indistinguishable from dozens of other villas just like it; and she had only moved into the Great Fortress with reluctance. At the time, the Great Fortress had been the largest edifice in the city, but it had been miniscule next to Thorn's Blue Palace.

Karalyn shook her head and turned away. She walked up the street that led to the Holdfast townhouse, passing well-dressed men and women and a squad of soldiers on duty. Few gazed in Karalyn's direction, and she almost felt as though she were invisible. She approached the front door of the townhouse, climbed the steps, and knocked.

A few moments later, a butler opened the door. 'How can I help you, ma'am?'

Karalyn smiled. 'Is Carden at home?'

'I am afraid not, ma'am,' he said. 'May I take a message?'

'Where is he?'

'I am not at liberty to discuss that with strangers, ma'am; my humble apologies.'

'I am his mother,' she said. 'I might not look it, but I am Karalyn Holdfast.'

The butler's eyes widened.

'You must have heard that I had to exchange bodies,' Karalyn went on. 'I know that Kelsey was here to tell the children about it. Well, this is my current form.'

A flicker of suspicion crossed the butler's face.

'You will also know,' said Karalyn, 'that Caitlyn remained with me in Colsbury Castle, while Carden returned here. If you like, I can recite the entire history of this townhouse, ever since it was purchased by my grandfather Godfrey Holdfast over fifty years ago. He bought it when he discovered that my mother was returning from Rahain, as he did not wish to travel back and forth from the Holdings. I was born here, in a room on the second floor, when my mother was living with my Aunt Celine. That was before Celine's husband Vince had been killed on the Sanang frontier. I wasn't here for long, though, and the next time I lived here was when I came to the city after my eighteenth birthday. I lived with Corthie and Laodoc, and we hid Belinda in the attic. We were forced out when Agatha's gods...'

'Please wait here a moment, ma'am,' said the butler.

Karalyn remained at the top of the steps as the butler disappeared inside the townhouse. She waited for a few minutes, then the door opened again.

'Hello, Caelius,' she said.

Kelsey's son eyed her.

'Do you know when Carden will be back?'

'I'm not sure,' he said. 'He's been out all night.'

'Out where?'

'The Kellach Quarter, I reckon,' he said. 'The butler suspects that you might be an imposter. To allay his suspicions, he wants me to ask you a few questions.'

'I suppose that's reasonable,' she said. 'I asked Caitlyn to come with me, but I hadn't realised that she would be needed to verify my identity.'

He gave her a wry look. 'Here's a question I have wanted to ask you for a few years,' he said. 'Why didn't you ever finalise your divorce? Legally-speaking, you are still married to Lucius Cardova.'

'It never crossed my mind,' she said. 'I was sad that my marriage to Lucius was over, but I wanted him to be happy. I wanted your mother to be happy, too; but when I returned to my own world I went back to the Sextant, and I... well, I forgot about the divorce.'

'You are indeed Karalyn Holdfast,' he said. 'Do you want to come in, Aunty?'

'I would like to wait for Carden to get home.'

'Might I offer a suggestion?' he said. 'Do this another time. Carden will not react well to you coming here unannounced like this. He has been drinking heavily since he got back from seeing you on Colsbury, and I have been unable to cheer him up.'

'Is he angry?'

'That would be the understatement of the year, Aunty. Tell me – did Caitlyn offer you any advice about this visit?'

'She told me that it was a bad idea.'

'And yet you came anyway?'

'Carden needs to know that I care about him.'

'I would be delighted to pass on that message.'

'Are you going to let me in?'

'I cannot deny you access to the Holdfast townhouse, Aunty, but I am working on my dissertation.'

'What are you studying?'

'Law. I thought you might have known that.'

'I have been negligent, as I am sure Carden will have mentioned to you. I am trying to make up for that.'

Caelius moved to the side, and gestured towards the interior. Karalyn walked into the townhouse. The butler was close to the kitchen door, his eyes still wary.

'This is definitely my aunt,' said Caelius. 'Could you please make her some tea while she waits for Carden?'

'Certainly, sir,' said the butler.

He walked into the kitchen, and Caelius showed Karalyn into the large front room. Kelsey's son had been working at the dining table, the surface of which was piled high with books and papers.

'Take a seat,' he said.

Karalyn sat down by the table and glanced over the papers. 'What is your dissertation about?'

'The long term implications of the Provincial Council's veto system as pertains to the lack of democracy in Rahain and Rakana.'

Karalyn raised an eyebrow. 'None of that made any sense to me.'

'Then I guess you haven't been paying attention to the political changes that have been taking place in the Empire,' he said. 'I suppose that's a trivial matter compared to the neglect of your children.'

'I am trying to make amends.'

'So you have said.'

Caelius sat down in front of the books and papers, then the butler walked into the room carrying a tray. He set down a teapot, cups, milk and a small bowl of sugar.

'Thanks,' said Caelius.

The butler inclined his head, then he left the room.

'You could have made that tea yourself,' said Karalyn.

Caelius eyed his books. 'Then what would the butler do?'

Karalyn filled two cups with tea as Caelius began taking notes from a large volume on provincial law. Karalyn poured some milk into her cup, and took a sip. She settled down as the room fell into silence, her nerves jangling.

Almost an hour had passed before the front door opened. Karalyn heard footsteps, followed by the hushed tones of the butler.

'She's fucking what?' cried a drunken voice. 'She's here – in the fucking townhouse?'

Caelius glanced up, then he got to his feet and moved himself round to the other side of the table, almost as though he was presenting himself as a barrier to shield Karalyn from the coming fury.

Carden burst through the dining room door, causing it to slam off the opposite wall.

'Let's be reasonable, cousin,' said Caelius.

'Why the fuck did you let her in, Caelius?' Carden cried. 'After everything I told you, and you still let her walk into the house?'

'It is her house, too, cousin,' said Caelius. 'Perhaps you should use your self-healing to sober yourself up. This is probably not the best time to be drunk.'

'Fuck you,' said Carden. He turned to Karalyn. 'Say what you have to say then get out.'

Karalyn stood. 'I wanted you to know how much I love you, son, and that I am so sorry for the years when I wasn't there for you and your sister.'

Carden snorted. 'You're too fucking late,' he said. 'I was six when you started disappearing from my life. Six years old. I barely saw you for years, and you vanished entirely when I was twelve. Thirteen fucking years of neglect cannot be washed away with an apology.'

'What I did was terrible, and I admit that,' said Karalyn. 'I understand your anger.'

'If you understood it, you wouldn't have come here,' said Carden. 'Go on, fuck off.'

'Cousin,' said Caelius, 'I don't want you to regret this when you sober up. Use your damn self-healing.'

'Stay out of this, Caelius,' said Carden. 'It's none of your fucking business.'

'We are Holdfasts,' he said, 'and this is Holdfast business.'

'You're an idiot, Caelius,' said Carden. 'Don't you realise what will happen as soon as my so-called mother dies and gets a better body? She will go straight back to the way she was, and Caitlyn's heart will be broken all over again. I won't let that happen to me. I refuse to let it happen.'

Karalyn nodded. 'Very well. I shall leave.'

'I never want to see you again,' cried Carden. 'Do you hear me? Don't ever come back here. Just leave me alone. I hate you.'

Karalyn bowed her head, then she walked past her son and left the dining room.

'Should I call you a carriage, ma'am?' said the butler.

'Thank you for the tea,' she said. 'I will not be needing a carriage.'

The butler opened the front door of the townhouse, and Karalyn walked back into the street. She suppressed the tears that threatened to spring from her eyes. Not in public, she told herself; she was a Holdfast.

She took out her Quadrant, then hesitated. She dreaded Caitlyn's reaction to what had happened and, like her, wanted to be alone for a while. She gazed at the Blue Palace, and saw a dragon circling overhead.

Halfclaw. Perhaps some company would be better than being alone. She watched as the blue and green dragon alighted onto the sturdy bridge that connected the two towers of the palace, then she brushed her fingers over the surface of her Quadrant. The air shimmered, and she appeared a few yards away from Halfclaw.

The dragon turned to gaze at her. 'Karalyn?'

'How did you know it was me?' she said.

'You have a way about you that remains constant between transformations,' he said. 'What ails you? I can smell the grief.'

'My son hates me.'

'I assume you are talking about Carden?'

'Aye. I have just visited him. He threw me out of the townhouse.'

'You are to be commended for trying, but you must have realised how angry your second son would be. The bigger surprise is that Caitlyn remained with you on Colsbury. She must have a very forgiving heart.'

'She does, but she is also angry with me.'

'Of course she is. Imagine that neither had been upset by your long years of neglect; imagine if they hadn't missed you, hadn't cared. Would you have preferred that?'

'No.'

'My beloved Frostback believes that you are being selfish.'

'She told me as much when I saw her earlier today.'

'Ah, so she has arrived safely on Colsbury? Did she offer to take your life?'

'She did.'

'And you refused?'

'It would mean having to take the life of another,' she said.

'Yes.'

'Do you think Frostback is right?'

'I do not have an answer to that,' he said. 'Can it be correct to hurt one innocent to save many others? I do not know.'

'Right now, my son is of more importance to me,' said Karalyn. 'I shouldn't have come, yet I am glad I did. Maybe Carden needed to shout at me; maybe he needed to get his anger out into the open. At least he knows I made an effort.'

'What will you do now?'

'I might stay here for the rest of the day. Caitlyn warned me what would happen, and I ignored her advice. I need some time to think about what to do.'

'The staff in the palace will no doubt be able to help you find guest quarters.'

'If they believe that I am who I say I am.'

'I will take care of that,' said Halfclaw.

The dragon walked to the western end of the bridge and poked his head through the large, arched opening.

'Courtiers of the palace,' his voice boomed, 'the lady on the bridge is Karalyn Holdfast, and you will treat her with all due courtesy and respect. You have my thanks.'

The dragon turned back to Karalyn.

She bowed her head. 'Thank you, Halfclaw.'

'I will be in the Eastern Tower,' he said, 'should you wish to talk to someone you know.'

'I will bear that in mind.'

She walked off the bridge and entered the Teal Garden. She had heard it being talked about on Colsbury, but the sight of the trees, lawns, flowerbeds and waterfalls gave her pause.

She heard someone clear their throat, then she noticed a small group of courtiers close by.

'Lady Holdfast?' said one.

'I would like to stay in some guest quarters if possible,' she said.

'Of course, my lady,' said one. 'I will show you to a clean set of rooms.'

Karalyn walked through the group of courtiers. One of them was hanging back a little from the others, and he was gazing at her with an odd smile on his face.

'This way, my lady,' said the courtier who had spoken to her.

Karalyn followed him up some steps and into a hallway that was open on one side to the gardens. He took a key from a pocket and unlocked a door.

'Thank you,' she said, as he handed her the key.

'We are at your service, my lady,' he said.

Karalyn walked into the apartment and closed the door behind her. She sat down on a low couch, put her head in her hands, and wept.

CHAPTER 32
THE LORD AND HIS MINIONS

Observatory, Viridia – 25th Abrinch 5281

Lindi stared at Konna and Esher. They were sitting outside on the terrace in front of the half-ruined observatory, and were talking quietly to each other as they gazed out over the vast forest below them. For some reason, Lindi didn't like how close they seemed to be, and their easy familiarity with each other annoyed her.

She caught a glimpse of Esher's left eye, and powered her vision into his mind. She examined the blocks that Cairney had placed onto his powers. Lindi knew that she would be able to remove them, but why would she wish to do such a thing? Esher wasn't her father; he was the most useless Ascendant in history. She wondered if she was jealous about his ability to use the Sextant. Perhaps she had been a little over-proud of being the group's only Sextant-user; a little too keen to show off. Regardless, Cairney had ruined that by bringing Esher to Viridia.

She turned to the last orders that Cairney had imprinted into Esher's head. He had said the same thing to Konna, and Lindi could sense the physical changes Cairney's words had made to Esher's mind.

You will not try to escape, and you will not try to harm yourself or others. That was what Cairney had said to them both, and they had been powerless to resist. Lindi would be able to free them from the compulsion but, again, why would she do that? If she followed Cairney through to the end, she would become a mighty queen. It was true that she found Cairney to be arrogant and overbearing, but did it matter, when the prizes on offer were so appealing? With Cairney as Emperor, the Holdfast gods would rule. They could get rid of the various forms of democracy, close the universities, destroy the stockpiles of god-killing weaponry, and get things back to the way they should be. If that meant having to humour Cairney for a while, it was a price she was willing to pay.

Esher narrowed his eyes a little, then he peered into the shadows where Lindi had been sitting.

'She's been spying on us,' said Konna.

'I have not,' said Lindi. 'Why would I spy on you, Konna? You bore me.'

'Do you want to join us?' said Esher. 'We were talking about what Cairney might do next.'

'I'm not going to discuss that with you,' said Lindi.

'She means that she doesn't know,' said Konna. 'If Cairney trusted her, he wouldn't have brought you here, Esher.'

'It's not my fault that you refused to help your brother,' said Lindi. 'When I am a queen ruling over a vast realm, you will be lucky if you are allowed to clean my toilets.'

'Could it be,' said Esher, 'that Cairney has compelled her to support him, but that she is unaware of this? I cannot see how any sane god would wish to follow a man like Cairney.'

Lindi laughed. 'That just proves how little you know, Esher,' she said. 'Why wouldn't a sane god wish to put a cousin onto the throne? Cairney ain't perfect, but he's better than any damn mortal.'

Konna smiled at her. 'But I thought you were going to be Empress, Lindi.'

Lindi shrugged. 'Compromises had to be made.'

'By you,' said Konna; 'not by Cairney.'

'I will still be a queen – what will you be?'

'But why now?' said Esher. 'Why not wait? I know of Lord Naxor's plan, and while it certainly aims for ultimate power, it does so without the need to overthrow the existing establishment. People will die if Cairney gets his way. And do you honestly believe the Imperial Army will happily switch sides if Cairney assassinates the Empress? What about the Imperial Marines? Thousands of them have already received the new Jackdaw weapons.'

'Do you hear yourself?' said Lindi. 'You counsel patience, and then you tell us that the new god-killing weapons are being distributed among the mortals as quickly as possible? The Jackdaws and the Battanaras are the reason we must act now; otherwise, it will be too late.'

'I do agree with that part,' said Konna. 'If the mortals keep improving their weapons, they will be able to obliterate us.'

'Then why don't you join us?' said Lindi.

'Because my brother is a sadistic, cold-hearted murderer.'

'I know,' said Lindi. 'We should be grateful that he's on our side.'

'The only side he is on is his own,' said Konna.

'All right,' said Lindi; 'let's say that your opinion of him is correct. Will it matter in the future? If Cairney is Emperor of the Sapphire Throne, then we can rule the other worlds that we can see through the Sextant; or we could even create our own. The most important thing, by far, is stopping the mortals from learning how to kill us. After that, we can argue among ourselves. We could join with the gods of the Dominion, and share the worlds between us.'

'This conviction that you both share,' said Esher, 'that the mortals are making weapons solely for the purpose of exterminating the gods – it is mistaken. The mortals don't want this. They want to live in peace and security; they want plentiful food and decent jobs. They want to live comfortable lives, and get married and have children. They aren't all conspiring about how to kill gods. I was a mortal, if you recall, while I lived in Jezra. Not once did I ever hear any mortal say that they wanted to eradicate the gods.'

'Lord Elmhirst thinks it is inevitable,' said Konna. 'He told us that he had seen this happen before, when mortals learn too much. At first, everything seems fine, but the wealth and power accumulated by the gods soon attracts envy and greed from the mortals. They want what we have, and they are able to take it from us by force. That's how it starts, and the more the mortals know, the worse the war that follows will be. The only way to break the cycle is to keep the mortals uneducated.'

Esher stared at her. 'What would your father think if he heard you say those words, Konna? Are you suggesting that we permanently oppress the mortals, keeping them down, forcing them to live as peasants or ignorant labourers? Our slaves, in other words? You think mortals should be our slaves? Isn't that why the Holdfasts fought the Ascendants – for the freedom to live however they please without the tyranny of the gods?'

Konna's features hardened in anger. 'I did not say that I wanted mortals to be our slaves. I was telling you what Lord Elmhirst thinks.'

'I like it when you argue,' said Lindi. 'Konna, you are only an inch away from what Cairney, Carter and I believe. I don't think it would take too much to persuade you to join us. But as for you, Esher, your views are hopelessly muddled. You have to pick a side; it's as simple as that.'

Esher shook his head. 'I would have thought, Lindi, that you would be more sympathetic towards mortals. Your brother has no self-healing – do you value him any less because of this?'

'Don't be ridiculous,' said Lindi. 'I don't *hate* mortals; I just think that the gods need to be protected from them.'

The air shimmered a few yards away, and Cairney appeared. He tucked his Quadrant behind his breastplate, and laughed.

'I found her,' he said. 'I was looking right at her, and she didn't recognise me.'

'Who did you find?' said Lindi.

'Who do you think? Karalyn. She is alone; she is vulnerable.' He glanced towards the entrance of the observatory. 'Carter; come here.'

Carter walked out of the building, covered in sawdust and sweat.

'I'm making chairs for all of us,' he said, 'but I need more timber and nails. Could I give you a list, brother? If yer too busy to go, then maybe Lindi could fetch what I need.'

Cairney raised an eyebrow. 'Stop wasting your time on trying to improve our living conditions,' he said. 'I need you to focus on the plan to take over the Empire, not on furniture.'

Carter frowned. 'But we need supplies brought up here just to survive. Food, drink...'

'Then we shall get food and drink,' said Cairney; 'forget the rest. Do we have any shackles?'

'Eh, no. We have rope.'

'Rope will do,' said Cairney. 'Get some ready. Lindi – to the Sextant.'

Lindi got to her feet. She didn't like it when Cairney snapped orders at her, but she knew she had to play along. She told herself to be patient. Everything would be better when Cairney took over. He would sit on his throne, while Lindi had an entire realm to rule.

She walked with Cairney through the chamber where the Sextant sat inert. Cairney withdrew the Weathervane from its scabbard, and inserted it into the flank of the device. The Sextant began to hum, and Lindi stepped forward, her palm outstretched.

'Wait,' said Cairney. I will tell you exactly what to look for, and what to do. Do not deviate from my instructions – is that clear? If you do, I will get Esher to do it for me.'

Lindi rolled her eyes.

'Karalyn is in the Blue Palace,' Cairney went on.

'The Blue Palace is shielded from Quadrants,' said Lindi, 'so I doubt that...'

'Be quiet,' he said. 'She is in an apartment off the Teal Garden. That area is not shielded.'

'Don't tell me to be quiet.'

'I will if you interrupt me,' he said. 'I find your argumentative demeanour amusing, Lindi, but if it starts to become tiresome, I will remove your self-healing and beat you.'

Lindi opened her mouth to protest, then she looked away. She was unsure if Cairney was strong enough to carry out his threat, but she wanted to avoid a confrontation with him. If their wills battled each other, and she was able to resist, then what would he do? He needed her to be subservient; anything less might be intolerable to him. And if his will triumphed over hers, and he was able to block her powers on a whim? She couldn't think of anything worse. Appease him, she told herself. For now at least, appease him.

'Karalyn is in an apartment on the second floor of the Teal Gardens, to the right of the central waterfall,' said Cairney. 'Use the Sextant to locate her, and bring her here.'

Lindi nodded, then she placed her hand onto the Surface of the Sextant.

What is your desire, Lindi?

'Show me the Blue Palace in Plateau City,' she said.

Cairney also placed his hand onto the device, as Lindi's vision clouded over. She found herself looking down on the enormous palace, and sent her vision closer to the middle bridge that spanned the gap between the two horn-like towers.

'This will soon be my home,' Cairney said. 'It was very considerate of Thorn to construct a palace worthy of the gods.'

Lindi laughed. 'Where will I live?'

'I have yet to decide that,' said Cairney. 'I was thinking perhaps that Dragon Eyre might be a suitable realm for you to govern on my behalf, Lindi. You are familiar with the ways of dragons. Proceed into the Teal Garden.'

Lindi sent her vision through the large, arched opening in the flank of the Western Tower of the palace, and gazed at the large gardens. She caught sight of the central waterfall, and moved her vision closer to the row of balconies jutting out from the apartments of the second floor.

'The windows to the left,' said Cairney.

Lindi's vision passed the ivy and flowerbeds, and passed through an open window. There, sitting on a low couch with her head in her hands, was Karalyn.

'Why is she weeping?' said Lindi.

'Her son Carden told her to fuck off,' said Cairney.

'That seems a little harsh.'

'Karalyn has been a terrible mother to her immortal children,' said

Cairney. 'I spoke to Carden yesterday evening. I disguised myself as a young marine officer, and enticed him into a conversation about his future. He might be willing to join us; he is angry and bitter, and his heart is ripe for rebellion. He would be a powerful ally.' He glanced at Lindi. 'Bring Karalyn here.'

'Sextant,' said Lindi, 'transport Karalyn Holdfast here. Do it now.'

The connection to Karalyn Holdfast has been broken.

'Don't give me your shit, Sextant,' she said. 'I can see her. Transport the woman I can see here. Do it now.'

The connection to Karalyn Holdfast has been broken.

'Fuck,' she muttered. 'The Sextant won't do it, Cairney. There's something about Karalyn that is blocking it.'

Cairney took his hand off the Sextant. 'Then we shall have to retrieve her in person.'

He walked to the side of the Sextant and slid the Weathervane out. At once, Lindi's vision of the Blue Palace ceased, and the Sextant fell silent. Cairney strode out of the Observatory, and Lindi hurried after him.

'Lindi and I are going to Plateau City,' said Cairney. 'When we return, we shall have Karalyn with us. Be ready with the rope, Carter.'

Carter frowned. 'And what are we going to do with Karalyn?' he said.

'I shall subdue her,' said Cairney.

'How?' said Konna.

'Ye cannae kill her, brother,' said Carter. 'It would be wrong, and she'd only come back stronger.'

'My plan depends upon keeping her alive,' said Cairney. 'We need her trapped within her current form; unable to die, unable to leave.'

'But how?' said Konna.

Cairney turned to his sister. 'Do you wish to help me? Perhaps later I will allow you to do so. Stand by my side, Lindi; I shall now assume the disguise of a soldier in the Imperial Guard.'

Cairney's form seemed to blur a little round the edges, and Lindi raised an eyebrow. If she squinted at him, she could see a hazy image of a different man – a man in the uniform of the soldiers on duty in the Blue Palace, but she knew it was an illusion; she could still see Cairney behind the disguise.

'Pyre's tits,' cried Carter. 'It works. It never used to work on me, brother, but it does now.'

Cairney smiled. 'My powers have been growing,' he said. 'Do you agree, Lindi?'

'Oh yes,' she said. 'I wouldn't have known it was you if I hadn't seen you transform before my eyes.'

Cairney eyed her, then he took out his Quadrant. 'We shall be back shortly.'

He activated the Quadrant, the air shimmered, then Lindi found herself in the Teal Garden.

'Why didn't we just appear in her apartment?' she said.

'Since we had to come in person,' said Cairney, 'I have decided to make a scene. The Empress will begin to fear me, if she learns that Karalyn has been taken. That would not be the case if she merely disappeared without trace.'

A group of a dozen soldiers and courtiers emerged from a building, attracted by the sight of Cairney and Lindi's arrival.

'Might I ask your business here?' said a courtier.

'You may,' said Cairney. He raised his hand, and the heads of every courtier and soldier exploded. More soldiers ran out from another entrance. Two aimed and fired their Jackdaw weapons, and Cairney was struck in the stomach. He staggered backwards, his breastplate pierced by the lead projectile. Blood flowed down from his waist, then he swept his arm from left to right, and the soldiers fell, their flesh melting from their faces.

Cairney glanced down at the hole in his breastplate. 'Thank you for the assistance, Lindi.'

'I didn't come here to kill soldiers and servants,' she said. 'Did that hurt?'

Cairney triggered his Quadrant, and they appeared on a balcony. Cairney swung open the door and they entered the apartment.

Karalyn was on her feet, her eyes wide as she reached for her own Quadrant.

'*Do not move*,' said Cairney.

Karalyn froze.

Cairney walked up to her, while Lindi lingered by the balcony door.

'What do we have here?' said Cairney. 'The last time we met, Karalyn, you were my jailer.' He laughed as he regarded her. 'I knew you would eventually make a mistake, but so soon? A fragile old woman? A mortal? This is almost disappointing, Karalyn – you are making it too easy.'

He slapped her across the face, and she fell to the floor.

'I told you that I would kill you,' said Cairney, as he lowered himself to crouch next to her. 'But, clearly, that would no longer be in my best interests. I want you to stay exactly as you are. *You may speak*.'

'Cairney?' said the old woman. 'Is that you?'

'Obviously,' he said, as he dropped his powers and revealed his true form to her, 'though it is nice to know that my disguise fooled you.'

'It is not too late, Cairney,' said Karalyn. 'Hand yourself over to the Empress, and tell her that you have changed.'

'You are right,' he said. 'I have changed. Eight years of living alone, fending for myself, has hardened me. My time in exile prepared me, Karalyn, for all that I now must do. I acted rashly the last time I tried to kill Thorn. I was overconfident; perhaps even a touch arrogant, and my plans were... they were terrible – let's be honest.' He gripped her by the hair. 'One can only learn from their mistakes; don't you agree?'

'You don't need to do this,' said Karalyn.

'Oh but I do,' he said. He tapped his breastplate. 'Do you see the hole? One of the Empire's new weapons did that. If the soldier's aim had been a little higher, he might have blown my head off. Can you imagine that – a lowly mortal soldier, capable of killing one of the greatest gods in existence? This is intolerable, Karalyn.' He reached out with his free hand, grasped onto one of Karalyn's fingers, and bent it backwards, breaking the bones.

Karalyn cried out in pain, and Lindi shifted uncomfortably.

'Let the pain fill your mind,' said Cairney. 'Beg me to heal you.'

Karalyn forced her mouth closed.

'*Beg me to heal you.*'

'Please, Cairney,' Karalyn said. 'Please heal my finger.'

Cairney laughed. 'No.'

'We're wasting time,' said Lindi.

'If you are squeamish about what I am doing, you should admit it,' said Cairney.

'I'm not squeamish, but I don't like it,' said Lindi.

Cairney shrugged, then he removed Karalyn's Quadrant from her pocket, and placed it behind his breastplate. He then moved down to Karalyn's left ankle. He put his hand round it, and squeezed. Karalyn cried out again, and Lindi looked away as she heard the old woman's bones snap.

'Now she won't be able to flee,' said Cairney.

He got to his feet, and took out his Quadrant.

'Where are you taking me?' whispered Karalyn.

'Viridia,' said Cairney, 'but you won't be there for long. I will be placing you into another location, one from which you will never be able to escape.'

'Viridia?' gasped Karalyn.

'Do you know it?' he said. 'What am I saying? Of course you know it. You know every world, don't you, Karalyn?'

He triggered his Quadrant, and Lindi found herself back on the terrace outside the half-ruined observatory. Konna and Esher were still sitting there, and both rose to their feet at the sight of Karalyn.

'*Sit back down and remain still*,' said Cairney.

'You got her,' said Konna, as she and Esher sat down again.

'How fucking observant of you,' said Cairney.

'You have hurt her,' said Esher.

'Again, I salute your observational skills,' said Cairney. 'I broke one finger and one ankle. Her bones are very fragile; it hardly took any pressure to crush them. It's amazing, isn't it? Look how weak she is. Karalyn the mighty; Karalyn, the greatest and most powerful being to have ever lived – humbled, frightened. In pain.'

Esher turned his gaze to Lindi. 'And you helped him. How could you, Lindi?'

'I didn't do nothing,' said Lindi.

'She is right about that,' said Cairney. 'Lindi was quite useless.'

'Why didn't you try to stop him, Lindi?' said Esher.

'She knows I am far too powerful for her,' said Cairney. 'She fears me, as it should be; yet her greed and ambition bind her to my side.'

Carter walked out of the building, a loop of rope held in his hand. He frowned at the sight of Karalyn.

'Behold our great enemy, brother,' said Cairney. 'Karalyn could have saved our father; she knows it – we all know it. Instead, she did nothing. She failed in her duties, her responsibilities to her kin, and this is her punishment. The rope will not be necessary. I will find shackles in the place where I shall next take her.'

Carter drew his gaze away from Karalyn. 'What place?'

'I will not say,' said Cairney. 'The fewer who know, the fewer will be able to have their heads read by Cael or Kyra. They will be harder to deal with than their mother. They will be searching for her; therefore, I have to place her where she cannot be found.'

'But we have to keep her alive,' said Carter.

Cairney smiled.

'If she dies,' said Carter, 'then...'

'I know what will happen if she dies,' said Cairney; 'there is no need to repeat yourself. Do you imagine for a moment that I haven't gone through this scenario a thousand times during my exile? – and yet you speak to me as though I were a child, brother.'

'I, uh... I didnae mean it,' said Carter.

'I am old,' gasped Karalyn. 'Whatever you do to me, I will not live beyond another decade, maybe two. When I come back, Cairney, I will not forgive this. I could have executed you after you tried to assassinate Kelsey and Thorn; I could have allowed Cael to hammer nails into your eyes. I didn't do either; I exiled you. I even supplied you with books.'

'I know,' said Cairney; 'I read them all several times over – even Kelsey's *History*. They were very useful, Karalyn; I learned much from them about how the Empire works.' He crouched next to her again. 'Did you ever dream that those books would help me to compose a new plan? The Empire is mine, Karalyn. You were the only barrier to my success, yet you threw away your advantage. Do you have anything to say to posterity? Any messages you wish to hand down?'

Karalyn reached out with her uninjured hand, and touched Cairney's arm. He raised an eyebrow, then a stream of blue flame appeared on his skin, rushing up from his arm to his bare neck, then his face. Cairney cried out in agony, as the flames swept over his body. He pulled his arm away from Karalyn, and toppled backwards, screaming, as his self-healing tried to contain the low, blue flames.

'What the fuck is happening?' Carter shouted.

'She has the Gift of Immolation,' cried Esher.

Karalyn turned her hand and pointed it at Lindi.

On instinct, Lindi raised her own hand. 'Sleep.'

Karalyn's eyes closed.

Lindi ran over to Cairney, then she sent a powerful blast of healing powers into him. Cairney squirmed and writhed. The flesh on his face was scorched and red, his eyebrows gone, as blue flames issued from his mouth. Lindi kept up the flow of healing powers, and the flames began to die down. Smoke belched up from Cairney's flesh as it repaired itself. Cairney cried out, and the fires were extinguished. He lay on the ground, panting and shaking, his breastplate charred, and his clothes still smoking.

Carter knelt by him. 'Can ye hear me, brother?'

Cairney opened his eyes. The burns on his face and neck were healing themselves, but he looked exhausted by the effort.

'You were struck by a Gunstian Gift,' said Carter. 'Karalyn is Gifted.'

Cairney's gaze went to Lindi. 'You... you were of some assistance; I will grant you that.'

'I saved your arse, you mean,' said Lindi. 'You're welcome.'

Cairney sat up, then he noticed that Karalyn was lying unconscious a few yards away, and his face contorted with fury.

'Who sent her to sleep?' he cried, as he rushed to her side. 'Which fool did this?'

'I did it,' said Lindi. 'The bitch pointed at me.'

Cairney slapped Karalyn across the face. '*Wake up!*' he shouted.

'What's the problem?' said Lindi. 'She can't do anything while she's sleeping.'

'You empty-headed imbecile,' Cairney cried. 'She can only use her dream vision while asleep. She could be talking to Cael right now.'

Karalyn stirred, and her eyes opened.

'*You will answer my questions truthfully*,' said Cairney. '*Did you use dream powers just now?*'

'Aye,' gasped Karalyn.

'*To whom did you speak?*'

'To my son Cael.'

Cairney clenched his fists and roared in anger as he got to his feet. He stared at Lindi, his teeth bared, and she backed away.

'I didn't know,' she said. 'Everyone told me she was powerless.'

Cairney walked to the edge of the terrace and stared out over the vast forest.

'They will be coming,' he said.

'Who – Cael?' said Carter.

'Aye,' said Cairney. 'Maybe... Maybe Lindi's stupidity can be turned to our advantage. I always knew I would have to face Cael at some point – why not now?'

He turned. 'Let us prepare ourselves,' he said. 'Today we shall capture not only the mother, but her son, too.'

CHAPTER 33
THE OBSERVATORY

Northern Aucteran – 9th Lexinch 1613

Cael gazed down from the flank of the mountain at the valley below him. He was sitting next to Elmhirst, and both of them had sent out their vision to examine the layout of the Gunstian encampment. The large command tents were in the centre, from where rows of smaller tents stretched out, filling an entire corner of the green valley. On an open stretch of field, Gunstian volunteers were training with swords and crossbows, supervised by officers and sergeants from the Gunstian army; while tucked away in another corner, and surrounded by soldiers, were close to two hundred Rakanese civilians kidnapped from Amatskouri.

'We will keep the plan simple,' said Cael, as he drew his vision back to his body. 'Battanaras first, to soften up the Gifted, then you and your death-powered gods can strike the centre to finish them off. The Aucterians and marines can deal with the volunteers, but two companies of marines will be diverted to release the hostages.'

'Shall we take prisoners?' said Elmhirst.

'There's no need,' said Cael. 'The bastards desire martyrdom; let's see that they get it.'

Elmhirst raised an eyebrow. 'I thought you were opposed to that sort of thing.'

'Are they civilians?' said Cael. 'They volunteered to kill our people, Elmhirst. They are armed combatants.'

'I'm not arguing,' said Elmhirst. 'Which end of the portal do you want?'

'I'll take this side,' said Cael. He pointed down the slope. 'I will position myself in that gap between the tents and the training ground, with the portal orientated towards the command pavilion. Remember, Battanaras first, then pile in with your gods. No warnings, no pauses. Have the Battanaras fired the moment the portal opens.'

Elmhirst laughed. 'I don't recall you being appointed as my superior officer, Cael.'

'The Empire has two hundred civilians down there,' said Cael. 'If it were the other way around, I would be happy for the Dominion to take the lead.'

'I was teasing you,' said Elmhirst. 'Your plan is sound. Shall we say ten minutes from now?'

Cael nodded. 'I will see you down there.'

Elmhirst got to his feet, inclined his head, and vanished. Cael took out his own Quadrant, and judged the distance and altitude. He quickly lit a cigarette, took a few draws, then stubbed it out. He knew that he would have to report to the Empress as soon as the operation was over, but he tried to keep that out of his thoughts. His priorities were the Rakanese civilians and the Quadrants stolen by the Gunstians – everything else would have to wait.

Cael stared at the encampment. If the attack was a success, then the threat from the Gunstians would be over; but if they managed to hold on to even a single Quadrant, then Cael had no doubt that they would rebuild their strength and renew their attacks. He tried not to allow his hopes to dominate his thinking. If, perhaps, he could prove to the Empress that the Gunstians were no longer able to assault the Empire, then she might back down over her command to destroy the Temple of the Great Mother. He pushed the thought out of his head and told himself to concentrate.

Cael got to his feet and activated his Quadrant. He appeared in the midst of the valley, less than fifty yards from the large command tents and central pavilion.

You cannot see me, he said in Gunstian. *You cannot see me.*

He could see officers and Gifted agents moving around the pavilion. As far as he knew, the Gunstians had two Quadrants left – were both within the encampment? Did they have others he didn't know about? He glanced over to the corner where the Rakanese civilians were being held. Gunstian volunteers were in the process of building a fence to pen them in – did that mean they were intending to keep them alive? The majority of the captured civilians were young men and women, people who had been relaxing on the beach before beginning their jobs for the day – buying coffee from the stalls, listening to the singers and musicians, and talking as though everything was normal. And then the Gunstians had attacked, and the nightmare had begun.

Cael felt anger flow through him. He checked his location, then triggered the Quadrant, connecting it to the one in Elmhirst's possession.

The air behind Cael began to move, then a black swirling void appeared. A few volunteers on the training ground stopped what they were doing to watch, then the void cleared, revealing four tiered rows of Imperial Marines. Each row held fifteen Battanaras, and Elmhirst raised his hand.

The noise almost deafened Cael, as sixty Battanara projectiles were fired at the same time. The projectiles shot through the portal, each aimed at the central tents and the large pavilion where the Gifted were based, then the explosions roared out in flashes of flames and billows of smoke. The centre of the encampment seemed to disappear amid the thrown debris and clouds of thick dark smoke. Cael stayed by the edge of the portal, as the sixty Battanara-wielding marines moved aside in quick order. Two dozen gods and demigods in armour poured through the gap, charging into the field. They raised their hands, and sent waves of death powers into the destruction by the centre of the encampment. Screams echoed then were cut off short. The gods and demigods drew their Tempest-edged weapons, and ran into the smoke. Next came the Imperial Marines, dividing into two as they streamed through the portal – some charging towards the volunteers on the training ground; the rest running towards the hostages.

You can see me, said Cael.

A marine lieutenant approached the edge of the portal, and Cael handed him the Quadrant.

'Keep the portal open until I return,' said Cael.

Aucterian soldiers with shields and pikes charged through the portal, and made for the training ground, joining with the marines as they cut their way through the Gunstians. Cael drew his Jackdaw, and ran in the direction of the hostages. A Gunstian soldier crossed his path as he tried to flee in panic, and Cael shot him in the head, the lead projectile ripping off half of his skull. By the hostages, the panicking Gunstians tried to flee or surrender, but the marines gave them no quarter. Cael holstered his Jackdaw and drew a sword, and joined the attack.

One hour later, every Gunstian in the encampment was dead. Marines were digging through the smouldering ruins by the centre of the camp, looking for evidence of slain Gifted agents and, more importantly, their Quadrants.

'Seven casualties,' said Elmhirst.

Cael kept his gaze on the rescued Rakanese civilians, as Aucterian soldiers handed out food and water canisters.

'Did you hear me, my friend?' said Elmhirst. 'We killed close to a thousand, for seven casualties, of which there were only two fatalities. I have already healed the five who were injured. Not a single Gifted agent had time to react to our attack – we were swift and overwhelming. Gods and Battanaras – what a combination.'

'I thought you were scared of our new weapons?'

'They terrify me,' said Elmhirst.

'The Empire will never use them upon the gods of the Dominion,' said Cael. 'We are at peace.'

'So you say, but you forget what is, to gods at any rate, an obvious problem. What happens a century from now? Mortals come and go, their governments change with the wind, and attitudes shift. Can you seriously promise that every future government of the Empire will think as you do? You say *never*, but you cannot promise *never* – such is the way with mortals.'

A marine captain approached. 'We have counted the bodies of at least seven Gifted agents, my lords,' he said. He withdrew two Quadrants from a pocket. 'And we recovered these.'

Cael exhaled in relief. 'Thank you, Captain.'

'A complete success,' said Elmhirst.

'I owe you for this, Elmhirst,' said Cael. 'You didn't have to give us the location of the camp, but you did.'

'I knew you would want to be part of any attack.'

Cael took the Quadrants from the marine captain, and handed them to Elmhirst. 'Take these, as thanks.'

Elmhirst smiled, then he handed one back to Cael. 'One each, I think, my friend.'

'Very well,' said Cael. 'I had better get the hostages back to Amatskouri.'

Elmhirst extended a hand, and Cael shook it.

'Gather up the marines and the civilians,' Cael said to the marine captain, as Elmhirst walked in the direction of his armoured gods. 'We shall first open a portal to Amatskouri, and that will require sending someone in advance, to control the other side. We shall...'

Cael.

He blinked.

Help me, Cael.

Mother?

Cairney has me; I am on Viridia.

Where?

On a mountaintop, next to the ruins of a large observatory, on a world called Viridia; a Doomed World. Please come; it has taken me longer than I had hoped to find you, and I am running out of time.

I'll be there.

'Sir?' said the marine captain.

Cael cleared his mind. His mother had gone.

'Are you all right, sir?' said the captain.

'Change of plan,' said Cael. He handed the recovered Quadrant to the captain. 'Use this to ferry the hostages to Amatskouri, then take the marines back to Yearning. I will be needing my Quadrant. Is that clear?'

The captain frowned. 'Aye, sir.'

Cael ran after Elmhirst, who was speaking to his assembled gods and demigods.

'Elmhirst,' Cael cried.

'Cael?'

'How do I get to Viridia?' he said.

Elmhirst raised an eyebrow.

Cael took out his Quadrant. 'Show me.'

'Viridia?' said Elmhirst. 'Why would you wish to visit such a place? The mosquitoes are almost as terrifying as your Battanaras.'

'Please,' said Cael.

Elmhirst narrowed his eyes, then he reached out and mimed the finger actions over the Quadrant.

'That will take you to the main settlement,' he said; 'it is the only one left upon that world, and it has almost been completely evacuated. The officer in charge is a Banner colonel by the name of Quintus.'

'Thank you,' said Cael.

He activated the Quadrant, and appeared on the middle balcony of the Summer Palace on Colsbury. Cole and Arrosa were sitting together by a table, and both got to their feet.

'How did it go?' said Cole.

'Fine,' said Cael. 'Load four Jackdaws; you're coming with me.'

'Where? Are we going to the Gunstian encampment?' said Cole.

'Not quite,' said Cael. 'Get me those Jackdaws and meet me back here. And put on a breastplate.'

Cole eyed him, then he hurried into the palace.

'What is going on?' said Arrosa. 'The Empress wanted to see you the moment you got back.'

'The Empress will have to wait,' he said.

'But...'

'My mother is in trouble, Arrosa,' he said. 'Listen to me – Cairney has taken her to a Doomed World called Viridia. That's all I know. She reached out to me.'

'But if Cairney has her... Cael, this could be a trap. What if Cairney ordered your mother to contact you? You should wait. Take an entire battalion; or take Frostback.'

'Cole and I can handle Cairney.'

'You could when he was sixteen,' she said. 'What if he's stronger? What if Lindi and Carter are helping him – that's three gods you will have to fight.'

'Then it's lucky I have a good aim.'

'But what's the worst Cairney could do to someone like Karalyn? If he kills her, she will be free of that Gunstian body; therefore, he will have to keep her safe.'

'Is it that simple?' said Cael. 'I can't leave her in Cairney's hands.'

'Then at least plug up your ears,' she said. 'We did that when we went to Ulna, and it worked – we couldn't hear his voice.'

'All right,' he said.

Arrosa eyed the other tables, then she walked over to a group from the legal department who were poring over documents. She spoke to them for a moment, and returned with a lump of red sealing wax.

'You should tell the Empress what you are doing,' she said.

'I can't risk it,' said Cael, taking the wax. 'Speed is the only advantage I have.'

'Unless Cairney knows you're coming.'

Cole ran out from the palace, carrying a large bag.

'I have four loaded Jackdaws,' he said, 'along with plenty of lead projectiles and packets of Ectus powder. Where are we going?'

Arrosa put a hand to her face. 'Don't go,' she said. 'I don't like this.'

Cael kissed her. 'I'm sorry, but I have no choice. We will be back soon.'

'You had better be,' she said.

Cael rolled his shoulders.

You cannot see us.

He saw Arrosa's face fall as Cole and Cael were rendered invisible. He stared at his wife for a moment, seeing her close to despair, and almost hesitated. He moved his fingers to his Quadrant, as Cole watched him, then he activated it.

The heat hit them like a wall, along with the oppressive humidity. Cael gazed at their surroundings – large piles of cut timber sat in yards, next to ramshackle wooden buildings. A few soldiers were sitting in the shade of a large tree by the edge of a forest that surrounded the small settlement.

'We are invisible,' said Cael, 'and we are on Viridia.'

'I have heard the name,' said Cole. 'A Doomed World. I am already sweating; this is worse than the Holdings in the height of summer.'

'My mother is somewhere on this world,' he said. 'Atop a mountain.'

'What would possess her to come here?'

Cael eyed his cousin. 'Cairney brought her. My mother has been captured, and we are going to rescue her.'

Cole said nothing.

'Well?' said Cael. 'Are you with me?'

'I am always with you, cousin,' said Cole, 'but there are hundreds of well-armed marines on Colsbury.'

'And hundreds of well-armed marines are far more likely to shoot my mother by mistake,' said Cael. 'While that might not actually be so bad, it's better if we go alone.'

Cole narrowed his eyes. 'Now I understand why Arrosa was looking so upset,' he said. 'Did she try to talk you into taking help along with you, is that it? And you refused?'

'We don't need any help,' said Cael. 'One shot, aimed at Cairney's head, and it will be over.'

'Are you going to kill him?'

'Of course I am going to fucking kill him,' said Cael. 'He has escaped, and the first thing he does is abduct my mother, when she is at her weakest. What else do we need?'

'What about Lindi and Carter?'

'Their fate will depend upon what they do when we bring Cairney down.' He gazed around, and saw a ridge of high mountain peaks in the distance. He triggered the Quadrant, and they appeared on a high outcrop of rock well above the treeline.

'That feels better,' said Cole, as a cooler breeze washed over them. 'My shirt is sticking to my back.'

'Start scanning the neighbouring peaks,' said Cael. 'Look for the ruins of a large building – an observatory.'

They sat on the rough ground with their backs to each other. Cael lit a cigarette but, again, he stubbed it out after only two puffs. He sent his vision across the vast mountain range, looking for anything that might resemble a built structure. He caught sight of a desert beyond the furthest reaches of the forest, then he wheeled back to the mountains for a closer look. Goats were scampering up a steep track, and birds were circling over the sweltering woodlands, but Cael saw nothing that looked like a building.

Cole tapped him on the shoulder.

'Aye?' said Cael.

'Four miles to the east of here,' said Cole. 'Ruins, and signs of recent habitation.'

Cael sent his vision out again, and raced it to the east. The four miles sped under him, and then Cael saw it – a collection of tall ruins close to the barren summit of a mountain. Some of the chambers had been re-roofed with fresh timber and thatch, and a ring of blackened stones on a terrace outside showed where a hearth had been burning.

Cael's vision entered the building through an open doorway. Several unfinished chairs were laid out on a workbench, along with tools and cuts of timber, and there were crates lined up against one wall. Cael went through into the next room. His mother was there. She was awake, but her left ankle was being bandaged by Konna and Esher. None of them were speaking. As Cael was about to enter his mother's mind, Carter and Lindi appeared. They were smiling and looked relaxed, and they handed out mugs of water to the others. Cael frowned, then he noticed the Sextant sitting in the corner of the room. It had been deactivated, the Tempest sword removed from its flank. Cael went back to his mother, and eased into her mind.

Do not react, Mother, he said. *Cole and I will be with you soon. Where is Cairney?*

He has taken the Quadrant and gone.

All right. Stay where you are; this won't take long.

Cael broke off the connection, then he turned, and saw Cole speaking to several squads of well-armed marines on the wide outcrop of rock.

Cole glanced at him, and shrugged. 'Sometimes, cousin,' he said, 'you can be too obstinate for your own good.'

'You went back to Colsbury?'

'No, I went to Yearning and collected the on-duty units who were ready to leave.'

'You needn't have bothered. I spoke to my mother – Cairney isn't here.'

'How should we feel about that? Relieved or disappointed?'

'It will make it easier, but he will still be on the loose.'

'Yes,' said Cole, 'but we will have separated him from the Sextant. You could then use it to find him.'

'Good point,' said Cael; 'although Cairney must have the Weathervane.'

'There are now plenty of Tempest swords in the Empire; one of them is bound to fit.'

'The others might resist us.'

'I cannot believe that Esher is there willingly,' said Cole. 'Remember how easy it was for Cairney to manipulate him eight years ago.'

'Then we'll assume that Esher might be under Cairney's control right now,' said Cael. 'As for Konna and Carter, and Lindi, we should assume that they are there willingly. We might be wrong, but we don't want to get stabbed in the back.'

'But neither should we kill any of them before they have had a chance to explain themselves.'

'Agreed.' Cael took out the sealing wax that Arrosa had given him. 'I don't think we'll be needing this; but we should be quick, in case Cairney returns. We'll go in – with your marines - and use the Quadrant to take everything and everyone out of there. We'll evacuate to Yearning – it's contained and isolated – and we can deal with Lindi and the others there without having to worry about Cairney.'

Cole opened his bag, and handed two Jackdaws to Cael. He holstered one, and gripped the other in his right hand, keeping the Quadrant in his left; while Cole had a loaded Jackdaw in each hand. Cole nodded to the officer leading the marines, and they began to load their own Jackdaws.

Cael waited until the marines were ready, then he triggered the Quadrant with one hand. The air shimmered, and they appeared on the terrace outside the ruined building.

'Take up positions around the building,' Cole said to the marines. 'Make sure no one gets in or out.'

'Aye, sir,' said the officer, and the marines split into two columns and began to encircle the ruined structure.

Cael and Cole entered the first chamber, and crept through it to the entrance to the second. Cael peered inside, but no one had noticed their arrival. He glanced at Cole, then both of them ran into the second chamber.

'Nobody fucking move,' cried Cael, his Jackdaw aimed at the small group.

Esher glanced at them, then he picked up an axe and charged at Cael, his eyes glazed over. Cael aimed his Jackdaw at Esher's head, then he lowered it, and fired. The lead projectile struck Esher above his right knee, tearing a chunk out of his leg and sending him flying across the stone floor. Lindi threw a wall lamp at the ground in front of Cole, where it exploded, then she unleashed her fire powers, sending a wave of flames rolling towards her cousins. Cole had to drop one of his Jackdaws to shield him and Cael from the approaching flames, his own fire powers battling against Lindi's. Cael dropped his first Jackdaw, and went to pull the other from his holster, when Carter threw a knife at him, using battle-vision to guide and power his aim. The blade struck the back of Cael's right hand, and the tip punched its way through his palm.

Cael grimaced in agony, and his thumb went to the Quadrant.

'*Do not move, Cael Holdfast*,' came a voice from the shadows.

Cael's left hand froze, his thumb an inch from the surface of the Quadrant. Cole raised his left arm, and fired his remaining Jackdaw into the thick shadows. The projectile hit the side of Cairney's face, ripping off part of his left cheek and spraying the back wall of the chamber in blood.

Cairney roared out in agony, and raced towards Cole. He ran through the battling wall of flames, and punched Cole in the stomach. Cole went flying backwards, then he hit a wall and fell to the floor, unconscious. At the same time, Carter took hold of Cael's left arm, and wrenched it behind his back. With his other hand, he pulled the remaining Jackdaw from its holster and pointed it at Cael's head. Lindi relinquished her powers, and the fire fell away to nothing. Cairney, the side of his face dripping with blood, turned to gaze at Cael.

'Shoot him, brother,' said Cairney.

Carter narrowed his eyes.

'Do I have to command you?' said Cairney.

'That wasnae the deal,' said Carter. 'We were never going to kill our cousins. Use the Sextant to exile them.'

'I'm with Carter on this,' said Lindi. 'We beat them fair and square; we don't need to kill them.'

'Those bastards blew half of my face off,' cried Cairney.

'Aye,' said Carter. 'Ye'll recover, but. If I blow Cael's head off his shoulders, he won't be recovering from that.'

'Marines!' Cael shouted. 'Get in here!'

Cairney stared at him, a callous smile on his face. 'The marines you brought with you are dead, and their bodies are lying by the walls of the observatory. There is no one coming to help you.'

Cael turned to Karalyn. 'Mother,' he said, 'why did you tell me that Cairney had gone?'

Karalyn looked at him, but remained silent.

'Karalyn and Konna have been ordered to say and do nothing,' said Cairney, 'just as poor old Esher was ordered to distract you. I suspected that you might try to talk to your mother before arriving here, and so I told her what to tell you. She has a remarkably pliant mind in that body.' He glanced down at the injured and unconscious Ascendant. 'I suppose I had better save him,' he went on. '*Esher, your self-healing powers are working again.*'

Esher didn't move, but the wound on his leg began to repair itself.

Cael writhed in Carter's grip. They were the same size and build, but Carter had battle-vision. Cael shot his vision out, and tried to enter Carter's mind. He was rebuffed. He tried the same with Cairney, with the same result.

Cairney laughed. 'Look at him,' he said. 'He is attempting to enter our minds. Oh, cousin, we had time to prepare for your visit. In that time, I went to Nom Karta and stole three sets of eye-guards. With my eyes protected, I am invulnerable, and yet the power of my voice still works. Witness. *Get on your knees.*'

Cael grunted as he felt the pressure of compulsion grip him. The pain coming from his right hand was distracting him, but he was yet able to resist. He staggered, but Carter held him steady.

Cairney frowned, and moved closer. He reached out and took the Quadrant from Cael's left hand. He smiled at his cousin, then he ripped the knife from the back of Cael's other hand and plunged it into his stomach, just under his breastplate

'No, brother,' said Carter, as Cael cried out in pain.

'That won't kill him,' said Cairney. 'It might get infected, but he's three-quarters Kellach Brigdomin; he'll survive.'

Cael swayed as blood seeped out from the front of his clothes. Only Carter's strength was keeping him on his feet, and his vision grew vague and hazy.

'Let go of him,' said Cairney.

Carter did so, and Cael fell to the stone floor.

Lindi walked over to Cole's body, which was slumped by the rear wall.

'He's still alive,' said Lindi, 'but barely. I will heal him.'

'Wait,' said Cairney.

Lindi froze, her hand outstretched towards Cole.

'I can't let him die,' she said.

'Save his life,' said Cairney, 'but nothing more; leave him unconscious. And block his powers while you are in his mind. Are you strong enough to do that, dear Lindi?'

Lindi frowned at him, then she prised open one of Cole's eyes and stared down at him.

Carter gazed at Cael. 'What are we going to do with them?' he said.

Cairney brandished Cael's Quadrant. 'I will put them somewhere where they will not be able to hurt us.'

'Where?' said Carter.

'I will not say.'

Lindi got back to her feet. 'Will they live?'

Cairney eyed them both. 'You two seem more concerned about Cael and Cole than you do about our great and noble mission. I will not kill them; you have my word. Now, Cael; listen very carefully. *Your powers are blocked. You cannot harm me; you cannot harm us.* Lindi, drag Cole over here.'

Lindi took hold of Cole's shoulders, and pulled him to where Cael was lying. She glanced at the wound by Cael's waist.

'He is going to bleed to death,' she said.

'Then fix him,' shouted Cairney; 'but just the bare minimum – do you understand?'

'There's no need to fucking shout,' said Lindi. 'I ain't deaf.'

Cael felt Lindi's hand touch his brow, then he sensed a great wave of healing flow through him. In his agony, he had found it hard to hear what the others had been saying, but it felt as though she was giving him far more than the bare minimum. The wound by his waist closed up and, for the first time, he was able to examine what Cairney had done to his mind. He felt for his powers, but they were gone.

'Did you block Cole's powers?' said Cairney.

'Of course I bleeding well did,' said Lindi. 'Check if you like. Oh, wait – you can't. You haven't got vision powers.'

Cairney glared at her, then he walked over to Cole and crouched by him.

'*Wake up*,' he said.

Cole groaned and moved on the stone floor, then he opened his eyes.

'*You cannot harm me*,' said Cairney; '*and you will speak only the truth. Are your powers blocked?*'

Cole stared up at him, then he nodded. 'Yes.'

Cairney smiled. '*Go back to sleep, Cole.*'

Cole's eyes closed, and his head slumped to the side.

Lindi rolled her eyes. 'I can't believe you thought I was lying.'

'Trust must be earned,' said Cairney, as he got back to his feet. 'I will be back soon.'

He activated Cael's Quadrant, the air shimmered, then Cael found himself lying on a set of wide stone steps, on the edge of a great plaza.

'People and priests of Gunst,' Cairney called out, his Gunstian flawless. 'Hear me. I have brought you two criminals. Hear me.'

The crowds in the plaza turned, as soldiers piled out of the Temple of the Great Mother behind them, their crossbows aimed at Cairney.

'I mean no harm to you,' said Cairney; 'I mean no harm to the noble people of Gunst. On the contrary, I am here to deliver Cael Holdfast and his cousin Cole Holdfast into your hands. Do with them as you please.'

The soldiers surrounded Cairney and he smiled at them.

'Who are you?' said a priest in long, flowing robes.

'I am Cairney, soon-to-be Emperor of the Sapphire Throne. I am removing the wicked Empress and her foolish advisors from power. Let this be an end to the raids upon imperial territory. Your argument was with the old regime; not with me. This point must be understood – I have brought you the Faithless One; in return, you shall cease your attacks upon the lands over which I shall rule. You would be wise to keep to the terms of this deal. Farewell.'

Cairney triggered the Quadrant and disappeared. Cael glanced up from the steps, his stomach and hand still in agony. Dozens of Gunstian soldiers were crowding round him and Cole, desperate to catch a glimpse of the son of the Demon Witch.

'It is the Faithless One!' cried a priest. 'We have him.'

The crowd in the plaza cheered, their hands raised in the air.

'He has dangerous powers, my lord,' said an army officer.

'Indeed,' said the priest. 'They will both need to be subdued before their public executions. Take them into the Temple of the Great Mother, and beat them both, but do not kill them. That moment must be preserved for the crowds of citizens to witness – you will not rob them of this.'

'Understood, my lord,' said the officer. He gestured to the soldiers. 'Hood them, and bind their wrists and ankles.'

Cael tried to raise his hands to protect his head, but they were dragged back, then a soldier kicked the half-healed wound on his waist. Cael cried out, then a hood was pulled down over his head, and everything went black.

CHAPTER 34
TESTED

Observatory, Viridia – 25th Abrinch 5281

Konna gazed down at Esher. His leg had finished healing, but the wound had been so grievous that the Ascendant remained unconscious on the stone floor. She knew that Cael could have killed him, and she was grateful that he had lowered his aim at the last moment. She glanced at Karalyn, who was sitting on one of Carter's unfinished chairs. The old woman looked exhausted, and she was clearly in pain from her broken ankle, but Cairney had forbidden Konna from healing her. The pain would help keep Karalyn awake, and that was his priority. Karalyn met her gaze. Neither was permitted to speak, and Konna wondered if Karalyn understood how reluctant she was to be there.

'He's gonnae be fine, sister,' said Carter. 'Esher's self-healing will sort him out.'

Konna turned to look at her brother.

'Why are you talking to her?' said Lindi. 'She can't talk back.'

'Aye, I know,' said Carter. He tapped his hand off his knee as he sat. 'Where the fuck is Cairney, eh? He's been gone for an hour. If Cael and Cole knew we were here, then others will be coming.'

'Who?' said Lindi.

'I don't know. Marines? They could be up in the mountains right now, aiming their Battanaras right at us, and the first we'd know is when the Observatory gets blown to fuck.'

Lindi leaned forward, a cigarette dangling from her fingers. 'Eventually,' she said, 'we might have to leave, to ensure the safety of the Sextant. I mean, what if Cairney's been captured?'

Carter pointed at Karalyn. 'And what would we do with her?'

Lindi narrowed her eyes. 'Do you know what Cairney was planning to do to her?'

'Nope.'

'You must have some idea.'

Carter shook his head. Lindi muttered something under her breath and got to her feet. She eyed the Sextant, then she began pacing up and down.

'If Cairney had left the Weathervane,' she said, 'then I could be looking for him right now.'

'He doesnae trust ye with it,' said Carter.

'No shit,' said Lindi, 'but I still have my Quadrant. I could move the Sextant, even though I can't use it. How long is the Weathervane; do you know?'

Carter eyed her. 'No. Why would ye ask that? Are ye thinking of looking for a different sword that'll fit it?'

'We might have to,' said Lindi. 'Let's say that Cairney has been captured, and marines are on their way here; if we had a sword that fit the Sextant, then we'd still be in business.'

'Yer dreaming, Lindi,' he said. 'If Cairney's been captured, it's all over. Me and you cannae take over the Empire.'

'Are you saying we should surrender?'

'If Cairney's been captured, then aye – what else can we do? We hand over Karalyn and the Sextant to the Empire, and beg for mercy.'

Lindi stared at him. 'It's too fucking late for that, Carter. We took on Cael and Cole, and beat them. There will be no mercy.'

'That depends on what Cairney has done with them both. He said he wouldnae kill them.'

'He said that because the rest of us were objecting. If Cael and Cole are dead... Shit.' Lindi eyed Konna. 'Stop looking at me like that. Do you know what? – I'm sick of you sitting there in silence.'

Konna felt Lindi enter her mind and, in an instant, the block preventing her from speaking was ripped away.

Konna gasped. 'I can talk again. How did you do that, Lindi?'

Lindi shrugged. 'It wasn't difficult.'

'You can remove Cairney's blocks?'

'So? Don't tell him; he won't like it. He thinks he's the most powerful god to walk the Known Worlds, but we all saw Cael resist the command to fall to his knees.'

'I thought that was because Carter was holding him upright.'

Carter eyed her. 'Nah. Cael was resisting; I wasnae stopping him from kneeling. His resistance only broke when Cairney stabbed him.'

'Surrender now,' said Konna. 'It's the only chance we have. Lindi – use yer Quadrant and get us the fuck out of here.'

Lindi said nothing, her eyes unsure.

'We're going nowhere,' said Carter. 'Not yet – it might feel like Cairney's been gone a while, but it's only been an hour.'

Lindi glared at him. 'But you just said that we would have to surrender if Cairney's been captured.'

'Aye, but has he been captured? None of us know. There's no point in panicking just yet. This is a high-risk game we're playing; let's not blow it.'

'What are ye hoping to get out of this, brother?' said Konna.

'It was revenge at first,' said Carter. 'Not very edifying, I know; but it was revenge against the Empress and Herald Kelsey that I wanted. Now it's changed. Ye were right about the weapons of the mortals – they're too dangerous. If we take over, then we can get rid of them.'

'Do you seriously believe that Cairney would make a good Emperor?' said Konna. 'Would he be a wise and generous ruler; one who protects and cares for his subjects? Once he's on the throne, he'll never vacate it. Ever. What will the Empire look like after a century of Cairney's rule?'

Carter shrugged. 'Who knows?'

'That's not good enough, brother. I'm not opposed in principle to a god becoming Emperor or Empress, but Cairney? He's fucking insane – you must see that. He wants to become the eternal Emperor, but the only way to achieve that is through massive bloodshed. Who will the army serve? Would the marines just stand by as Cairney wipes out the Imperial Court? I know Uncle Naxor can be a sly wee prick at times, but his plan makes the most sense – we get what we want without having to kill anyone. And what about Esher? Cairney will use him to carry out his dirty work, and we know how that will end up – with Esher's death. And Karalyn? We had better fucking hope that Cael and Cole are all right; otherwise, Karalyn will kick our arses when she returns.'

The three of them turned to look at Karalyn, who was watching them all from her unfinished chair.

'I didn't want any of this, Karalyn,' said Konna. 'I fucked up when I helped Edgar steal the Sextant.'

Lindi snorted. 'You barely helped at all.'

'Aye, it was you,' said Konna; 'ya sleekit wee bitch.'

'Fuck you,' said Lindi. 'At least I picked a side, while you kept dithering one way then the next. If only you would make up your bleeding mind, Konna, instead of feeling sorry for yourself.'

Konna laughed. 'You haven't picked a side,' she said, 'you're trying to play both sides at once. You pay lip service to Cairney, but then ye keep things from him at the same time. Cairney can see through yer act, or if he doesn't, he soon will. And then, as soon as yer of no more use to him, he'll drop ye.'

'Blah fucking blah,' said Lindi.

The air shimmered, and Cairney appeared in their midst. Before Konna could react, she felt Lindi's presence in her mind again, and the block preventing her from talking was put back into place.

'Where have ye been?' said Carter.

'Preparing,' said Cairney. 'It is time to leave Viridia. Our enemies will soon discover our location, as I can hardly believe that Cael wouldn't have told someone where he was going.'

'We'd already worked that out for ourselves,' said Lindi.

'And yet you waited for me to return,' said Cairney; 'how touching.'

'We talked about leaving,' said Lindi. 'We thought that you might have been captured.'

Cairney laughed. 'Captured? By whom? Karalyn has been subdued, and Cole and Cael will no longer be troubling us. Who could possibly capture me?'

Carter got to his feet, and began to gather his tools together, throwing them into a large canvas bag.

'Where did you take them?' he said.

'What was that?' said Cairney.

'Cael and Cole,' Carter went on; 'where are they?'

'I didn't kill them.'

'That's not what I asked.'

'I made a deal with the Gunstians,' said Cairney. 'In exchange for them stopping their raids on the Empire, I gave them Cael and Cole.'

Carter and Lindi turned to stare at Cairney, then Konna saw a tear roll down Karalyn's cheek.

Cairney smiled. 'I don't know why this seems to concern any of you; they were our enemies. What else are we supposed to do with enemies?'

'They're our cousins!' Lindi cried. 'You had no fucking right to do that.'

'You are wrong,' he said; 'I can do whatever I please.' He brandished a Quadrant. 'We are leaving.'

He triggered the device, and the air crackled. Konna fell to the ground, as the chair she had been sitting on remained on Viridia. She looked at her new surroundings. They were in another stone chamber, but the walls were partly green with moss, and the air was far cooler. Light was coming in through cracks in the ceiling, and a ray of sunlight was striking the inert form of the Sextant. Karalyn had also fallen to the floor, and she was nursing her broken ankle, her features contorted with pain.

'This shall be our new home for a while,' said Cairney. 'Carter, do you recognise it?'

Carter narrowed his eyes. 'We need to talk about Cael and Cole.'

'No, we don't,' said Cairney. '*Never mention it again, Carter*. Let me ask again – do you recognise where we are? You have been here before.'

Carter blinked a few times, then he gazed around. 'Are we back in Kellach Brigdomin?'

'Obviously,' said Cairney. He eyed Konna. '*You may speak again.* Where are we?'

Konna cleared her throat. 'We are in the ruins of the Fire Temple, next to the Mountain of Pyre, close to where Lach, Domm and Brig meet. Uncle Naxor brought us here years ago.'

'Well done,' said Cairney.

'The blood of Cael and Cole are on your hands, brother,' Konna said.

'Aye,' said Cairney. 'Do you think I care? It was Cael and Cole who subdued me eight years ago on Ulna. They had it coming. It's Cael's own fault, though; if he hadn't butchered hundreds of innocent Gunstians, then they wouldn't have been so desperate to catch him.'

'Could we not have gone somewhere that isn't in bleeding ruins?' said Lindi.

'There is plenty of fresh water down here, and we can bring food in by Quadrant,' he said. 'These ruins were partly excavated by a team of Domm around a decade ago – there are tunnels leading out onto the flank of what once was the Fire Mountain; alas, the Rahain somewhat diminished its height during the invasion. That was nearly sixty years ago, Lindi.'

'I don't give a shit,' said Lindi.

'Why would you?' he said. 'It's not your history; it's ours. My father's father fought here during the final siege. This is where he was captured and enslaved. The population of Kellach Brigdomin has never fully recovered to its pre-invasion level; and yet no one cares about getting revenge on the Rahain any more. The same will happen after I take power. Aye, some will have to die; possibly many – but give it a generation or two, and the mortals will have forgotten. Konna and I will be leaving with Karalyn and Esher now. Carter and Lindi, you will remain here. You may explore the tunnels and caverns, but do not leave the Fire Temple.'

Lindi said nothing.

'I know that look in your eye,' said Cairney. 'What schemes are you dreaming up, Lindi? Perhaps I should take your Quadrant before we go, to reduce any temptation.'

'Keep your hands off my Quadrant,' she said.

'Where are ye taking Karalyn?' said Carter.

'I will not say,' said Cairney, as he kept his gaze on Lindi. He took two steps towards her, and she took one step back.

'You're not getting my Quadrant,' said Lindi.

'I don't need to take it,' he said. '*Lindi, you are not able to operate any Quadrant without my express permission. You will use one only if and when I order you to, and on no other occasion.* That should do it.'

Lindi's eyes widened. 'You utter bastard!' she shouted.

Cairney laughed. 'Aye. That I am. *Get on your knees, Lindi.*'

Lindi fell to her knees, and Konna frowned as she watched. If she was play-acting to fool Cairney, then her act was convincing.

'Are you loyal to me?' said Cairney.

'Yes,' said Lindi.

'Say it.'

'I am loyal to you, Cairney.'

'Tell me that you are my faithful servant.'

'I am your faithful servant.'

Cairney nodded. 'Carter,' he said, 'keep an eye on Lindi while I am gone.'

'This is bullshit,' said Lindi. 'Did I not prove my worth in the fight against Cael and Cole? Did I not save you when Karalyn tried to have you immolated? Did I not rescue you in the first fucking place? I've done more than Carter to help you, and you bleeding well trust him.'

'Carter is my brother,' said Cairney. 'If he disagrees with me, he tells me. Whereas, with you, Lindi, I cannot escape the feeling that you are hiding your true intentions from me. But, you are right – you have helped me, and that is the reason you remain alive and by my side. Keep it up, and earn my trust.'

Lindi glared at him as he walked over to Karalyn, Esher and Konna. He gazed down at Karalyn's ankle, then he turned to his sister.

'I have decided to allow you to help me, Konna,' he said. 'Think of it as a test. If you pass, then I might remove some of the restrictions I have placed on you. Try not to fail.'

He activated his Quadrant, and the air shimmered. The temperature immediately increased, though without the oppressive humidity of Viridia. Konna gazed up. Before her was the largest building she had ever seen. It was also one of the most featureless. There were towers and turrets, but they were rising from a flat, smooth block, as though an enormous slab of granite had been dropped onto the ground.

'We are in the Holdings,' said Cairney. 'This is the Palace of the Almighty; the abode of Edmond, the Second Ascendant. Do you know what is special about this building?'

'I have heard of it,' said Konna. 'Edgar was a prisoner inside, along with others, including that bastard Ward.'

'That's right – but it's not what I meant,' said Cairney. 'The secret of this building is how it was constructed. Only Edmond knew the interior layout; nine-tenths of the entire structure is solid stone, and the internal passageways and rooms are distributed randomly, making it impossible to access the inside with a Quadrant. One cannot vision inside, either, as every opening has been covered with multiple layers of specially-designed gauze. Air can flow in and out, but not vision.'

Konna frowned. 'Are we placing Karalyn inside?'

'We are.'

'But, what will happen when she dies? Her spirit won't be held back by gauze.'

'Very true,' said Cairney. He gazed down at Esher. '*Wake up, Ascendant, and get to your feet. You will do what I command; nothing more, nothing less.*'

Esher's eyes opened, but they were glazed over. He got to his feet, then he remained as still as a statue. Cairney picked up Karalyn and slung her over his shoulder. The old woman grimaced in agony, but no voice came from her lips.

'She is so light,' Cairney said. 'I can barely feel her weight. Come on. *Follow me, Esher.*'

He set off, walking along one massive flank of the grey, plain palace. Konna glanced to her left, at the foothills of the Barrier Mountains. Colsbury was in that direction, though Konna wasn't exactly sure how to get there. She followed Cairney and Esher, keeping a few paces behind them as she tried to fathom her brother's plan. She could see how the Palace of the Almighty would be a useful place to hide Karalyn, but that didn't solve the overriding problem of how to prevent her from dying. Part of her was curious to see what her brother was going to do, while part of her wished to flee as far away from him as possible.

She examined the blocks in her mind. The strongest was the restriction on her running away, and the weakest was the prohibition against harming others. She began to pick at it, like scratching the edge of a scab. Being able to harm others would not help her against Cairney, but she had to do something. Maybe the other blocks would be easier to remove if she could rid her mind of that one. Was there any point in even trying? Konna felt beaten down, and it was hard to believe that she had been in Nom Karta only that morning, before Cairney had arrived to throw her life into turmoil.

She was repulsed by Cairney, disgusted by Lindi, and disappointed in Carter. Whatever way events turned out, her life was in ruins.

Cairney halted by the building's only entrance, halfway along its southern flank. The entrance was sealed shut, with no visible join between the stone of the gate and the stone of the grey, granite walls. The only way to tell that it was an entrance were the vestigial remains of an old drawbridge that protruded from the side of the building in various places.

'*Esher*,' said Cairney, '*your stone powers are unblocked. Open the gate*.'

The Ascendant raised his hand, and Konna sensed the flow of powers leaving his body. Cracks in the side of the building appeared, forming the outline of the stone gate, then it began to lower and open as though it was hinged at the bottom. The gate struck the ground with a low rumble, and Konna peered into the interior of the Palace of the Almighty. Cairney stepped onto the gate, then he walked inside, disappearing into the darkness. A few moments later, a hallway was illuminated by several wall lamps, and Cairney re-appeared, a lantern in his free hand.

'*Esher*,' he said, '*your powers are blocked. Go to sleep, and wait for me here*.'

Esher's eyes closed and he fell to the grass. Cairney gestured to Konna, and she followed her brother into the building.

Cairney led her along tunnels and hallways, ascending some stairs and descending others, until Konna was completely lost, her sense of direction subsumed by the sheer weight of the granite enclosing her.

'How do you know the way, brother?' she said.

'Don't call me that,' said Cairney. 'I have been in here before; that was not the first time I have asked Esher to open the main entrance for me.'

'You were here eight years ago?'

'I was. Did you ever wonder why I was so often missing? Did you never wonder where I might have gone?'

'I had assumed you were working on your plan to start a war between the Empire and the Dominion.'

Cairney laughed. 'Perhaps I should have been doing that, then my plan might have been better. This place has always intrigued me. How did Edmond live in a building such as this? It is ugly, cramped, miserable and dark. Every hallway looks the same; every chamber is featureless and drab.'

'He was paranoid,' said Konna. 'He hid himself away in this palace to remain safe from the other gods.'

'Aye. He was scared of them. I will not be a fearful ruler. I intend to live in Thorn's Blue Palace – her one true contribution to the Empire. I will not hide behind thick walls of granite.'

They came to a chamber so large that the light from Cairney's lantern did not reach the ceiling or the far walls. The room had been fitted out with furniture, but most of it was broken, and all was covered in a fine layer of dust.

Cairney placed Karalyn into a wooden chair, then he drew a knife and stabbed the old woman in the stomach.

'What are you doing?' cried Konna.

'Have patience,' said Cairney, 'and watch the master at work.'

He pointed at Karalyn, who was gripping her stomach in silent agony as blood seeped through the front of her dress. The wound healed, and Cairney stabbed her again.

'She weakens every time I do this,' said Cairney, as he healed her again. 'Do you know why I need her to be weak?'

Konna said nothing as Cairney plunged the knife into Karalyn for a third time.

'Each time,' he went on, 'I take her closer to death, without letting her die.'

'But why?' said Konna. 'You are making her suffer for nothing. Her body is old; she cannot survive this.'

'This latest body of hers is merely a vessel,' he said, as he stabbed her again. 'She will not remain in it for much longer. I am draining her reserves to exploit a singular weakness. Karalyn herself gave me the book that taught me what to do. I read the testimony about what happened to Karalyn on Zamata, from an eye-witness who watched her friend Lyla of the Dragon Corps be murdered and raised from the dead by a dragon. And what did the dragon do next? Come on; you must know this part.'

'He placed Karalyn's spirit into the body of Lyla.'

'Ah, so you have also read Kelsey's second book?' said Cairney. '*A History of the Sapphire Empire*? In my opinion, it's better than her one about the Star Continent.'

'There were no details in that book about what exactly happened.'

Cairney healed Karalyn again. She looked close to unconsciousness, but Cairney revived her.

'It mattered not,' said Cairney. 'Kelsey's new book led me to a woman called Cisca, who is married to the president of Zamata. She was there. She saw what happened. Karalyn is not at her strongest when she is incorporeal. She can use vision skills, and she can persuade people, but that's all; nothing more; and I am wearing eye-guards. I need her to be weak when I finally kill her, so that her disembodied spirit can be forced into another body against her will, as was done on Zamata.'

He stabbed Karalyn again, and blood seeped from her lips. This time, Cairney waited for the old woman to almost die, then he sent a small amount of healing into her.

'It's a tricky balance,' he said, 'but I think it's working.'

'Are you going to force her into another body?' said Konna. 'Whose? No one else is down here, Cairney. You can't possibly be thinking of my body.' She took a few steps back, and eyed the door.

Cairney laughed. 'Of course I'm not thinking of your body; you are far too powerful a vessel for Karalyn. She would immediately rise again, stronger than ever.'

'Then whose?'

Cairney got to his feet, the knife still in his hand. 'I want to introduce you to someone I found in the dungeons below us eight years ago. Many think that this palace is now empty, but there are still hidden areas that are yet to be explored.'

He walked into the corner of the room and opened a door. He crouched down and picked up the form of an emaciated woman, her body almost skeletal, then he carried it across the room and laid it down onto a table. Konna stared at the body. Strapped to the woman's gaunt face was a restrainer mask, and dried blood and pus had marked channels down her sunken, withered features.

'This demigod is still alive,' said Cairney. 'Isn't it remarkable how self-healing endures, despite the pain, despite the lack of food and water?'

His hands went to the buckle at the back of the demigod's head, and he ripped off the restrainer mask. Konna felt like throwing up, and she had to wrench her gaze away from the two holes in the demigod's face.

'It's not a pretty sight,' said Cairney. 'The shock of removing the mask might even kill the poor bastard, and we can't be having that.' He touched the brow of the demigod. 'There; she has stabilised.' He walked back over to Karalyn, who was lying in a pool of her own blood a few yards from the table.

'*You may speak, Karalyn*,' he said, '*but you are unable to hurt me*.'

Karalyn gasped and choked for air.

'Do you have anything you wish to say?' said Cairney.

Karalyn looked into his eyes. 'I... will not forget...'

Cairney raised an eyebrow. 'You'll not forget what? This? Me? You can remember this for as long as you like, Karalyn; it is of no concern to me. Are you ready to die?'

'Do it,' gasped Karalyn.

Cairney frowned. 'Perhaps you are still too strong.'

He stabbed her in the neck, and her blood gushed over his hand. He pulled out the knife, and waited. Karalyn choked, then fell silent.

Cairney touched her, and the wound on her neck healed.

'I can't watch this,' said Konna. 'You are a monster, brother.'

Cairney ignored her, then he rammed the knife into Karalyn's forehead, driving it deep into her skull.

'There she goes,' said Cairney. 'Any moment. Now. *Karalyn, I order you to enter the mind of the demigod on the table. You cannot flee; you cannot harm us. Enter the body of the demigod*.'

Cairney grunted, as though Karalyn's deceased spirit was waging an invisible war on his mind. Konna crouched down, as Cairney staggered back.

'*Enter the body of the demigod; I command you!*' Cairney cried, then he screamed in pain. 'I do not submit!' he shouted. '*Enter the body of the demigod; you cannot resist me.*'

Cairney stumbled to the floor, then he sprang up, and ran to the table. He gripped the restrainer mask, and pushed it back down onto the face of the demigod, driving the two nails into the bloody eye sockets. He buckled the strap, then staggered back. The demigod's ancient body writhed on the table.

'*You cannot block your own self-healing, Karalyn; I forbid it,*' shouted Cairney. '*This is your new home, for all eternity.*'

The body on the table stilled, though the demigod's chest was still gently rising and falling.

'I am victorious,' said Cairney, then he crashed to the floor unconscious.

Konna got to her feet. All was still, except for a low whispered groan of agony coming from the emaciated demigod on the table.

Was Karalyn in there? No – such a thing was surely impossible. But hadn't Cairney been right; hadn't she been entrapped before?

'Karalyn?' Konna whispered.

The mouth under the mask opened. 'Kill me, Konna.'

Konna stepped back, her hands trembling. Her gaze went to the knife embedded into the old Gunstian woman's skull. She walked over to the body, the fourth inhabited by Karalyn. She pulled the knife from the head of the old woman, and walked back to the table. She gazed down at the demigod, the fifth body to be inhabited by Karalyn; then she raised the knife.

She hesitated, the block preventing her from harming others restraining her actions. Konna exerted all her strength, and tore the block away. She cried out in pain, then she readied the knife again. She would have to remove the head, she realised, and the thought made her sick.

'I am sorry, Aunty,' she said. 'I am doing this not to hurt you, but to free you.'

'Kill me,' whispered Karalyn.

Konna drove the knife down, aiming for the neck. A hand shot out. It gripped Konna's wrist, and broke it, sending the knife falling to the floor.

'You treacherous bitch,' said Cairney. 'After all my efforts, all my struggles – you choose once again to betray me. *Your self-healing is blocked.*'

He punched Konna in the face, and she flew backwards. With no self-healing, she remained on the floor, her face in agony, and her wrist burning with pain.

Cairney gathered a few things, then he walked over to Konna. He rolled her onto her back, and placed a knee on her chest, pinning her down.

'I am going to restore your self-healing in a moment,' he said to her; 'but for now I want to enjoy seeing you suffer. You could have been a queen, Konna – a mighty queen. Instead, I shall leave you here with Karalyn; won't it be nice to have some company?'

He held up two long nails and a hammer.

'You might wonder why I happen to have these with me,' he said. 'The truth is, I was hoping to use them on Cael, but I decided against it. Let the Gunstians tear him to pieces. So now I am going to use them on you. It's a bit primitive for a restrainer mask, so I will have to chop off your hands first; I hope you don't mind, but I can't have you pulling the nails out as soon as I've gone. *Your self-healing is unblocked. You cannot hurt me or move.*'

Instant relief poured through Konna's body as her injuries began to repair themselves. Cairney picked up the knife, then he held down her left arm and cut through the skin, muscles and bones, severing her hand.

Konna screamed. Cairney repeated the action, holding down her right arm until he had cut through the wrist. He threw the two severed hands into the corner of the room, then he smiled down at her.

'It's time for the nails,' he said. 'Your self-healing will be so busy trying to heal your eyes, that your hands will not grow back. I will shackle both you and Karalyn to a wall before I go, but you will be in so much agony that you probably won't even notice. Anything to say? No? Very well, Konna. This is what happens when you fail my test.'

He showed her the nails again, then he positioned one just above her left eye.

'Goodbye, sister,' he said.

Down swung the hammer.

Thump. Thump.

AUTHOR'S NOTES

NOVEMBER 2025

Thank you for reading ***Yearning for Evermore***; I hope you enjoyed it.

This book was a joy to write, as the ideas for it had been formed a long time ago, and I felt as though I was just writing out what I already knew had happened (if that makes sense!). It is also the first book of the final trilogy of the series; and not just Magelands Empire, but the entire Magelands story. The *Evermore Trilogy* should perhaps be seen as one long story, rather than three separate ones, and each book begins the day after the previous one ends. For ***Yearning for Evermore*** itself, however, events start eight years after the end of ***The Lost Ascendant***, and, after an absence of four books, we return to Karalyn's point-of-view. In many ways, the story of the Magelands is the story not just of the Holdfasts, but of one Holdfast in particular – Karalyn.

RECEIVE A FREE MAGELANDS DOMINION SHORT STORY

Building a relationship with my readers is very important to me.

Join my newsletter for information on new books and deals and you will also receive a Magelands Dominion short story that is currently EXCLUSIVE to my Readers' Group for FREE.

www.ChristopherMitchellBooks.com/dominion

ABOUT THE AUTHOR

Christopher Mitchell is the author of the Magelands epic fantasy series.

For more information:

www.christophermitchellbooks.com
info@christophermitchellbooks.com

Printed in Dunstable, United Kingdom

73567943R00297